THE OBLIQUE PLACE

Caterina Pascual Söderbaum

THE OBLIQUE PLACE

Translated from the Swedish by
Frank Perry

MACLEHOSE PRESS
QUERCUS · LONDON

First published in the Swedish language as *Den skeva platsen*
by Albert Bonniers Förlag in 2016

First published in Great Britain in 2018 by

MacLehose Press
An imprint of Quercus Publishing Ltd
Carmelite House
50 Victoria Embankment
London EC4Y ODZ

An Hachette UK company

Translation sponsored by

The moral right of Caterina Pascual Söderbaum to be
identified as the author of this work has been
asserted in accordance with the Copyright,
Designs and Patents Act, 1988.

Frank Perry asserts his moral right to be identified as
the translator of the work.

ISBN (TPB) 978 0 85705 723 5
ISBN (Ebook) 978 0 85705 725 9

Designed and typeset in Haarlemmer by Libanus Press
Printed and bound in Denmark by Nørhaven

I should have liked to see you before you became improbable.
War feels to me an oblique place.

Emily Dickinson to Thomas Wentworth Higginson
(Letter, February 1863)

Swedenborg somewhere has an image akin to her "oblique
place" where he symbolises evil as simply an oblique angle.

Thomas Wentworth Higginson ("Emily Dickinson's Letters",
Atlantic Monthly, October 1891)

For Rita

CONTENTS

Part One
Shadow Rose Shadow

Hotel Garni Sonnhof, Bad Ischl, Salzkammergut, Austria, the Beginning of July, 2006, Morning

The door of the glazed veranda is ajar, behind the transom windows, pinned down by the invisible steady rain, the garden is breathing beneath the particular kind of stillness that comes with the passage of water through air, and beside the tall dark hedge the cloudy surface of the pond is quivering under the needles of rain like a secret pulse; the blackbird that kept singing through the dawn from the old yew tree outside your balcony can still be heard, the song brings with it the smell of soil and wet grass and lays itself like a warm compress over the ice-cold odour of cellars and mould from your dream, in the deserted conservatory where the three of you are sitting on your own (a large camellia with shiny dark-green leaves and bright red perianths in the middle of the room, a black piano by the half-open door of the French windows) breakfast has been laid but it is as if the morning were not quite able to penetrate the mist green tones of the light and the entire room were tilting towards the night, the hum of the rain hanging in the air like a lingering nocturnal trace, as though not only the gleaming piano and the abandoned bar were missing the night-time comings and goings while still harbouring vestiges of the people and the music that continue to sap the bluish-green mist from the garden floating like a breath above the empty table and the rumpled tablecloth on which you spilled coffee, above the china coffee pot and the broken eggshells beside the plate, above the rag doll lying on its stomach, above the half-finished chocolate, above the gold-painted numerals carved into the large wooden block with a metal key on the end of a grubby cord, but the entire four-storey building you have spent the night in as well. The landlady who put out the coffee and bread disappeared inside the hotel long ago, beyond the kitchen regions where she could be heard clattering for a while, she may have had things to do in a laundry whose whereabouts you do not know, one flight down perhaps, an extension of the spiral staircase that brought you down to the ground floor and through a long wide corridor to this glazed veranda with an open door that a cold draught is coming through. The coffee is cold now as well and is beginning to taste bitter, the rain-drenched air turns your little daughter's hair frizzy, the curls falling dully over her shoulders, and to smooth out the straggling strands of hair that stick out you slowly run your hand in drawn-out strokes over her scalp and neck, the caresses release a sweet powdery scent of soap in your mind, a velvety mixture of vanilla and amber, of saltwater and sun-warmed skin that trickles like balm inside your ribs. In the chair opposite, he, your husband, lifts his coffee cup to his mouth and lets his gaze fall inside as if to confine it there, to allow it to rest on the bottom of the round interior which it does for a few long seconds, until he puts the cup down and it collides against the saucer with a clink, then he looks up and straight at you instead, settling the entire weight of his dark-brown gaze on your eyes – which are of a muddy greyish-green colour, with a vein of gold that clashes with the green closest to the pupil – and you know that he is planning on keeping it there, that he is not going to drop his eyes, not yet, although you drop yours almost immediately and the moment you have done so you also realise that there will be reproach in his gaze now that he has sniffed out your nightmare that is lying between you unspoken, unspoken but like a wall and that that dream, which he can sense like running water through the movements of your eyes, is making him feel disappointed, angry, making him feel alone, lost, in the wrong place, as though you were suffering from an illness that was self-inflicted and you were refusing to do anything about it. Beyond his head, which you are looking at against the light, the tall dark-green hedge that rises in the background behind the windows screens the garden from everything except the thin strip of grey sky gleaming above its edge, you watch his face from the corner of your eye, it is hanging there at the periphery of your vision as large as a moon; though it is the brilliant actinic light of your dream that comes flooding in now, as if reflected off whitewashed houses with roof terraces in much more southerly latitudes (for a while you thought it was a kindly light, a memory of a different journey you had been on together), then you could see the crocheted lengths of white cotton yarn that were hung so absurdly along the walls of that room, *beneath* and not above the oblong window (like a crack) beyond which shone a blue sky (named *heaven* in the dream) that made you screw up your eyes, it was those crocheted expanses of stars and chain stitch pinned beneath the window sill on the inside of the room that signalled danger, accentuated almost immediately by the figure that had let you into that harshly sunlit room (a whisper in the dream called him "the Rabbi") and you remember turning away from that breach towards heaven to see an iron door ajar and then you remember as well that it was from that dark gap behind your back that the freezing smell of cellars and mould and something choking like exhaust fumes came pouring out during the night, beneath the notes of the blackbird's song, and tainted everything.

The muted rain shower is prolonging the night, your child (she is only partially open to what is outside herself) is moving her hands slowly, as if she were within another dream, or a memory perhaps, you have to protect her, keep her *outside* it even though the rain is forming a skein of airborne water. A horn blares from the station at the bottom of the hill and over the loudspeaker a voice is announcing a train whose destination you cannot make out. The steady rain is now falling more heavily behind the glass panes, and from the tall yew glistening in the downpour where the blackbird was perched large heavy drops are falling onto the pond, rain bubbles are becoming visible in the water; then the train rolls into the little station on the other side of the veil of rain, the coaches that make up the train so close that you can hear the thumping of the wheels against the stone grooves, the whistle of the train burns its way into your ear canals and is followed almost immediately by the screeching of the brakes, the shrill sounds whirling inside the tunnels of your ears as piercingly as if they were trying to turn themselves into light, to be transformed into the razor beam of a searchlight ransacking your brain.

"¡Mira, una merla!" he says having got up from the table and taken the child with him, the two of them are standing inside the half-open door looking out at the garden, he is on his knees beside her so that their heads, which you can see from behind, are at the same height, his hand extended and the finger pointing towards the blackbird pecking its way around the thick trunk of the yew, he tells her that there aren't any blackbirds at home on the farm and even though it is so black, it sings very beautifully, almost more beautifully than any other bird, although your daughter does not seem impressed by the coal-coloured bird, not even by the yellow beak a worm is dangling from, she is probably thinking about the hoopoes that live year round on your plot of land and whose orange heads and startling black and white wings she sees almost daily bobbing this way and that over the lawn and under the fruit trees. You are thinking that the onomatopoeic Catalan name *puput* (poo-poot, poo-poot) manages to convey both the colours and song of the hoopoe through its syllables (like sunlight shining through the petals of a flower) and that *merla*, too, has a singing sonority that *blackbird* (a dry dull blackness rather than trills and cheeps) lacks, the Spanish *mirlo* has the notes of a song in it as well, although something (the "m"?) also lends the word a sheen of black velvet (the black velvet between the stars of a winter night).

"We can go over to the pond later, once it has stopped raining," he says to the child and then you get up from the table as well. "I'm going up," you say, "I forgot the tablets," and start making for the stairs, tentatively, as if you were encountering resistance, and you think about the beginning of this trip, when you were coasting so smoothly along in the car on the way to the airport despite your damaged hand and then you also remember the white butterfly (the white bandage reminds you of the wings of the white butterfly) that appeared from nowhere in the opposite lane while you were driving through Colomers, the neighbouring village where you buy bread, and had not yet had time to pick up speed, the unsuspecting zig-zag motions of the wings that you tracked as the distance increased in the rear-view mirror and you can see quite clearly, lingeringly, in a kind of slow motion, the abrupt collision of the fluttering white spot that had been tracing rosettes as it were in the air with the wind-screen of the dark oncoming car. And then you raise your left hand to the banister and a shooting pain in your damaged ring finger (which must have overextended a muscle or a joint – you have forgot-ten that that hand no longer properly functions and you are not supposed to use it – in order to adapt to the shape of the banister as you grasp it) makes you look down at the hand which is bound to a metal splint and has a large brown iodine stain on the bandage and then the dream you had the first night in Salzburg starts to flicker before your eyes, when you were approaching a large, long and narrow table with a glass syringe in your hand, with bloody scratches across your knuckles, the table was covered in sand and growing out of the sand was a rolling landscape of mountains, forests, and plains, there was even a lake, the landscape was slowly rising, like water gently rocking or the ribcage of someone asleep, the hand holding the syringe, dark clotted blood along your fingers, was twice the size of the mountains and the trees (mainly pines) and you pushed the long needle in at various points, over and over again, the needle sucked up the grains of sand and your magnified hand, always in the foreground, deposited them onto a microscope, the grains were magnified, they caked together and fell apart, they built structures, they looked like cells or like letters, lumps began to form, you dropped them into a test tube and the liquid in the tube turned blue-green, the same colour as the lake, longer than it was wide, that was glittering in the miniature landscape like a comma; you woke up as a black locomotive came out of a tunnel on the periphery of the model landscape. You are moving upwards, the staircase is a broad spiral of low wooden steps that work their way along the spine of the building between bumpy whitewashed walls, there is no view out, neither up nor down, just the spiral motion, so you make for the light falling through a window at the back of the landing; the passage between the first and second landings is along the corridor of the first floor, lit by the window at one end of the corridor is a thick hall carpet that absorbs the sound of your steps, just before the next set of stairs is a large hand-painted linen cupboard and opposite the linen cupboard a wall covered in hunting trophies and black-and-white photographs, and then a large painting of the building in pastel shades, with some people standing in front of it dressed in folk costume, two women in ankle-length hooped skirts and a man in short leather trousers and a feathered hat, from the Thirties or Forties to judge by the hairstyles, the facade from that period is recognisably the same even though the photograph has been taken using an obsolete technique, there is too much cyan in the sky above.

In the bathroom where you go to get water you are struck by your reflection, the white bandage around your left hand sends a flash through the glass, a diagonal line that runs right through the figure that is you, the alien hand makes your whole appearance unfamiliar: Who is this person with that damaged finger of yours? Who are you here? The present is a place without colour, like the white spot in a chromatic circle, a superposition; you see the full moon above the Dolomites the night you crossed the border on your way to this place, half-lying on your side with your throbbing hand in your lap, the moon huge and distorted above the mountain tops while you groan and hold your hand as if it were a suckling baby, and the silver ribbon of the asphalt that seemed intent on leading you deeper and deeper into the mountains, where horses are snorting and plunging over the edge and the clatter of rain is the clatter of a machine gun. Without taking your eyes from the mirror you shove two capsules into your mouth, letting them lie on your tongue until the taste gets too bitter, you are thinking about the calf that ripped open and broke your finger on the farm at home the very morning you were supposed to fly to Venice and start the journey here, about the rope the finger got stuck in, about the several hundred kilos of fear that made the calf yank at the rope when it felt the lasso around its neck, and your hand got caught between the rope and the rusty pole in the stall so the upper part of your finger snapped, and you are thinking that the pain, your pain, came such a long time later, not until the evening. Then there is a knock on the door.

The bandage is piled in the sink, before you pour iodine on the cut you wiggle the nail that was detached at the root, when you press on the tip of the nail a hidden spot jumps under the skin of the third joint, the outer phalanx, just above the last joint of the ring finger, up and down like a swing; you spray iodine over the stitched-back nail and reapply the metal splint, he helps you wind the bandage several times around the splint that keeps the finger straight, but when that has been done it turns out to press too hard and the bandage has to be reapplied. The child is standing in the doorway looking at you, you wonder if this is an image that will stay with her, Pappa bandaging Mamma's bad hand in a strange building, a place in her memory whose contours will in all likelihood be erased; your daughter's brown eyes are often unfathomable, in photographs they sometimes possess a distinct expression of grief, but now they are bright with anticipation and under her arm she has the book you bought yesterday after the visit to the Imperial Villa (with its six hundred mountain-goat horns along the walls on the main staircase and the portrait of his wife (Sisi) in his dressing room, she is wearing a white lace dressing gown and her long tresses have been let down, across her shoulders like a broad cloak that falls all the way to her knees, in the middle of her chest two strands of her hair are tied together at the same height as her heart; the portrait was positioned on an easel in front of the desk at which Franz Josef signed the declaration of war against Serbia in the summer of 1914), your child is standing there and the lovely fall of her curls is twisting along both sides of her throat and you smile and say, yes, you're going to be reading the book about the Empress with the long, long hair in the car together while Mamma drives to the new hotel you're going to stay in tonight, it's next to a lake with very clear blue-green water you can swim in.

Haus Schoberstein, Weissenbach am Attersee, Salzkammergut, Austria, June 2006

A certain distance was evidently required for the building to become visible, you have driven past the place several times, followed the waterline all the way to the neighbouring village of Steinbach without managing to see a single building even vaguely reminiscent of the three-storey villa in the photograph you are holding, the glittering lake has been rocking alongside you the whole time just a few metres from the winding country road, the sun is high in the sky and the colour of the water is an opaque bluish green, a colour also called turquoise, cyan and aqua, *water* that is, redundant therefore or a tautology, *water in water*, these various attempts to capture a colour composed of two other colours, blue and green, and you are thinking that Gustav Klimt painted the ruffled surface of the Attersee in a great many different versions, with the light slanting at a low angle more often than not, every summer he would row out early in the morning to paint in the middle of the lake in his flat-bottomed boat, the point of view from water to land, the square canvases made up of 98 per cent water and just a narrow strip of sky or land at the very top, and it may be because you have been distracted by thinking about Gustav Klimt's watery landscapes as you look for the house along the lakeshore on the outskirts of Weissenbach that you fail to see it, by the idea that unlike in Vienna what Klimt painted here summer after summer was the natural world, never any portraits of women, neither naked nor overloaded with clothes, but water for the most part which is after all just a way of trying to capture the light itself, and while you are driving along the narrow road squeezed between the lake and the burgeoning green vegetation at its edge that Klimt too would have driven along many times, you remember the autochrome plate in which he is standing beside the same lake in his ankle-length painting tunic (*"Gustav Klimt sur les rives de l'Attersee, vers 1910, Plaque autochrome Lumière de Friedrich Walker, collection particulière"*), something about that indigo-coloured tunic must have etched its way in, something gloomy about the colour, like an omen, sporting that faun-like beard of his, the painter is standing there looking towards a point outside the picture with a severe expression, not turned towards the water but towards the land, to the edge where the faded grass is growing inwards towards a deciduous forest, as if he could see something he objected to, his fists clenched beneath those long puffed sleeves. At Weyregg, at the midpoint of the lake, you turned round and drove past Steinbach for the second time, the cyan-coloured water always on your right this time, at the turn-off to Weissenbach, which is now in front of you rather than behind you, the road bends and the lake suddenly stretches across the entire windscreen and that is when it happens, when you see the building that had been obscured, when you choke back a cry or whisper so fiercely it makes your vocal chords burn and you throw yourself forward so your sunglasses touch the windscreen. Beyond the bobbing expanse of aqua-coloured water, right in front of you, some way up the wooded mountains the white building you have travelled all this way to visit is looming, that distinctive projecting turret is unmistakable: Haus Schoberstein, Villa Schoberstein according to some sources. You have found it; part way up the immense cliff (Höllengebirge – the Mountains of Hell? – on the map) the building's moon-face is taunting you, the narrow shadow you can make out has to be the large veranda visible in the image, like a smile. A stab of fear, the swell of the lake just a little more pronounced, as if it were the house that had discovered you.

*

A few minutes later and you reach Weissenbach, stopping the car on the shore road, opposite the small town's hotel, a building hard to place in terms of age whose sign proclaims it to be the HOTEL POST, you had stopped here yesterday while trying to find the house, then as now the water was lashing the pier, throwing up metre-high columns and spattering the parked cars, the silver-coloured Renault you hired in Venice a few days ago along with one or two others.

Your child is sleeping on the back seat, it goes without saying that the hunt for the house cannot be undertaken while she is awake, sleep is a protective shell.

You have both been sitting in silence in the car for a while, your eyes fixed on the private jetty that caught your attention the first time you were here: it is square-shaped and covered in a lush, well-maintained lawn, an elderly couple were sitting there yesterday on garden chairs side by side reading the papers, you have never seen a jetty like this one before, like a backdrop, part of a working stage set. After a while you reverse out of the car park and turn 180 degrees towards the vertical cliff from which the house takes its name: Schoberstein, and drive up a little hill and turn off to the left just round the corner from the Hotel Post to park in front of the kitchen entrance, behind a green rubbish container standing in the shade. On the right-hand side the ground rises a metre or two above your heads, up there is where the land belonging to Haus Schoberstein begins. A member of staff walks from the kitchen door over to a van and peers in your direction, but then soon goes back inside again.

"There are no *bearers of secrets* up there any more," you say, and wish he would try to smile. Slowly, with your good hand, you place the video camera and your new digital one in the shoulder bag. The car park is just as empty, the sun is broiling, you try out the word *Herz*, here the word for heart is *Herz*, your heart is beating rapidly. You close the car door carefully behind you so as not to wake her, she is breathing heavily inside the car with the heating on.

A half-landing stairway cut out of the rock leads up to the property, after the last turn you are standing on the edge of an English park, the greater part of which is in shadow, the trees are a mixture of pines and firs and right at the back next to the cliff face is an immense copper beech. It is apparent that the building is connected with the hotel in some way, presumably it is used as a conference centre, no single person can be seen in the vicinity at this moment, the lawn has been weeded and is well tended, there is no long grass swaying in the breeze, which reinforces the impression of absolute stillness, a gravel path draws gleaming lines across the ground, the gravel here is white too, although you notice that it does not stick to your soles as the gravel (or was it ash?) in Treblinka is said to have done.

The path curves beneath the beech tree, you get out the video camera and press PLAY. Facing the mountain you film the huge copper beech, when you arrive beneath it you look up at the canopy, layer upon layer of branches reaching up towards the sky, there is a wooden bench beside the trunk and it frightens you, as if a voice might emerge from it, that may be why you start talking quietly into the camera, tentative and indistinct to begin with, there is a kind of protection in the silence it feels uncomfortable to abandon. It will be difficult to hear what you are saying afterwards (. . . *sixty-six years* . . .), particularly at the beginning of the tape, the camera pans shakily towards the house (*There . . . the balcony and the veranda . . . the side wall overlooks a fish pond* . . .). In focus a circular construction of coarsely polished granite. A long tracking shot zooms in on the fish pond, the water is opaque and mud-coloured. Cut from the fishpond up to the house. A quick panning shot from the basement to the top. Just below the roof there are reflections from the sunlight dancing on the water, the sunbeams form an undulating pattern that simply freezes solid on film, not one of the still pictures captures it.

A clear blue sky.

The black motion of a swallow cuts into the image, it flies this way and that above the billowing reflections of the water, in and out under a beam. How old does a swallow get? How many generations of swallows have used the nest under that beam? If evil is an oblique angle, what is time? What kind of geometry does it possess?

It was all drifting on open water.

You turn around, from the veranda the Attersee is a blue strip shredded by white sails. The Rose Wind is blowing across the lake, ruffling the surface. You wonder where the roses are, what kind of roses the wind is sweeping across the lake.

Villa Schoberstein, the Hitler Government's
Recreation Facility
for T4-Staff members, Bad Ischl-weg 1, Weissenbach
am Attersee, Reichsgau Oberdonau, Ostmark
(Austria under Annexation), August 2, 1943, 6.00 a.m.

"If only everyone was like you, Unterscharführer Seidel." The book-keeper Klara Deneke's words come back to him on this last morning, who was she comparing him with in her thoughts? Miete? Mentz? Josef Vallaster? He's from the area after all so he'd be bound to come here when he could and she can't really have been thinking about Frank and that fair boyish face of his that would surely have charmed Lorent's former secretary when she sighed like that, besides he's got a whore in the village and would never bother making the long trip here. In his mind S.S.-Unterscharführer Kurt Seidel runs quickly through his colleagues, which of them has taken the opportunity to stay at the holiday villa? Apart from the married ones, a lot of them stay at the camp while they are on leave, exchanging goods and services with the Polish women who gather at the fence; although what's it to him, why bother about what some conceited typist thinks of him? He brushes the whole business aside and turns his gaze outward instead, towards a landscape irradiated by the play of light off a vast still lake, once again he notices the way the summer clouds are reflected in the great glass pane that is the Attersee at this time of day, before the wind has picked up, the clouds are snow-white cottony formations and remind him reluctantly of Boelitz's hair (a dependable young man nonetheless, maybe because they share a background in the police force), in his mind's eye he can see the glint of Boelitz's bone-white hair as he stands on the ramp, his eyebrows and lashes are faded as well and give off tiny golden sparkles when the sun shines through them, Boelitz on the platform, sober and correct, his hair gleaming as he issues directions in a reassuring though firm voice, just like the policeman he essentially continues to be, oh well . . . S.S.-Unterscharführer Kurt Seidel takes one last deep drag as he looks at the glassy lake dotted with cumulus clouds that extend all the way over to Unterach on the other shore, the village he sometimes rows over to in a newly painted rowing boat, if only he had time he would have jumped into the little vessel and made his way out to the centre of the lake to float in the enormous inverted sky that is now expanding at his feet, what a sight he saw when he came down to the jetty a while ago: the sky doubled, dropped, to put it bluntly, across the surface of the lake; the mirror effect is opening up the firmament before him, row upon row of shining cumulus clouds are sketching a kind of heavenly valley above the water, the water no longer water but air, the weightlessness of the clouds, snow-covered mountains or gigantic tufts of cotton wool, continues to enthrall him and for a fraction of a second the delusion, the hollow feeling in the pit of his stomach that says a fall from up there would be identical to the incomparable sensation of flying, gets the better of him again. It occurs to him almost immediately afterwards that there is also a practical side to the notion: he can save this beautiful illusion and summon it up if . . . when at death's door, when he is about to be devoured by what he conceives to be the cellar-like darkness of death, which could happen at any moment, after all, at any moment he could be reassigned and forced to board one of the troop transports that pass through the railway junction at Małkynia rather than get off there; at the thought of the small station where he has seen so many army units and military supplies pass by on their way to the front, a few short kilometres from the river where he goes to swim, the word "Stalingrad" occludes the image of the lake like a solar eclipse and blacks everything out; he throws the butt into the water, the cigarette end floats for a second or two before coming apart and sinking; at any moment, though, a bombing raid could blow them all apart or the partisans could launch an attack, or death could strike the way it struck Max Bielas on the calmest of afternoons, stabbed as he was by a worker-Jew when he least expected it; if death comes creeping so slowly through his body he has time to see the black wave coming he can place the vision of this heavenly valley between himself and the onrushing darkness like a hand-coloured film, reassuring notions of dying form part of a soldier's equipment after all, like cigarettes, preserved meat and dressings. And endless rounds of drinks in the stone hall named Valhalla are not in his nature, on the contrary, all he feels when occasionally he goes to the mess is revulsion. A splash cracks the surface into concentric circles, the rings reach the water-lily leaves floating in clumps near the jetty where he is sitting, the long ridges and knots of the rough grey-bleached boards scrape the back of his thighs as he reaches for the gold lighter that has become a kind of amulet; he lights a fresh cigarette, spitting out a flake of tobacco. *Bug!* He loathes the very name, he tries to keep his eyes fixed on the clear greenish-blue water clucking against the jetty beneath him, but it is a brown Polish river he is seeing, the mud churned up by those disorderly, bleating Ukrainians; the jolting and the racket of the squeaking wheelsets is already preying on him, all the stops and the changes of train, the singed smell, the overcrowding and the sweaty feet, the suppressed fear of being strafed which is another form of cold sweat all the time on the nape of his neck, the smouldering fires and the fences clad in pine branches where he is headed that limit your field of vision wherever you look; his reluctance to make the journey is being converted into a sluggishness in his limbs, a hollow sensation in his midriff that leaves him almost breathless; how he wishes he could stay with this lightness meeting his eyes, drink in for one more day the cool fresh smell of the mountain, over a thousand metres high, that descends like mist from the cliff face at his back, the cool, fresh mountain smell that meets that of the water here by the lake and makes the air almost floral, *rose-like*, which may well be why the wind over the lake is called "the Rose Wind" by the locals, that has not occurred to him before. S.S.-Unterscharführer Kurt Seidel, whose

leave ends in exactly twenty-four hours, is clinging to these percep-
tions as though they were implements he could actually hold, wedges
set into a rock fissure that could keep him suspended over this place,
and in one last attempt to prolong the few minutes left to him before
he has to get to his feet and walk up to the house and finish packing
and put his uniform on he applies himself to predicting the atmospheric phenomena that will occur here in the next few hours, after
he has left: the wind will pick up just before nine, the Rose Wind
whose name he now feels he has invented, named for the very first
time, and the Rose Wind will then shatter the reflection of the sky and
make the surface of the water crinkle into millions of tiny opaque
waves (by nine o'clock he should already be on the first train); then,
as the sun climbs, the bluish-green colour of the lake will intensify,
the blue of the inverted sky will become earthly water, cloudy but
turquoise in any case, like a gigantic jewel casually left around for
everyone to look at, without any greed, without any intense or heady
desire to grab it for your own. What happens next, just after nine?
Here, with no warning, his predictions go off at a tangent and he finds
himself on the platform where the carriages will be standing at around
nine, in front of the painted clock which always shows a different
time, always the same wrong time of day: six, as the time is now or
rather what the time was when he came down to the jetty. He reaches
for the watch he placed in one of his sandals, it shows 06.17, the
second hand is moving, time is not standing still here after all, he
looks out over the water as if it could offer some kind of corrobor-
ation, in the movement of the large white cumulus clouds perhaps,
though he can no longer see a radiant heavenly valley, not even a fallen
heaven, but rather the metre-wide pipe on "Ascension Road" in the
Upper Camp, as though he had got lost in a system of passages running across several different floors that all ultimately lead into each
other, the flow of his thoughts has got stuck as if at a crossroads and
he experiences this immobility of mind as a kind of ache, a forceful
pressure on his frontal lobe, a pressure he tries to balance through an

act of will by sucking air and smoke deep into his lungs, he takes a few quick drags until his thoughts start flowing again and soon the words are coming to his rescue, spinning out the red thread so he can find his way back: *Attersee, Rosenwind, Höllengebirge*; he pronounces the names slowly, committing them to memory along with the other names, folding them syllable by syllable, meticulously, the way he folded his shirts earlier, because he will not be coming back to this place (fewer and fewer transports are arriving, the one with the Bulgarians from Thessaloniki was the last major one and that was a while ago, at the end of March, the week after his birthday, a sense of bodily calm was restored to everyone that day, the gold-Jews in particular) but then there is another lull and his departure is in the air again, like the muggy soil-saturated smell of summer rain and thunder that rises after a storm and that storm does have a name, Stalingrad, a name with a rotten smell that used to hover like cigarette smoke over the tables in the mess throughout autumn and spring ("High time the Wehrmacht had to fight a Rat War, like we've been doing the whole time!" followed by Bolender's dry guffaw, like the sound of a seam being ripped open) until the day it was finally admitted that the entire Sixth Army had been destroyed, building by building, house by house, in that "Rat War", and here he is now, all too aware that he is being crushed between two places without prospects, that there are no other prospects than the elusive beauty of the view before him. In the end the presence of the building and the three-peaked mountain becomes so strong he can feel it on the back of his neck, he will soon have to get up and go and it is as if that vertical Mountain of Hell, as upright as a wall carved out of the rock, were telling him so. Villa Schoberstein, another name to take with him, from one hell to another, hell can be flat as well, a region in the heart of the forest walled off by fences, a few short kilometres from the border and with the Russians far too close to the river; he is thinking about the suitcase he smuggled out on his last leave and which is now under a bed in Prenzlauer Berg, and about his last conversation with

Stangl, the Kommandant has a tendency to confide in him, most recently he pointed out, with the nasal pronunciation typical of his Austrian accent, that they had a lot in common and then took the trouble to come up with a long list: the police background came first, of course, but also the fact that he is the only person, apart from the Kommandant himself, who borrows the books they get sent. It was there in his office that Stangl let him know he had applied for a transfer a long time ago, that Wirth had mentioned an anti-partisan unit in Italy, and he promised to make sure that he, Seidel, would get to go with him. An unusually broad-winged gull crosses his field of vision with a screech, it is unusually white too, no black lines decorate the tips of its wings, the whiteness appears to be related to the clouds it is flying between, the bright-yellow beak opens for another piercing cry that slices across the silence like a knife, Kurt Seidel watches the gliding flight of the bird for a long while, the perfectly delineated wings flap every now and then until it is a white spot far off at the same height as the black onion dome in Unterach, silence falls once more over the landscape, the world seems to have been deprived of all sound and motion, besides the lake and its constantly changing light spectacle it is this silence he will miss most, the din and the responsiveness of his senses in Treblinka get on his nerves, the screams of the women and children that the singing of the caged nightingales cannot cover up, on the contrary, they erupt into the trilling of the birds like boils and the tune gets distorted by squeaking notes that jar and the deformed birdsong continues to wobble for the eternity of the three hours it takes to deal with a transport like woozy black swarms hovering among the pine trees. He gets to his feet, it is getting late, he gathers up his things, right by his cigarette case and the gold lighter with its ornate inscription, just a few centimetres from the notch where he wedged the first of his cigarette ends this morning, the large scorch mark from last night's bonfire glistens, a black wound now on the wooden boards, a few hours ago the flames of a fire burning in a zinc tub lugged down from the house; while he does up the watch strap around his left wrist he can see head nurse Gertrud's dainty watch against her own coarse one, the thin black-leather strap digging into her flesh; then other arms, rough, loose skin, plum-coloured cones on heavy white breasts he had sucked to hardness under a sweaty sheet, the sour smell of the secretions from a sticky bush of hair; he thinks about the way women's voices set their stamp on a room, their movements leave their imprint on a place, an entire landscape, like throwing a large stone into water, the presence of women changes the frequency of the wavelengths in a space, the flower beds and zoo Stangl had them construct during the spring when there were so few transports are an expression of the essence of the feminine, the night-ingales and the deer, the finely carved benches set out here and there in the garden invite reflection and stillness, animals and flowers femi-nise a landscape, they serve as passive, beautifully coloured currents of a secondary form of energy, still and receptive like water, a female energy that would otherwise be entirely lacking there. He recalls some of the wives and the nurses doing exercises early in the morning on the lawn up at the Villa during his first stay, in the summer of '41, they performed them all in white, wearing very short skirts, like the girls on display in "Wochenschau" before the war; the old times and the new continuing to live on in one another, that may be why he can now see images of the rear courtyard in the Prenzlauer Berg of his childhood where he once kissed a girl, the courtyard faced the abat-toir, there were always a lot of children prowling around the loading bay of the slaughterhouse and war veterans rooting through the waste bins, like the corporal with the disfigured face they called "the Monster"; Kurt Seidel, born in Berlin in 1912, has lived long enough to recognise a familiarity about the body parts of the different people he has encountered, as if nature did not have an endless array of them at its disposal and provided you live long enough you were bound to come across a mouth, a smile, a gait or a pair of hands you have come across before in one or several other persons: the parts of the body as reminiscences of other lives (that Tchechia, who had worked at the garrison for a bit but had to go back to the hospital ward for the worker-Jews: the sheen and the waves in her red-blonde hair, her hands, her way of moving them and the shape of her fingernails, hadn't they seemed familiar to him?), these reminiscences might be secret signs: only what sort of sign? An omen? That his life, like a circle, is now nearing its end? He starts to walk up to the house, as a final farewell he conjures up images of the gang that was partying here last night in the light of the flames; Walther's accordion and all the commotion they made on the jetty must have travelled right across the lake and disturbed the guests at the hotel, good old Erwin dancing up close to his Maria the whole night long (her frizzy hair like an aura of uncarded wool surrounding that permanently smiling face, that face resting against the man whose body hair calls to mind the image of a bear's pelt), they make a nice couple, there is something age-old about their attraction to each other that makes you think of folk tales: "Beauty and the Flying Architect", good old Erwin Lambert is going to marry her, make no mistake about it, as soon as circumstances permit, you can see it in the way he looks at her and the way she welcomes his looks, yesterday in the dining room downstairs they were telling him about the day they met, in the dining room at Schloss Hartheim, as it turned out, he had come to convert the instal-lation, they ended up at the same table and it was love at first sight, despite the difference in their ages, he must be at least fifteen years older than Maria, they plan on getting married in Linz, they have already been approved by the Racial Purity Board and are near the top of the list for an apartment in the Führerstadt; Kurt Seidel recalls that Maria went up to her room to fetch some pictures taken on Agfacolor film she had been able to buy through the photographer at the hospi-tal, they caused quite a stir because colour photographs are a rarity, there were pictures of the Führer's visit to Linz in April, Maria was smiling among the crowd on the Nibelungen Bridge, in a blue dirndl that looked so lovely in colour, the Agfacolor brought out some marvellous shades, as it did from the bright-red gleam of the Blood

Flags that fluttered at intervals along the railing of the bridge, an equestrian statue of Siegfried was outlined against the clear sky above the entire scene, and level with the horse's hindquarters one of the flags was flying above Maria Brandstetter's head like a veil the wind had got all tangled up, as if she were already a bride, it was just that the veil was red, an involuntary association with fresh blood evoked some misgivings in Kurt Seidel when he saw it although he brushes them aside now, thinking about the two of them, Erwin and Maria, sitting there holding hands saying everyone was invited to their wedding, and he is also thinking of the way the characteristic kindliness in Erwin's eyes turned shiny with a vast and deep joy. Unterscharführer Kurt Seidel takes his leave of all these figures as though they were still sitting round the table at the Hotel Post, all of them fit to burst from laughing, Maria's head in its red bridal veil resting happily against Erwin's chest; soon after he reaches the rear courtyard of the hotel where stone steps lead down to the recreation facility's park whose dark-green shadow welcomes him (the baroque blue sky now screened off) with a raw dampness that caresses the bare skin of his shoulders, as though the foliage were a weight on his head he drops his eyes to his sandals, the gravel path he is walking along merges with the path he runs along every morning, past the root cellar and the exercise ground for the Ukrainians, he usually runs at this time of day, well before the arrival of the transports, into the pine forest and back by the road that runs in a straight line between the section for the worker-Jews and the garrison, finally he turns onto the 800-metre long cement road that bears his name, Kurt Seidel Strasse (how proud his mother would have been that he had a street named after him, even though it is just a short stretch in a little forest clearing in the General Government, he does not think about it much himself although he does occasionally mention it to her in his sleep); the Ukrainians run as well and use his road as a track, at the end of April one of them almost broke a record, just behind John Woodruff's time of 1'52.9", they were pretty full of themselves afterwards. Kurt Seidel thinks about his own youth, and how things might have turned out for him if he had had the chance to enlist in the Air Force Academy in Gatow or Dresden, in which case he would most definitely not have ended up in the pit of the Reich's stomach, its stinking anal orifice, he pictures himself in an Air Force officer's uniform, like the ones worn by the young officers he saw on the streets of Dresden when he was a transport leader for *Die Sonne*. Though there is at least an 800-metre stretch of road in this vale of tears that bears his name, he supervised the work himself, by God he did, like so many of the other construction projects and improvement works in the Lower Camp: the lawns and flowerbeds bordering the asphalt road, the staff quarters, the watch towers and the gate in the Tyrolean style (not the painted clock on the platform, however, that was Kommandant Stangl's idea); they spent all of the months of March and April on the avenue, surveying, excavating and laying the foundations, forced to endure the fumes from the cement that smoothed out the gravel laid across that dead Polish soil. Although he feels nothing for the zoo, he is thinking about it as the path curves under a hundred-year-old copper beech, the bizarre conceit of having two hundred nightingales in cages is one he finds disturbing, animals in general make him nervous, particularly the squirrels and their large rats' eyes; a glimpse of the white riding jacket worn by the Kommandant peeks from among his thoughts the same way it did between the bushes while he was watching the naked people from the mound on the other side of the fence, then he remembers the way he saw things a short while ago, the way he conceived of the hand-coloured heavenly valley and wonders what the naked ones protect themselves with against the waiting darkness. Though worst of all are those revolting transplanted squirrels and the havoc they cause among the children up by the pipe. He passes the veranda, the faint clatter of cups and dishes travels through the open doors of the dining room, once he is inside the hall the front door slams shut behind him as if to confirm his own view: what happens up at Camp II has got nothing to do with him, he has *never* been an operative there.

*

The smell of smoke is still thick inside the dormitory despite the regulations and despite his having left the window wide open. His suitcase is also open on the unmade-up bunk, Gomerski is lying open-mouthed on the upper one, knocked out, insensitive to the sounds and noises of the world, he arrived from Sobibor the day before yesterday and was celebrating noisily on the jetty last night, Seidel cannot bear him, he would have requested a change of room if he had been staying longer, it is not personal, the cremators have all been marked by what they do, coarse and disrespectful like that obnoxious Vallaster. S.S.-Unterscharführer Kurt Seidel changes into his uniform trousers, with an easy swinging gait he moves over to the handbasin at which he has to stand bent slightly forward in front of the low mirror and rubs pomade on the spot where a dark-blonde tuft coils up from his scalp, he then combs the cream carefully through his still-wet hair with a tortoiseshell comb, the tip of his chin kept tucked into his throat so he can see what he is doing, he had a shave before his swim, he inspects the cut on his right jaw, it has stopped bleeding. The comb, the razor and the rest of his gear he stuffs into his washbag and pushes the bag in its turn into the suitcase, next to the sandals and the wet swimming costume which has been rolled up and tucked into one corner, it is bound to smell of mildew when finally he gets there. Then he opens the wardrobe and takes out the leather jackboots he made sure to have polished the same day he arrived, but it is almost impossible for him to put them on, his feet have swollen. He sits down heavily on the edge of the bunk and pushes one of his feet inside while having to tug repeatedly at the leg of the boot before his heel goes in all the way with a thud. Gomerski snores loudly as if he were deliberately taunting him. The procedure is repeated with the other foot. With both boots on he walks around the little room several times in order to sink properly inside them, forcing his resisting feet to get used to being cooped up, he goes back to the wardrobe with creaking steps and takes the neatly pressed grey shirt off its hanger before putting his arms through the sleeves, he pulls the tie around and under the collar and knots it, then he puts on the field-green uniform jacket, does up the five buttons from the top downwards and folds the collar over so his perfectly centred tie is visible. He has to do the last bit in front of the mirror above the handbasin. He recalls an image of himself dressed in the white coat he used to wear when he was transport leader in Sonnenstein. It was an innate quality he possessed, without the slightest effort he could inspire confidence and exude kindness and calm, people trusted him, that is how it had always been, it could be because he was well built and tall or because he conveyed that natural authority in his manner, through his eyes, as someone had once tried to persuade him, he cannot remember who any longer. Finally he hooks the metal tongue into the black leather belt, his service pistol has been secured and is in its holster and he is holding his cap under his armpit, with the peak, the skull and the eagle insignia facing outward. Aware that this is the last time he will be coming here he slams the door shut, hoping the noise will wake Gomerski.

He carries his suitcase down the stone steps with a casual, almost trotting gait, but his boots creak so much that the people sitting closest to the door eating breakfast in the dining room turn in his direction, from the corner of his eye he catches a glimpse of the couple who arrived late the evening before, when almost everyone had finished dinner and Maria had been handing the album around, he recognises the woman, she is a doctor's secretary, Dr Lonauer is sitting next to them with his family, his wife on his right, her glossy dark hair is arranged tightly around her pale narrow face as if she had also just been for a swim down in the lake and it was still wet, the son has dark, lively eyes. Then he turns left towards the exit. In the entrance hall he has to hold the door open for Ilse Haus who tells him that his car is waiting and wishes him a pleasant journey: "You're leaving us in the nick of time, Herr Seidel, all the records are on their way here from Berlin, the head office has been hit by a bomb and the entire staff have been forced to camp out in a shed in the garden for several days."

Then she disappears along the corridor behind the staircase and into her office.

Outside, the vault of the vast sky he had been observing down by the lake is still bulging with cumulus clouds, like a church mural, he looks at his watch, twelve minutes past seven, just as he becomes aware of the sound of a bouncing tennis ball. The doctor couple from Vienna are already playing on the court opposite the main entrance, behind the sparse vegetation that screens off the court he can make out the white clothes the players are wearing, the waiting car is parked by the high fence around the tennis court and while he is walking over to it the driver makes the German salute with a rather loose hand, failing to extend his fingers with full force, but he decides to turn a blind eye and hands him the suitcase before getting in. From the right window in the back seat S.S.-Unterscharführer Kurt Seidel casts one last look at his surroundings, one of the kitchen maids is out early feeding the rabbits by the half-buried greenhouse on the right, just a metre or so away from the high barbed-wire fence that shields the plot from the public thoroughfare below, he can see the white kerchief dipping towards the cages, there may be rabbit stew for dinner, as on his first evening. That leader of the Photographic Section in Berlin, Wanger – Wagner? – the name escapes him at first, Franz Wagner, a small, mild-mannered man who used to spend time over there by the cage, feeding the rabbits with vegetable leaves as big as sheets; while the car is reversing he winds down the window, for a moment there is no sound from the tennis court, but through the dark branches he can see the female doctor preparing to serve, the match would appear to have got going again, the sound of the racquets striking the balls accompanies him for quite some distance beyond the steep curve of the drive that leads away from Villa Schoberstein, and then it is as if his thoughts suddenly become stuck between the two sounds, as though the cadence were trying to trap them: a hush occurs between the first and the second beat, the brief silence between the first and the second bounce of the white ball, his vision is being trapped as well, it gets stuck on the woman's white skirt, which rises like a beat of wings in the air above her thighs as she hits the ball back, and the same hush is forming between the words *white* and *skirt*, white-skirt, white-skirt, it is as if that reverberation were occupying the interior of his cranium, and when he thinks about that he can see the craggy face of the rock wall he has been living beneath for a couple of weeks, the steep cliff face of the mountain that loomed high above the building and above them all, rock-wall, rock-wall, like a cupped hand, a vice-like grip. It is not until they are approaching the broad, shallow river flowing along both sides of the road outside the little town of Weissenbach that the stacked-up words work loose. "Honk!" he yells to the driver because some of the people from the villa are standing in the stream, water up to their ankles and long fishing rods over their shoulders. Mayrhuber, wearing Lederhosen, is in the middle of the stream, he waves, as do the Hackel couple, he can see old Emil wobbling with his arms extended before they all vanish behind a curve. Emil is off to the Western front, he is supposed to report next week, after being married for only twelve months. He has no clear memories of Hedwig from his time at C16, he cannot help associating her forgettable face with the stench that could hit you when you opened the rear doors of the buses. He looks at his watch, he can feel his toes at the bottom of his boots pining for the cool water he is leaving so inexorably behind him, his toes twist inside their black socks, thrusting upwards so the nails scratch the inside of the boot, the water is so bloody cold, that has to be the only drawback of the Attersee, and the fact that it is so far away these days. Though he prefers Rosel Kaufmann to Ilse Haus, she has already filled the villa with high-ups like the Lonauers and that doctor couple on the tennis court. They stop at the crossing and before they drive out onto the main road to Bad Ischl he can see a convoy bearing down on them from the left, his driver pulls onto the road with plenty of time to spare and as the two limousines and a large green Saurer BT4500 with a covered bed passes them he twists his neck to the window opposite to try and catch a glimpse of the passengers, but all he can make out is the familiar radiator of the lorry. This has to be the consignment of records all the way from Berlin, already here, crate upon crate packed with certificates and reports, rolls of film and photographic documentation, binders filled with employment contracts, including his own. Without understanding why at first, he feels unsettled at the thought of the Central Office moving in to Villa Schoberstein, it feels like a kind of trespass, tress-pass, tress-pass, his thoughts get stuck again, tress-pass, tress-pass, he repeats to the rhythm of the engine and can see once again the mountain looming behind Villa Schoberstein and the cliff terrace where they all sat drinking beer in the evenings while the sun went down behind the peaks.

"The holidays'll soon be over," the driver says suddenly from the front, like an echo of what Klara Deneke had recently announced – *Soon there won't be any holidaymakers coming here*– and while he is listening to the driver change gear he is watching those manicured typist hands of Klara Deneke's, the habitual nature of the gesture as she signs and passes a receipt to him. Far from feeling gratitude for the interruption he is suffused by a wave of panic, he closes his eyes firmly as if that could make time stand still, put a stop to what he can see in his mind's eye, the three weeks he has been away for is far too long, the reality he imagined waiting for him frozen like a still will have had time to alter over and over again. Inside the body of the car the engine turns over more rapidly and it is as if the same horsepower were making time run riot, he almost screams when he realises that: everyone can be replaced, gone, even the wife of the Kapo, that woman Tchechia and her red hair. He takes a deep breath, looks out through the window, it is Monday today, just an ordinary Monday, the journey is a long one, best remain calm.

Hotel Seegasthof Stadler, Unterach am Attersee, Salzkammergut, Austria, June 2006, Evening

The lake is a plate of glass, an immense blue-tinted lid of silence, and the evening sky is emptying its light into it, it is the lake that is the source of light, the sky just a reflection; between you and Haus Schoberstein there are now vast expanses of water.

You take off the bathrobe you borrowed from the hotel and it falls to the jetty almost without a sound. It is cold, the tricot film of the black swimming costume leaves your back bare and as the damp in the evening air moves across it, the skin feels as if it has been scraped off. You are watching the low smoky mist gather once again in the centre of the lake, at the same spot, though smoother now, where fluttering metre-high veils of mist, intertwined like girls clasping each other by the hand, executed a ghostly ring dance at sunrise; you were astonished then by the crazed fluctuations of the mists towards the invisible hole they disappeared into one after the other, the higher the sun rose the wilder the dance became, the greater their haste to dash to the point where they were sucked down. Now they are rising again. On tiptoe you raise your arms towards the high vault above your head and that is when you see his swallow dive from the springboard at the top, suspended beneath the open sky at the summit of a hill not far from Tibidabo, not far from the point where the city begins to slope all the way from the mountains down to the port; he flings himself upwards in his one-piece bathing suit that is black like yours, it is him, but long before he became your father, you know there were still bullet holes in the swimming pool. Before he begins to drop he hovers for a moment with arms outstretched and his spinal column flexed outwards. You lean forwards and aim for the open shaft. An enormous pressure is blotting out every sound except that of your blood. Then the water opens and you can see the old rooms in Lérida flooded like in a shipwreck, the walls of photographs, the portrait in the hall, the pile of records on the floor, the flounces of your christening robes swaying in the current. You spread your arms and float, your arms gleam in the leftover daylight as they clear the way, you swim through the long corridor that ran from the entrance to the illuminated stairwell, through the hall to the best room and the sunlit sitting room, into the nursery without a view. Then you stop again, your spinal column flexed outwards, the hair around your face like seaweed. The whole of the lake is resting on your back.

You come up to the surface, from the evening water that is lapping against your eyes you observe the line of land, the severe contour of the Schoberstein mountain. You swim slowly, half your face submerged, just your eyes, forehead and the crown of your head still in contact with the air, the cold cuts into your hands, your body slices the water, when you sink it is an act of will, the difference between tightening your muscles and letting go and you let go, you fall sharply through the water, blindly, your vertical body a luminous knife through patches of bluish-green. His body up on the springboard against the evening light, those transparent blue eyes, as if there were only harsh, chlorinated water under his skin, you open your jawbones wide and the scream comes rolling out of the depths like a wave, you are hurled backwards, it is the force of the scream that hurls you backwards as you unleash it

YOU
ARE
ALL
DEAD!

On the jetty afterwards your head is heavy, your legs half in and half out of the water. *Sonámbula*. Sleepwalker.

Hotel Seegasthof Stadler, Unterach am Attersee, Salzkammergut, Austria, June 2006, Morning

Your five-year-old daughter cannot reach over the balcony railing so she is kneeling on a garden chair beside you looking out over the lake, or peering down at the garden perhaps where there are swings and a large lawn; your right hand is keeping watch, spread across the hollow between her shoulder blades, resting on the undulating sliding surface that is covered by her long hair, you know that scent well, vanilla and something nutty and tangy that is somehow connected with your own skin, her soft corkscrew curls, hollow the way letters are (letters you constantly decipher with your hands), give elastically when your fingers squeeze them, you have never had to cut that hair, or bleach it with corrosive acids in the middle of the night (lacking any protection other than the dark). On the opposite shore the colossal grey silhouette of the triple-peaked Schoberstein is sharply outlined, a mountain with three peaks can also be seen from your home on the farm: Canigó or Canigou as it is called on the French side, snow-covered in winter and well into spring when the scampering calves chase one another, kicking out their back legs in a frenzy to drive the winter cold from their muscles; the sky here is high and clear the way only spring skies are down there in the south, as they were when your child was born at the large county hospital on the coast, the dogs ran down the lane to meet you as you arrived, the mulberries were still just small green buds on the trees, in a few years the child would be eating the ripe purplish-red berries straight from the ground, like the vixen that had started to turn up at night and the flock of starlings that invaded the lane one summer after an unusually severe winter, but it was still only March and the child was lying silently in the pram you were pushing to and fro under the mulberry tree and along the wall of old cypresses behind the kitchen garden, up to the sloping cow pastures from where you could see the Pyrenees and the white top of Canigó, a blend of lavender and rosemary in the air and the acrid sour-sweet stench of pig manure that rose from the neighbouring farmer's fields. Your mood was as unrelenting as that stench (it floated in through each and every window that was left open), you dragged the pram up to the newly delivered calves like a sleepwalker, and the unrelenting pain you felt like a weight on your chest stretched tight across your breasts and trickled down secret paths into the milk ducts and you were afraid that so much inexplicable and unexplained grief would make your child ill, she was otherwise so healthy, the one person no-one could take away from you; though you were still haunted by the gipsy woman who ran past you on the pavement in the city of your childhood with her little son flopping in her arms, you were on your way to school one morning when she crossed your path, you had only managed to take a couple of steps out of the front door, the woman was weeping though not that loudly, more like a whimper or a suppressed moan (as if she was saving her energy for an even greater pain), her bare soles were making more noise as they slapped against the paving stones and the asphalt with a wet whipping sound that drowned out the buses and the cars driving down the street, and you stopped and turned around and watched the woman's black soles as she rushed out into the traffic to move at a slant towards the Red Cross hospital, one of the boy's slack arms dangling with every step, you stayed where you were (turning up in bare feet at school was a recurrent dream that filled you with shame) and watched her barefoot running as though you had been bewitched, convinced those feet would leave burn-marks on the hospital steps. Many years later as you came out of the hospital in Palamós with your newborn child in your arms, you could see those black soles again, as though they might come running past at any moment and point the way to an approaching catastrophe, this was shortly before Easter and a cold northerly wind was blowing, white-topped waves were picking up even between the piers inside the port, at the farm the dogs barked like crazy when the car drove up under the mulberry tree whose branches were swinging in every direction, spots of sunlight through the swaying leaves formed a carpet of moving patterns along the gravel road; something (the homecoming or the barking and the wind and the patterns of sunspots on the ground) made you think of the wall-to-wall carpet of flower petals along which the military parade was supposed to pass during *La procesión del Corpus*, the adults were wearing their Sunday best and the children white or black leather shoes, in front of the town hall the city's giants made of wood and papier mâché were standing still, they had not yet begun to spin and dance, their hollow bodies without bearers, empty, it was like a tent under the queen's skirt but one whose top was infinitely high, a transparent pane gleamed through the material of her skirt at the height of her lap, you were standing on one of the cross-pieces that held the trunk together in order to reach the camouflaged peephole, through it you could see the soldiers arriving in their dress uniforms, striding across the pattern of petals in their black boots, with your father at the front, next to the soldier carrying the flag, marching and swinging his right arm so that the white glove reaches the height of his shoulder, the purple silk sash set diagonally across his chest and the plume whose long bristles you sometimes comb with your fingers dangling against his hip alongside the steel sword you know is very heavy and always very cold, you are shouting from inside the casing of the cardboard doll and with every step the soldiers take, red and white rose and carnation petals fly up an inch or two across the ground, you keep shouting but he cannot hear you, he keeps marching beside the flag, his gaze fixed on some point straight ahead until the procession has gone past and the street is empty. The petals have turned into piles of debris, it is absolutely silent, there are no longer any traces of rose or carnation in the air, nor of rosemary or lavender, when they sniff the child in your arms the dogs fall silent as well.

"Pappa!" Your child is using the whole of her arm to wave. "You and Pappa should go and swim now," you say and let her get down from the chair.

When you close the door behind them silence fills the room like a flood of afternoon light, you follow that light to the bed with the orange-brown bedspread and sit on it, at the foot, with a degree of expectation, as if something were about to happen. Your choosing that particular spot has to do with the light, the square of sunlight that is painted on the floor in front of the open balcony resembles the square that was formed in the living room of your childhood home, it was smaller and fainter in the winter when the sunlight made the mottled green flagstones flow like the water in a stream across the floor, during the spring and summer the corrosive light opened glowing islands of shiny whiteness that burned the soles of your feet, although the sun poured all year round into the large, square-shaped room that faced south. In the otherwise dark and damp flat the living room was a kind of courtyard, the long, straight corridor that began in the hall and swerved towards the front door on the right led to it as well. The living room also contained what you might call the apartment's hearth: *la mesa camilla,* the low round table with a thick cloth that reached all the way to the floor and beneath which was an electric firepot with a cylindrical element in the middle. When the current was turned on the element shone with a bright golden-red light from the centre of its aluminium dish, like an orange left behind in a cave, the hot chamber that was formed under the cloth while the firepot was on, and the thin black cord was plugged into the equally black point on the wall, was also cavernous and forbidden. Even so, you lifted the cloth whenever you got the chance to observe the burning orange from a distance, on your knees you could see the deadly light that was nevertheless the source of so much that was good because the raw chill that made the clothes in the cupboards damp, verging on wet, in the winter and formed pools of condensation under the beds made you feel heavy and long for sleep; the radiant firepot was an antidote to that somnolence, a caged sun from which heat was extracted though to touch it meant burns and something deadly called "electric shock", and you could get *cabrillas* too if you sat close to the firepot for too long, fluid-filled blisters on your legs, like Doña Enriqueta who ran the shop in the basement, *cabrillas* sounded like little goats to your ears. You took your meals at the round table all winter, the toast with orange marmalade your mother made in a large saucepan in the kitchen and that you, dressed in the dark-blue uniform and the regulation Gorila-brand brown lace-ups with rubber soles (also known as "gorillas"), had for a snack when you came home from school, and the soup served at lunchtimes when your father came home from the barracks. The cloudy soup with its coating of fat and the shapeless lumps that you loathed.

"Eat up," your father said.

"It'll be easier if you think about something else," your mother said and after you had counted to ten you shoved half a spoonful into your mouth even though it was hard to think about anything else, at best you managed to focus your thoughts on the caged sun under the table, you did this by moving the rubber soles of your gorillas closer to the burning element and the heating of the rubber that warmed your toes meant the gorillas turned furry and got huge slab-like teeth and started howling fitfully, screeching at the flames that surrounded them.

At the other end of the T-shaped corridor, past the square hall that was like a cavity, to the right of the front door, were the two best rooms which faced the street and the north, they were permanently submerged in a greyish light and almost always empty. The room on the left might have been called the drawing room in a more affluent home, but its nondescript furnishings, an ochre-coloured corduroy sofa and en suite armchairs around an oblong marble table, also contained the crown jewels of the home: a North African tapestry and two animal skins mounted above the sofa and beside them, as though it had been the knife the skins had been cut off with, your grandfather's dagger from the war in Russia even if neither "war" nor "Russia" were words your seven-year-old brain could grasp, the only thing you knew about war had to do with the soup, it was because of "the war" you had to swallow the greasy liquid with those slimy lumps lying in wait for you. Although the circles that spread out from the words when your father spoke them, the quivering around his mouth and on those narrow lips, would have been perceived by you as a smile, and the ripple across his eyes, which were blue the way water is blue, as though someone had dropped a stone into them. Sometimes when you were alone in the best room you went over to the wall-mounted dagger, the sheath was made of grey metal that made you think of the bowls engraved with reindeer and sleighs your mother had brought with her from her homeland. Between the sheath and the blade was a spiral of something yellowish-white and shiny that brought white chocolate to mind and was called *marfil* (ivory), and chocolate was something you did know about, it could turn the strange object that belonged to a dead man you had never met into something you could understand to some extent, the notion that one part of the knife contained stale rock-hard chocolate also had an effect on the man in the photograph your papá must have called "father" (though never "Papá" surely?), just as the knowledge that this apparently very strict man who was dead had cast a shadow over your father lent him a hidden and disturbing side, your dead grandfather encapsulated a life you knew very little about. One thing you did know, though, even if it is unclear how you had found out about it: somewhere in that large, dark flat in Barcelona where your father grew up was the explanation as to why your parents, but not you, always slept with the bedside lamp switched on. The explanation would have to be either there – in the dark corridor full of brooding

49

shadows and as long as a night – or in the black-and-white photographs of the desert that had been stuck neatly into the album with
snakeskin-patterned cardboard covers. If you moved your hand from
the dagger to the reddish-brown antelope heads mounted above the
sofa you would be transported to another era in your father's life,
the skins had belonged to gazelles in the Sahara desert, that much
you knew, the proof of the gazelles' previous existence was to be
found in two faded rectangles. The fact that your childhood home
was made up of different rooms in time, rooms only your parents
were familiar with but whose memory and access to which they
preserved on the walls, in furnishings and photographs, was something you learned early on, the rooms your present lives occurred
in were inserted in those other past rooms that could at any
moment be folded out from various objects in the home. Your own
memories and thoughts were wedged into the joints between those
invisible rooms, where they would lie dormant for years and years.
The skins of the Dama gazelles told you about a time when your
father was no-one's father, when he had already plunged towards
the bottom of a swimming pool that would swiftly be dyed with
blood after a dive from the topmost springboard (which was the
reason his long nose was perfectly crooked and made his face seem
so strange when seen from the front), when you tired of other games
you could climb onto the sofa and run your fingers with or against
the nap of the Dama gazelles' skins, if you stroked against the nap
circles and ridges formed that you would smooth out afterwards,
as though to console the flayed and crucified animals (it was not
for nothing your father had shot them), you used to draw on the
skins with the tips of your fingers and the sensation of roughness
which that evoked would rasp across the smooth vowels of the name
El Aaiún, the word trembling like hot air at the boundary between
understanding and mystery, *el* was the masculine article so many
nouns were linked to in Spanish, *el* was like the familiar street you
follow without any great thought as to where you are going or like

the road you think you know well but which then takes you to a new and unfamiliar place: Aaiún, Aaiún was both real and unreal at the same time, it stood for sand and heat and the familiar smell of the barracks, but for something unfamiliar as well, like the open word *África*, so full of crackling sounds, like the crunch of the bread with margarine and sugar on top you were given as a snack after school.

"*¡Viva la muerte! ¡A mí la Legión!*" he would still sometimes yell at home, especially at weekends when the gramophone was turned on. The records were piled next to the bone-white artefact, usually on the floor, those legionnaire songs the parties ended with, one had to be sung very quickly, as if at a run, "*legionarios a luchar, legionarios a morir*",[1] while the other was so melancholy, slow and swaying, "*El novio de la muerte*", "Death's Bridegroom", as all the legionnaires were, your father said, him too, not just the man with a dark hollow on his cheek and a black patch on his eye who was tacked to the wall and called *El Fundador*, just like the bottles of cognac that came with a vinyl disc with two songs on each side and had the same little jingle before the beginning of each one, "*Fundador el coñac que mejor sabe, Fundador, porque es seco y es suave, Fundador, está como nunca, está como nunca, ¡Fundador!*"[2]. "Legionnaires are always singing," he said, "they sing when they go into battle to keep fear at bay" (you were allowed to be afraid but never cowardly, never *cobarde*, and the grin with which he pronounced that word was more frightening than anything else), though the legionnaires would also sing when they were wounded and in pain, which you could do as well if you fell over or hurt yourself, or had toothache, just like the Great Legionnaire there on the wall who had lost an arm and an eye and got a bullet through his heart, and just kept on singing through it all. *¡Legionarios a luchar, legionarios a morir!*

1 "Fight, legionnaires, die, legionnaires!"
2 "Fundador, the cognac that tastes best, drink Fundador, it is dry and mild, Fundador tastes better than ever, better than ever – Fundador!"

Grandfather's tall black bookshelves were in the best room as well, and contained books and more albums, only men were included in the photographs in the one with a snakeskin pattern, never any children or women, men who, apart from your father, were all ugly, there were legionnaires and men in turbans, but animals as well, camels and dogs, and especially a little puppy whose name, GRIFA, was written in blue ink in your father's handwriting at the bottom of a photograph. In another picture he is sitting with the full-grown black mongrel above the sign on the wall of the fort:

LEGIÓN
FUERTE HAGUNIA
CONSTRUIDO
POR LA II BANDERA
1938

And the gazelles. *Las gacelas dama*, large princess-dogs with horns and long slender legs.

On another page of the album he is standing beside the metre-thick stone wall holding up both gazelles by the horns, the one he has in his right hand, higher than the other, so high that its front legs are extended in the air, is pointing its face and its half-open muzzle upwards, towards the white sky, its eyes too, while the other gazelle is closer to the stony sand and its head, which has slid into your father's shadow, is held out straight at the level of his hips, from where the large mournful eye looks out of the picture. He is smiling, the legionnaire's cap is aslant, the way it should be, it is kept in place by a leather strap under the chin, his shirt has been unbuttoned down to the broad black belt with the bronze buckle, on the breast pocket of the shirt is a white rectangle with two stars topped by a thick black border. You thought that the stars stood for gazelles, a star for every gazelle killed, like a badge, your father was the sort of man to have killed two gazelles. The picture underneath it shows seven Dama gazelles stretched out on the sand, the head of one gazelle on the rump of the one nearest to it, all the bodies turned in the same direction.

Behind the dead antelopes is a large group of men, some of them bareheaded, some with hats on, others wearing kepis, two of them are dressed in kaftans, one is wearing a dark turban wrapped around his head and throat. Your father is standing beside the man in a turban on the left side of the picture, he stands out from the group because of his height, his bearing, his entire appearance. He stands out in every picture. All the other men are ugly, some are old, everyone is always shorter than him, a fat man who really ought to have his shirt unbuttoned has obstinately tried to button it over his spare tyre, but he can scarcely do it up.

"*¿Por qué los legionarios se quieren casar con la Muerte y no con mujeres? ¿Tú ya no eres legionario porque te casaste con mamá?*"[3]

In the next two photographs your father is about to ride a dromedary. A Berber in a dark turban and kaftan is helping him to mount. Your father is wearing shorts, his long legs are very suntanned. In the background is the entire perimeter of Fort Hagunia's stone wall, the one against which he is displaying the shot gazelles in the first picture.

If Death had to choose a legionnaire, she (*ella*) would choose your father, he was the most handsome legionnaire of them all although Death loved the animals most, in the snakeskin-patterned album there were only dead animals.

"Though in wartime you kill *enemies*," he said. And then he told her about the good old days just a few years before he was born. An aristocratic lady arrived at the headquarters of the Foreign Legion intending to open a hospital and care for the wounded, a Red Cross hospital like the one on the other side of your street. She was so

---

3 "Why do legionnaires want to marry Death instead of women? Are you no longer a legionnaire because you married your mother?"

high-born, the lady, that she was a friend of the then queen. The Duchess of la Victoria was dressed in a dazzling uniform with a thick white wimple on her head, like the nuns in your school although their wimples were black, not white like the Duchess', and the general welcomed this lady with a large basket of red roses.

"Only, do you know what was under the roses?"

(a shake of the head)

"Two severed heads!"

La duquesa de la Victoria worked as a nurse for several years afterwards, and though she may have been an aristocrat, almost a queen herself, she would shave and wash the bodies of the dead legionnaires with her own hands.

Pontevedra, Galicia, Spain
the Night of July 13, 1936

We got to Pontevedra the same night that Calvo Sotelo was murdered,
the two boys will say long afterwards when, as full-grown men and
one of them at least a pensioner, they talk about their memories
of the war: *Llegamos a Pontevedra la misma noche en que mataron a
Calvo Sotelo.*

On the night of July 13, 1936, as they are approaching the fruit
warehouse on the Atlantic coast that is the final destination of a
journey that began almost a week before in Barcelona, José Calvo
Sotelo, the right-wing political leader, was abducted from his apartment building at Calle Velázquez in Madrid and shortly thereafter
executed with two shots to the back of his head inside a van a few
blocks away. The body was dumped only minutes later at the capital's
Eastern cemetery.

The right-wing politician who has been murdered this night, or
is about to be murdered, was born in Pontevedra, the town the boys
are now approaching, dozing in the front seat of a Ford truck laden
with crates of fruit. What the men, who are eleven and nine years
old on this particular night, will mean by their words is that it was
fate that brought them at the eleventh hour from revolutionary terror
(Barcelona) to safety (Galicia), to the part of Spain, that is, where
the military revolt would immediately succeed – or at least not
immediately fail – even if the machinery behind the revolt had already
been set in motion long before Calvo Sotelo was murdered, which
occurred as if by chance – the first two men on the list were not in
their apartments when the death squad turned up, Calvo Sotelo, on

the other hand, was, he was at home when the executioners knocked on the door and was therefore the one to be kidnapped and shot in the back of the head not far from Calle Velázquez and then left at the entrance to the nearest churchyard.

That it was fate which would place them right there and then, if only symbolically perhaps, at the centre of events remains unstated, though it may be the most important aspect in the view of the men, who are still just boys and can have no idea how significant this night on which they arrive in Pontevedra will turn out to be – for the official account of the war by the victors, for their own lives.

It is, in fact, the boys' father and not fate who has anticipated events and left his wife and daughter in Barcelona to take his two sons to the part of Spain his contacts in the military have assured him will not mount any resistance when the armed forces rebel. That the armed forces are planning to rise in revolt will come as a surprise to no-one, least of all their father, who has been a member of the banned *Somatén* since 1931 and has been acting as liaison between the rebellious factions of the military. And he is already in the know, he has been since long before this night on which the right-wing leader Calvo Sotelo is being liquidated inside a van in the centre of Madrid.

The engineer and entrepreneur Salvador Pascual Juliá, raised by the parish priest in Sarriá, who for some unknown reason would become his guardian, is at the wheel, driving a truck along the deserted streets of Pontevedra, the engine is sounding more strained here, as if it had to work harder between stone facades and over cobblestones than driving along the country roads that over the past few days have taken them through fields, over mountain slopes and across shrub-steppes; the street is straight and narrow, and at the end the familiar outline of a baroque church of remarkable design can be made out: rounded like a shell.

As the truck is approaching the church the noise of the engine gets louder. The older boy – who is still awake – identifies the low gear and makes a motion in the air as though to engage second, a gesture that contains the memory of a sequence of similar hand movements carried out just a day or so ago, when both his brother and he had to test-drive the Ford on a dusty and desolate earth road on the steppes of Los Monegros; the dust whirled up so thickly in the cab they had to tie their handkerchiefs over their noses and mouths, the boy is thinking about that now, the three of them in the cabin, *forajidos* on the run from the law, their laughter got stuck in their throats with the dust; he is thinking about the round steering wheel that could be spun left or right just as you pleased, an eternal symbol of freedom spinning crazily in a landscape that was no longer their tame homeland but a country created by words and illuminated by inner visions that were brushing themselves down, blocking nostrils and inducing coughing fits while the bed of the truck heaved up and down and the columns of dust rose behind them like exclamation marks.

The rust-brown truck brakes to a halt and the engine dies with an abrupt sound. A little square opens before them and in its middle, above a wide set of steps, rises the tall and slender silhouette of a church with a curiously curved facade, the older boy has never seen a church like this one, round instead of straight. The echo of the din made by the crickets that has been combined day and night with the groaning of the engine in the course of the journey reverberates through the boy's head as the humid silence of the square pours in through the windows.

"*¡Despierta a tu hermano, hay que darle gracias a la Vírgen!*" He is supposed to wake his brother, and, inevitably, the Holy Virgin will have to be thanked. Once he has spoken, their father begins to smooth his creased and wrinkled shirt, tucking it inside the waistband of his trousers, then he reaches across to the glove compartment on the left-hand side of the steering wheel. The older boy, Salvador, also known as Sal, watches his father get out the pistol that has been

57

brooding in its leather case in a kind of hibernation, their father has taken it out of the compartment and then put it back every time they have got out of the truck, as if it were a living thing that needed to be cared for and exercised, a thing that could wake up at any moment, the boy is thinking, and with the image of the polished leather case shimmering like a black fur coat in his mind's eye he obeys his father and twists around towards his brother who is leaning against him, asleep. A quick drop of his left shoulder makes his brother's head fall forward so that the sleeping body is thrown off balance.

His newly woken brother wonders where they are. When he is told they are going into a church, his eyes immediately open wide in shock.

"*Això no és Barcelona,*" Sal whispers in Catalan though he is more interested in watching his father, who for his part is listening attentively, expectantly, his eyes turning now to the right and now to the left of the church, gripping the pistol firmly in his hand. Sal is also looking at the darkened windows from which light could shine at any moment, he is watching the closed doors through which people from the Federación Anarquista Ibérica and the Confederación Nacional de Trabajo should sooner or later pour.

Abruptly the taste of peaches fills his mouth, the juicy half-dissolving flesh trickling down his throat, he can track all the over-ripe peaches he has devoured this evening, tracing their meandering journey through his body that, just like theirs, seems to be reaching its end right now. The sudden pressure against his rectum tells him he is going to have diarrhoea and that his bladder is full.

His father's eyes are fixed on the rounded church entrance. There is a clock up on the left tower, standing in for the moon on a starless night: it shows twenty past two. Then he turns towards them:

"You're to stay here," he says, *¡Vosotros os quedáis aquí!* – the harsh-sounding language of whistling, guttural consonants that he has recently begun to employ even at home – and goes on to tell them that if he is not back on the half hour he wants them to run and hide somewhere (*bajáis del camión y os escondéis donde podáis*) and that they should head for the water (*id hacia la ría*) and ask for the warehouse of the Seoane family.

Without waiting for any reaction to his instructions the father steps down onto the street, he stands for several seconds by the driver's door, looking in every direction except that of his children; so he is unaware when he starts moving away that Salvador, the elder, has to empty his bowels and bladder, or that José María, the younger, is struggling with something that is making his throat burn and his body tremble all over. Sal goes on watching his father without saying a word and sees him stand for a second or two by the wing mirror, he can see the back of his father's head reflected in it, his father who is turned towards that section of the long straight road that lies behind them. Afterwards, during the year the children spend as boarders with the Seoane family, when the war is no longer a machine to be set in motion but a reality that has become the everyday, a reality in which the executions by firing squad on the riverbank that the boys witness together with other children half-hidden behind a wall have also become everyday, he will remember the profile of his father's face as he stands there at the end of the Calle de Michelena, his head beside the wing mirror of their Ford, which is fully laden with fruit that has ripened far too quickly under the black canvas over the truck's bed. He will always associate the buzzing of flies, the flies that have been laying their eggs with every passing day of their trip in more and more of their cargo of fruit, with the stab of pain he felt as his father, without trying to catch their eye, turned towards the Peregrina church and left them in the truck.

Salvador, who prefers to be called Sal and has discovered a kind of liberation in that short but spacious nickname, a name that encompasses an entire ocean, because the ocean is full of salt and that is what Sal means, salt, feels deceived, he never thought that the great moment of parting would arrive like this, so unexpectedly and abruptly, so without warning or preparation, like a sudden death, like a death without a long illness and without any stench, a death that provokes cries and tears, not a death that evokes darkness and rosary prayers in large cold rooms with the blinds drawn. Sal stays in his seat watching his father's silhouette all the way across the square, sensing his brother's trembling, knowing tears are already flowing down his brother's cheeks, knowing he has to hold back his own tears, the drawn-out scream that is rising from the opening of his stomach and approaching his throat. He must not scream, because if the Reds come he has to save himself and his brother, *if the Reds come they will have killed Papá* and his father will be lying somewhere inside the curved church bleeding to death and in that case he will have to gather a strength he does not feel he possesses, he does not feel able to move a single muscle, only if Papá has not come back when the little church clock strikes the second quarter, he will have to gather his non-existent strength and carry out a long sequence of moves, so many moves that he will never be able to manage, the first move will have to be to take his brother's trembling hand, the second move to reach out with his own right hand and open the door of the truck, the third to pull himself and then his brother out, the fourth and fifth to get his legs moving and run, the sixth to run away from *him*, their father lying dead in front of the altar at the feet of a Madonna with an incinerated veil and a bullet-riddled face, the seventh move is the resting motion, the moment when he has to stop and find a hiding place, a hiding place in a city he has never set foot in before. It is now he decides he can no longer keep it in. The boy christened Salvador, "the Saviour", but called Sal, salt, feels deceived, deceived more by his own stupidity than by the world, by his own body more than by life, the fury he feels is turned against himself, against his lack of authority and real strength, and the very idea that this trip was going to be an adventure, the most incredible one he had ever been on, how could he ever have believed anything of the kind?

It is at this point that he opens the door, he undoes his fly and gets out his member and aims at the wall on the other side of the narrow pavement, it takes a moment before the signals arrive from his brain and a stream can flow in a broad arch that hits the spot where the wall and the pavement meet. Rage makes him bold, he raises and lowers the tip of his penis so the jet of urine hits the wall at different heights, the noise of the urine raining now on the wall, now on the pavement, becomes a splashing sound he wishes were as hard and dry as a whiplash.

There are five strokes left before the church clock strikes the second quarter as arranged, the church tower stands out against the night sky and Sal finds it difficult to believe that this is the same sky they saw on the desert steppes in Los Monegros, it seems inconceivable now that that tattered bit of sky around the pointed church towers can be the same night sky they lay beneath outside Bujaraloz, beside the green saltwater lake they had bathed in that evening, utterly inconceivable that all three of them could have lain there on their blankets under the star-studded sky, a sky with so many brilliant points of light, so wide and deep and dense with stars it was like an abyss above their heads, as if the sky were sucking them upwards, or as if it were coming loose from its moorings – his father was convinced that God was the mooring of the sky – to fall on top of them like a suffocating quilt. It is now he gets down to stand with feet firmly planted beside the van, the open door like a shield against a frontal attack by the Reds. His younger brother starts shaking his head.

The "tongue of the sea" their father had mentioned, *la ría*, a sort of deep estuarine inlet that only exists along this coast, like the word *ría*, the estuary and all its islands, the clinic where the sailors have to wait in quarantine, the beaches of white sand . . . Sal takes a deep breath to get a whiff of the Atlantic he has never seen, but can detect no smell of ocean, no smell of a sea that is in any way different to the sea he swims in when he trains with his swimming club in la Barceloneta, the sea that clucks and gurgles, brown and stained with oil, between the great ships and freighters in the port of Barcelona: he cannot find his way home, only back the way he has come, if he had to run towards the inlet to try and find the Seoane family's warehouse he would have no idea in which direction to set off. Through the lowered window he can see the clock of the church tower, five strokes left. His father's features under the open sky are all he can see in his mind's eye, his father had shaved in front of the truck's wing mirror by the verge of a road outside Burgos with only the edge of light on the horizon for illumination, it was not until then he had felt he could stop wearing the proletarian disguise he had decided to shelter beneath. Astonished, Sal had watched his old face emerge with each swipe of the razor, the face clearly defined in the mirror, the road in the background coarse-grained, blurred. Then he returns to the saltwater lake they had spent the night beside on the outskirts of Bujaraloz, his father still unshaven, feral, the surrounding landscape dry, the way he had read that a desert was supposed to be, the reflection of the moon in the water, the deafening song of the crickets, how unrecognisable he had felt his father was when he laughed, when he splashed José María and him with toppling cascades of water, the taste of salt as they floated open-mouthed and on their stomachs in the lake, like caimans lying in wait, the roughness of his skin as they sat drying afterwards in the night breeze. Where did the salt come from? They had eaten peaches to rinse away the salinity that clawed at their gums.

"Come back," José María hisses and asks him to shut the door, his voice about to crack again. But Sal does not want to get back inside what he feels has become a rat trap, he can taste overripe peaches in his mouth once more and the pressure on his rectum builds again as if the long clump of loose excrement had woken up and was bent on goring its way out. Four strokes left, he would rather shit himself than face the Reds with his pants down. He tries to find relief in his memories, in the privy on the other side of the chicken run at the tavern in Bujaraloz where they ate lentils with pork, the drops of sweat beading on his forehead and across his back while he did his business, even the chickens had looked listless when he came out, enveloped in flies, the chickens had their eyes shut in the sandpits they had managed to excavate under the Ford his father had parked beneath a ramshackle arch. When he returned to the dining room the stout landlady was interrogating his unshaven father about the strikes in Barcelona, the "B" on their number plates had not escaped the innkeeper's quick eye, *huelga*, a forbidden and loaded word, and a treacherous kind of word as well, all those punishments he had had to endure in school for the tricky silent "h"s he forgot to write, but he has seen *huelga* stamped on poster after poster across the city, ¡HUELGA! and that silent "h" has become imprinted on his mind like a drawing or an image, just like the memory of the stout woman's daughter, the way the black-haired girl had blushed as she set the over-filled plate in front of him, her thumb rhythmically inundated by the brownish wash of the lentil stew across the rim of the plate; he is leaning back against the door with his eyes on the church entrance and is astonished that he can remember all of that now, the girl's pale, perfectly white skin, the dark shadow over her lip, her prominent nipples beneath the lemon-yellow blouse, the outlines of her small immature breasts. And it is then, at last, as his member stiffens as a result of the light almost unintentional contact with the girl's body in his mind that the unendurable pressure of the contents of his intestine retreats.

Almost at the very same instant the silence is shattered by a dog's bark and a yapping cloud of muzzles and tails rolls across the square from the right, the burning clump Sal has been battling against is reversing further up his large intestine in defeat, Sal catches a glimpse of the mottled-grey bitch forced up against the church steps the second before all her escape routes are cut off, the steps an unwitting ally to the six, seven dogs that have pursued her there. Just as most of

63

the bitch's grey pelt disappears beneath a black hunting dog twice her size the church doors open and a solitary male figure the boys immediately recognise as their father comes out. Their father comes briskly down the steps, when he gets to the bottom the pack has rolled unintentionally towards him, the boys watch their father kick his way through the whirling cloud of dogs and their raucous barking is overlaid with whimpers and howls. Their father's foot must have hit some of the soft parts.

The little church clock strikes the half hour.

Is that their father smiling? Walking towards them with his shirtsleeves rolled up? Sal begins to move around the open door to the truck he has been sheltering behind, but José María tries to stop him – "*No marxis!*"[4] He implores him.

Sal pays him no mind, they are in no danger now, so he halts the movement he had begun and runs over to join his father at the end of the street, José María realises at this point that he has to extricate himself from the paralysis that has been affecting him ever since their father left them alone in the cab. As if his hands and feet had been tied behind his back and gone to sleep, he shuffles sideways across the seat towards the open door, but as his legs are dangling outside the truck they feel as if they are made of glass, they would shatter into a thousand pieces if he jumped down now, and so it is in the middle of a balancing act, turned away from him and tottering, that he sees his father again, or rather, that his father sees him again, from the back. And as if his father understood he addresses the trembling boy in the language they speak at home, around the dinner table and at bedtime:

"*¡Apa, baixa, Josep María!*" Get down now, he says using the softer consonants and closer vowels of Catalan (*¡Anem tots tres a veure a la Verge!*)[5] and then he tells him how radiantly beautiful the Holy Virgin is and that the church is still intact (*L'església està intacta*).

4 "Don't go!"
5 "Let's go and see the Virgin, the three of us."

Intacta, inmaculada, impoluta, in spiritus sanctus, infierno, I.N.R.I., *incienso, incarnatus, in albis, íncubo* . . . Sal is hallucinating words, that is what he usually calls it, *alucino palabras,* whatever he means by that. What he is doing is seeing the "i"s strewn across the cobblestones, luminous white "i"s all the way to the church, as his father and José María walk hand in hand slightly behind him, his brother fumbling for the words to the questions he manages to stammer out, their father whispering brief answers, Sal stamps on the "i"s forcing them further inside, deep inside, their words, as if putting out cigarette ends, one "i" for *intacta* (untouched), one "i" for *inmaculada* (unsullied), one "i" for *impoluta* (spotless), one "i" for *incienso* (incense), one "i" for *infierno* (hell), one "i" for I.N.R.I., *in albis* has actually got nothing to do with the church, but Father Ramón often uses the expression as does Father Sergio, so in that sense it is religious, all the priests at school used as much Latin as they could, the poor cowards, in a cold sweat at the pulpit while the workers were chanting their slogans outside, thinking they might set fire to the whole school, burn them inside so their dirty priests' robes that smelled mostly of sweat and something else, something sour that rose behind them with every movement they made, would catch fire and extinguish that musty smell of theirs. Apart from Father Llorenç though, he was a mystery, he smelled nicer than the finest soap, and when he came close to Sal, stood over him, leaning over his exercise book, Sal could feel ants creeping across the back of his neck and over his scalp and a sudden drowsiness would come over him that he could do nothing about. Father Llorenç smelled clean in a way not even women could smell, only Isabel, the nun at nursery school had smelled like that, the white wimple beneath the long black one always smelled freshly ironed, a scent that was acrid and sort of white in colour, and she also had transparent skin, smooth hands without veins, as though she no longer needed blood, because Sister Isabel was saintly or simply kind, all the things the blackfrocks went on about without understanding them at all: *abnegación,* self-denial, and

Father Llorenç was kind in the same way, his hands were never quick to lash out with the ruler, they never lashed out with the ruler, and they could take on the shape of pointed leaves when he blessed them, just like Jesus' hands in the catechism, no cutting remarks ever passed his lips nor did any word meant to frighten them, his lips were smooth and calm like the beach at la Barceloneta early in the morning when it welcomes the slow rocking motion of the sea, no demons fucking (*íncubos*) ever passed those lips nor did any hellish visions (women being raped or allowing themselves to be fucked by demons), he never frightened or revolted or wounded them the way the other blackfrocks often did, those goddamned blackfrocks with their club feet and their crossed eyes, those pathetic strands of hair combed across their bald scalps, their endless bowing and scraping to the headmaster, the venerable Pater Anselm.

When they enter the church Sal is expecting it to reek of burning, and although there is a smell powerful enough to irritate his nostrils, it is of incense, and below the high altar in the nave shaped like a cross are several lit candles that are also giving off smoke. Otherwise there is just a naked bulb to the left of the altar to produce the faint yellow light, a dull glow filtered through a stillness resembling that of water. No traces of destruction can be made out in the dense submarine gloom, no overturned confessionals or statues, even the barking of the dogs is subdued and falls silent, everything is water-soaked, immobile.

His father nudges him and his brother forward along the central aisle towards the reredos. From a distance the Madonna looks rather small on her perch high up between the golden columns, the embroidered floral pattern flowing down her ornate dark velvet robes glimmers in the semi-darkness, as do the tiny silver points on the upturned edge of her hat. Sal has to suppress a laugh when he sees the round Napoleon hat on the head of the icon, she looks to him as if she is in disguise, an eccentric combination of a shepherd and a general. There is no glint in her eye, though, as the Madonna glares down at them from beneath the star-strewn brim, her lips only slightly parted, and her hair is not made of painted plaster or wood but of real hair arranged in thick chestnut-brown curls. She reminds Sal of the doll his younger sister Rosa was given on her last birthday, and he can see himself climbing up to the pedestal and lifting down the Virgin doll and then running off with her in his arms to the Ford that is parked under the moonless night and putting her on a bed of overripe peaches and melons, for the heavy dark-red mantle to scare away all the flies that are beginning to buzz in the darkness.

"It's just, why the hat?" José María finally dares to ask when their father has told them about his most recent trip to Pontevedra, this was in May and the Festival of the Body of Christ, and the Holy Virgin made her appearance all in snow-white, with a cape and hat made of shiny white satin, like a queen, like one of the noblewomen who fled across the Bay of Biscay to Galicia during the French Revolution (. . . *huyendo de los comunistas de aquel tiempo*), fleeing the Communists of that time.

In 1958, Sal, an officer in the Spanish Foreign Legion, would think about the Holy Virgin in the Peregrina church during the marches across the desert at El Aaiún or beneath starry nights in Larache, the heavy velvet cape would be flapping in the rowing boat that took him across the Lukus river to the distant shore where the horses of the arms smugglers stood snorting. And when his men, exhausted and high on *grifa*, sang the hymn "*El novio de la muerte*", "Death's Bridegroom", on their way home to the fort, it was her face that appeared to him first.

Hotel Seegasthof Stadler, Unterach am Attersee, June 2006, Afternoon

The illuminated square on the floor has almost entirely faded and you get up from the edge of the bed, but as you start to move towards the side table in the hall he comes in, wearing battledress, the black-and-white puppy in his arms; the jacket that flares above the black leather belt "smells of tiger", that is how he puts it: *huele a tigre*. You think it smells of something else entirely, war maybe, that is after all what he does with his soldiers when they bivouac up in the mountains, sulphur and explosives, a sour-sweet smell of firewood, when his clothes smell that way you know he has been on manoeuvres (*de maniobras*) and then you can also see the broad barracks square at the military academy for N.C.O.s in Tremp, you see the bends up the cliff to Talarn, the light bulb in the room where the rain came in, heavy drops falling close to your face that roll on into your ear canals, the little boarding house at the mercy of a great storm, the landlady Lola leaning over so her mouth is hovering close to your eyes, the raindrops wandering deeper inside the labyrinth of your hearing; the light on the ceiling of the bedroom burns all night long, it has a crocheted skirt around the bulb, the falling folds of crocheted yarn mean the storm outside is less audible, you forget that the black beams are not water-tight, drop after drop slips from the rotten wood you keep your eyes fixed on during the thunderstorm, first the drops fall mutely onto the starched sheet next to your pillow, then there is a metallic sound as they are collected by the washbasin with an enamelled blue edge; *talarn, talarn* your tongue does somersaults confronted with the "n"; *talarn, talarn* like the church bells this morning, *talarn, talarn*, church bells during the long night you were too little to remember, though your entire body remembers, from the slanting scar on your abdomen to the geometric figures in a long corridor conjured by the fever or the ether you were given during the makeshift operation carried out on a Saturday night by an inebriated military surgeon who was actually on leave that evening, the rasping noise as a bulky white cylinder approaches, looming larger along the pitch-black tunnel. *Talarn, talarn* (your tongue does a somersault), is there some knowledge to be gained from the names of places where you have been on the point of dying? You lay there flat and unmoving with your eyes closed as if you were asleep, death was not supposed to strike sleeping children. When, almost grown up, you hear your grandfather's letters from the lake south of Novgorod mentioned you will hear raindrops drumming on a lake with a bottom of white enamel, in his letters he wrote about an old Russian woman who was cutting her daughter's hair outside her cottage beside a melting snowdrift while everyone was waiting for the people in Leningrad to give up.

He bends over and puts the dog down onto the sun-splashed paving stones, the rubber soles of his boots squeak against the mottled-green floor and the scrape of the puppy's claws makes a cold noise as if it really were the rippling water of a spring your father had put him in. He tells you he found the puppy huddled by a grey rock near a stream in the Arán valley, in a little village close to the border called Bosost where a small army of Reds was making a vain attempt to invade Spain long after they had lost the war. So it might be a good idea to name the dog Arán or Bosost though you can christen him what you like.

"Tessy," you say without batting an eyelid.

"Only it's a dog, not a bitch, do you see?" He has turned the puppy round so the greyish-white abdomen and the black-haired sheath are visible. Though what you see makes no difference, you want him to be called Tessy and so he will be.

Tessy's fur had a nutty smell of bread crusts, you ran your fingers against its nap and drew your thoughts on his skull and believed he understood them; sometimes you took him on expeditions to the north side of the apartment to play with the mounted heads, you explained to Tessy that the Dama gazelles lived in the Sahara desert and Tessy allowed himself to be stroked, unperturbed by the fact that the Dama gazelles were dead. The degree of coarseness of the antelopes' prickly hair would be weighed against that of the white patches on the coat of the dog, with you standing upright between two poles of fur like a container and transferring water from the streams and rivers of the Pyrenees to the thirsty animals of the Sahara.

Let's play everyone lives!

The Dama gazelles often insisted on remaining in their stiff-furred state. On the floor were the grey gramophone and the piles of scratched records. Some days the antelopes remained permanently flat as if they had heard the shrill trumpet from the fort in El Aaiún and just wanted to listen to the singing of the legionnaires. *Soy un hombre al que la suerte hirió con zarpa de fiera, soy un novio de la muerte . . .*[6] Sooner or later you would get tired of them. You and your dog would then abandon the sand-coloured sofa and move over to stand beside the black bookcase, leather and gold were what counted now, not sand and fur. "*Quo vadis*, that's Latin, Tessy, a dead language, languages die too, you know. *Kaputt* is German and means broken, wrecked. Mother knows that because she comes from a country far from here where they speak a bit like in Germany. *¿Sabías que casi morimos en Hamburgo? Hamburgo está en Alemania.* We almost died in a car crash when we were on our way there. Sit still. Sit still, I told you! When Moumoú comes we'll teach you Swedish (*sueco*). I'm going to show you something very special now." Tessy wags his tail and rivets his eyes on your hand shifting towards the bookcase to get down the book with glossy cardboard

6   "I am a man that Fate has wounded with an iron claw, I am a bridegroom of Death."

covers and a watercolour drawing on the front, he sniffs excitedly at the book which unlike the red leather-bound volumes with gold lettering, the ones your father had had bound, smells simply of dust: "*La fille du capitaine*," you say, reading the title aloud as if it were in Catalan. "This book is about me, you see, because I am a girl and my father is a captain."

"The water was so cold she's gone all giddy," your husband says as he comes into the room and puts the child down, father and daughter tickle and chase each other, the laughter has been at work inside them for a while now which leaves you on the outside. "She ought to have a hot bath," you say, and take her by the hand.

The deafening stream is filling the bathtub while your hand becomes a dolphin tickling the child's calves or a dangerous shark biting her toes. The water level rises to the point where her thighs are below the surface, "Lie on your back," you say, so the heat can penetrate her body more quickly, the waterline reaches her belly, distorting the true lines of her body, a sense of unease is rising through your chest, the shark chases her toes more and more slowly, the shark becomes distracted, the child stops laughing, you stop seeing your child in the bathtub, all you see is the water rising too quickly. You turn off the tap. She sits up. A single drop falls and it is as if even the steam were echoing. Apart from that the silence is absolute now that the water has stopped running.

One day at the height of summer you were called into the best room. You and Tessy had been sitting in the cement tub on the balcony with the water up to your waist when your mother came out to tell you to hurry in to the television room because something very important was on. *Drip, drip, drip* . . . your feet running along the corridor, *click, click, click* . . . Tessy's claws scraping against the tiles. Your father was sitting in his shirtsleeves in front of the television set.

"*Hoy los americanos han pisado la luna por primera vez. Ven. Ahora*

lo enseñarán. Eso es la luna, ¿la ves? Acuérdate de este día. Acuérdate."[7]
Remember this day. One summer.

La luna.

You can remember the spot where you were standing, half inside the room, the door on your right and the television on your left, you remember the direction your father's voice came from, from the green armchair in the corner, at an angle to your grandfather's dagger and the animal skins. You cannot remember where your mother was although you usually remember her voice hovering behind you. The astronauts were moving so slowly in their white suits, you recognised the black space from the dark tunnel of the delirium that is endlessly reproduced in your nightmares, it gives you the creeps and you begin to feel cold and hug yourself, digging with your index finger between your ribs as if that could make the floating figures move faster, as if you could make time go faster and things happen by pressing on a secret spot inside you.

You leave the child swaddled in towels in her father's lap and get out the loaded video camera and your notebook. You flip through to the last note:

They were ordinary people. The people who stayed at Haus Schoberstein were normal people for the most part, the way most people are: comfortable, limited, indifferent.

It all took place as though it were perfectly normal.

7   "Today the Americans have landed on the Moon for the first time. Come here. They're going to show it. That's the Moon, do you see it? Remember this day. Remember it."

Château Bardou, *Secours Suisse aux Enfants*
Maternity Hospital in Elne, Pyrénées-Orientales,
France, the Free Zone,
July 11, 1941

The girl born yesterday evening is going to be called Amèrica, can you really be called that? Randi Tommessen is waiting in the middle of a long, narrow room with a single bed against one of the sides, there is a desk as well aligned with one of the two windows giving onto the massif of Les Alberès, beyond it, to the southwest, the Pyrenees and the border with Spain, or Catalonia as Joana, one of the mothers, pointed out last night when they were up on the roof having a look, Randi's hand was pressed firmly against one of the iron-framed panels of the remarkable glass dome that crowns the chateau because the terrace lacks walls and railings. The light in the matron's office changes over the day (unlike the room she shares with Edith Wild and the other midwives because it faces north and enjoys a steady greyish light), this is only the second time Randi Tommessen has been inside Elisabeth Eidenbenz's combined office and bedroom, the first was the day before yesterday, in the afternoon, shortly after she arrived, and then the shutters were closed against the noonday sun that would otherwise have been pouring in to make the oblong room as hot as an oven, now the early morning air is cool and clear, in the course of the dawn the blue-green outline of a majestic mountain has been emerging from the haze (*I've named my room after that mountain, Canigou, you may still be here in October when the peaks are covered with the first snows, there's this perfect white gleam of snow then above the still-green valley, it makes me think of my childhood in Zurich*), the open window lets in a cool almost chilly current of air, and the leaves of the plants and papers are flapping in

73

the draught with a kind of even rhythm (*At first the fleeing Spaniards all got shoved together on a beach sectioned off by fences, without any shelter from the wind or rain, and you've no idea yet how the north wind can blow here, it can reach speeds of 120 km an hour, the sand cuts into your skin like sharp nails. The mothers told us they buried their children up to their necks in the sand to keep them warm*). Señorita Isabel, as she is called by most of the mothers, is sitting with her back to her, finishing off the writing of a report, the straps of her apron overlap in a large white cross, it may be one of the row of newly washed white aprons someone was ironing in the kitchen yesterday. A butterfly with white wings flutters in through the wide-open windows and hovers for a moment over Elisabeth Eidenbenz's head, which Randi Tommessen is looking at from behind at an angle, her nape bare and bent forward over what her hand is writing, the parting that divides her skull into two identical halves, the narrow light-brown plait that runs across the crown of her head, the spasmodic flapping of the butterfly's wings that somehow makes it clear that the sea is far away . . . On one corner of the desk is a camera, Fräulein Eidenbenz always seems to have it in the pocket of her apron, Randi watched her get it out and snap a series of pictures of the mothers and children in the garden yesterday. A guitar is propped against the wall closest to the bed (*I'll never forget the first delivery, the girl was called Pepita, we still hadn't got a single midwife at that point, eventually we got Madame Ida, an indefatigable sixty-year-old lady, who had to deliver women day and night, an average of four children a day, now Madame Fillols gets sent to us from Elne when we haven't enough staff of our own, she can play the piano as well and makes a brilliant addition to our little orchestra. Have you met Vladimir yet?*), on a stool a gramophone with a record that is perfectly still and gleaming against the light: the blackness of the Bakelite, so dense and impenetrable, fragile yet firm, at once attentive and expectant in its horizontal resting position, or rather, its forced immobility, makes Randi Tommessen think of a beetle on its back though she is also recalling the drawn-out keening of the cello music that poured into the feeding room the previous morning (*Every morning we play the prelude of the first suite to the mothers while they're breastfeeding*) and then she remembers the young Fräulein Eidenbenz smiling, that astonishing gap between her teeth and the three deep wrinkles at the corners of her mouth as she talked about the music and the man who performed it (*That's Pablo Casals, no-one has ever recorded Bach's cello suites before. He's a Catalan, living in exile in Prades, which isn't far from here. He came to visit us but sadly I wasn't here then and I never had the pleasure of meeting him, but we did get 300 French francs and a letter*), tacked up with two drawing pins above the gramophone is the letter whose lower edge trembles every now and then in the cross-draught. Randi Tommessen glanced through the letter when Elisabeth Eidenbenz received her the first time and talked in that choppy way of speaking she has about the services provided by the maternity hospital and how it is organised (*At first we took in Spanish refugees from the camps in Argelès and St Cyprien, but now soup kitchens for the children in other camps are coordinated from here as well: Rivesaltes, Bram, Gurs, because they're being filled with the deported from the whole of France, refugees from all over Europe are being sent to them, a large number of Gypsies and Jews. A lot of the Spanish civilians who managed to get out of the camps were sent back after* l'armistice *as well: we recognise a lot of them unfortunately, children who were born here in good health come back like skeletons, the need never ends. We don't just take in women about to give birth but now also convalescents and severely malnourished children*), Pablo Casals' letter flaps in the draught as though it were making a half-hearted attempt to free itself and fly off with the butterfly that is fluttering nearby and has still not found its way out, she recalls that it is dated March 17, 1940, and addressed *to Sra. Dña. Elisabeth Eidenbenz, Directora de la "Maternité Suisse", Elne*; that much she understands, the rest of the long letter written in a narrowly slanting hand is in Spanish and she has not learnt that yet, not in the few days that have passed since she got off the train in Perpignan and Edith Wild met her on the platform, although she can get by with her French, well enough to distribute the powdered milk and peaches in the milk hut the Swiss aid organisation has set up over in the camps, or to pull the long and unwieldy pram loaded with up to five children through the garden of the maternity hospital or cut cabbage, cauliflower and green tomatoes for bottling in the kitchen garden together with the domestic staff and some of the mothers as she did for a while yesterday before supper, after helping to make the four newly arrived expectant mothers feel at home (*I haven't had a bath in a tub for a whole year* – her voice dissolved into tears – *or been able to wash my hair properly*), then Edith came to get her and showed her the way up to the roof terrace where they stood looking out over the magnificent countryside while she gave Edith an exhaustive report of what her own first day had been like, totally unlike anything she had imagined at the nursing academy in Zurich, they could both agree on that and laughed together. Randi Tommessen thinks back to the tile-lined corridor where Edith, her instructor in obstetrics at the time, had told her she was going to Southern France as a volunteer, this was in November last year, the decision was announced just before her departure, she left the academy a few days before Christmas, Christmas here, Randi is thinking, in the letters Edith sent her later she wrote about the greenery in the garden that kept going all year round and about the much-needed sunshine the malnourished children could bathe in even in January, but above all about the extraordinary atmosphere in the maternity hospital, "a women's colony, an oasis," that made up for all the hard work: she wrote that twenty-one children had been born during the first fifteen days of the new year and that at the time of writing she had had no sleep for forty-eight hours because most of the deliveries occurred at night, but when she did get a chance to go to bed, she would do so feeling perfectly happy, "helping, Randi, is the greatest happiness". Elisabeth Eidenbenz is folding one of the sheets of paper she has been writing on and stuffing it in an envelope. "I've just got to write a short letter, please have a seat, I'll be finished soon," and that gap between her teeth is visible once again. Randi Tommessen feels forced to admit to herself how keen she is to gain Elisabeth Eidenbenz's trust, to make herself worthy of it; the sewing machine and the other things the Norwegian Quakers have been sending to Elne over the years, food and clothing too, but the sewing machine most of all, appear to have been enormously appreciated by everyone and she cannot help but feel a little proud of that, when Elisabeth went around introducing her to the breastfeeding mothers she told them in Spanish that she was Norwegian, like the sewing machine they had been given: *"¡Randi es noruega, como nuestra máquina de coser!"* A half-truth in fact, because Randi's mother was Swiss, from Zurich. *"C'est la Suisse, ça!"* Randi would later hear Fräulein Eidenbenz tell two gendarmes who rang the bell, with those words resolutely denying them the right to enter and take someone away who was on the list they had with them. Señorita Isabel is very young and short in stature, often shorter than everyone else, with narrow shoulders and a slender, almost flat chest, and yet she radiates a great sense of authority. The sound of pen scraping against paper can still be heard and Randi Tommessen, who has sat on one end of the bed and can now see Fräulein Eidenbenz's face from the front, is thinking that a magnetic field is created by the proximity of this woman, everything is affected by her energy, even objects seem to take on an inherent motion. Singing can be heard from the kitchen garden, Randi gets up to look, a woman whose name she does not know is picking tomatoes and putting them in a large basket she is carrying in the crook of her arm (*Up to now we've always tried to extend a mother's stay until her papers are ready so she and the child can avoid having to return to the camp, but most of them can only stay for two weeks now, compared with the average of three months they used to get*). You can hear various tasks being performed throughout the building, Randi knows that the gramophone will soon be moved two floors down to the spacious room in which the mothers feed their children in the mornings and where the meals and other activities like sewing also take place (*The women who come here have been treated like prisoners of war or criminals,* aucune considération, *they are guarded by gendarmes and until very recently by Senegalese, who have a very bad reputation. The first thing they did was to split up the civilians and the military, with the result that in Argelès, for instance, there are two camps, with the river serving as a natural barrier, and the families are split up too, the men from the women and children, which means that the women are unable to protect themselves from the assaults of the guards, we had a black baby born here, just to give you an example. Which is why being together, singing and celebrating the various festivals is so important*) and after lunch it all moves on to the rooms where the children sleep, to the smaller room called "Madrid", where the newborn lie in baskets, like silk cocoons, under lengths of white muslin close to the white-painted wall, and then on to the broad and beautiful "Barcelona" where the slightly older infants, on their backs in fruit boxes that have been converted into cots, sleep in the shade of the cooling branches that rustle beyond the window (*I feel so calm once I've been in to see them*) and Randi Tommessen has a sense that what Elisabeth Eidenbenz feels, surrounded by her children, is a kind of covetousness and that she may keep counting them over and over again (*346 children have been born alive since the first week of December '39, when we got access to this building. We had a house in Brouilla at first, though at the very beginning, before we inter-vened, the women gave birth in some disused stables outside Perpignan or in the camps. I'm not exaggerating when I say that most of the children would have died if not for us, that's how malnourished most of the women are before they come here. Many of them have told us they were not even given water during the first five days and a lack of water is still a major problem, there are pumps now, but there's still salt in the water. The first day I was allowed in to the beach camp at Argelès I saw this one woman screaming, she was carrying a lifeless infant, in total desperation*

78

she had given the child a feeding bottle with sea water in and the baby had died. One of the first women we took in here cried for days after her delivery, we couldn't understand it, she had given birth to a perfectly healthy baby and here with us she and the baby were given food and warmth, it turned out she was crying for another woman, whose baby had died there on the beach and she had seen the woman digging a pit in the sand in which she was forced to lay her child). The white butterfly keeps hovering over Elisabeth Eidenbenz's head, as if the woman writing were one of the intensely fragrant rosemary bushes down there in the garden where the nappies and sheets are hung out to dry, they are surrounded by a swarm of the tiny cabbage whites fluttering in the sunshine (*Some progress has been made, there are huts, water pumps, health care, work arrangements and a school that the internees organise and run by themselves, and we've been given permission to set up a special hut for the mothers as well as a soup kitchen. There are fewer and fewer refugees in Argelès now, the ones who are left are to be moved over to Rivesaltes, north of Perpignan, where we also have a hut with a resident nurse who will soon be getting reinforcements in the shape of an additional nurse, but the hunger and suffering are still extensive. Sixty children have died of gastroenteritis this last month in Rivesaltes alone, people are literally dying of hunger, but there is also tuberculosis and typhus, so we've been forced to set up and run* La gota de leche *(the drop of milk), when we hand out a glass of milk every day to each child under sixteen*). Randi Tommessen is beginning to feel a deep resentment tightening around her forehead as she recalls the queue for the milk hut, because it felt as though the only thing that existed were eyes, *devouring eyes*, eyes like holes, round holes like the hole one of the boys had in a cardigan that was much too big, tied round his skinny trunk with a piece of string, a little round hole as though a bullet had penetrated the left shoulder blade, it had to be a cardigan he inherited, a cardigan the boy had had handed down from an adult, because who would want to shoot at a child? The hole might not of course be the result of a bullet but Randi Tommessen is beginning

79

to doubt that she will ever be able to deal with all the visual impressions crowding in on her, or be able to move among the barracks made of wooden planks and corrugated iron and greet the children as cheerfully as Bethli does (it is Edith who calls the matron Bethli), or keep at it the way Elisabeth did among the queue of emaciated children dressed in rags, children with grey skin who scratched their heads and their bodies, calling them all by name (¡Hola Manolita, Gilbert, Eulàlia, Toni, Margarita, Josep, Wladyslaw . . . !). For Randi Tommessen reality seems to have fractured into tiny pieces, little facets ten centimetres to a side like the rectangular screens that separate the groups of barracks and the beach from the sea as well; the sea could be seen behind the latticed fence that ran between the beach and the water as though trapped in a kilometre-long fishing net, and the waves came rolling in towards the beach as if the sea were trying to pound its way out of its imprisonment, with the blind rage of a natural force, a natural force that many of the interned would sit facing (*We've become experts on the sea, before we set up the sewing workshop in Argelès there was nothing to do there, and no way of making money, we used to count the waves to forget the hunger, we used to study them, we compared them with the waves of the day before, with the waves that followed and we'd be sitting there facing them, staring at them, so we compared the way their colour changed depending on the time of day and the sky, the wind, what direction it was blowing from, and when we weren't studying the waves, we were counting the peaks of the chain of mountains, their number varied with the light, you could count thirty-three mountain peaks on a fairly clear day, on others the peaks used to merge with one another as if they were a viscous mass, a bluish-brown dough I wanted to just bolt down, I was so hungry I used to imagine the mountains melting and becoming edible, if I looked at them long enough it was as if I could get them inside me and in some strange way I used to feel like I was almost full*), the sea that at any moment could roll out its highest waves, vertical ones like walls of foam and wash away the women sitting round a sewing machine making clothes on the beach, and wash away the four-year-old as well who was playing while tied to the sewing machine by a long white cord. *The wind is called the Levant,* her father had told her when they got down to the promenade after the long and violent storm in Nice, *it makes waves that roll in all the way from Egypt and Turkey, you see, from the opposite end of this sea, we might find things that come from very far away, they could have been lying on the bottom of the sea outside ancient Alexandria or the coast of Crete, imagine that!* And her father wanted her to walk along the endless beach with him to see what discoveries they could make, she had been eleven the autumn they travelled to Nice and unable to come to terms with the waves she had seen the day before from the veranda of the hotel, breaking against the promenade, raging away at it, lifting and shattering the stone benches under the long avenue of palm trees, at first she refused to walk along the beach, she was afraid of what the sea might do and afraid of what it might have cast up from its depths, and now she was afraid of the children's eyes, of what they could see and what they had been forced to see, she was ashamed of what they might see in her, of her well-fed, well-dressed body, of the smell of soap her hands gave off, of her clean, cared-for hands, of her clean and freshly ironed apron, of the Swiss passport that allowed her to come and go as she pleased, across countries and in and out of their prison, she was ashamed and revolted by all the things the mothers had told her up on the roof terrace the night before and the things she could read between the lines, she was nauseated by the barrier of excrement that stretched along the water's edge the first harsh winter and gave off a stench and spread disease, by the Senegalese who masturbated behind the women who were forced to do their business crouching with their drawers pulled down for all to see (Salope! Salope! Putaine! *they yelled at us*), by the terror the children felt when the guards entered the barracks at night and forced themselves on their sisters and mothers, by what the mothers must have felt when the children were forced to witness the assaults and because the children had to watch one night when their mothers defended themselves with sticks and bottles and killed one of the guards.

"That's it," Elisabeth Eidenbenz has turned round, she is smiling, her high, squarish forehead is broad, two unplucked and perfectly straight eyebrows of equal thickness draw a boundary between it and the rest of her face, one of her brows is somewhat higher than the other. There is nothing mawkish or feeble about genuine charity, charity is shown by the person who can remain steady and acts purposefully and never hesitates, Randi thinks and remembers her father's bony fingers as he pointed out the details in the frescoes by Giotto in the Arena palace in Padua, his square nails and the veins visible along the back of his hand which made them look as though they had been sculpted out of stone, the way he opened his hand and cupped it as if to receive the heart that the stout figure of Caritas is receiving from God the Father in the far right corner of the fresco, a heart whose aorta has clearly been chopped off and that is as big as a cow's.

"Once we've done the milk round, we've got to go in to Elne and register this week's births, and while I do that, you should go to the post office and the market. José has got too much to do today so we're going to have to do the shopping, here's the list, tell them you're from *la Maternité suisse* so they don't try and trick you, they can tell from the uniform but it's worth pointing out the fact in any case." They're bound to respect her, Randi Tommessen thinks as she remembers the looks the gendarmes gave her at the barrier to the camp.

"Watch out for the old ladies at the market, they can count faster than a maths teacher and they've got a coin purse where you have a heart."

Randi Tommessen takes the shopping list that Elisabeth Eidenbenz gives her and recalls once again the basket of fruit that Giotto's *Caritas* is holding in her hand, as well as the envelope addressed to the *Schweizerische Arbeitsgemeinschaft für kriegsgeschädigte Kinder* in Bern.

Elisabeth Eidenbenz turns around and puts the camera in her pocket, then she picks up the gramophone, together they leave the room called "Canigó" and look in on both "Madrid" and "Barcelona" to check whether any of those caring for the infants has packages or letters to go to the post office or to the camps. A mother whose name Randi Tommessen has not yet learned passes them an envelope while saying something that Randi cannot make out, the words, however, unleash a sudden chorus of voices from the other women in the room, several bursting into song: *¡Ay Carmela, Ay Carmela!* One of them sways her arms over her head and taps her fingers against her palms as though she were playing castanets. Elisabeth Eidenbenz explains that it is a popular revolutionary song that was sung on the Republican side. Randi accompanies the matron to the ward called "Córdoba", one of the patients there wants to send a letter she would presumably have written at dawn, in the light of the long window she has by her bed, the pen is still on the sheet and falls to the floor as the woman reaches over to give them the letter. Randi cannot help noticing the address because the word AUTRICHE has been spelled in underlined capital letters: *Miguel Ángel García, K.Z. Mauthausen. Reichsgau Oberdonau, Linz. Ostmark.* Randi Tommessen is marvelling at all the threads that run from this sunny provincial spot, from this small, walled community with its four town gates and its unexpected cathedral and attached cloister that floats above the upper part of the town (if only she could show her father the fantastic carved buttresses) from where narrow lanes wind towards the lower part and the imposing Salle Héléna on the left side of the *route nationale* where the market is held on Fridays and in whose vicinity the midwives of the maternity hospital, despite the cathedral bells tolling both the hour and every quarter, try to catch some rest after their shifts in the little room Elisabeth Eidenbenz has hired for the purpose in a damp stone building opposite the

83

Porte de Perpignan, the northern gate, a building that even now in July exudes a pronounced smell of mildew. From this half-elevated, half-submerged town the threads run all the way to a provincial part of annexed Austria, the threads get stuck to each other, from one camp to another, she thinks, from Argelès to Mauthausen, the threads harden too, turning into steel, they are tied together into latticed nets, the fence that closes off the several-kilometres-long beach in Southern France stretches all the way to a lake district on the other side of the Alps, the Nazis have reached all the way here and so has their barbed wire.

Elisabeth Eidenbenz is on her way down the stairs towards the dining room where the mothers will take their seats in a while and Randi goes with her, step by step down the staircase bathed in light, the daylight pours in through the wall of glass that allows a clear blue sky and the green tones of the garden and the fields outside, with their dark rows of poplars and closely planted cypresses, to become part of the building. Randi Tommessen keeps pace with Elisabeth Eidenbenz's rapid little steps, her eyes sweep past the posters featuring Swiss Alpine landscapes that decorate the white walls, but they look up almost immediately through the broad shaft that encloses the staircase to find the glass dome that lets in the sunlight in vertical cascades, the glass dome up on the roof of the building where she sat through the dusk yesterday evening, barefoot, her legs tucked under her on the warm tiles. Surrounded by leguminous plants and heads of garlic set out to dry and her journal open in her lap, she had smoked cigarette after cigarette on that broad terrace without railings, without a barrier to cut off the view. After a while the woman who was going to give birth to a child who will be called Amèrica had started screaming, she screamed at regular intervals, wave after wave of labour pains that rose from the confined space of the room bizarrely called "Marruecos" two floors below. When the evening star began to shine above thin slivers of horizontal crimson clouds, she was joined by Edith who arrived with the wooden funnel in one of her hands and told her it would be a while yet before the labour entered the transitional phase, that was why she was coming to join her for a bit. Joana turned up soon after along with Celia and Wilma, the German Communist, and a woman called Aurèlia, another Communist, who was a teacher and spoke glowingly about the educational reforms of the overthrown Spanish Republic, she had to serve as an interpreter for Joana and the cook María Sardà, who did not have a child though she came from the camp as well. "*Cel rogenc o pluja o vent*"[8] – there'll be wind or rain tomorrow, María had predicted at the sight of those flat clouds like dashes, they were sitting in a circle on the outside of the glass dome and Aurélia had been trying to teach them the correct pronunciation of the Plough in Spanish, *el Carro*, with a strongly rolled "r" that neither she nor Wilma nor the Polish woman Mala, who arrived later with her three-year-old when the sky was already studded with glittering pinheads, managed to achieve. And then Joana had told them about a classical epic poem in Catalan, because Canigó had been the sacred mountain of the Catalans since time immemorial which made it particularly painful to be imprisoned in its vicinity, the epic celebrates the broad, bowl-shaped mountain, likening it to the petals of a magnolia in flower, Randi Tommessen had thought that sounded beautiful so she noted it down. Randi kept offering her cigarettes around but only Wilma had accepted, immediately putting two of them in her pocket. "Offer them to the girls in the camp instead, they can exchange them for something to eat on The Avenue," Joana said with sudden seriousness, because she had been employed at the maternity hospital after she had given birth to her child and now had a good life, her husband was a doctor besides and got called here from the camp when required and she was able to see him often. Mala had been sitting half turned away from them with her little daughter in her lap, pointing out the names of the stars in Polish (*Wielki Wóz . . . Polaris*),

8 "A reddish sky means wind or rain."

the little red-haired scalp pressed against her mother's chest in order to follow the finger that was drawing lines between the glittering points; Randi had watched as their silhouettes were thrown against the curved night sky, a sky that was resting on a circular horizon and she had been admiring the strength of mind required to survive in Mala's situation, homeless, stateless, with a three-year-old in her lap and a newborn boy down in "Madrid" who was so feeble when he arrived he did not even have the strength to eat or cry.

Voices can be heard from the kitchen, speaking Spanish, she recognises María Garcia's nasal squeak and Celia's more indolent timbre, Elisabeth peeks in and says hello while Randi remains in the doorway. In her white uniform with the little round Swiss brooch prominently displayed on her apron María Garcia is making up the feeding bottles, Celia is helping her, at the stove María Sardà is boiling water in saucepans, the smell of coffee still lingers from breakfast (the new arrival, Ines, the same woman who cried in the bath yesterday cried this morning too when she was given a cup of coffee with hot milk and ended up swallowing both the milky coffee and her tears one after the other).

The breastfeeding room seems forlorn in a morning light that brings with it golden-green reflections from the peach grove out in the garden, Elisabeth sets up the gramophone at the short end of one of the simple, oblong, white-painted wooden tables, some of them have obviously been knocked together from left-over packing cases; Elisabeth aims the horn of the gramophone towards the large mirror above the bare mantelpiece made of mottled pink marble. Randi's gaze is drawn towards the reflective glass surface as if it were capable of displaying something other than what she can see with her naked eye, a different room dating from the period when a cigarette-paper manufacturer had this chateau built and furnished, when the dining-room table might have been made of shimmering red mahogany and the gleaming crystal facets and candles of a chandelier could be seen

86

in the mirror inset between two flat and fluted columns. Randi prefers the room the way it is now, pared back and with flaking light-coloured paint, its uncarpeted bare wooden floor and the rough wooden benches on which women from different countries sit together as if on church pews, the birthing of children a religion, because here breastfeeding is a kind of singing, a kind of prayer. Eat of my body for it is Life. All those medieval wooden Madonnas she had looked at baring their breasts to the Christ child. And once again Randi Tommessen can hear the scratching of the pen that fell to the floor in the room called "Córdoba" and the impulse to write makes itself felt, if only she could sit here and get out her journal, set down one of the thoughts *hovering with extended wings over the waters of the soul* as she had seen it put so beautifully in a novel she had read. At the very moment, however, when that impulse, towards that place inside she most wants to be, is at its strongest, screams and cries can be heard and Nurse Bertel comes rushing down the stairs to call Elisabeth aside. Elisabeth goes back upstairs with her and Randi is left alone, her peace of mind gone, she is back in the camp looking at the wooden huts and the open latrines that spread disease and infections, the barrack for the mothers that is twenty-four metres by four with sixteen beds for the pregnant and sixteen for those who have just given birth and that also houses a children's section, a dining table and a pantry (*We're so glad you've come, we're currently expecting a lot of deliveries in July and August. The Tech overflowed its banks last spring, you see, the water took entire buildings with it, we were spared here, but Perpignan and the camps were badly affected, it did a lot of harm, but it also meant that the fences between the camps for men and women collapsed and disappeared in the course of a few days . . . and now we're faced with the consequences*). Grotesque visions force their way through the words doing their best to cover the worst of it just like the sand that blows through the gaps in the wooden planks of the barrack walls: where did the copulating couples go during the flood, in the midst of all the devastation?

87

Debris and water, a sodden blanket. *Copulating*, though? Dogs *copulate*, is it anger she is feeling? Contempt? Would it be so wrong to lie with your husband, or a man you were attracted to, even if the embrace were taking place in hell? Randi Tommessen pictures in her mind the pouring rain, the screaming children, things floating and sinking, saucepans, clothes, rats, children calling out to their mothers. Betrayal piled on betrayal, betrayal on top of sand and brown water while mucous membranes are being rubbed together in pleasure. The consequences. How can anyone bring children into the world in circumstances like these? What is she supposed to do? Randi Tommessen gets out one of the cigarette packets she stuffed into her apron pocket but remembers straight away she is not supposed to smoke in front of Sister Elisabeth. What is she doing here? Has she really bitten off more than she can chew? That phrase calls forth an image of her own mouth, her lips stretched in an ironic smile although the smile is invisible when she stands in front of the mirror. She inspects her face, the bonnet, her fingers fumble at the band putting it to rights, the broad parting slices across the centre of her light-brown hair and disappears under the fabric as if into a tunnel. You were the one who got yourself here, she is thinking, who forced yourself along the whole of the long road from idea to action. *Constantia. Constantia*, you've got to be steadfast, to persevere. Though what emerges between the flat, fluted columns of the mirror is another female figure from Giotto's frescoes: she has lost her footing and is falling backwards with one raised arm that is sticking out beyond the frame.

Below the beautifully curved staircase of the Château Bardou is a black car with Swiss number plates and large white capitals painted on the boot: AYUDA SUIZA. Like Elisabeth Eidenbenz's room, the delivery room and the dormitories, it too has a name, but Randi Tommessen has forgotten what it is.

"And here comes the *tramontana*! The North Wind! Although in its milder summer version, in winter the air turns so dry it crackles, forcing its way into every cranny, the children become fretful and anxious." Elisabeth shouts the words as she turns past the bonnet and heads for the boot. The luggage space is filled with packets of powdered milk and large buckets of water, as well as a couple of crates of peaches and one with large ripe tomatoes the head gardener José has just brought in. Elisabeth Eidenbenz has told her the car was left behind by the flood of Spanish refugees that crossed the border two winters ago. Two winters ago Randi Tommessen was in Paris, reading in the papers about the hordes of people fleeing across the border, from the moment she saw the photographs of the female militias in *Vu* in the summer of 1936 she had followed the events in Spain (the heat in the little room on rue Vavin, the greenery of the Luxembourg Gardens floating in the light). She read the special report on a bench in the park, it was on the next page that she found the advertisement showing two women in laboratory coats set within the sphere of a gigantic lens: *Apprenez la photographie!* COURS DE PHOTO-FULD-PUBLIPHOT. She made up her mind there and then, her gaze slid across the large pond in the Luxembourg Gardens while she was putting together the wording of a telegram: PHOTO-COURSE STOP 450FR STOP THANKS STOP RANDI. Followed by the move to the 18th arrondissement so as to be closer to the school on rue Simon Dereure, the lemon-yellow walls of the rented apartment on the crest of rue Rochechouart, the long nocturnal conversations with Gertrud Fehr and her husband Jules who have since moved the school to Lausanne. Though she never felt comfortable in what turned out to be those far-too-worldly circles, they took her even further away from that core she was seeking, something she vaguely defined as "a place she could feel was the centre of her life", and yet she had felt as far away from that place in Paris as in Zurich or at her father's home in Oslo. She also lacked the driving force, a genuine interest, and above all she lacked talent. No-one really understood how much she loathed the technical side

89

of photography – the light metre, the developing fluids, the anxious wait to see the result. Growing up with an art dealer had left its mark, she wanted to see faces and bodies emerge, slowly, as if from brushstrokes, or in the form of a description, word by word, because she does not even paint (her journal is her only work, a work in progress as far as she is concerned, at least), snapping pictures of human models (those *instantanées*) often made her feel panic, when she then developed the pictures she felt the bodies had been trapped in that moment (*l'instant* – such a lovely word all the same), and the instant, time, she associated with air, oxygen, the oxygen in a photograph does not last long, a face has more space in which to breathe in an oil painting, a portrait in oil is ongoing and progresses through various versions, through layer upon layer of paint. Although the greatest space is to be found in words, the bodies can move among the words without ever being suffocated, a sentence, an entire page, an entire novel, will never keep a body trapped, or close all the pores like that shiny photographic paper did, words leave intervals, ways out. So she went to see her father in Oslo (her fourth attack of gallstones was the pretext) and her trip coincided with the capture of Barcelona by the Spanish Fascists in January 1939, the newspapers she read on the way were filled with images of thousands of loyalists and civilians crossing the border over the mountain passes, wounded, frozen, a great many older people and children, she remembers the girl with the amputated limb featured on several front pages, now it turned out that many of them had got no further than here, that they were the people she had seen yesterday on those appalling beaches. Hundreds of them still, imprisoned between the fences and the sea, hundreds of rows of white huts, her sandals treading across the sand to the milk hut with an escort of two gendarmes, she and Elisabeth accompanied by a squad of internees carrying the bags of powdered milk and buckets of water and a huge roll of grey-coloured cloth.

A scent of lavender or it might be *Kölnisch Wasser* hangs inside the car, Randi Tommessen is at the wheel for the first time, Señorita

Isabel, the teacher from Zurich, is giving instructions from the seat beside her. "Second gear is a bit stiff, bear that in mind," her starched apron rustling faintly with every movement. Wait a moment! I have to have a word with Guillermo, and Elisabeth sticks her head out of the lowered window to speak with the young man with frizzy hair and narrow almost amused eyes astride a bike with a cart attached to the rear wheel. Elisabeth draws her head back into the car as the air is filled with dust whirling in the cross-draught. "That was Guillermo, he's been with us since 1939." The smell rising from Randi Tommessen's own apron is of freshly pressed clothes that have been drying in the sun, it rises to her nostrils with every obstinate jerk of the gearstick as she tries to engage second, whatever the resistance is it finally gives way and she manages to get up to the right speed along the short stretch before the end of the road where she has to stop at the crossing and change down to first while the car is filling with the dust from the gravel the wheels have thrown up and that the north wind is blowing inside, then she has to struggle to get back into second once more as she swings out onto the tree-lined main road. When the car is at last moving smoothly in a higher gear Randi lets go of the breath she was holding, Elisabeth is sitting lost in thought, her features flicker in the greenish-yellow light sifting through the row of plane trees alongside the ditch, in the semi-darkness under the canopies each interval between the trunks casts rectangles of white light that carve out Elisabeth's profile as they come and go, lending it a ticking, throbbing presence in the confined space inside the car. Faces are rarely finished, they are just on their way to completion, death that is, she thinks, like a reminiscence of Gertrud Fehr's nocturnal observation on the sofa at rue Rochechouart, the sofa with its high armrests screened them off the way this car is screening them off from the trees and the landscape outside; but death is nothing, death is effacement, *solarisation*, the term appears in her mind, its black border surrounding bare skin. Like a name, she thinks, a name that is an over-exposure, a blazing irradiation, the Mackie line around a body, *l'effecte Sabattier,* she smiles, lost deep in thought. Language may conceal (*La parole a été donnée à l'homme pour déguiser sa pensée*) but names illuminate, burn, they are on fire. Randi Tommessen can feel that the Ford is obeying the steering wheel and recognition arrives with that sense of security, as well as a momentary desire for the most beautiful automobile in the world, a Buick Y-Job, the 1938 model, that was parked in the snow, its dark curves and straight steel lines gleaming outside the front door of her building when she arrived home in Oslo. But even as Randi Tommesen was walking up the staircase on Løvenskioldsgate after spending three years abroad she knew that this homecoming was temporary, it was a habit of hers always to leave lights on when she left home and now it felt as if she had come back only to turn those lamps off, to turn them off before the Germans came as it would turn out, that afternoon three years before when she had taken the night train to Paris the lamps had been glowing in the hall and the drawing room as well, the lights were turned off when finally she got home and inserted the key and opened the door, but her collection of pumps was still there arranged as it always was, along one wall of the corridor, pair after pair all the way to the bedroom, some silver lamé dancing shoes made her stop and bend down, as if she were seeing them for the first time, then she ran her finger along the pair next to them, the black velvet gleaming, the sheen undimmed: no dust, none either on the decorative wreath on the tiled stove in the drawing room but a note from her father:

Welcome home,
p.s.: I've paid the electricity bill.

Randi's cheeks are burning now, flushing wildly with shame, as if her skull were made of the same glass as the windscreen her eyes are peering through or as if the road stretching in front of the bonnet were a screen on which her thoughts were being projected and

Elisabeth, who is sitting silently beside her and rubbing something between her fingers, was able to read them while she is thinking them. All this wastefulness that her life has been, the irretrievable extravagance that is lost for ever and can never be undone, never channelled into something useful, like food and soap and clean water or an enduring action, *food*, she cannot remember a single day in her life when she has been hungry, not *really* hungry, the kind of hunger the women up on the roof were talking about, one that turned your skin grey and stopped your liver and kidneys working and kept your brain trying to sate itself on illusions, the starvation that turned the bodies of little children into living skeletal corpses with distended stomachs. As if Elisabeth really could read her thoughts Randi can feel her silence preying on her like condemnation, and that it is preying on her more deeply and more potently than her own which is not silence at all, and is therefore unbearable.

"You christen everything here, the rooms, the car, everything's got a name, *c'est drôle ça!*"

"*Morsomt?*" Elisabeth says, turning to face Randi.

"That's right, *morsomt*," Randi Tommessen replies. "It's a lovely notion. Taking your homeland with you wherever you go. I understand that the halls have the names of Spanish cities, but why is the labour ward called 'Marruecos'? Doesn't that mean Morocco?" Randi can see the long narrow room in her mind's eye, like a tube almost, with its birthing bed, a windowless, claustrophobic space, so unlike the high-windowed hall in the academy where they practised doing mock deliveries with a jointed doll that was pulled out of a leather mock-up of female genitals.

"'Marruecos' is Morocco, that's correct, it was the first of the birthing mothers who came up with it, they were thinking of Franco's African Corps and his *guardia mora*, his Moroccan bodyguard, who spread terror wherever they went. Apart from that though the idea of christening things is a leftover from the time when we were working in Spain to evacuate the civilians from Valencia and Madrid.

93

We arrived in Spain in a bus and four trucks loaded with humanitarian supplies, they all had names. The bus was called 'Zwingli' after Ulrich Zwingli. The trucks were called 'Pestalozzi', 'Dunant', 'Wilson' and 'Nansen'. Those names had an explicit purpose: evacuating civilians through a war-torn country with those white signs on was a way of campaigning for peace. We're still using Dunant, it's the one that distributes the supplies from the central depot in Toulouse."

"Only what did you say this car was called?"

"That's a different story," Elisabeth Eidenbenz smiles, "it's called 'Rocinante', like Don Quixote's poor nag." Elisabeth Eidenbenz extends her legs and stretches out her body to retrieve something from a fold in the pocket of her white apron, Randi thinks it is the camera, but it is something that rustles instead, a piece of paper.

"We have less and less freedom to manoeuvre with the German occupation of the Northern zone. Do you want to know the names of the children to be registered today?"

"Of course."

"Ellen Jacqueline, born June 22, August, born June 23, Harmonia, born June 26, Felipe the same day, Locadia, born on July 7 and then Amèrica who was born at half past eleven last night. Amèrica, that is both beautiful and sad. Like an indictment."

"I was awake when the child was born, the night sky was marvellous, all the stars were out, a few of us were sitting up on the terrace talking until midnight."

"Starlit nights mean the *tramontana* here."

Randi Tommessen can hear how tired Elisabeth is from her voice and understands that she read out that list of the names of the newborn more for her own sake than for Randi's, that she needs to remind herself of what she is accomplishing and why. *Harmonia*, *Amèrica*, an accusation or an invocation, an attempt to deliver yourself from despair. We're going to get out of here, your name will get us to America, my baby. Get us to him, your father, who is already there. On the other side of the sea. Mexico. Veracruz. You give birth to lives and you demand life for them, a promise of life at least. *Ellen Jacqueline* tells a different story, there's resignation there: live my life, take my name with you, I've come this far, no further, *Ellen* turns into *Jacqueline* or *Jacqueline* carries *Ellen* like a weight across her shoulders for ever. *For all time.* Randi Tommessen is sighing now as well. Breathing in air and searching along the line of the horizon in memory. Can you see the boats sailing out of Marseille from the beaches of Argelès and St Cyprien? Children are playing in the filthy sand, the mothers are staring at grey puffs of smoke that disappear where the sea changes element and becomes sky, air, a colourless dream. Veracruz.

"You can do it . . . if you stop brooding about it," Elisabeth Eidenbenz says unexpectedly and without turning towards Randi. She keeps her eyes firmly on the road instead, while squeezing what she is holding in her hand, rolling it between her thumb and index finger. For a moment Randi Tommessen thinks it is a rosary she is holding, but then immediately changes her mind, Elisabeth is Swiss, the daughter of a Calvinist priest, besides, no rosary can be seen, what pops up between her index finger and thumb turns out to be a walnut, shiny from the persistent polishing of her fingers. Randi Tommessen is not brave enough to ask if she is a believer, or to question it. She knows that Elisabeth Eidenbenz misses the conversations with her father, she knows that her father is ill, but not if it is serious, she supposes so, she knows that Elisabeth went to stay with him in the spring. And she can see that she is tired, that her nerves are worn by the intense pressure of constantly having to overcome setbacks and find solutions where no solutions seem to exist, of having to improvise all the time. She watches Elisabeth rubbing the shell of a nut whose kernel resembles a human brain, and she thinks that that must be what God's hand is like, if there is one.

"I've only just begun to train as a nurse . . . Edith Wild talked about your work here in such glowing terms I just felt I had to come

95

and help. I really do want to help. That word has acquired an entirely new meaning for me. I may not have what it takes, though. I may be too fragile. I keep asking myself if I really belong here. I'm not like the rest of you." There is silence for a while in the car as they pass the sign to Argelès.

"In Barcelona, during the panic and chaos of *la Retirada*, the Retreat, I lost touch with my group, they went off towards the border in the trucks loaded with refugee children while I got lost in a strange city in chaos and tried to contact the administration every way I knew how, without success. After two years of hard work, of seeing children dying or being orphaned during the bombing raids my pacifist ideals had been demolished, how could this happen again, after Verdun? After all our efforts? I was completely disheartened and I was literally dumb and blind for the two days I lay in a bed in a simple guesthouse near las Ramblas. I lay there on the bed without sleeping or being properly awake, I just closed my eyes and kept sinking deeper and deeper, it was as though all the buildings I had seen hit by bombs hadn't actually collapsed until that moment. The fatigue was so intense I thought I would die, because I did not have the strength to resist any more. But at the very bottom of that resignation was something other than the end, there was a room there, a well, that's where I get the energy from to help the innocent, that's what we're going to be handing out when we're in the barracks distributing reconstituted powdered milk: the water of life. For the sake of simplicity I call that room 'prayer'. Even though I'm a pastor's daughter, I really hadn't understood the importance of prayer before that. What you need to bear in mind is that no-one is forcing you to be here. You are free. I think you're the only free person in Europe at this moment. Whether you are strong or weak is something you have to decide."

Is Elisabeth disappointed in her? Randi Tommessen does not feel free and she is ashamed of the badges of freedom she does possess – the passport, the money. No, it really isn't that simple. She doesn't come from the same kind of background as most of the other nurses. Maybe that's it. Children of priests, almost the whole bunch. It has to be that. Being fed conviction along with your mother's milk. She barely remembers her own mother and her father is no priest, he's an agnostic, a doubter (*The extent of the region of the uncertain . . . will vary according to the knowledge and the intellectual habits of the individual agnostic*). She does not want to be faced with demands, what she needs is understanding for the confusion she is feeling, not demands. How could anyone say she is free? The knot on the nape of her neck that keeps the bonnet in place is chafing her skin as though an entire colony of lice had invaded the roots of her hair there at the back, she is bound to have picked up lice when she went into the camp yesterday. She raises her right hand to the back of her neck and has a good scratch, prepared to undo the knot or even take off the bonnet, her forehead itches as well and she has to move two of her fingers to keep rubbing the spot until she can feel the nails have scratched two red tracks above her eyebrows, which is why she takes off the bonnet in the end, keeping a tight hold on the steering wheel to stop herself tearing off the apron as well along with the white uniform that commands such respect. If she entered the camp half naked the gendarmes would be able to paw at her body with those obscene looks of theirs. *Salope! Putain!* The humiliation would appease something inside her, *salope!* She would feel more worthy of the people locked up inside. She ought to go and stand in front of the barrier and yell at the guards to take her instead, take me and let them go, they haven't done anything, they're children, let them go, they're women and the elderly, let them go, take me, *take me!* Let them go. She sees herself running barefoot between the huts and setting them on fire, she sees herself at the head of a group of women and children with a torch in her hand while she leads them through the raised barrier, they walk along the avenue of plane trees that leads away from the beach up to the village and out onto the road to Elne, they are moving slowly along from the opposite end of

97

the long way she has ahead of her, she is moving with them as well, at the head of a gaggle of children, she can see herself from a distance, the double of herself, that is, walking in the opposite direction to the one she is currently driving. Ten or so metres further on and she is forced to brake to allow a flock of sheep to cross the road. Randi leans her entire upper body against the steering wheel and bursts into tears, she opens the car door and gets out of the vehicle. The sheep wander slowly past the bonnet, in close formation, the head of one resting on the rump of another, the white-spotted shepherd's dog that is barking to drive them on nips a straggler on the back leg before it notices Randi, when it sees Randi standing by one of the tree trunks that edge the road it runs over to her and snaps cautiously at the pleats of her skirt and at her right sandal. The dog is a long-haired bitch with drooping ears and a pointed nose. The sheep are accompanied by a stifling smell of tallow, but it is the bitch's split face, half black and half white, aiming its pointed nose and a look of absolute conviction at her, one of the amber-coloured eyes is encircled with black, the other with white, that distracts her. Africans believe that the nose of a dog possesses magical powers, they crush the noses of dogs and hyenas to powder in order to contact the spirits and to gain insight, to become clear-sighted, if only she could be clear-sighted now, if only she could put on the dog mask hanging in her father's cabinet.

Elisabeth Eidenbenz comes over to her and puts a hand between her shoulder blades, then stands there silently, waiting. The white bitch runs off, called away by the shepherd, and starts barking with renewed vigour at the sheep lagging behind.

"You can help me as well," Elisabeth says, her hand still touching her back, "I need someone who knows how to develop my pictures. You realise that the photographs I take are the most convincing argument we have, both against the French and for our office in Bern. I've managed to extract more than just one permit from the prefect, thanks to my camera, they still have enough of a sense of shame to be terrified of the international press. I need you, someone who knows how to develop film. I'll write to Marcel Dubois in Toulouse tomorrow and apply for the necessary equipment. We'll save a lot of money in the long run, money that's needed for milk and food. Headquarters in Bern have got to be persuaded every so often as well and they need to *see*, with their own eyes, not just in words, what is happening here and what they are collecting funds for. Do you see?"

Back in the car, Elisabeth Eidenbenz turns the radio on only for them to hear the familiar notes of the Radetsky March, so she immediately turns it off.

"That is Radiodiffusion Française, they mostly broadcast martial music when they're not reading out biased news reports. Although on Saturdays we usually listen to Radio Andorra which only broadcasts classical and popular music, a lot of opera and variety acts, tomorrow you'll see how lively it gets, the Spanish women love the announcer, 'Mademoiselle Aquí', because she's a Spaniard in exile too, her real name is Victoria and she's got an incredibly difficult surname with two of those lisping sounds, Zorzano, but they call her Mademoiselle Aquí because she always starts by saying *'Aquí Radio Andorra, la radio del Principado de Andorra'*. It gets going at a quarter past eight in the evening with *Le quart d'heure de l'auditeur*, when the audience can listen to their requests and we all take our seats then in the large hall. Sometimes one of us will have written to Mademoiselle Aquí and things really get animated then, believe me. The evening often finishes with dancing."

Randi Tommessen turns her head towards Elisabeth Eidenbenz and meets her eyes beneath those unplucked eyebrows, the short straight nose above that broad smile, the gap between the two large square front teeth. Before either of them can say another word they both laugh, they laugh so much that tears fill Randi's eyes once again.

The Staircase, C/ Balmes 33,
Lérida, Spain,
Early Spring 1971

When the clock above the grey-painted doorpost struck one, the three-hour lunch break began and those pupils at La Anunciata school who were allowed to eat lunch at home could take off the obligatory light-blue overall with white edging and transparent plastic buttons that protected the navy-blue uniform from chalk dust and stains of various kinds. You took off your overall and hung it (largely unstained) on a hook at the very back of the classroom, then you lined up to follow the stream of girls going out under the clock that doled time out to you (it was a round and cold metal clock you never felt was on your side but on that of the Dominican nuns and the portrait of Franco and the Crucifix) and continued along the wide-arched corridor to leave the school grounds by the back way, through the gate, that is, on the other side of the orchard the sisters had planted in rigidly straight lines, the soil between the plum and the peach trees was covered in coarse gravel that left a grey film on your dark-brown lace-ups, alias the gorillas, the times you played tag or hide-and-seek in there, which was actually forbidden. That gate opened onto a broad expanse of empty land overgrown with high grass and wild fennel on both sides of a beaten track, in late spring the fennel flowered and the stalks turned juicy green and tasted of aniseed when you chewed and sucked them; now in winter the frozen stalks were brownish and covered in white snails. The newly constructed Ricardo Viñas square that began where the wasteland ended was paved and took up an entire block, it contained a low, rectangular carp pond, a competing school (with higher fees than yours, its pupils had check uniforms in a black-and-white pattern that was considered more stylish than the sober navy blue of La Anunciata's), the Lugano café on one of its sides and next to it a doctor's surgery in front of which the queue of people wanting to be vaccinated that summer cholera broke out stretched as far as the circle of stone benches and oleander bushes that formed the centre of the square. During every break the first weeks after the Christmas holiday a large contingent of La Anunciata's pupils had flocked into the pine grove on the lookout for the robber El Lute behind the burnt-out house (*la casa quemada*), you were there as well staring in total silence at a ramshackle hovel with blackened beams that appeared to be staring back at you with a peculiar kind of defiance. The rumour that the robber El Lute, whose real name was not known, had been spotted in the province of Lérida following his latest escape on New Year's Eve, had spread like wildfire and you were drawn, all of you, to the metal fence at the western perimeter of the school playground to try and locate him, convinced that evil would call to evil. You had to remain absolutely silent and not move your eyes away, not even blink, that was the unwritten rule as you faced the abandoned house, only in that way could the invisible appear, you all knew that without anyone having to tell you. There was an inexplicable difference in altitude between the pine grove and the ground beneath the abandoned shack and the elevated position you were forced to adopt as you observed the ruin in silence helped lend your serious game a sense of imminent danger. The metal fence that marked the boundary of the school grounds to the west had been erected only a couple of metres from the partly collapsed outer walls of the burnt-out hovel, if there had been a space to turn, a threshing floor or a little garden in front of the house it now lay where you stood, buried beneath the Dominican nuns' imposing elementary and grammar school for girls. On the days none of you want to do skipping or play princes and princesses (the girls who play the prince – it is always the same girls who are unanimously assigned that role – take off their blue overalls and do the topmost button up around their necks so that the overall hangs across their shoulders like a cape while the princesses – the vast majority, which means that the competition for the few princes is intense – take off their overalls and tie the sleeves around their waists to create greater volume in the uniform skirt) you go to the haunted house beyond the pine grove, no matter whether a bandit hunted by the Guardia Civil across the whole country is suspected of hiding there or not; in one corner where the roof has collapsed the sky is reflected in a pool of water on the uneven flagstones, many years of rain have failed to wash away the soot that has left patches on the walls like sores, you sense a movement out of the corner of your eye, at the edge of the pool shaped like a lens that glitters inside a window set with bars, a wing, a cloud, you are expecting the fleeting sight of a face, plaited hair, an old toy. As if the pool were a mirror to the past and it were still being played out there now, on the other side of the charred rooms, the side you cannot see but that is revealed in glimpses on a trembling film of water.

"¿Por qué la quemaron?" says Fanny on your left. "¡Pues para castigarla, tonta!"[9] a voice whispers impatiently.

On clear mornings cobwebs can be seen between the frozen fennel plants the frost is draining the life from and turning brown (the mist is usually thick along the track and runs wet fingers over the bare skin between your socks and the uniform skirt); now, in the middle of the day, it is as if the spiders have folded up their nets and taken them away because nothing can be seen between the stalks, the unconstructed land between the school and the square is more than ever a place that has been but is no longer, a place waiting to become something, an interval, a limbo (like the thing the white-clad nuns in their black wimples say Masses over) but you prefer it to the hard flatness of Plaza Ricardo Viñas whose bright paving makes

9   "Why did they burn it down? To punish it, of course, silly."

your eyes ache when it is sunny and that you hasten to cross at an angle, cutting straight through the oleanders at its heart and all their names (*adelfa, baladre, rosa laurel* and *yerba mala*), everything about them (the leaves, the stalks, the flowers and seeds) is poisonous. On one of the days you stood there keeping an eye out for a glimpse of El Lute you tore off one of the pink flowers and shoved it in your pocket (in case El Lute should suddenly appear), they say the poison is so powerful your heart just stops, you begin to vomit and get diarrhoea and die soon after, that's what happens to sheep, goats and horses (dogs don't like flowers, thank heavens, just grass every now and then) but what about El Lute? How are you going to get him to eat part of the flower if he should suddenly spring into view? Will it be enough to throw the flower in his face? You think of your hand that has touched the poisonous flower, your hand is now dangerous, tainted, you mustn't touch anything when you get home, you mustn't stroke the new black puppy that still hasn't got a name.

Your street, Calle Balmes, begins at one corner of the square with the side wall of Señor Primitivo's grocer's, its shutters are painted a yellowish shade of brown, inside you are served by Señor Primitivo, a tall fellow with a prominent stomach that forms a long curved bulge under an overall that is light brown as well, he always has a pencil behind his ear. His wife Estrellita is permanently smiling at his side, dressed in a similar light-brown overall, it is just that hers is several sizes smaller because she is only knee-high to a grasshopper, her head a long way below his shoulders, and her face set behind a voluminous bust that appears to be held in check by two of the brown buttons on the overall; she has a lovely name, though, Estrellita (little star), and she paints her lips a brilliant crimson and has plucked eyebrows that arch round her black eyes like a bow and she coats her curly raven hair with pomade as in the films of yesteryear, because they say she was an artist during the war (*era cupletista durante la guerra*) and your parents say she keeps trying to look the way she did when she was young. Señora Estrellita also has a short, worn-down pencil behind her ear though it cannot be seen under all that hair. Sometimes you get sent to the grocer's to buy toilet paper or a packet of margarine, if there is no other customer in the shop the couple move over to you like a perfectly coordinated duo, the identical overalls lit from the side by the refrigerated display counter, as if they were taking their places for a number together onstage, and Señora Estrellita leans towards you while clapping her hands and then resting them under her bust. "*Hola, guapa, ¿qué quieres, cielo?*"[10] Though usually it is Señor Primitivo who handles the long wooden pole with the hook on one end to pluck items off the topmost shelves (the walls of the shop are covered from floor to ceiling in wooden shelves), he raises one hand and the pole sways up to the top and pinches a toilet roll wrapped in yellow cellophane, the hook is then quickly released so the roll falls off the topmost shelf with a kind of graceful flip and that particular brand's design of a red elephant does a kind of pirouette in the air. Señor Primitivo is locking and bolting the door from inside as you pass the shop, he says hello in an inaudible voice from beyond the glass pane of the door, as if he were speaking underwater, and you can see the bubbles rising from the corner of his mouth and Señora Estrellita in the space behind the shop floor stirring the stinking war soup everyone has to eat because the people who lived during the war were so hungry. You are not the least bit hungry.

The narrow, green-painted entrance you go through is wedged between Doña Enriqueta's bag shop (she lives a couple of floors above you) and her husband's cycle-repair business which always exudes a thick smell of rubber. You only need to press the handle lightly for the door to open, the graffiti-covered corridor that leads to a staircase bathed in daylight is long and narrow and painted halfway up in a dark green the same shade as the entrance, the edge where

10 "Hello darling, what would you like, my love?"

the green-painted part shifts to flaking white is a long way above your head and the bare bulb hanging in the middle of the corridor gives off a dim light as if it were a sun seen from a depth of several metres under water, which is why that darkness has something slimy about it, and why you always move through at a run, the graffiti that has been scratched into the surface glows like secret organisms on both sides of your face, the incised words floating against the green like an affirmation of a threatening and hidden presence in the same way that the presence of algae both indicates and makes possible the existence of the monstrous creatures that live off them. The plastered staircase at the end of the underwater light, in contrast, is bathed in a steady dry gleam, like a soft beach welcoming you, the banister set into the wall is whitewashed and catches the white light falling diagonally through the ground glass in the windows on every landing. Your front door is on the second floor, the first door on the left, balancing as it were on the edge of the last step of the staircase, and it is right there, on that last step, you always stop to check to see whether that could possibly be pee on it. And it is then the boundaries start to become fluid, the staircase is as much a recurrent element in your nightmares as it is on the way up to your apartment, so the fact that you come home from school to eat the lunch soup together with your parents and ring the bell on the shiny door with the honey-coloured varnish (that flows and keeps flowing while you are waiting for the door to open) often gets mixed up with the scene you dream in which you walk up the staircase that is bathed in light and ring on the doorbell, you ring time and again while your eyes trace the brushstrokes of the varnish down to the floor and the pressure on your bladder becomes more and more acute; sometimes the door is not opened and then you have to let the stinging warmth of pee trickle between your thighs, it runs down to the inside of your knees where the regulation white socks absorb some of it, the urine then continues relentlessly down towards your shoes and winding one leg round the other to try to stop the gush of liquid does not help, though you do it anyway, even if it is in vain, the sticky trickle winds between your legs no matter how much strength you use to oppose it and finally reaches the gap between the sock and the sole. But sometimes when the door does open you do not recognise the woman standing there. Nor do you recognise the hall or the tiles on the floor, the colour of them is entirely wrong, and you have never seen the woman before. It is the right staircase but the wrong door.

Then you remember the turkey.

It was your father's batman who turned up with a live turkey the week before Christmas, he rang the doorbell with a sack in his hand that he tried to hand over in the hall, the sack was moving and giving off little noises, your mother could not bring herself to take it, the batman would simply have to find a place for it, but where? It would freeze outside on the balcony, your mother maintained, the batman then asked for a piece of string, your mother came back after a while with a ball of blue yarn. The young batman who had remained immobile with the sack in his hand while facing the severe expression on the man whose portrait was hanging in the hall then poured the contents out of the sack and into the small hip bath in the bathroom and out came a tangled pair of wings and a rubber neck that looked like a curved tube with a head on one end. The orderly grabbed the turkey's legs and turned the bird upside down and after a couple of quick turns of the blue yarn around one of its legs he tied it in a knot and then fastened the thread to the hot-water tap, which was very rarely used in any case. It was the maid Maria who opened the door a week later, by then you had got used to having one of the turkey's eyes staring at you every time you went to the toilet though you refused to begin with and had to use the cold enamel potty that left a numbed mark on your behind. Lately, however, you had felt brave enough to go in and sit on the toilet seat, you looked at each other, you and the turkey, you thought that you had the same posture in common at least, crouching with your knees towards your chest. Maria opened the door when you came home from school one day at lunchtime and you saw the turkey running for the first time, you were scared at first, but your fear soon turned into a kind of exhilaration, the moment you came in the front door the bird ran out of the kitchen, it ran towards the light pouring in from the balcony in the living room at one end of the corridor, then you noticed something dangling on one side of its neck, you saw it a second or two before the bird collapsed in the middle of the living room, its eye was still open when you reached the spot on the speckled green floor where the turkey had fallen, it was the head that had been dangling so oddly, it was lying there upside down at the end of its slit throat and was still attached by a little flap of skin, you close your eyes, you press the bell and press it again, when you raise your face a woman is standing there, you do not recognise her, she has fair, shoulder-length hair and her arm is in plaster all the way up to her biceps, it is dark in the hall behind her because evening has fallen, an autumn evening, you were in the school playground waiting for your mother to fetch you after school, but she never turned up, the playground was emptying of people and light at a relentless pace, as if someone were pouring the light out of a bottle and you were the last drop that remained, you stayed standing there in the light left behind (it existed in your head, everything else was darkness) for a very long time, until the lamps in the main entrance, beneath its pillared and arched vestibule, and the windows in the section for boarders began to glow, and the older girls could see that you were standing in the middle of the playground, waiting for the person who had forgotten you. You drag yourself over to the lit glass entrance with its carved iron decorations (it is the feeling of shame you are dragging, it pulls you in the opposite direction, towards the dark, but you have no choice, she is not coming now) and it is the short nun who usually stands behind the counter in the office who opens up. *No llores, no llores, telefonearemos a tu casa.*[11] One of the older boarders went home with you, your mother

[11] "Don't cry, don't cry, we'll telephone your home."

looked as though she had just woken up even though it was eight o'clock at night, two long creases across her cheek and eye from the pillow, you are kicking at the door now, kicking and kicking to make her wake up, wake up wake up wake up you're not supposed to be asleep when I'm at school, you're supposed to clean and do the washing up and make the food you have to do the washing up the kitchen is dirty you don't do the washing up you just lie there all day long and you feel so ashamed as though under your breastbone your body were on fire and so were your cheeks and your eyes only better to be ashamed than just stand here better to stand here and wait than end up in the wrong building a building on the other side of the courtyard that all the balconies look onto your balcony can be seen from this apartment's balcony what you do not know is how to get to the right door your door the one that is now on the other side of the courtyard all the doors look alike after all although why you walked up the staircase the way you always do to find someone behind the door other than your mother all the staircases are the same all the doors are the same and the corridors lead everyone from one set of stairs to the next always to the left of the last step where a large pool has formed and it is pee no doubt about it because it smells of pee and it smells of saliva on the transparent plastic button you are sucking on God how revolting you suck on the buttons of your school overall the way Fanny does she smells of spit all of her does her fingers and her breath when she comes up to you in the queue and when you see her buttons on the blue-striped school overall it makes you feel sick as if you were going to puke better to puke than stand here with pee squelching in your shoes better to better to better to you are so miserable your heart is going to burst sorry it doesn't matter if you haven't washed up let me in let me in let me in I have to come in otherwise I'll die you know that because you were close to death when you were two and your appendix burst (you think of your appendix as a sand-coloured puppy that has not yet opened its eyes) you've heard it said a thousand times how the army doctor at the camp in Tremp was so drunk your father had to slap him twice and force several cups of coffee down him and then shove him under a tap in the officer's mess and turn on the cold water, *¡O la operas o te parto los cojones!*[12] and you remember the long dark corridor where the sound of squeaking made your teeth ache and the large white cylinders slowly getting closer with a rocking sideways motion a yellow cylinder and after it a large bright square they are moving along the black corridor with that terrible squeaking getting closer and closer your jaws ache as if they had been drilled with nails and you block your ears because the scraping sound of the approaching figures makes you feel sick better to vomit than hear that sound and see the figures coming towards you so close to your eyes right up to your mouth your face better to die than better to die than that shame and you lick your tainted hand filled with poison first one finger then two then you lick the palm with a long greedy tongue you lick and lick your hand sticky like a dog because you are never going to have to meet El Lute after all.

12   "If you don't operate on her, I'll cut off your balls."

Country Road Outside Wels, Oberdonau,
Ostmark (Austria during the Annexation),
Schloss Hartheim Psychiatric Hospital Staff Outing,
March 1941

"If everyone could look this way," Bruno Bruckner, head of the hospital's photographic laboratory, is not laughing though perhaps he should be, almost all the others are, laughing as they shiver in the raw March cold, laughing because the outing in the hospital coach brings out something childish and high-spirited in them, laughing out of habit, there is usually a lot of laughter in the workplace, laughter is so much more than it is thought to be, he thinks and swears at the flat light lying like a lid above the heads of his colleagues, at the crust like cracked nails at the edge of the road that is forcing him to hold the camera a little unsteadily; from beneath his remarkably heavy brows he observes the restless group standing in unruly fashion in front of the coach. He has another go. He measures the light for the third time and sets the aperture and the exposure time, one of them has climbed up onto the bonnet of the coach the better to be seen, though she is not looking in his direction even so, Fräulein Hintersteiner's pale red fringe appears to be permanently turned away, he has just taken a close-up of her perched on the radiator like a figurehead, her feet on the shock absorber and her hands behind her back holding on to the large metal star, her upper body hanging forward, although the normally aloof secretary to the hospital director seems to be in a sparklingly playful mood today she is ignoring him, not even when he moved closer with the light meter and held the black oblong box beneath her face, a little above the V-shaped neckline of her white blouse, would she stop laughing at Gomerski's clowning about and look into the camera instead. "I'm going to press the button any moment now! Don't you want to be in it, Hans?" But the driver Hans Lothaler, who is smoking in the driver's seat and has not the slightest intention of being in the chilly air, sticks his head out of the window and shouts that it is much too damn cold, there wouldn't be any snow on the hills otherwise, would there? And urges Bruno Bruckner to get a move on because time is moving on and they have only got as far as the outskirts of Lambach. So Bruno Bruckner finally takes one last picture even though a handful of the ten or so people standing in front of him (a lot have remained in their seats on the coach) are looking away and even though Helene Hintersteiner is ignoring his request yet again and turning her laughing face all the way towards Franz Mayrhuber instead of towards the camera. Which means he now has two pictures in which Dr Lonauer's sandy-haired secretary is looking away from him, looking at someone else, that is, first at Hubert Gomerski who started throwing snowballs at everything and everyone as soon as they got off the coach for a cigarette break and now at the balding Mayrhuber (not even the latter's bald pate offers any kind of consolation, it actually makes his own scalp with its thick brown hair seem like a handicap, a badge of inferiority) and while everyone is getting back on board he realises that Nurse Maria Raab is also standing close to Mayrhuber (not that he has any intention of looking straight at them, out of the corner of his eye, however, he can see Maria Raab's unruly light-brown fringe close beside the high blonde hairline of Mayrhuber's shiny forehead and the two of them sitting down in the seats right at the back) and he remembers with an involuntary shiver Maria's broad hips resting heavily on his knees the other evening during the little impromptu party in Dr Renno's office, and that afterwards she kept giggling as she walked with him under the archways for a whole turn around the castle courtyard and they were already French kissing on the steps up to the second floor, he was permitted to run his hand up between her thighs even as she was leaning back against the balustrade, and she was soaking wet and her labia were soft and smooth and as slippery as snail meat between his fingers. So how can things have turned out like this? As though everyone were totally ignoring him? A flash of pain hits a spot behind his right eye and runs right across the top of his head like an incision and he can see a point light up in his slit-open brain where he has located the seat of the pain in his mind's eye, it shines like a window in a darkened street, a brilliant white spot in the area the doctors are busy mapping and that he is beginning to recognise although the bloody and peculiar convolutions of every brain he photographs, like the streets of a constantly changing city, are strangely unlike those of the next. Just as he is getting back on board and standing by the door looking in some confusion for a seat, (his heavy eyelids more like a bloodhound's than ever) the secretary of Dr Lonauer, the hospital director, offers him the one next to her and although she does not sit down immediately but turns to stand facing the rest of the staff and begins to count them, Bruno Bruckner, the hospital photographer, has no difficulty adjusting to the sudden change in his circumstances, quite the reverse, his mood immediately improves, he sits in the seat the hospital director's secretary pointed to, in the front row next to the window, and as Hans Lothaler restarts the engine and the coach careens back out onto the road the pounding behind his eye seems to be gradually diminishing in force and he feels he has every reason to recall his great good fortune at being given this position last year, and the fact that he earns 300 Reichsmark a month for doing a job that includes very nice trips like this one (board is included with his salary – good food that would taste so much better were it not for the perpetual stench that forces its way in almost everywhere and that is at its worst on the way to the dining room – and so is lodging, a double room he has to share with Sepp Vallaster, an unpredictable fellow, in a castle, besides, in a small quiet village not too far from his home in Linz and all the further from the front in consequence). And in that light, the light of Fräulein Hintersteiner's sandy hair and that toffee-coloured constellation of freckles, even Wirth, the supervisor, a crazed veteran who goes around yelling as if he had grenades in his hands that were about to explode and storms unannounced into the darkroom to inspect the images floating in the developing trays with those furiously myopic eyes of his (the never-ending triptychs he has to take of every patient), becomes an obstacle that can be surmounted; and while Lothaler is picking up speed and the coach is humming along in a higher gear he tells himself that the fellow does at least have a sense of humour, of the coarsest sort, it is true, but humour all the same, after a couple of glasses at least, that lunatic Wirth had been as funny as anyone at the party the other evening; and then a snatch of a tune from Walther's accordion comes back to him (the poor sod had had to sit his rump on Dr Renno's desk almost the entire time and play his tunes for them into the wee small hours) and drifts around his head like a puff of wind along the winding gritted road.

At the outskirts of Lambach Helene Hintersteiner interrupts an animated conversation with the relatively recently appointed photographer Bruno Bruckner in the seat beside her, a young man she finds surprisingly pleasant despite his heavy brown eyes and drooping lids and whose refined and engaging manner she has not become acquainted with before now; she gets to her feet with a smile, buildings have taken the place of the open countryside, the coach is rumbling up the slope to a sleepy little town and she is in an almost ridiculously good mood, when she raises her right arm high above her head to get the staff's attention she does so with a girlish sense of expectation, as if she were waving from a pier to a docking ship, which turns her smile into an ill-considered mixture of self-mockery and embarrassment; so she smiles, smiles broadly and not even Dr Lonauer's face, hovering above her thoughts like a neatly drawn cumulus cloud, has the power to restrict the widening of her lips, her mouth like a drawbridge being let down. She knows what she is going to say and she is waiting for the moment when Hans Lothaler will turn into the marketplace in Lambach so she can ask him to stop in front of a long, curved row of houses that occupies one whole side of the square: she is going to speak to them now, like a military commander, a Joan of Arc leading the staff of the castle out and across a deep and putrid smelling moat to the open and glorious fields of history; advertising images in saturated colours (cherry red, emerald green) are beaming at her from the wooden shutters of a tobacconist's (*Berlin raucht Juno*) and a house wall (*Persil bleibt Persil*), the luminosity of the images works like a catapult on the first sentences of her speech, the words are hurled out on a high note that comes from the top of her throat and makes her voice, as she notices straightaway, sound too bright, too shrill. But there is no going back, so she goes on to announce that Alois and Klara Hitler lived with their children over there, on the second floor, between 1896 and 1897. Those dates are still echoing inside her skull as she realises something has gone wrong, it could be her pitch which is too high, or the words rasping across her throat that sound off-key, lacking any resonance, or the fickle indifference of her audience, because they are continuing to talk among themselves with only a few giving her their full attention. The smile stays in place, however, wobbling across the lower part of her face (which now feels heavy) and she clears her throat and tries to shift her voice downwards, towards the vaulted chambers of her chest where she hopes the words will take on a darker timbre. With a deep breath she makes a new start and tells them about the magnificent monastery where the eight-year-old Adolf Hitler became a member of the boys' choir and served as a chorister, the words are echoing roundly and fully through her airways as far as she can tell, the way the singing of the boys' choir must have echoed under the vaulted arches of the monastery (*This unique setting has very recently been inaugurated as yet another of the Reich's many newly established teaching institutes for national policy where the youth of tomorrow will be instructed in the lofty ideals of the Thousand-Year Reich*) but only the rows nearest her appear to be listening, right at the back that Raab woman is laughing shamelessly at something Mayrhuber has just said and not even Gomerski, who has been sending indecent looks her way the last few days, has been listening, he is not even looking at her. Dismay is tying itself in a knot around her epiglottis, it feels as though she has dropped the reins and is losing any sense of control of her speech, which was intended to bestow a higher purpose on today's outing, as well as any desire to proceed, in the final stretch one of her sentences falls so flat it drops almost at her feet (*Because we have no intention of disturbing the lessons under way we will not be visiting the monastery*), she sounds like a defeated general, lacking in energy and without any will to communicate. All that remains is a brief run-through of practical matters, which she performs briskly while turned towards what are now the shapeless spots of colour on the advertising posters so as clearly to signal her refusal to have any further contact with her audience: "Make sure to buy cigarettes or anything else for that matter here in Lambach, because we will not be making any more stops before we get to the Attersee and that will not be until the afternoon."

Twenty-year-old Anneliese Neubeck sighs, she has, of course, been listening attentively to Fräulein Hintersteiner, her immediate superior in the large office upstairs where she works with thirteen other typists, but the market square in Lambach reminds her of her home village of Waldkirch im Breisgau, in far-off Baden-Württemberg, far too many miles from here; besides, it is the first time she has left the hospital since she started working there and now, finally outside the cramped stinking castle, she wants to go home more than ever, her clothes are already loose around her waist because she can't so much as eat, that nasty smoke is so horrible and revolting and sticks to your clothes and gets into everything else, the others complain about it too, but they seem to have got used to it and they can even joke about what happens to the patients, in the dining room of all places, the cremators are the worst, she just can't understand . . . It looks as though Fräulein Hintersteiner feels uplifted by what she is telling them about the Führer, it's hard to imagine him as a little choirboy, just one among all the others, that solitary figure always high up above the people, her parents will be very proud when they hear she's been to the square where the Führer played as a child, she's going to write and tell them, there's so much else she's not allowed to tell anyone after all, everything is so secret and she did sign that contract, if only she'd known then what goes on in that place on the other side of the wooden planking down there in the courtyard. Hauptmann Wirth's wide-eyed stare when he threatened her was like a raving madman's, she's not allowed to say anything to anyone at all, some of them say they've looked through the peephole, but now the doctors have put a stop to that which is a good thing, she's not planning on ever going into that place, the ashes the relatives are given aren't even those of their departed, her jaw dropped when Hanni Pfeiffer said that, they get mixed up with the others and could be anyone's, and not everything they have to write in the official letters of condolence is true. *Think about it – thirty people can't all have died of pneumonia on the same day at the same time*, besides, no-one actually gets treated in the castle, they just get driven there all on the same day, although Fräulein Hintersteiner is nice, strict but nice, which is why she tries to listen attentively and appear interested because some of the ones at the back are talking and giggling and she feels sorry for her, it's not like that at the castle, everyone looks up to her there, even the doctors address her with an exaggerated – slightly suggestive? – politeness, that has got to be because she's so pretty and girlish although they say she's over thirty, she wishes she had that sandy kind of blonde hair curling round her face like a wreath, if her boring chestnut-brown hair at least had a bit of body, not that there's anything she can do about her prominent eyes or her mouth, but her hair could have a natural curl, a kind of compensation for the ugliness she's been endowed with, Hanni has offered to lend her her curlers and help her pluck her eyebrows like a bow around her eyes, *Nature's mistakes are for Man to correct* she said, but she doesn't know if it would feel right, what would Father say, God, the racket they're making at the back, Fräulein Hintersteiner is looking embarrassed now, it's painful to witness, a lovely and talented woman like that and they don't respect her, she's going to pay closer attention to show Fräulein Hintersteiner that she at least is fully focused, which is why she runs her tongue over her teeth that go dry if she forgets to compress her lips every so often, *so clench your teeth then, lass* Mother says she looks stupid if she doesn't do that, she says it even though she's got a good head for figures, she forces her upper lip against her lower one so the lips meet in a tight fit and her large overbite can no longer be seen, you can look stupid and absent-minded even if you are top of your class, I wonder if Fräulein Hintersteiner was top of her class as well, her voice has got stuck in her throat and is barely audible, which means Anneliese has to look away so Fräulein Hintersteiner won't see her own embarrassment mirrored in her eyes, and it is as Anneliese turns her head to the left that she notices the new transport leader listening attentively to what Fräulein Hintersteiner still has to say (that was it – she's got to buy envelopes and stamps!), was his name Franz, Franz Gindl? She has seen him a couple of times from the draughty window in the office on the first floor, the window looks onto the road and the turning spot the Gekrat buses have to pass, she associates his profile with the striking of the keys against the platen and with the phrases she writes over and over again on the false death certificates, he started work last month as well and doesn't seem to have really settled in either, the meals are the hardest because there's a fixed seating arrangement and hardly any of them can be bothered to talk to her. As though he had felt her eyes settle on his profile Franz Gindl looks in her direction, Fräulein Hintersteiner has just finished speaking and a lot of them get up and move towards the exits but he remains in his seat and doesn't stop looking at her, he even smiles. A sudden palpitation makes Anneliese turn her head in the opposite direction, then she gets out her purse, she's going to buy postcards and stamps at the tobacconist on the square as well as a couple of packs of those expensive round cigarettes people smoke in Berlin to send to Father, poor Father, who imagines she is doing so well for herself. *Berlin smokes Juno*, the white letters are glowing at her against a red background as she approaches the tobacconist's, that's where she'd run away to if she could and take the lift to the cafeteria on the fifth floor of the KaDeWe department store Nurse Gertrud told her about on the way to the dining room, she was trying to be friendly, to comfort her, in a way, she's from Brandenburg and doesn't have a thick accent either, not like the people from around here.

Persil bleibt Persil, Nurse Gertrud is looking at the elegant lady parading past in her white gauze dress with twin girls also dressed in white on either side of her and sees a flash of Hildelein suddenly standing in the doorway to the veranda, her dress dirty and wet and shot through with the light from the garden (*Mutti? Wo ist meine Mutti? Mutti!*), just the memory of the exquisite tiny buttons that adorned all her dresses makes Gertrud's nostrils flare and inhale the pungent scent of lavender and starch in the nursery; the girl was trembling, raindrops were glistening like sparklers on the sunlit lime tree in the park, the hem above the specially made boot was filthy with mud, there were grass stains and blood you couldn't get out all over the rest, the expensive fabrics and lace that little Hildelein's club foot dragged through the dirt all the time (*Mutti? Wo ist meine Mutti? Mutti!* followed by that harsh grating noise as she struck the keys of the Countess' piano with her malformed hand.) Leaning heavily against the back of her seat, Nurse Gertrud Blanke lets her thoughts drift as she feels around with the tip of her tongue the blister that has erupted yet again on the inside of her cheek; Dr Lonauer's gorgeous secretary is urging them to get off the bus and shop in the square, and most of them are doing as they have been told. But she doesn't need anything and would rather stay lost in thought in the warmth now that the new and confused young typist she has taken under her wing has left the seat beside her for a little stroll in the world of the Führer's childhood, that might do her good, their operation has been blessed by the Führer, like she said, *What is currently secret will become the law of the land when the war is over, didn't Hauptmann Wirth tell you that?* she said to her and it obviously lightened the load a bit, it's like that for everyone to start with. Though it is painful to think about Wittstock and the family who employed her, when Frau Dora entered a room there was a kind of radiance suddenly hanging in the air, the materials were lighter then, before the war, the dresses had these panels cut out and flounces on the sleeves or at the shoulders that flew up every time you moved and Frau Dora was a dragonfly in any case, all long and slender and forever swathed in bright silk gauze and chiffon, like that woman in the advert for washing powder, even the scent of lily of the valley that she left trailing in her wake was brilliant white, as though whiteness was all she wanted you to think of in her presence, which you did. But Hildegard was made restless and cross by that smell (*Mutti! Ich möchte mit meiner Mutti sein*), she used to stalk it through the house like a dog. As if she was actually amused, Gertrud Blanke suddenly snorts while running her right hand across her pinned-back hair to make sure that nothing has come loose: what an absurd notion! Frau Dora go out and buy her own washing powder?! Nurse Gertrud straightens up and pulls in her stomach, but the advertising image with its emerald-green background and white human figures is still aglow in her thoughts like a dimly burning bulb, *Where are you, Hildelein? Where's Gertie's little elfchild now?* She can remember every tiny pleat and every piece of lace in the deformed child's white dresses, there were seven of them hanging in the velvet-lined wardrobe, drenched in a scent with blueish notes, and she can recall the lace collars on all of them, their patterns and shapes, real lace on the whole bunch, even the wrong sides of the collars had to be stitched according to the pattern of the lace without any rows of stitching

visible as though the perfection of the dresses, with no wrong side
at all, could compensate for the defects of that little body; and
she remembers the socks made of crocheted lace that were neatly
arranged in a drawer of their own on little linen cushions stuffed
with lavender, the socks she had to get onto the twisted foot every
morning, and those fiendishly tiny buttons that slipped out from
between her fingers, every transport has made her afraid she will
find those initials embroidered on a vest or some item of underwear
as she is sorting and folding the patients' clothing, mind you, Hildegard is no longer a child, she would be in puberty now, and bound
to have started menstruating ages ago, the very thought of Hildelein
having to get on a Gekrat bus and then be herded into the changing
room, being forced to take off all her clothes or be undressed . . .
thank God she has escaped having to welcome her and speak reas-
suringly to her while undoing the back of her dress and removing
both it and her underwear and silk stockings and the vest that would
all end up in a sack, she will have to be even stronger now, little
Hildegard, strong enough to strike back and kick out with that heavy
boot of hers, after all, she used to do that even then, in Wittstock;
no, not little Hildelein, thank heavens, not the *Elf Child, the Princess,*
naked in front of that Bruckner, that half-Italian with the horrible
eyes, photographed by him from every angle, Hildelein's huge blue
eyes glaring in fury at the doctors, not Hildelein shoved into that
cramped chamber together with the other naked people and Sepp
Vallaster's hand on her crooked back before he slams the iron door
shut and Dr Lonauer or Dr Renno, not Dr Renno, turns on the
gas. *Once there was a hand that wasn't like anyone else's, it couldn't
play God's instrument, it couldn't write beautiful songs to God or hold
a brush to paint God's creation, and the little hand wept and asked
God: why did you make me so unworthy? And God shone the light of his
eyes on that little unworthy hand and said . . .* Gertrud Blanke breathes
deeply into her lungs as if to shore up her failing backbone while
raising a hand to her face and wrapping her fingers around her cheek

to protect it from the cold of the window pane, she has forgotten the end of the Countess' bedtime tale to her inferior child, what could God's reply have been, gifted as she was with wealth, beauty and talent? It had something to do with the wind and the butterflies and the rain and sunbeams and the clear source of the Danube, or some other source, something about the unworthy hand being just as worthy as all the other aspects of God's creation. In the mornings Hildelein would be lying there like an angel her blonde locks strewn across the pillow and the rest of her body hidden under the eiderdown only to appear later in the day stained with blood and dirt, the French windows wide open, Hildelein in the doorway, the ankle-length dress brown with mud a long way up above the lace edging and large green patches around her thighs and knees, the stains were a brownish-red on her chest because she had dragged herself over to the hole under the hedge in the kitchen garden to dig up some scraps of flesh she was holding in her arms, the raindrops were glistening on the lime tree in the sunlight, as if God were trying to prove that he could see everything, Hildelein said they were newborn rabbits she had saved from the gardener's dog, an overweight, pale-coloured Labrador, among the gnawed body parts was one living baby rabbit, she had hit the dog with her deformed hand, hard and flat like a spade, and saved the last of the litter, it was lying there on that flat, twisted hand as if on a tray, and with her good hand, so like her mother's with those aristocratic fingers that played for the rich and the powerful at expensive *soirées musicales* where they drank French Champagne, she was patting the trembling little pile of fur, with slow rhythmical taps, almost impossible to distinguish from the patter of rain against the tops of the trees in the park . . . Poor Anneliese has come back, her cheeks rosy from the cold and with a bunch of postcards and envelopes in her hands. The coach sets off and Anneliese shows her the postcards she picked out, some are from Linz, the Nibelungen Bridge and views across the Danube, because this little dump is not somewhere you'd ever want a postcard from, she lets the girl chatter on about who is to get which card, she is so young, only just out of the nest. The coach drives alongside the monumental monastery where, according to *die Hintersteiner*, Hitler sang in the choir as a little boy, four storeys of regularly spaced dormer windows, she counts up to eight windows in each wing of the building, the courtyard of this castle must be ten times bigger than the one at Hartheim, Dr Renno's flute music would never be able to disperse the stench here, *our contribution to the war effort* as Hauptmann Wirth calls it. As luck would have it the new transport leader starts chatting to the girl and she can stop pretending she is interested and turn back towards the window although she is mostly looking inwards, she can see Dr Renno dressed in his best uniform without the white coat on top, standing in the narrow castle courtyard as he usually does on Sundays, his back to the planks and the brick chimney that has been added on, slightly bow-legged as he plays his flute under the high, floating rectangle of sky, he gets going just before Mass begins in the musty little church in Alkoven, he plays as if he were performing a prayer service just for them at the hospital even though hardly anyone stops to listen under the archways, he plays as if he believed that his music could diffuse the smell and offer them absolution of a kind and somehow, she thinks, that really is the case, the notes whirl up and take with them the incinerated human flesh into the clouds, if you go with the music the smell no longer feels as invasive and a sense of calm can develop, as if the music were carrying the smoke away and making it easier for all of them to breathe; she sighs, and for a second or two her airways are entirely clear, opened by a flowing melody. Then she closes her eyes, while the coach forces her large, heavy, 42-year-old body to shift sideways so her shoulder hits the window pane and the memory of Dr Renno's boyish, almost baby-like face fills her mind's eye, he is closing his eyes as well, his lips pressed against the cold silver mouthpiece of the flute, his lips half-open, shiny with saliva, his tongue forcing its way in to slide around the inside of her mouth, licking and sucking hard at her nipples and smearing her breasts, so swollen and fat, as he says, oh how he squeezes them and chews on them, her naughty little boy, so touching as he struggles on top, that little arse she shoves so hard up inside her, and when he takes her from behind, he seems possessed then, she does too, her on all fours and him thrusting so hard that the smacking of his flesh against her rolls of fat is a crack of thunder inside the room and her breasts are slapping and bobbing wildly beneath her, and then the abrupt deceleration as he is forced to restrain himself, thrust more slowly so he does not come too quickly, him barely moving, and her, knocked silly, she is, *you randy great she-cat* ...

The Hall, C/ Balmes 33, Lérida, Spain

There were three doors and a corridor off the hall, when you came in the front door the doors to both the best rooms were on the right, they were usually empty when you weren't playing in there or when there weren't any guests. To the left of the front door a windowless corridor led past the kitchen, your bedroom and the bathroom to the sunny living room that faced south onto the gallery and the rear courtyards of the block, and sunlight came pouring in through the glass doors of the gallery and halfway up the hall, which is why the light in the corridor was always a backlight that somewhere in the middle met the grey light that filtered through the best rooms which faced Calle Balmes, this grey light also brought with it traces of the pewter objects that were on display in there and was bound therefore to have a cold metallic tint. At some point along the short passage between the kitchen door and the nursery the flood of southerly light from the living room would triumph over the metallic greyness of the northern side, and it was in that particular section of the corridor that the entry to the subterranean nest of black ants was to be found, the hole they disappeared into was a crack between the skirting board and the mottled green tiles on the floor; one late summer you would often be sitting there observing the activity of those large, gleaming ants, you even built rooms around the entry with clothes-pegs set on their edges, by creating those sunlit roofless spaces you hoped to lure out the queen who brooded on thousands of eggs in a huge, dark chamber you imagined lay beneath your bed, but the queen never emerged into the light and for the worker ants who hurried between the kitchen and the entrance to the invisible system of passages your outdoor rooms were simply barriers and they couldn't be bothered to spend time in them, unless you placed crumbs of something edible inside, which you used to do in one of the corners furthest in. You saw this one ant once whose appearance differed from that of the identical workers: it was a flying ant with a large abdomen and long brown wings that rose from the vestibule you had constructed out of pegs and flew on wobbly wings towards the open balcony door in order, as you had been taught in school, *to bite off its wings* shortly thereafter and establish a new colony somewhere else. Sometimes you saw your mother as a flying ant like that, who had flown from her ant heap in northern Sweden, touched down on an island where Spain's highest mountain lay as well as a cliff edge above a bay from where your mother had looked out across the ocean all the way to Africa together with a young man who belonged to one of the richest families on the island and who wanted to build a house for her on that cliff but she had flown onwards and had not bitten off her wings until she reached the continent, here in your rather boring hometown, where there were no mountains or seas, just La Seo de Urgel, a cathedral on a low hill whose clock tower was marked by large black holes from the war. It was more evident on some days than others that she believed she had flown in the wrong direction or that she missed her wings, she would walk along the passage between the rooms as though she had not bitten them off yet, as if she had not yet laid her one and only egg that was you, and was still trying to get up into the air, but then it would all go wobbly and slurred and her breath would smell sour and bitter like crushed beetles mixed with the wine you had to pop down and buy at Señor Primitivo's and it would end with her going to her room to lie down. She blamed her migraine attacks on all the car crashes she had been in and the accident in the lift when she had almost lost an arm. So when you found yourself in the hall on returning from school you were only too aware of your situation: in your almost black school uniform you were an ant too, at school you might have been a silent and anonymous worker ant, at home you were one of a kind, a crown princess ant whose brown wings were still in training to fly far away some day. Inside your room the toys were piled along the walls, the dolls, half-naked like grubs, were waiting for you to come in and give them life, but the room was too dark, the high window gave onto a narrow lightwell that scarcely provided any illumination at all and you had no desire to sit and brood on your imaginary worlds in there, in the subdued daylight the toys turned slimy like eggs coated in a sticky jelly, the life of a queen in that gloomy child's bedroom was not for you, you preferred the destiny of the flying ant and used to colonise first one pole of the apartment and then the other: the living room to the south or the best room to the north, if you were going to play with your Barbie dolls imported from Andorra and Sweden you went north, to the best room, and on the way there you passed the hall, a small rectangular space submerged in semi-darkness, as though the greyish-green submarine light from the staircase at the entrance to the building and the long corridor you always ran through had overflowed and risen all the way up here. There was a table in the hall but no wardrobe or hat shelf or even hooks, the hall table was fixed to the wall opposite the front door, that wall made a right angle together with another blind wall, the square that was formed by all the intersecting lines and angles was made up of only two unbroken walls, the other two sides were provided by the front door and the doors to the dining room and the best room with its Iberia-brand gramophone and the Dama gazelles, doors that were always open and through which the oblique rays of light that fell on the little hall space came, only when the front door was opened was a beam of light projected from the whitewashed staircase onto the wall where the hall table was fixed that illuminated both the table and the framed portrait that hung above it. The hall table was in fact an old plinth on which a medium-sized sculpture of Saint Anthony with the Infant Jesus had once stood in your paternal grandparents' apartment on Calle Balmes in Barcelona (a wider and longer version of the same Calle Balmes you lived on in Lérida), the saint had been deprived of his base and was tucked away on a chest of drawers in your room, you went past the plinth, however, every time you went to the best room and it reminded you of a baptismal font which is why there was something devotional about that hall with its illusory waterless font that was not a font but served instead as a kind of pedestal for the portrait above it. And a faint odour used to hover there too, of camphor and of relics, of the tongue of Saint Anthony, that is, which had been preserved perfectly fresh and full of blood thirty years after his death, your grandmother had told you (*Al abrir su sarcófago treinta años después de su muerte encontraron su lengua incorrupta. ¿Sabes qué significa "incorrupta"?*).[13] If someone were to cut open your skull and inspect the convolutions of your brain there would be a hollow spot in there, something known as a *lacuna* in medical language, where the brain matter had been discoloured by the greyish-green light in that hall. Because children never forget, even if they do not always understand what they remember.

It must have been at the beginning of the autumn of 1962 that you were christened and your father had his portrait taken at home with you in his arms, in the photographs of that day your christening robe tumbles in a cascade of flounces from the fold of his arm, like a tiny snow slide. To judge by the photographs the portrait that would later be hung above the plinth had not yet been accorded such a prominent place, its own chapel, but shared space instead with other portraits of military men stuck with drawing pins onto one wall of the living room, above a camp bed covered in a camel-brown woollen blanket your father had acquired during his years in the Sahara. That wall forms a kind of thematic centre in a series of photographs from your christening day, arranged across two pages of the family album from that time. In one of them your father is in full dress uniform standing

13   "When they opened the coffin thirty years after his death they discovered his tongue was incorrupt. Do you know what 'incorrupt' means?"

beside the wall, his right arm raised as he toasts the portrait. The photograph next to it shows your father out of uniform with you in his arms, in the long christening robe, swaddled in masses of white fabric, staring gravely into the camera (only a few weeks old but without either curiosity or fear, just a steady enquiring look that suggests you know the person behind the camera), you, the cause of that toast, are being ceremoniously presented to the men in uniform. Among the portraits can be seen the one-eyed legionnaire, Millán Astray, *El Fundador*, the man who was supposed to have yelled ¡*Viva la muerte!*, Long Live Death, Death who was the betrothed of every foreign legionnaire, their wife-to-be, and your father therefore the Bridegroom of Death, *El novio de la muerte*, as the legionnaires' anthem was called, and Death had tried to come for you soon after, still but a child, Death that lit black embers in your stomach, a fever that plunged the valves in your heart into darkness and that you would remember in nightmares. Francisco Franco, *El Caudillo*, the Leader, can also be seen in the black-and-white photograph of your christening day, the same man you would see every day above the blackboard at school, a young general in battledress in the photograph and not the old boy in his ceremonial attire that hung in the classroom. The battle cry then was ¡*Arriba España!*, Arise Spain! Arise? As if Spain were a lazy or sleepy or sick woman just lying in her bed all day. The fact that you thought of Spain as a woman was not only because of the feminine ending –a in *España* but also because you thought that the Iberian peninsula really did look like a woman in profile when you traced it in geography lessons and coloured in the fifty-four provinces with their Spanish names, never the Catalan ones (yours was called Lérida, for instance, and not Lleida as your father preferred to call it). Spain looked like a rather strict woman with her hair tied back (the knot was the southernmost part of France) and a curved and pointed nose (the tip of her nose the province of Lisbon and its deep estuary). Spain apparently had or had had a tendency to lie down (to lie ill, to lie asleep, to lie dying) because *she* constantly had to be told to get up from that reprehensible horizontal position. The long dagger with its ivory handle and pewter scabbard with an engraved swastika that would subsequently be hung in the best room next to the Dama gazelles and whose handle made you think of white chocolate can also be seen on the wall in the photograph of your christening day. Above the dagger can be made out a portrait of your grandfather in a third kind of uniform, the uniform of the German army, what was noticeably different about it were the eagle's wings on the cap and the medals on the chest. It would be many years before you understood that the men's uniforms had different stories to tell, the same way the school uniforms in your town told you which religious school the pupils attended and therefore what degree of prosperity their families enjoyed; the uniforms could simply be read, like the titles of the books in the best room that you used to borrow to build houses for your imported Barbie dolls; the red volumes of *Historia Universal* that remained stable when you placed them on the floor and leant them against one another at various angles to form the walls of the house you were trying to build for your dolls, and the other smaller books that were not part of a series but existed each in its own right: *La fille du capitaine*, "The Captain's Daughter", whose title you imagined referred to you, and had the beautiful watercolour on the front, your favourite book; *Kaputt* was a tall volume you used as a table for your dolls most of the time, the word sounded dashing and appealed to you though you knew it meant *broken, wrecked*. Another favourite was *Quo Vadis*, *Quo* sounded like the cry of an owl (*Quo quo!*), sometimes it would serve as the backrest for a model of a sofa whose seat was *Kaputt*, even though the dark-green colour struck you as too gloomy and then you would lay the slimmer *La piel* against *Quo Vadis* like a throw; the covers of *La piel*, which meant "The Skin", were made of a matt and rather rough, faded pink fabric and went better with the sophisticated costumes of the Barbie dolls. It did not escape you that the same writer had written *Kaputt* and *La piel* because his name was so

striking: Curzio Malaparte, you could not help dissecting that surname in your head as: *mala* (evil) and *parte* (part, direction or place),
Mala parte: *Evil place* or (from) *an evil direction.*

A special place among the books on the antique bookcase with
decorative carvings, an inheritance from your father's father that
like the sculpture of Saint Anthony had previously been housed on
Calle Balmes in Barcelona, was reserved for just a few volumes bound
in red leather, and although there were several of these you remember one in particular. Both the title and all the names (there were
several sharing the space) were printed in gold and you can distinctly
recall how confusing it was to see your father's two surnames printed
on the lower edge of the spine although the explanation, when it
came, was very simple; he was the person who had had that copy
bound, which was why both his surnames were on it, PASCUAL PASCÓ,
in capitals, above double lines in a zig-zag pattern that made you
think of the cross-stitch you practised in the sewing lessons the nuns
gave you at school. On the upper part of the spine inside a panel set
off by the same suture-like system of interwoven lines was another
name in capitals engraved in gold, HITLER, and under that name a
dash, in gold as well, to separate the author from the title below it:
MI LUCHA, "My Struggle". The bookbinder had got the letters a
bit awry, though, both HITLER and PASCUAL slanted slightly downwards, especially HITLER which was not perfectly centred either in
its oblong panel set off by gold stitches. Inside the sober and restrained
red covers the paper was heavy but of poor quality and had yellowed
as a result, the paper had become sand-coloured like parchment
along the frail roughened edges most of all, the original covers
the red leather ones replaced had been removed but it was clear
from the back of the flyleaf that there must have been a photograph
inserted

Photo: Hoffmann, Munich

which would have been a portrait of Hitler in all likelihood because Heinrich Hoffman was Hitler's official photographer. And below, at the bottom of the page

Traducción autorizada por la
Editora Central del Partido Nacional Socialista
Franz Eher Nachflg. G.m.b.H.
Múnich-Berlín
Alemania

On the flyleaf your father's name is associated with Adolf Hitler's once again, his entire name this time, in the form of his signature in blue ink, there is a long line above the author's name and beneath it is the address and a date:

Salvador Pascual Pascó

ADOLF HITLER

Balmes 297, 2°
1942

MI LUCHA

Traducción directa del alemán
Distribución para España
Avila. San Roque 13

The copy contains an introduction on page 7 by the anonymous translator who dates the translation to March 1935 (*EL TRA-DUCTOR, marzo de 1935*). A new introduction to the second edition follows on page 11 signed this time in October 1937, and in reverse order: *Octubre de 1937, EL TRADUCTOR.* The concluding paragraph of the second introduction reads:

> *HITLER, MUSSOLINI y FRANCO son los orientadores políticos de una nueva Europa, porque al defender la individualidad de sus nacionalidades rechazan la absurda tendencia – contraria a la cultura humana – de querer hacer del mundo civilizado el conglomerado de un internacionalismo informe.*[14]

So the translation into Spanish of Adolf Hitler's *Mein Kampf* was completed just over a year before the military revolt took place that would lead to the Spanish civil war. Your father acquired a copy of Hitler's *Mein Kampf* in 1942 but does not appear to have read a great deal of the book, the notes in the margins and the underlinings end by the second chapter. Apart from both the frequently underlined introductions attributed to the translator, your father seems to have read only the first and second chapters: *En el hogar paterno* ("In the House of My Parents") and *Las experiencias de mi vida en Viena* ("Years of Study and Suffering in Vienna"). This may not be that remarkable as in 1942 your father, who was born in September 1925, was only seventeen years old. The Second World War was still going on and was far from over. Leningrad had been under siege for twelve months, your grandfather would travel to the front as a member of the Blue Division at the end of January 1942. Presumably his seventeen-year-old son acquired a copy of *Mein Kampf* when his father left to serve with the German army. But the craftsmanship does not look as if it dates from the Forties. Your guess would be that your father was an adult when he had his old copy bound, at some point in the 1960s, when he was a captain in Franco's army. So

14 HITLER, MUSSOLINI and FRANCO are the political lodestars of the new Europe because they defend the individual character of their nationalities and thus reject the absurd efforts – which run completely counter to human culture – to transform the civilised world into an amorphous international agglomeration.

why that toast at the christening? Because Adolf Hitler is the final figure on the wall of uniformed men, his A4-sized portrait – a typical product of the Hoffman studio – occupies a central position in that constellation of images and is also the largest, it is surrounded by the founder of the Spanish Foreign Legion Millán Astray, the dictator Francisco Franco and your paternal grandfather, an entrepreneur who changed profession to become a soldier during the Spanish Civil War and enrolled in the German Wehrmacht when Franco permitted the formation of a corps of volunteers (mainly veterans of the Civil War and young students) after Nazi Germany attacked the Soviet Union; and you recognise the Hitler portrait from the hall, it was the one hanging in a bronze-coloured frame above the plinth that used to belong to the eloquent Saint Anthony, Adolf Hitler's right eye looked into the distance beyond the windows onto Calle Balmes, it was Adolf Hitler's face you passed every time you went to play with your dolls in the best room or put the gramophone on, it was on Adolf Hitler that the bright beam of light from the staircase fell whenever the front door was opened. Although during the entire nine years you lived in Lérida you never heard a single word said about the figure hanging in that elevated position in the hall so you never bothered to find out who he was or what he was called, he was just there, like a part of your home you simply took for granted.

Schloss Hartheim Psychiatric Hospital, Reichsgau, Oberdonau, Ostmark (Austria under Annexation), July 1941, Night

She is so deep inside the dream the darkness that enfolds her feels like yet another of its twists and turns, she thinks she is still seeing the long echoing tunnel that the child soldiers, whose distorted mouths were hideously daubed with crimson, were marching along in their shabby Wehrmacht uniforms, their unbuttoned collars swaying in the beam of light from the chink in the door she had watched them through; for another fraction of a second she continues to try to fit the sounds she is hearing into the white room with a high panoramic window that showed a glaring blue sky and white domes in an entirely whitewashed city the children – or were they dwarves? – were marching past on the other side of that half-open door (she is still astonished by those crocheted curtains that hung *beneath* the oblong window, from the sill down to the floor); and as she puts her feet down she is convinced that the floor is tilting towards a large pit in the centre of yet another room in her dream, one she entered after visiting the first, because she believes herself to be in the same room like a convent cell with a vaulted ceiling in which she was sitting in the dream, on a rib-backed chair by a window that gave onto a cloister and from that cloister the murmur of a fountain could be heard. But once Helene Hintersteiner becomes aware it is wooden boards and not a stone floor her toes are touching she realises she is not in the room she dreamed of but in her bedroom in the castle and that the screams and the blows (hammer blows?) she can now vaguely make out among the muffled ambient sounds are coming from another of the staff bedrooms. Her fingers blindly grope for the little chain on the bedside lamp, and in her sudden excitement at being freed from the delusion she now realises she has been experiencing for the last few minutes (*I can't really have been dreaming we're losing the war, can I?*) she knocks over the glass of water that has gone flat overnight on the table and it falls to shatter on the floor, she does not usually put the glass so near the edge, did she drink from it in her sleep? Misgivings are not the kind of thing she is prepared to entertain, so she calls upon the decisiveness she is known for to banish the anxiety and her feet are soon fumbling comfortably around for the slippers by the bed. *Ow!* She notices too late that the right slipper is not just wet but contains a sliver of the broken glass, one of the bits of glass has just penetrated the hard layer of skin in the arch of her foot, slicing into the ball and the stab of pain throws her back on the bed with her arms in the air and with a sense of her own scream being absorbed by the noise going on outside and of everything criss-crossing and getting mixed up in this thin-walled old castle – Good lord, how is she ever going to get out there to see what is going on? She simply has to. As the secretary to Dr Lonauer she has a certain responsibility in his absence, and what appears to her then is the meandering main road that runs along the water all the way home to Linz, with the Danube on the left, exactly as Dr Lonauer must see it every evening when he drives home to his family while in her case it is only every now and then, she has not had any leave for six weeks now. "He really ought to spend the occasional night here just like everyone else!" she hisses while inspecting the bleeding gash with her foot pointed towards the light of the little lamp, it is a deep cut, and a painful one, the glass has got wedged halfway under the bone she can see it glisten when she raises the edges of the wound between her thumb and index finger, it will be impossible to remove without pincers, she observes, only she does not pluck her eyebrows, there are pincers in the surgery, she will have to ask one of the nurses to help her, or even Dr Renno himself perhaps, good thing *he* is here at least, although God knows where, she thinks, feeling a grudge at both doctors now, though she has to stop the bleeding, that's the main thing, the wound is throbbing, it may need stitches. Leaning her heel against the floor she limps across to the chair over which her dressing gown has been folded in two, there are still cries and screams from outside above the rumbling and hissing that might be a storm, a storm without any thunder, *we are floating*, she thinks, as if that muffled rumble might be affecting the very foundations of the building, dismantling them even. She sits down heavily on the chair and digs out a large man's handkerchief from a pocket, it is one of her father's old handkerchiefs which her mother embroidered ages ago, while they used to sit alone with her, she and Johann (Johann always at her side) not knowing whether their father was still alive, *this wretched war and here I am sewing for the dead*, she remembers her mother's deep sighs as she folds the handkerchief twice around her foot and pulls it tight, *the good ones always go first*, how right she was, her mother's sighs become her own. She makes a double knot with the corners of the handkerchief, and now their Johann as well, the bloodstain spreads quickly across the blue thread her mother used to embroider the initial "H" with, the cotton is almost immediately dyed red, the feeling of loss assails her as though it had been lying in wait under the chair, she gets to her feet taking her weight on her heels, how is this going to work? How is she going to put her shoes on tomorrow morning? Going into the office in slippers would be unthinkable, the idea makes her shudder, it would be like standing naked in front of the director, and she is already feeling fragile, she picks up the dressing gown and puts her arms into it, no matter how cordial he is to her she would never choose to be that exposed in front of him, and she can see that narrow meandering road along the Danube once again and his black Daimler-Benz parked outside the doctor's mansion, he stoops so unbecomingly in that civilian suit of his that flutters around his frame as if there were not a muscle on his body, his uniform suits him so much better, it lends him, his entire person, a firmness of character, it lends him the muscles and subcutaneous fat he lacks. Coming up with that particular phrase, which she feels is rather well put, improves her mood, only then it is the bony face of Dr Lonauer's wife that emerges with its high cheekbones and black buttonholes for eyes, she can see her meeting her husband in the hall dressed in the brown fox-fur she turned up in at the castle last spring, when there was still a crust of snow over the fields, and she remembers the ridge of large teeth and her glossy hair, lank and dark, as if it were always greasy or wet. *What with two small children it's perfectly understandable really that he won't stay here*, she thinks with the deep red-leather seats of the Daimler stamped on her retina, *not in this whorehouse!*

Once she opens the door she realises that rain is pelting down violently beyond the arches and she is struck by a pungent smell of wet soil, piled closely on top of the other smell, the acrid sour-sweet stench that is still there underneath the stifling scent of rain, or maybe everything is just so steeped in the stench that she is always prepared for it, that it lingers in her nostrils even when she closes the doors behind her, *does it smell in here? Is there a smell? Can I smell it now?* Though no, the stench appears to have gone, the downpour must have been going on for a long time, *while I was asleep*, she thinks, astonished at the force with which the rain is lashing the hundreds of thousands of small tiles that cover the hipped roof of the castle like scales. And then suddenly a howl can be heard above the tumbling cascades of water, the same noise that woke her and got her out of bed, it floats across the oblong shaft at the centre of the castle building through the darkness that is gleaming silver from the rain with a kind of burning luminosity. "BLOODY HELL ...!" A few steps is all it takes and she is at the balustrade looking upwards, she is searching for a chink of light or some other clue to the origin of the voice, but the rain has immediately torn the scream to shreds along with the pain it conveyed, as if it were the rain behind it, and she has no idea which floor the cry came from, the second or the third. For moment or two she remains at the balustrade as if spell-bound: the water is tumbling over the tiles, like a torrential mountain stream, the steep slope of the roof evokes the same hollow feeling she gets in her stomach when she is on her skis, looking at a sparkling white ski slope as it winds down the mountain, the torrents are plunging towards the gravel on the cramped courtyard of the castle and the roof covered in thousands of small scales feels eerily close and animated, the hard carapace of a primeval beast that could come to life at any moment, if she reached out her hand she could touch it and her arm would be grabbed by the plunging water, dislocated by its monstrous power, and she is afraid that that horrible and smoking object that has been constructed in the courtyard will not stay whole, that the crematorium chimney erected as a temporary measure is going to collapse when the beast awakens. She raises her eyes then towards what she sees as the underneath of the grey night sky, the crematorium chimney slices into it and so does the brilliant sphere of the massive clock tower, round and white like an artificial moon. "Heaven's privates," she says, and a brown sludge oozes out of that revolting phrase, revolting and completely *alien* to her, so alien she needs to take a step to the side to render it harmless and to stamp it into pieces, she takes a step to the side and starts moving resolutely along the gallery towards the stone staircase. She immediately feels an ice-cold pain shoot through her left foot because her slipper is standing in the centre of a pool of water that has formed between the docks in the balustrade. "There's going to be a flood," she suddenly declares with a clear head, the rain will inundate the ground floor and the installations, and she can see the arched pillars in the reception room half-submerged in water and the sacks of clothes floating half-opened like boils that have burst in the muddy water, and the white uniforms the nurses wear all soiled and brown and floating round their waists, some of the nurses almost hysterical, like that namby-pamby Raab and the greedy and bad-tempered Gruber, her purse clenched tight in her pocket and full of gold teeth, all of them crazed with terror and revulsion as the cold water carries along items of the patients' clothing that wrap themselves around their thighs. And the urns in the rear courtyard that are supposed to be driven four kilometres away to be tipped into the river floating off over the plain as well, *the Danube will have risen all the way here*, and she pictures herself and the other employees clinging like shipwrecked survivors around the chimney that sticks up from the courtyard like a mast, she can see herself at the very top, sickened by the heat that the rough surface of the bricks gives off, her bleeding foot slipping and sliding and unable to find a toe-hold on the sharp edges; and she even finds herself envying that German woman from Cologne, her sole companion in the book-keeping section when she had just started working here, for getting away in time to avoid the deluge (How slyly Fräulein Weber had arranged her escape and in what a calculating way. Though she looked so modest and so ordinary. She had never given any hint of her intentions, there had never been a single word of criticism!) and a vein of bitterness, of indignation is attached to that unwelcome envy, when it was realised that the quiet little typist who shared a desk with her for an entire six-week period had absconded while on leave she had felt outraged and betrayed. She arrives at the foot of the staircase and then has to rest the upward-bent foot, trying to keep the toes continually pointed into the air, the extended ligaments under the arch of her foot have already been overstretched and she supports her heel on the first step while the ligaments relax and gathers her strength before hobbling up to the next floors. At that moment some white knee-socks appear in the gap at the top, followed by shiny leather trousers and finally the rest of a man's body lit from the side by the weak lamp that illuminates the staircase from above, Sepp Vallaster's large, square-shaped head and thick wavy hair at the very top against the light. "He's like a horse," she gasps to herself in the shadow of Vallaster's jutting upper body and the harness-like leather braces on his trousers seem to bear that out.

"What is going on, Vallaster?"

"Nothing to worry about, that Berliner Schmidtgen has gone a bit crazy, bad blood if you ask me."

"Is Hauptmann Wirth in the building?"

"I haven't seen hide nor hair of Wirth since we got the order to carry the urns up to the attic. Or of Dr Renno for that matter."

It must be the weather keeping Wirth away, Helene Hintersteiner is thinking, the roads are probably impassable. For the first time since she woke up she wonders what the time is, which is odd in itself because she makes a point of always knowing it. Dr Lonauer had given her advance notice that several transports of a new kind were due this week, they should be arriving around half past four. She looks at Vallaster's hairy wrist, on it is a gold watch. There are a lot of watches in the building, a little piles of clocks and wrist-watches among the other little piles Anne Marie Gruber watches over, Gruber and that black Danish hound of hers, necklaces, gold crucifixes, medallions, there are even small piles of Christian statues, *Look, Fräulein, what I found*, Helene Hintersteiner remembers the cleaner Rosa Haas' coarse leather-brown fist level with the breast pocket of the striped apron, at first she thought that what her chapped hand was closed so carefully round was a young bird, *It won't matter if I keep it, will it? It would be unchristian to leave it just lying there on the ground like a turnip*, then she watched the hand opening and in it was a little white statuette of the Holy Virgin with a deeply ridged white mantle and blue belt, black crusts of mud glistening along every ridge, on the little platform on which the figure stood could be read: Lourdes. *That comes from France, Rosa, from a little village in a mountain range called the Pyrenees*, she remembers informing the woman and that Rosa Haas immediately raised the statue to her lips and smacked a kiss on the mantled crown of its head and then ran a black-edged thumb over her forehead to make the sign of the cross and then rapidly made another with sweeping strokes over the whole of her face and down to her chest.

"What is the time?"

"Ten past two," Josef Vallaster replies. "I'd best get on with my business," he adds and moves towards the staircase to the ground floor, trotting, tail-heavy, in his white knee-socks.

The clatter of a typewriter from within the main office on the opposite long side can now be heard above all the other noises, this endless compilation of statistics that continues without pause, night and day, just who is supposed to be up there tonight? She sets off towards the second floor, where she can see silhouettes moving behind the arched pillars along the opposite short end and continues to hobble along, uneasy about who she will encounter in the dark, the patter of rain feels like cotton wool laid over her ears and she thinks her sight has been dimmed too, but she can hear voices and noises from inside several of the rooms she passes and the whole thing makes her feel exhausted and furious, people have a right to be allowed to get some sleep after all. That ache beneath her sternum is something she calls lack of sleep *and it's the second night this week!*, she is definitely going to be making a complaint to Dr Lonauer though at the same time she is thinking that the rain makes people as restless as the rats that are swarming in every corner, *I'm going to complain to Hauptmann Wirth as well*, though that option scares her and makes her falter just where the arched hallway makes a ninety-degree turn to the left . . . *unless he's already there, of course.* At the same moment she hears sounds coming from the staircase at her back and when she turns she sees Anzinger and Vallaster panting up the steps, each with an urn on their backs: "Serves them right!" just slips out of her because she is so intent on maintaining her distance from them, she is not like them at all and something inside her needs to be told that. A door that may have been standing ajar is suddenly closed, she has time only to see the black gap between the door and the sill, not that it matters, she knows exactly who lives in there. She covers the last stretch to the crack of light that cuts across the stone floor of the archway without breathing, without wanting to think about anything at all. But then her brother Johann appears to her for one lightning-swift instant in a brown uniform, smiling broadly beneath his freckles, just as in the photograph they took the day she joined the party. Then she is at the door from where the light is coming. The door handle has been torn off and is on the floor not far from the doorstep. What strikes her first as she pushes the door open and steps into the room is that Nurse Maria Raab (it would be her, of course) is sitting half-naked on the edge of the bed, and as she had so recently done herself, must have thrown on the dressing gown although Mitzi Raab's is half-open allowing the deep gap between the huge udders of her breasts to show and below the belt, loosely tied around her waist, the lower part is gaping, exposing a pair of large fleshy thighs and a dark and scrubby bush. Lips parted in readiness for her words to exercise their customary authority, Helene Hintersteiner's brain continues to register the details, like the fact that the cremator Otto Schmidtgen is sitting on the edge of the bed next to Maria Raab, his weeping head leaning against the nurse's spongy bosom (she is soft and porous like a sponge, everything about her is fluffy and absorbent, even her small round eyes are like the round holes in a sponge) and the fact that Schmidtgen's crooked bird-like nose is wedged halfway inside the abyss between Raab's breasts and that blood has been smeared across the woman's skin; as well as the fact that Maria Raab's right arm is wrapped around Otto Schmidtgen's head and her bloated fingers are stroking his pallid grey temple while she is swaying her upper body gently as if she were trying to rock him to sleep. Sickened by the whole scene Helene Hintersteiner shifts her eyes to the lanky and loose-limbed figure of Hubert Gomerski who is standing some way away from the bed. Then she takes in the hammer that has been chucked into the middle of the floor. Hubert Gomerski gives an apologetic shrug when he meets her eyes, as if it were way beyond him too.

"You are disturbing the peace of this house in the most improper and offensive manner and I am definitely going to have to report this."

"BLOODY OLD COW!" Otto Schmidtgen has unexpectedly raised his head from Maria Raab's bosom and, his throat extended as though his neck had been dislocated and he were unable to turn it, twisted it a half turn on its axis. "SO GO DOWN THERE YOUR-SELF THEN."

Maria Raab tries to force down his shoulders and turn him back towards her, but there is no stopping Otto Schmidtgen.

"THIS LOT WERE SHAVED. EVERY SINGLE ONE OF THEM. EVERYTHING SHAVED, EVEN THEIR PUBIC HAIR!" His Berlin burr is twisting in spirals towards an even shriller tone. "AND PACKED LIKE SARDINES SO I FOUND THEM STANDING, *STANDING*, DO YOU GET THAT, MISS PERFECT?" The man's voice is curling upwards as if there were something to be found high above. "WHAT SORT OF PEOPLE HAS YOUR BLOODY DOCTOR GONE AND BROUGHT HERE?"

"Mind your tongue, man!" Helene Hintersteiner leans back against the door to keep it shut.

"AND THIS LOT WEREN'T EVEN IDIOTS!"

"What if Captain Wirth comes along?" Maria Raab whispers.

"WHY DON'T YOU GO AND BLAB TO THAT BASTARD SO HE CAN SHOOT ME RIGHT AWAY!"

"Don't talk like that," Helene Hintersteiner says to him in a tone of command while peering furtively at Maria Raab.

"THE BONE CRUSHER IS BROKEN! WHAT THE HELL AM I SUPPOSED TO DO? YOU TELL ME. GO ON, TELL ME, YOU BLOODY STUCK-UP COW!"

Otto Schmidtgen's hoarse squeak erupts into tears and snot that end up going down the wrong way and unleash a fit of coughing. Helene Hintersteiner turns to Hubert Gomerski, her eyes appealing to him to deny what she has just been told.

"The rain is making it a lot more difficult for us down there,"

Hubert Gomerski says in his Rhineland Plattdeutsch and pauses with a pouting of his lips and a raising of his eyebrows, "We've got technical problems, the chimney isn't drawing properly and the electrical crusher is broken, Otto here has been trying to crush the bones by hand while it's being repaired . . ."

"Thank you for that information," Helene Hintersteiner interrupts, she is an office worker for Christ's sake, she had been promised the position of head of the book-keeping section, that was *the only reason* she came here, what other people do is their affair and why is it so difficult for people to keep to their own domains? If only everyone could just do their jobs. There are more partitions than just those wooden planks that close off the castle courtyard, there are partitions between her domain and that of the people who receive and handle the patients, she works *upstairs*, in administration and in the doctors' office, where all the books are, the university theses from Heidelberg, proper knowledge, the work of Dr Alfred Polz in three volumes, of Dr Martin Ulrich who raised the moral question in 1923 (*Dürfen wir minderwertiges Leben vernichten?*),[15] of Dr Fritz Barth who identified the related issues as early as 1924 (*Euthanasie. Das Problem der Vernichtung lebensunwerten Lebens*),[16] serious approaches to the problem, because there are problems involved, she cannot deny that, only the biggest problem is what is going on *here*, not that there is ever anything about what goes on *here* in the academic books. The three in front of her, on the other hand, operate *down there*, an entire world separates her from them, a stone staircase with high worn steps in particular, shiny and concave from repeated use, from feet tirelessly running up and down them, like Vallaster and Anzinger carrying their urns. And as if that were not enough, the wall of wooden planks that cuts right across the courtyard is another barrier that divides them, the planks are there so that no-one can see those entering for treatment, so it can never have been intended that she

15 "Can we destroy inferior life?"
16 "Euthanasia. The problem of the destruction of those unworthy of life."

who works in the office one flight up should have to know anything at all about what occurs on the ground floor. The boundaries have been staked out and they are crystal clear. So why then does everyone insist on violating them? They keep letting the cat out of the bag all over the place, in the dining room, in the bedrooms, when everyone should just keep their traps shut.

"The problem is there's a lot of transports expected this week," Hubert Gomerski goes on with a grin and his hands stuck deep inside his pockets, trying to fill the embarrassing silence, he is aware that the lovely doctor's secretary is squirming in discomfort at his words, which is why he is smiling, he realises the tender conscience of the doctor's secretary is tormenting her just as if he were pinching and twisting her stiff nipples, somewhere there under her floral-print dressing gown.

It does not escape Helene Hintersteiner that Gomerski is trying to find her weak point, the spot where she might give in, but she has no intention of giving in, she has no intention even of closing the collar of her dressing gown even though she realises that is where he thinks he has found a chink, that would be like admitting she can see what he sees and that she will never do, not now and not here and not anywhere else, she never sets foot outside the office when the buses arrive, she did it once, she was forced to go down to the reception room, Wirth forced her to do it at the start, and she would do anything not to have to do it again, Wirth knows that, and he knows he can exploit the fact whenever he wants, fortunately her appearance works in her favour and she has that innate authority at her disposal, to resist him with, people tend to look up to her, that has helped until now, both Hauptmann Wirth and Dr Lonauer respect her, even Police Constable Franz Stangl is on her side, he may be the one to take over Wirth's duties so that is just as well, they all know she does not want to go down there, although it is Wirth alone who decides who has to go down there and who does not. He makes that decision every day. Only she is never going to go down there and touch them again, touch their clothes, undo their disgusting buttons, if she is by a window when a bus arrives she turns away and walks as slowly as she can over to the bookcase where the binders are lined up to demonstrate that that is where she belongs, among the files and stencils, or she will move across to one or other of the typists (she was in charge of fourteen typists for a while, but the operation is shrinking) to correct them, there is always someone to correct because the girls are young and usually careless, they find it hard to concentrate, they become curious and get distracted by what is not part of their domain. "The only thing I want to know is what has been going on *here*! Why is he bleeding?" Before anyone can answer her eyes have shifted to Otto Schmidtgen who appears to have fallen asleep against Raab's breast, a full-grown man, he must be fifty, his nosebleed is beginning to stop, his lower lip has swollen. Sixty bodies, shaved, hairless, her inner vision has been entirely taken over by what the badly bruised cremator yelled for all the room to hear, crowded into the gas chamber, she does not want to see them, the tiles smeared with excrement, how can that woman hug him like that? The inhuman stench, she rolls her eyes behind closed lids and takes a couple of steps across the room, her hand pressed against her belt, she takes a few even breaths, *Sonderbehandlung 14f13*, the list was lying on Dr Lonauer's table the day before yesterday, she takes a deeper breath, at the top of the A4-page *K.Z. Mauthausen*, not idiots but prisoners from the quarry outside Linz, she tilts her throat back so as to inhale more air and remains standing there for a moment with her eyes open on the white ceiling. *Though there's not that much difference between them and our usual patients*, Dr Lonauer explained. She had seen S.S. men walking around the garden when she came back from Schumann's with milk and cheese, they were questioning the cleaner, Rosa Haas, who was digging up potatoes in the kitchen garden, and then she saw another two S.S. men in the guardroom, one of them wanted to know which farmer she had bought the cheese from and asked her to point out the farm to him because he wanted to buy a bit too, *Paragraph 14f13 basically covers the same groups, those ill in body and in mind, those not fit for work, in other words. Fräulein Hintersteiner must remember that we are at war, why should the Reich allow itself to be depleted by enemies who are unable to work? It is simply the law of nature or basic maths if you prefer, since you're a bookkeeper, work it out for yourself, work out how much each patient costs per day. It's either our soldiers or those of the enemy . . . so? Who should the resources go to?* The S.S. car drove off in the evening, the men who had thanked her for the tip were loading the sacks of clothes – *Not that there were any valuables in there for them to sort,* Anne Marie Gruber snorted afterwards in the dining room, *not likely, still, if they take the clothes back to the camp that means less work for us.* Helene Hintersteiner calls up an image of the large black hound that is Anne Marie's permanent companion, how strange that the dog had kept quiet through all the commotion, then she recalls the dreadful downpour, it must have muffled the sounds and the smells. Fatigue threatens to overwhelm her.

Maria Raab meanwhile has been making the most of the fact that the hospital director's secretary has decided not to interrogate her in particular as to why Otto Schmidtgen is bleeding, she answers all the more freely and willingly in her own head, where the answer is self-evident, she presses Schmidtgen's head against her breasts, clasping it in both arms, and replies inwardly without stumbling, without a shadow of doubt, clear-sighted as if she were standing by a window looking out across a white landscape full of details your eyes can take in at a single sweep – plains, hills, church steeple, road: the poor man is bleeding because there's so much out of order here. Schmidtgen is bleeding because he and the other cremators have got to shoulder the heaviest burden and because the place was full of S.S. men yesterday and because he went and got blind drunk afterwards and because Bruno was in here with her when Otto knocked on the door because he really needed to see her as well and when he couldn't, he started banging on the door with the hammer which drove Bruno crazy . . . Everyone is bleeding. She is too, she thinks when she notices the bloodstain on Helene Hintersteiner's slipper, everyone is bleeding, then she giggles as she thinks about Otto calling the doctor's secretary *a stuck-up cow*, which is true after all, it's because of her no-one dares say how things really stand: that the ones who arrived yesterday weren't cases in the usual sense, they didn't come from some institution but from a concentration camp, they had to be able to talk about that among themselves at least, didn't they? They were foreigners, besides, there were Spaniards among them, they kept looking at them and shouted *Spanisch Spanisch* before they got shoved away, Gertrud Blanke had hysterics in her room afterwards, Gertrud Klähn and Elizabeth Vallaster were trying to calm her down, she was screaming that they were being guarded by S.S. men and they all had the same striped clothing on. *What's that got to do with us?* Poor Gertrud kept screaming the whole time, they were forced to give her some brandy and smelling salts because she was quite beside herself. Elisabeth is right that she's mentally unstable and should be moved from here, but Hauptmann Wirth is not going to hear another word said about that, seeing as how he flirts with her and calls her "the Lady", and everything . . .

"He got punched! Nothing serious," Hubert Gomerski replies, interrupting Maria Raab's train of thought, she looks up at him and sees him glowering at Helene Hintersteiner with an expression of defiance, with exactly the same sneer as when he was standing outside the door next to Otto when Bruno opened it. Bruno! He's going to be sulking for the next few days and refuse to visit her for a while, a loud "Oh!" slips out of her, followed by a deep sigh.

Gomerski looks straight into the doctor's secretary's blue eyes, it's a bloody shame she keeps herself to herself, the stuck-up bitch, typical that she should be so hard to get, the prettiest female in the whole place, and she knows it, that has to be why, only fuck, she came close to giving in last spring, during the bus trip, it began with him chucking a snowball down that V-neck of hers and she obviously liked it, kept giving him looks all that day, he thought he was going to be quids in that night in the villa on the lake, but when it came to the crunch she was like a different person, since then she's kept him at arm's length, wrinkling that freckled little nose of hers and behaving like she was someone special. And here she is trembling in her nightie and what wouldn't he give to be allowed to pull it up, part her legs, those straight legs like stems she's normally so steady on (only what's the matter with her foot?) and thrust himself in between her hips and ride her, grabbing those small soft tits of hers a bloke could hold in the palm of one hand, his erection is so huge he has to shove both hands in his trouser pockets to distend them so it won't be noticed, although he feels exposed in any case, as if his stiff member (*Feel how hard it is. And that's your fault, you little whore*) were peeking through his eyes as much as through the cloth of his muddy trousers, because he had actually been in Anzinger's room since he'd offered to share his part of the extra ration they got after night duty when they heard the hammer blows and when they came out of the room Schmidtgen was standing there pissed as a newt banging on Mitzi's door and he realised right away this was not going to end well because that Bruno was inside going at it so hard with Mitzi the fucking bed sounded as if it was going to collapse, that's what he and Anzinger had had to listen to long before Otto started hammering on the door, and so he had a try at persuading Otto to go with him to the other room for a spot of brandy when that fucking Bruno opened the door sporting an erection like a stud horse and then Schmidtgen went beserk and charged head first, small as he is, at Bruno's midriff, which wasn't a good idea because Bruno is bigger and wasn't as drunk as Schmidtgen so he gave him a bloody good hiding (*Next time you'll get that hammer right up your arse, you wanker*) and took off, he barely had time to do up his trousers and then he was gone, right terrified of Wirth he is that cocky bastard, he thinks, and can picture Bruno

Bruckner once again in the doorway without any trousers on and sporting a huge erection that was pointing diagonally to the right, at the two of them who were just standing there open-mouthed like a couple of idiots, or Schmidtgen's mouth had dropped open while he himself was grinning is the way he remembers it, and Anzinger had already scarpered back to his room because he doesn't give a damn about anything very much and he's taken care of in any case, even if he was alone this evening because his Anne Marie was in Ybbs looking after her sick mother, and he looks down at Helene Hintersteiner's tightly knotted belt and wishes he could undo it and get in there and suck all the juice out of her, he likes women who stand straight with both feet planted on the ground, when they fall boy do you know about it, like when you bring down a fir tree, and somewhere he can hear leaves sighing and creaking like when Father cut down a huge pine tree up in the forest, and once she's lying there on her back with the whole show dripping he'd like to plunge his tongue deep inside her before sticking it in, so his face gets a proper soaking, and he can revel in the taste of that little cunt. "What happened to your foot," he asks without looking away from Helene Hintersteiner's face.

"Oh yes, I noticed that too," Maria Raab interrupts with some effort from her corner, the voice that just floated out into the room has taken her by surprise, she cannot comprehend it, that that voice which *is* her, the voice that is always with her, grinding away in her head, should feel so unfamiliar the moment it slips out of her mouth.

Her speech is slurred, Helene Hintersteiner is thinking and turns towards Maria Raab who is looking at her with a stupid smile, and the rage that was just about to engulf Helene Hintersteiner begins to gather in a fresh wave, extremely close to the surface this time, she absolutely loathes drunken women. And who's going to help her get the bit of glass out now? Raab is under the influence and where her room-mate is God only knows. She can sense the wrinkles forming on her forehead, and feeling the skin creasing up there closest to her thoughts serves to counterbalance the rage that is further down, somewhere above her stomach, and keep it in check. "Is Nurse Elisabeth on leave?" she manages to get out at last and can feel herself regaining control.

Maria Raab nods vigorously while slowly twisting out of Otto Schmidtgen's embrace and urging him to silence with a hissed *Shush*. "He's gone to sleep," she whispers, followed by a little giggle. Otto Schmidtgen is lying on his side halfway up the bed, snoring with his mouth open.

He actually does appear to be unconscious, Helene Hintersteiner thinks and can't be bothered to stand there a moment longer, she is desperate to leave and is already at the door when Hubert Gomerski asks if he can be of any help, as she is clearly limping.

"Thanks, I can manage," she says, stepping over the sill with a little hop before Gomerski has time to respond and say *Well then, good night, Fräulein Hintersteiner.*

The broken door is left ajar and she can hear him offering to stay with Maria Raab to keep watch over the drunken pig lying on her bed, she can hear him call her *Mitzi*, and can also hear Maria Raab, who has just been called Mitzi, laugh and say *How kind of you, Hubert* and then *Only you'll have to offer me a cigarette first.* Slowly, her body supporting itself on her right heel and with the bunch of keys jingling in her hand, she gets down the stairs to the first floor and hobbles along to the doctor's surgery, she will have to try to clean the wound at least and bandage it until it can be looked at.

Inside the doctor's surgery she is enveloped in a silence that feels like a fall, as though she had tumbled into a well, all the books seem to form an insulating carpet, and she can see the moss-covered walls in a well so that as her eyes flick across the spines of the books (*Die Euthanasie und die Heiligkeit des Lebens. Die Lebensvernichtung im Dienste der Medizin und Eugenik nach christlicher und monistischer*

Ethik)[17] she thinks she can hear the slow reverberation of drops falling off the walls towards the bottom. When she comes back out into the arched corridor a while later the rain has slackened, what remains is a hissing, a soothing breathless murmur suspended in the air, though Helene Hintersteiner is not soothed, what she can hear all of a sudden (rhythmical thuds are echoing across the courtyard) breaks in on her with the abrupt energy of a wall of fire and makes her walk over to the balustrade. She knows where the sounds are coming from, from that room one flight up where she has just been, and she knows what the sounds mean, it is one end of the bed slamming remorselessly against the whitewashed wall so that the wall of fire burns every millimetre of skin and every softly breathing membrane all the way inside her private parts where fluid and mucus are pooling thickly and throbbing as they move downwards. She presses one hand hard against her swollen labia, she closes off the opening to her vagina with flat fingers as if to block the large ball of mucus that is trying to ooze out and sticks her head into the shaft at the same time to let it hang there under the rain that drums lightly against her face. Every thud of the bedstead is thrusting against the walls of her vagina. *Sterilisation und Euthanasie. Ein Beitrag zur angewandten christlichen Ethik*,[18] the title of the book brings coolness with it where the rain failed to help, it was written by Professor Fr. W. Schmidt, a modern book, she reminds herself while pressing her fingers up in an even firmer block, printed in the year they took power, which she knows, because every now and then she seats herself behind Dr Lonauer's desk and reads it as she does many of the other older books in the hospital. Then the clatter of typing starts up again to distract her ears, it sounds much closer and mercifully is superimposed over that other noise, muffling it.

17   "Euthanasia and the Sanctity of Human Life. The Destruction of Life in the Service of Medicine and Eugenics according to Christian and Monistic Ethics."
18   "Sterilisation and Euthanasia. A Contribution to Applied Christian Ethics."

The Internment Camp at Rivesaltes,
Pyrénées-Orientales, France, the Free Zone.
From Friedel Bohny-Reiter's Journal[19]

Elne, November 11, 1941

Fortunately the journey went well, no mean feat in these times. And up to now everything has gone well for my little Spaniard who suffers from heart disease. We were welcomed most cheerfully at the maternity hospital and they were thrilled at the children's clothes we brought with us – not to mention the Swiss chocolate. [. . .]

Rivesaltes, November 14, 1941

Little by little I am becoming familiar with my work – it is not easy to achieve anything in the face of such prodigious misery. I have gradually been getting to know the mothers and the children; the women come to me with their requests – one after the other.

My first job in the mornings is to distribute the rice. Our Spanish cooks and the boys prepare it before 8 o'clock. We pour it, still steaming, into buckets and go from barrack to barrack. Today the wind was blowing so hard in the camp that the cart almost overturned. It is the barrack for the sick that depresses me most. We have so little to help them with, other than a bit of food and they need so much. People lie on their beds in dresses, jumpers, shirts stiffened with

---

19 Friedel Bohny-Reiter, *Journal de Rivesaltes 1941–2* (a translation from the original German of the Journal). Friedel Bohny-Reiter arrived at the camp as a volunteer from the *Schweizerische Arbeitsgemeinschaft für kriegsgeschädigte Kinder* on November 12, 1941.

dirt, often without any sheets, on soiled mattresses. While we fill the empty tins they hold out with rice, they track us with their hungry eyes. I think about all the resources I would have in Switzerland that could do so much good here. Even if it were only a few cigarettes. So many wishes – often not expressed – that seem impossible to realise.

The most distressing thing though is the infirmary for little children. There they are, their pale faces like those of the elderly, lying on their little wooden beds, without sheets, nappies, their backs and their little legs often covered in wounds and boils. I have been racking my brains for a way to help them. When we give the children clothes and nappies, they get stolen. We cannot say anything because it is the French nurses who look after them. I can see only one solution: to send some of them to our maternity hospital in Elne. We have to wage an endless battle with the French head doctor on behalf of the children. I feel so discouraged every time I leave the infirmary.

November 29, 1941

It keeps raining, the camp is being transformed into a town on water. You really need boots to get to our barrack. The water is forcing its way in at various points. Dreadful weather for our people. Their shoes, already in a bad state, are soaked through. So almost all the children turn up with feet blue from cold, wrapped in rags. It is hard not being able to help but we have no shoes. Will our Federal Council respond to our requests for clothing? If those people could only take a single glance at our camp.

I found a fifteen-year-old yesterday in the boys' barrack with hollow eye sockets, no eyeballs and stumps for hands – "a bomb", they told me. My heart sank – the only thing I could do for him was to change his shirt for a warm vest and put our last pair of socks on his feet.

First Sunday in Advent

It is Sunday.The storm raged all night long and lashed the rain against our windows. When I tried to get out of bed this morning, I had to put my walking boots on: my room had been turned into a lake. The entire camp looks like a town on water. They will be useful though for distributing the rice.

Advent – if only we could have a little of the spirit of Advent in the camp despite the rain, the storm and the destitution.

I went out to distribute the rice with Francisco and Rafaela in spite of the rain and the storm. It is still warm in our barrack, elsewhere the beds are standing in water and the mothers did not dare to hope we would turn up with the rice. So they were all the happier when we did.

The rain continues to fall; the camp is a wasteland. In our barrack we have to keep filling buckets with water every couple of hours, but one of the doors has been nailed shut – our little dining nook is the only spot that is dry.

The conditions are difficult for our assistants. My little "driver" has not got shoes any more, and because the water has got in through every hole, the poor boy's feet were freezing. I gave him a pair of my woollen socks and my ordinary shoes – he was beaming with happiness.

The stoves burn poorly in this weather, and the rice was cooked an hour too late. When we got to the school there were such shouts of joy at the sight of the hot rice that I had to ask them very forcefully to be silent. Yet again I had to see all those little frozen bodies, all those little naked feet blue with cold. The worst thing is that we cannot help; we have no shoes left at all. To cap it all the cold weather is here. Let us hope that our appeal to the President of the Confederation will be granted, because winter promises to be terrible.

In the barrack for the sick, my women were lying there with their coats on (if they had one). They tried to light a fire in the children's infirmary but there was so much smoke that very soon you could not see the children anymore.

December 5, 1941

The cries of joy today when each of our schoolchildren received a head of lettuce. The Gypsies were the happiest – most of them ate it right there and then, without washing it, right down to the stalk. It looked so comical as they set off with their lettuces under their arms. The guards were less happy, because the ground in J-block was covered with lettuce leaves.

Permission has been given for two infants to be sent to Elne. We almost had to go on our knees to the head doctor to get that. There is always some ray of hope though – particularly with the children. Whenever I head for barrack 41, when they see me in the distance, they shout "Ola, la Suiza, la Suiza".

December 6, 1941

There was quite a commotion today.

At 7.30 I rushed off on the bike to the infirmary to see how the departure of the two children for Elne was going. There was not a single nurse in the infirmary! No-one knew if the baby had had his bottle. I had to stand firm. Little José had nothing to wear apart from two short-sleeved shirts and a nappy. I hurried over to our barrack to fetch shirts, nappies and a woollen blanket, dressed the child myself and held the miserable little infant in one arm while I steered the bike with the other towards the waiting lorry. The mother followed behind us weeping, helpless. When we got to it we discovered that the woman who was supposed to go with him was not leaving. Who was going to accompany little José? Without hesitating I shoved the other woman holding the two-year-old into the vehicle and I took José myself and we left for Elne. The others would have to manage without me and Elsi is used to dealing with the unexpected.

At Elne I saw all our dear colleagues again hard at work. I saw our children from the camp in little clean beds on the terrace in the sunshine, their cheeks round and rosy.

So our work is not for nothing – even if I could get only two out. That does make up a little group after all. I undressed my protégé who I had battled so hard for – a tiny skeleton appeared, skin red and inflamed all over his legs and up his back. It was enough to make you weep. I was so incredibly glad to see him lying there comfily in his bed once he had been washed. And once he had been given that precious mother's milk.

Barely an hour's chat with Bethli, Gret and Bettina. Then I said goodbye to several of the women who were such desperate and miserable mothers when I got to know them in the camp and who have begun to come back to life here.

I had to walk on foot from the Rivesaltes station, an hour and a half across the fields – the evening was extraordinarily beautiful, the stars, the moon – and I was so grateful.

December 8, 1941

Work, work – we have so many projects on the go. We can send two children to one of our children's homes.

We are also going to set up a sewing room next to the Swiss barrack. The women in the camp will be able to sew dresses and underwear for themselves there with the help of Madame Darcau. There is also going to be a carpentry workshop in the same barrack – that is a good thing. It is vital to have work and distractions in the camp – something to energise body and soul. Apart from that we have a great deal to get ready for Christmas. Let us hope the toys arrive in time.

Elsbeth is also doing good work. Yesterday she took a rucksack with her and went out for a walk with thirty of the boys. It does our children good to be out of sight of the guards – to be free – in nature. Every living thing gets completely suffocated in the camp – people, souls, plants – there are no fields, no gardens, no trees.

Good night, my hands are stiff from the cold – I have been writing in bed but my mind has been warmed by ideas and projects – tomorrow I have got to tackle the murals our "painter" failed to finish.

I have almost no time left for thinking about my home, the mountains, Christmas, my friends. Though when I can, I do so intensively.

December 10, 1941

I was just about to write my report on J-block when my little guests appeared to have breakfast before the journey to Banyuls.

December 13, 1941

I am tired, so tired – but we managed to get things done today all the same: the work on our sewing room and our cobbler's workshop in barrack 13 is proceeding. The stove has been installed; lamps, tables and benches have been fitted. I kept running back and forth while this was going on from the supply clerk to the barrack and from the barrack to the supply clerk. You can only beg for one thing at a time. Then I finished painting the carpentry workshop, as usual with a crowd of onlookers around my feet. The little Spaniards turn up the moment something out of the ordinary occurs. It probably looked rather comical to see the Swiss nurse in her white wimple standing on a ladder holding a paint pot and a brush.

I had some free time between four and five p.m. and painted a watercolour from a small photograph. It was taken in Valle Verzasca – did I really go there once? I stuck the watercolour up onto two boards that had been painted. I also turned over the soil in our little "garden" in front of the barrack, two tiny beds of carnations, that is. A little bit of soil, a little bit of life in the camp does us good.

There are only twenty minutes left before one in the morning – one more day of work, another day of effort, a rewarding day. I can only give thanks that I have the chance to work here. Goodnight.

December 15, 1941

A new notebook, a new page. I began the previous one in Florence. I experienced so much joy, so much happiness there that I could write about in its pages. What does this one have in store for me? Here where there is so much to deal with, day after day. Those days I spent on my own immersed in work were so lovely. Barrack 13 is finished, the women are at work – shoes and underclothes are being produced. We will be getting new supplies today. Olives, sauerkraut, firewood, powdered milk. You have to have experienced working in the camp to know what it is like, having to be everywhere, keeping an eye on everything – down to the last detail, and not hesitating to go and tackle the various people in charge yourself.

Yesterday was Sunday. In the morning we distributed the rice in the nurseries. At ten I went to sing in the barrack for the sick along with twenty-two Spanish children. It made me as happy as everyone else to hear those bright voices. They are not exactly spoilt for that kind of thing, my invalids.

Between one and four p.m. I sat in the sun outside the barrack, and for once had time to let my thoughts wander to those I love. That did me so much good! It was a mild sunny day. Our dog Guioz was lying beside me with her two puppies – and her family was surrounded by a flock of little Spaniards. Now and then one of the women would come and sit next to me for a chat or for a bit of comfort. A real Sunday.

We rounded it off by lighting the advent candles and drinking tea with our supper. We are so happy in our warm little room. If only the same were possible for everyone here.

Today I took a small boy over to our barrack and gave him our last pair of old shoes. His eyes shone when I gave him some socks as well. It is those eyes, the children's eyes, that keep me here. If I had only the adults to look after, I would fall ill.

The orderly in the men's barrack came to get me to look at someone who was in a very bad way. I could see at once that he was dying. He had been in prison – God knows for what offence – and the lengthy period of starvation had proved the *coup de grâce* for an already frail old man. His eyes were lifeless, his forehead ice cold. There was no-one at his side. I asked what his name was, where his wife was – he could no longer answer and there was no-one who knew anything about him. I kept talking to him, I took his cold hand in my warm ones, so that he could feel that someone cared about him at least, but he failed to react to anything. When I returned two hours later, he was dead. Thanks be to God.

I am alone in our barrack. Elsi will be arriving at Rivesaltes at half past eleven. I will cycle the two hours it takes to get to the station. Though I am dead tired, I am immensely glad that Elsi is coming back. I feel I would soon drown in all the work if I had to do it on my own. I am weeping for the very first time, that is how tired I am. I long to lie down on my beloved pallet but I cannot leave Elsi to make her way here on her own in the middle of night.

December 16, 1941

So at half past ten I got on my bike and rode off. The night is pitch black. I can barely make out the uneven road – I end up among the vines more than once – until I reach the main road, beyond the camp district. All of a sudden there is a voice in the dark: "Stop, where are you going?" It is one of the guards. I dismount immediately, show him my pass, he questions me in detail about the reason for my nocturnal excursion. Suddenly he drops that tone of command and instead gives me some directions. I laugh – they are all the same. The possibility of openness exists in the depths of every human heart – you only have to know how to find it.

Night welcomes me back. Kilometre after kilometre. Not one living soul, not one building, not one light. Above me the stars, and in the beam of the little torch lashed to the front of the bike our white cross is dancing against its red background. A profound sense of being protected comes over me – nothing can happen without *Him*, *He* who keeps us all in His hands. Where have I felt something like that before? Ah yes, I remember now: it was when I was hiking down the Oberalpstock, that labyrinth of crevasses. It is when distress, loneliness and danger are at their greatest that God is closest.

The scattered lights of Rivesaltes are approaching. Now I can see the station, the train has already arrived and Elsi appears. Our return journey is interrupted by three policemen – it is almost merry. We sit in our nook at home and chat late into the night, making plans for the new work we are going to do.

Schloss Hartheim Psychiatric Hospital, Alkoven,
Reichsgau Oberdonau, Ostmark
(Austria during the Annexation),
Sunday, January 4, 1942

Rosa Haas pulls the door in the entrance to the castle towards her as she shoves the large iron key into the lock, but the door meets resistance and refuses to shut properly, she is forced to push the door open again and bend down to clear snow from the doorstep with two of her rough fingers, hardened from handling cold water and lye over many years, by sharp grass and acid soil from all the vegetable harvests she has sown, weeded and dug up in the course of her life; her face halfway to the ground it occurs to her that she is fifty-four years old, fifty-five this autumn, and that she has started feeling giddy when she makes certain movements, and when she mops under the beds she has begun thinking about her age as she does when she cleans the high windows with six panes each, thirty-six window panes in the dining room upstairs alone, or when she dusts the curtains in the doctors' office, those sky-high windows that force her to raise her arms in the air so her heart pounds and everything goes black before her eyes almost. Once upright again she takes a breather, the snow she pushed aside has formed a clump in her hand, she squeezes it and the snow moulds itself to the bent joints of her fingers and the ridges of her skin like a cast, she can see a couple of pebbles sticking out of the lump of snow she has compressed into ice, she throws it away and closes the door, turning the cold key twice and dropping it into the pocket of her coat, it makes a muffled thud before ending up askew, then she turns around: a curtain of large wet snowflakes is between her and the castle park, already streaked white by this first snow; almost simultaneously she begins to hear metallic-sounding notes that seem to be coming from the other side of the door, first a short snatch that is broken off and then picked up again immediately before winding casually up into the air in a long beguiling sequence – ah, that would have to be him, wouldn't it, the young doctor, playing his flute. She has heard it mentioned, she might even have heard the music before, but never this close, only at a distance, if she had not gone into the kitchen to return the dish she had taken home during the week she would have been on her way to Mass long ago and not been listening, by this time – what could it be now? – she must have spent too long in the kitchen with Linchen and Marianne Lenz, she would usually be halfway to Alkoven. The notes of the flute are merging with the snowflakes in a way that makes her think of the singing in the church she is going to, of how it sort of rises between the walls and is lit up by the windows; for a moment or two she is tempted to stop and let herself be filled with the whirling light, with the soughing of the flakes and the notes that are blending together, but then she is filled with unease instead: letting the music go straight up in the air as he does, allowing it to trace the same path as that horrible smoke . . . And now there's all this whiteness as well. She feels far too visible in her dark-grey woollen coat in the midst of all the whiteness, the white building, the flat landscape turning white, it feels as though the music might disperse the dull winter shroud, *der Hochnebel*, the fog she sometimes imagines shields them from God's eyes. Rosa Haas makes the sign of the cross and begins to trudge towards the village in her baggy galoshes, she soon passes the bench under the espalier where the staff usually sit in the sun during the period from March to October, she often glances over at them while digging and weeding the garden, she remembers big-busted Hanni especially, always smiling in her floral dress on that bench, that floral dress is the one she remembers her the most in, maybe because it looked as if she had won a prize at the tombola when she walked around the office in her floral dress and with one of those urn things in her hands, the people who work inside have it pretty cushy on the whole when they're off duty, mobile cinemas, and parties and a lot of flirting about, good thing her daughter Trudi keeps well away, sometimes the park looks like the walkways in Vienna her Trudi wrote about in those first letters she sent, a long while ago now, the apartment of the family she was in service with overlooked an old park "with broad walkways that form a star as big as the whole of Schloss Hartheim", that's what she wrote, "full of families with children and courting couples on Sundays", she doesn't know if she still lives near that park, she was so tight-lipped when she came home at Christmas, and she didn't want the watch or the shoes, best not worry too much, girls get full of themselves when they start working in factories, *I'm not bowing to anyone,* she had said, *the times are changing,* if Hans could have heard her, sometimes it sounds as if she has taken up politics, but she keeps quiet and hardly ever writes anymore, just as long as she doesn't turn up with a bun in the oven . . . Odd to think now the snow is landing on the green-painted boards that it can get so hot on that bench, she has even seen some of them sitting on it in their shirtsleeves the last few years, while working a patch opposite in the kitchen garden, a lot of the men in those short leather trousers, that stocky driver, Hödl, the one with the fleshy thighs, who spends ages just leaning against the fence smoking, doesn't have to pull his weight, not him, while she rakes the soil or shakes the potatoes out of mounds of earth and other people are doing whatever they're supposed to inside. Some of them come over to her after a while, in search of shade beneath the trees and for a bit of a chat as well; it's mostly the typists she remembers because they're the ones she sees more of, on the whole the nurses keep behind the wooden planks and hardly notice she's there, though they're nice enough when they do turn up, they walk arm in arm between the beds, she sees the typists when she cleans the room they work in on the upper floor, there's always someone in there, no matter what time she gets there, not that there are that many left now, not like before. Anneliese's a sweet girl, she was supposed to be getting married this weekend in Purgstall, into that Franz's family, they've been in love ever since she started working here, they're a decent couple in any case, not like some of the others, even the older doctor is having it off with one of the nurses, Linchen said during the big Christmas party when she'd had just a bit too much, dearie me. *They go at it like rabbits. Like rabbits, I'm telling you.* Summer is still a long way off in any case, Rosa Haas thinks as she turns right and leaves the avenue, it seems to take longer with every passing winter, she feels a yearning for the potato flowers and the carrots that glow like flames when she pulls them up from the rich soil. This war never ends either, *this war* she is thinking, but remembering the other one, when she was young and strong and had small children, with another on the way, only then the war was further off somehow, that Hitler . . . She passes the side entrance on the left where the idiots get brought in and a wave of something she cannot quite define rises from her chest all the way to her forehead, what there's no doubting is that the wave is largely made up of tiredness, that insidious heaviness in her chest and limbs. Good thing it's Sunday and there's no bus standing there because she would rather take this road to the village than the other, the one past the lawn on the eastern side, she avoids the eastern side where she saw two of the cremators emptying out the urns filled with ash (those good-for-nothing Germans they brought in who've got no shame, too lazy to carry the ash off to the river like poor Lothaler has to), especially after she pulled up the clod with the French Madonna in last summer, the one from the Pyrenees, like Fräulein Hintersteiner said, ever since that day the Lord's two colossal hands have been sinking into that terrible stretch of grass every time she passes it and those godly hands have been kneading the ash and soil together, just the way she did the mince and the fat for the rissoles at Christmas, God forgive her. She makes the sign of the cross and wonders what shape the Lord will give those poor *unworthies* next time around, and will their mothers recognise them in a new and more worthy form? Will the Lord Himself be able to recognise them, know who is who? She has reached the sloping terrain at the rear of the castle that leads to Dorfstrasse and there, on a little patch of ice, her left foot slides away from her, she feels something whirl in her belly that sucks her stomach in and a force on her spine that yanks her backwards, though she does not fall, she does not fall but manages to stay on her feet, even if there was a terrible crack and a stabbing pain around her kidneys as she whipped her trunk round to keep her balance. She walks slowly down the rest of the slope, snatches of music can still be heard rising from the castle while she digs her heels into the ground so as not to slip again, she hurries as best she can because it feels like that shameless music is trying to point her out.

She is finally out on the public road, the slowly falling snowflakes form a wet carpet she ruins with every step. After a few minutes there is a gust of wind that drowns out what remains of the doctor's flute and rips apart the mist hovering in front of the solitary houses, soon all that can be heard are her dragging steps, heavier with the snow that sticks to the soles of her shoes, and her breathing which is making her bust heave beneath her scarf, though why isn't she seeing anyone else on the road? There aren't any footprints in the snow in front of her either. She pulls the scarf tight under her chin and hopes that the church clock will soon be sounding the third quarter to confirm that everything is the way it's supposed to be, that she isn't late, that she hasn't got the time wrong, and that it's not the wrong day, New Year's Day falling in the middle of the week has mixed up the days for her, as though Sunday had already been and gone, this Sunday just a memory of another, one she might simply have dreamt. It would be good to be wearing the watch right now, but for some reason she never puts it on. As luck would have it, though, she can feel the stabbing pain strike in her lower back every time one of the galoshes makes her step go awry, the sharpness of the pain helps her to remain calm, every stab proof she is not dreaming. Steyrmayer's large black wooden barn comes into view at the crossing, the Holy Virgin inside the sentry box with a roundel on the crest of its roof, just before she turns into Kirchenstrasse she makes the sign of the cross towards the blue patch that is the Madonna's mantle, catching sight at the same moment of a Pinzgauer horse harnessed to the cart with a fur thrown over the upper part of the vehicle, and out of the corner of her eye she watches Steyrmayer and the hired hand carrying grandmother out to the waiting carriage, so she's definitely not late for Mass. She takes in that realisation as reason triumphing over the confusion of anxiety and it helps her to trudge more securely along the church road towards the train viaduct she can already see; relieved, she inhales and exhales the cold air in deep breaths, let's hope there won't be too much snow on the tracks at least, she thinks while picturing the postman's bag of letters, she hasn't had a letter since three days before Christmas Eve, not that her sons are much for writing. She tries to imagine Anneliese's wedding instead, a serious girl that one, hard-working and always so friendly, she gets up from her chair right away to let her mop under her desk, with a real show of respect, as if she didn't feel there was a difference between them or thought she was better just because she sits upstairs hammering away at the black contraption, let's hope Franz Gindl gave her a really nice wedding in his home village. Rosa Haas can see them coming out of the church, or maybe they got married in the town hall, you never know these days, arm in arm beneath an arch of raised arms, that at least you could take for granted, they look really nice together, Anneliese and Franz Gindl, she can see the girl's shy smile, they are lucky he's an orderly, so he can avoid ending up at the front, if her own Franz had been one she wouldn't have to feel so worried, but all he can do is care for the horses and tend the fields, like his father, may he rest in peace, Frau Krautgartner has promised to find them somewhere to live in Alkoven. And there is Elfriede Krautgartner coming out of her grocer's shop on her way to

Mass as well, she barely says hello, always doing that knitting for the Winter Relief behind the counter, as if trying to make herself out to be better than everyone else, only when was she ever going to have time to knit any socks? Besides, it wasn't as if she hadn't held her tongue just like everyone else when the S.S. men called them all together in the town hall. Rosa Haas walks cautiously up the few steps that lead to the church entrance, afraid now she no longer needs the reassurance the pain brought that there will be a nasty twinge at the base of her spine if she lifts her feet too high or too fast. Just inside the entrance she shakes out her woollen scarf and brushes the worst of the snow from her coat, the people who usually attend High Mass are all inside, a musty smell of damp woollen clothes hangs in the nave and tickles her nose and takes her back to the place she has just panted and groaned her way from, though there's no stinking smoke smouldering there today, that's the best thing about Sundays, all the more reason to forget that building now she's here, she thinks, and dips her finger in the holy water. She looks up at the vault of the church, she has got nothing against God seeing her in this place, she lifts her eyes to the leaded windows and the crucified figure behind the altar. Oh Lord, my God, can You see me now?

The priest has not yet appeared at the altar, that new one she has no confidence in at all, it must be a good six months at least since she last made confession, what was she supposed to say? What could anyone say? Elfrieda Krautgartner, who has been twenty paces in front of her the whole time, is only now reaching the third row of pews and about to take her seat, having said hello to Schumann, the mayor, who is easily recognised by his white hair and that short dark moustache of his she cannot see, because she is looking at him from the rear; she is sitting right at the back, closest to the exit, to avoid being looked at by all the others and so that she cannot see them thinking: That's her, the one who works *in there.* Her eyes alight on the floor of the church and it is as though the brandy bottles and the cigarette stubs were lying there, the stained sheets rolled together in large bundles, most of the cremators are gone now, the one who is left will be sleeping it off while the young doctor is playing the flute, the staff party just before Christmas was as grand as a harvest festival, she had to work overtime helping out in the kitchen for two whole days, because a lot of them were stopping work, even that horrible man Wirth who gave her the job and just yelled orders and kept rolling his eyes; she is not as afraid of the new director, though she prefers Herr Stangl, the handsome lieutenant who lives in Wels, he is really friendly and modest, they say he's happily married and has small children, Marianne says he's always talking about his wife and children, he's doing the right thing not living at *the rabbit castle*. The sole of a shoe that is angled towards her under the pew diagonally opposite her grabs her attention. Anne Marie Gruber and that black hound of hers pop into her mind's eye, as well as the sacks of clothes and other items the hound and his mistress kept watch over, not that there was anything that stuck up woman wouldn't swipe for herself. And she got no thanks for not saying a word, for not telling on her, those pumps made of the finest calfskin with low, rounded heels and the line of tiny nails in the sole, she did get given those, she'll admit, so her Trudi could have a nice Christmas present when finally she came home for a few days, only that was nothing in comparison. She was too nice, too stupid more to the point, the brandy bottles Hauptmann Wirth keeps, kept, under lock and key in the storeroom are the only desirable thing left, apart from the tins of food and sugar, we'll have to see if this new boss is more generous, she still hasn't learned his name, there are so many people coming and going all the time, she can't keep them all separate in her mind . . . Though there are fewer and fewer people working there, who knows how many will come back after the Christmas holidays, there won't be anything valuable arriving anymore, that's for certain . . . With a sense of relief Rosa Haas sees Father Seidel coming out of the sacristy and bowing before the altar, bowing, bowing again, all this endless bowing and scraping, Trudi is right. A sudden rumble from the pit of her stomach brings her tiredness out in a rush, as if she were hungry or as if the tiredness and hunger came from the same spot in her body, and while she isn't hungry this false hunger makes her think of the row of skinned rabbits Linchen was jointing when she went into the kitchen a while ago, chatting happily with Marianne Lenz she was, Marianne who was peeling potatoes, what wouldn't she give to be able to go back to the time when she cooked her own meals on Sundays, for Hans and the children, no wonder Marianne is happy, young and healthy as she is and with a husband who is an accountant in the building, not a soldier somewhere at the front, though they're both members of the Party, of course, not one day goes by that she doesn't put her Party brooch on, it's the ones who do the talking that dare the least, as her Hans used to say, may he rest in peace, who suffered so towards the end, good thing no-one decided to "release" him, he got to die a Christian death in his own bed. *That is the very thing that separates us higher beings from the other races and the animals*, Marianne chided her once, *that is what language is for, to ennoble our existence, you do understand the difference between "rissole" and "meatball", don't you, Rosa?* What a plague all these new meanings are, *release* and *treatment* and God knows what else, as though it wasn't just the body that was ageing but language itself was determined to leave you behind as well, back there, in the past, in the days of her youth when she felt she was at the centre of her life, not pushed aside like now, as if everyone was overtaking or running away from her, rushing towards a world she can no longer understand. Though sometimes the others, the younger ones, seem to get tired of it too, it's mostly people like Marianne Lenz and her husband who use the other words, *mercy killing, release*, not even that Hintersteiner creature does, even though she is so proud of being Dr Lonauer's secretary, not that her Hans would ever have worked in there, not even as a plumber like Barbl, the way Barbl refused to burn the bodies was almost impossible to credit, he was supposed to have stood up and yelled like a madman when Wirth tried to force him to, who would have thought it, given how frail he looks, though Hans said that all the time too, the strength is in your head, it's your head that decides what you can do and what you can't, the same way courage lives here and then he struck his large hand against his chest. Rosa Haas presses her fist against the top of her stomach pushing down hard under her scarf, life hasn't been easy, Hans, she doesn't know much about that courage business, but she plans on having the strength, on surviving this war as well, like they survived the last one together, that's the sort of thing you just have to make your mind up to do. And that's what she had told the boys as well, they've managed to survive this far, Rosa pulls her fist out from under her scarf and clasps her hands together in her lap, she bows her head and closes her eyes and thanks the Almighty for all the letters she gets from the front, most recently the two just before Christmas Eve, one from each of her perfectly healthy sons. The hardest thing is that the names of the places they write from mean nothing to her, she doesn't get any pictures. All she can see is a long trench filled with mud and water, and rats gnawing at bits of something black she forbids herself to look at, although Anneliese, who helps her read the letters, says that war isn't like that anymore, that the soldiers aren't in trenches this time. Now Father Seidel wants them to pray for the sons and fathers in Russia who are defending us from God's enemies. Rosa Haas counts herself lucky that none of her sons are dragging themselves through the snow outside a city whose name she can't even make out, she feels certain Anneliese never read that name aloud to her, Legrad, it isn't often she gets invited in to listen to the radio, though she'd like to be, then she might be able to follow the whole thing better. She was born during the Old Emperor's time, but her world has always been a small one, they've always been simple peasants tending their animals and their fields, she has never been beyond Alkoven, never even got on the train to Linz. They've got people from all over the world coming here now, the most recent consignment was foreigners, red Spaniards.

Spaniards! How did they end up in Alkoven? Are they soldiers? Oh my Lord, have we really got the right to make no difference between human beings and animals? And what if the Russians do the same to our soldiers? That's not something Father Seidel talks about. She is still thinking about that as she makes her way home to Hartheim number 28, the row of houses on the other side of the castle park where she has been living alone since her husband died of cancer the year before the Anschluss, Trudi moved to Vienna to work in service for a family with relatives in Alkoven, and the boys enlisted in the army shortly afterwards.

When she arrives at the hospital grounds an hour or so later there is no flute music whirling through the air and it has stopped snowing, instead she meets Helene Hintersteiner just beyond the entrance to the castle, she is coming from the direction of Annaberg and is wearing trousers and boots and has a short beige jacket on top of a bright-blue knitted jumper with a check pattern, she recognises the clothes from the photograph Fräulein Hintersteiner has upstairs in her room, beside the miniature of a party banner that has the word Linz carved into the flagpole, in the picture she is on a pair of skis in an Alpine landscape together with some other skiers, she is posing as if she were a famous sports star, one of the ones in the ladies' magazines she saves in a pile.

"*Heil Hitler, Frau Hass.*"

"*Grüss Gott, Fräulein Hintersteiner.*" The ruddy gold hair of the doctor's secretary is shining like a halo around her head, not even the chalky mist manages to make it look lifeless and dull, on the contrary. Rosa Haas suddenly feels unsightly and dark all over again, ugly, used up, tired and old.

The Visit, Ymergatan 7, Uppsala, Sweden, August 2006

You can follow your mother's movements around the kitchen from the sounds that reach you in the living room: the heavy wooden drawer that catches when you pull it so the cutlery makes that shrill, concerted rattle. The more muffled rattle as she sticks her fingers into one of the compartments to get out a tablespoon or retrieves one of the small butter knives with hand-painted porcelain handles she inherited from your grandmother – she laid the table before you arrived so the knives and forks are already on the bright-green damask tablecloth, it too inherited from her mother; the cupboard doors she always leaves open – especially before, when you were a child and living in Spain – and that click, almost soundless now in this Swedish flat, as she opens and closes them to get out a serving dish or a colander does not escape you either. You know that if you go into the kitchen in a while, closer to the final stage of the food preparation, at least one of the cupboard doors will be open wide, cutting off the flow of light at a perpendicular angle, and the cutlery drawer in the built-in wall cupboard will be hanging halfway out into the room, like a visual – if nothing else – obstruction on the way to the dining table – the kitchen is not large, and longer than it is wide besides. So you plan on staying where you are until the food is ready to be served, the mess that tends to spread around her used to infuriate you (your fury was as fleeting and as easily ignited as paraffin), now the rage is more viscous and runs deeper (a kind of emotional rock oil). You are sitting in the living room with the photograph album you took down from the bookcase open in your lap, it has been many years since you last looked inside, immediately you recognise the ticklish sensation in your fingertips as you run them over the light-brown textured cover, the smell is also particular and very familiar, the album smelled the same way when you were a child (What kind of smell is that? The photographic paper? The chemicals in the old pictures, some of them black and white, some in Kodak colour? The nondescript quality of the cover, a sort of plasticised cardboard?). The smell brings back the fascination you used to feel with what was between the covers, you would often look through the album when you were living in Lérida, you remember the longing you felt for everything that was behind you in time, life before you could remember and see it for yourself, the places your parents lived in before you were born, her, your mother's, clothes and hairstyles, and the way she would occasionally be so present in the pictures, now and then a huge smile at the camera and those lovely blue-green eyes (you knew they were blue-green although the photographs from the time when you did not exist were in black and white) that were looking straight at you and yet far off at the same time, past the observer, her forearm straight up like a flagpole, her elbow supported on a café table and her hand nonchalantly at her side, the cigarette between her fingers, tar in her mind and tar in her lungs (those long car journeys when you always felt sick from their tobacco smoke), those eyes of hers that were never *there*, that were never filled, never satisfied, that never stayed.

The album is open to two pages dated October 1962, there is no more specific date but all the photographs appear to have been taken on the same day, your christening day, you would have been a little over a month old. The photograph you wanted to see is on these two pages, among five others, originally six, one has come unstuck and disappeared, the memory of this picture was what made you ring and invite yourself to dinner, and you have just discovered that your memory was wrong, your memory has merged two images, superimposing one upon the other, made one picture out of two.

One of the photographs (which you did not happen to remember but find interesting anyway) is a group portrait taken on the daybed (a single bed pushed against one of the short walls with a round bolster along the long wall) covered in the Moroccan blanket made of coarse brown-and-black woollen yarn with broad white stripes your father acquired in the Spanish Sahara, you are all sitting on it: your parents, smiling at each other, Chi Chi the dog, already your father's companion at the fort in El Aaiún (only the dog is paying attention to the person behind the camera), an infant in a christening robe that is supposed to be you. There is a powerful current of sympathy flowing between the two adults in the picture, a shared understanding radiates from their eyes and mouths despite their not touching one another, the face and body of the man are seen from the front, they are turned towards the camera, but he is looking to the side, at the woman, his pose reveals the crooked line of his nose, the way the corners of his mouth are turned upwards; she is in the centre of the image and on the middle of the chaise longue, seen from the side, her face in profile (she is looking only at the man), she sits with her slender, pale (no stockings on?) legs drawn up and her feet in shoes on top of the blanket, as though the chaise longue were a river bank or a jetty from where she was observing the other people, her family (the man is perched on the very edge of the chaise longue with the dog and the infant on either side of him as if the three of them were seated in a little narrow flat-bottomed boat), her upper body is supported by her left arm which cannot be seen in the image while her right arm is resting on her hip or stomach; unlike your father, who is holding both the baby and the dog, she is not touching anyone, she is complete in herself, her body forms a closed system, her gestures feeding back on themselves, they begin and end in her. Between the woman who is sitting on the imaginary jetty and the man who has the infant in his left arm is the dog, of uncertain pedigree, the brown fur turning black on its back and the tips of its ears, you would hear a lot about that dog when you were growing up, the dog that had to be sacrificed for your sake, so you wouldn't get distemper as well and die, your father's right hand under the chin of the still-healthy dog; shifted to the right side of the image, seen only by the camera, you are resting in the crook of your father's arm, your white christening robe merging with his white shirt, your gaze (a guess at best) is aimed at an indeterminate point in the air straight in front of you, the one your recumbent position allows; the dog, whose nose is not yet oozing pus and blood and that will be killed by a pistol shot from your father's service revolver hours before its lungs start drowning in fluid or the sequence of epileptic attacks begins, is the only one looking at the camera, its black ears folded down. You do not remember that dog although you do remember all the others that came after it and all the names you gave them, naming the dogs your father brought home would be your privilege.

The glue the lost photograph in the series was attached with has left a hole in the paper, a hole large enough to stick two fingers in, so you do and the fingers end up on the other side, it is Christmas there, now and for ever, the Christmas of 1962. It is still your father who is holding you close to him while your mother sits to one side, observing, you are lying nestled on a shelf on your father's body, in a hollow between his face and his shoulder, like a puppy trying to find the beating of the heart in the jugular vein, like the puppy that no longer exists. The energy of love is tangible in every gesture and detail, as if it was conveyed by the light itself and lay somewhere beyond the laughter and the touches. You do not want to see any more, you turn the pages back to "octubre 1962" in blue ink in your father's characteristic handwriting your own would be so like. The photographs are spread across two yellowed pages but form a sequence, all of them were taken in the same room, although from different angles, and the people, with the exception of your father, are wearing the same clothes, not only you who can be seen in your christening robe in four of the five pictures (in the fifth one your father is alone and raising his glass towards the portrait on the wall) but also your mother – in a dark outfit part of which is a short jacket with large round buttons which, in another of the photographs, are made to sparkle by the camera flash at the same time as the dog's eyes – your grandmother, who, to judge from the sheen of the cloth appears to be wearing a silk dress (the images are in black and white and the following detail can only be a guess, but the dress is probably blue, because almost all the clothes your maternal grandmother possessed were blue, various shades of blue). Her shoes, unlike your mother's which are surprisingly or perhaps quite unsuitably light coloured, are dark, maybe black, what is light coloured about your grandmother is her snow-white hair tied back in a chignon and the pearl necklace that had slipped a little to one side in one of the pictures, the one in which she is holding you up to the camera and simultaneously twisting her trunk aside and pulling her face back so as not to obscure the view of what she clearly takes to be the most important subject of the picture: her first grandchild, who is yawning hugely in her flowing christening robes (Oh how they must all have laughed. The baby bored and tired of the celebrations, so touchingly unaware of its own leading role), the long folds of the ornamental train falling to brush against the moiré floor tiles that you know were green, green tiles with veins of yellow. During the hot summers when it was impossible to spend time outside until the sun had set you used to run in bare wet feet through the rooms, sometimes wearing your grandmother's thick reading glasses that distorted your vision and opened pool-like hollows in the floor, a perpetual flood was taking place on the shimmering green tiles and sometimes it would drag the whole building to the bottom along with it, you had seen an entire village lying under water (that was from a train window on the way to Tremp from Talarn), the church tower stuck up above the waterline of the artificial lake as if it were sinking in front of your eyes, while you sat in an old train pulled by a steam engine that crawled up between the mountain passes and over a rickety bridge, so rickety the train had to stop every now and then; the evacuated and abandoned village moved into your games, you could see the under-water houses and rooms where clothes and toys floated with the current, the inhabitants swimming along the streets, in and out of the buildings, the girls sitting on the swings, black hair floating upwards like algae seeking the light, the first time you saw the church tower sticking out of the lake was one summer, the windows of the trains had been lowered, a powerful cross-draught whirled around the compartment and you got a speck of coaldust in your eye.

There is something odd about your father's clothes in these photographs: was he in civvies or in uniform during the baptism ceremony in church? Was the picture in which he is so impeccably kitted out in his dress uniform taken immediately after they returned home, before he had time to remove the jacket and in that case why isn't the picture the first in the sequence? Did he change into a black suit afterwards? He wears a white shirt with a narrow dark tie in two of the photographs, in one of them a dark suit jacket over what could readily be interpreted as the same white shirt and the same narrow black tie, it is only in the fourth picture in the sequence that he is dressed in uniform, his captain's cap (the three stars are visible) under his arm, his eyes turned towards the camera, his mouth creased in a huge smile that exposes the whole of his upper row of teeth, although the extraordinary, the crucial thing is what is on the wall, that is why you are here. The same portrait that would later hang in its frame in the hall is hanging there, above the chaise longue, above the happy family. The portrait has simply been stuck to the white plaster wall with five drawing pins (three along the lower edge of the Hitler photograph), without a frame, the round steel of the pins gleams in the flash of the camera, the metal point invisible, pressed into the plaster; the same pointed motion through something softer and more innocent than the sharp steel is burrowing into your mind: the baby swathed in gauze beneath the wall of honour proudly displaying Hitler and the Nazi dagger that would later hang in the

178

best room and remind you of white chocolate, the whole thing hovering at an angle above the crown of your head, and in the photograph beside it your father in uniform, his hand lifted towards the same wall, raising a glass to the portrait of Hitler in his winter uniform with a thick fur collar around his coat. And you are the cause and object of the toast. The impression formed by the composition is that a toast is being made in the course of a ceremonial celebration. Your father could plausibly be supposed to have just uttered the words *Heil Hitler* a second or two before the person behind the camera snapped the picture (your grandmother presumably). You have the photographs in front of you, now and then, over the years, you have found yourself believing you might just have dreamt them (that you had dreamt what you were remembering; your father raising a glass to Hitler on your christening day, with you on one arm and a glass in the other hand). They had hung Hitler above your head like a guiding star. The sight of the tin dagger with the swastika carved into the hilt that is positioned slightly askew above your forehead haunts you, the entire wall with Hitler and your father's toasting hand and the dagger and the other warlords rising above your dark-haired skull with its still soft and open fontanelle haunts you, has been haunting you ever since the day your own daughter was born and she lay in your arms.

You shut the album. Fontanelle, fountain, fontana, a *spring*, water. And as though it might help or console or protect, as though the words could distance, remove or prevent, cleanse even, wash, erase and eradicate, you decide to look up *fontanelle* which gives you a reason to get up and move, over to the bookcase to gain time, your mother continues to clatter saucepans and cupboards in the kitchen, she calls out to ask you if you want a glass of wine while you are waiting, you are still alone with the photograph album and Hitler and the toasts and your father's smile, and your mother's complicit indifference on that imaginary jetty, the family in the lake that has to go under.

The first entry listed for the Swedish word *fontanel* is an obsolete medical term for the wounds that were made *with a knife or a corrosive substance or Spanish fly* (a drug extracted from the beetle *Lytta [Cantharis] vesicatoria Lin.*) on the upper arm and inside of the thigh and held open with what were known as fontanel peas or fontanel plasters or Spanish fly plasters, the aim being to expel diseased fluids along with the pus that would be drawn out. So, not spring water, no purifying water was poured over your scalp (a new baptism), what this confirms instead is the image of a suppurating wound (the photograph of your father toasting Hitler on your christening day).

You open the album again to those two pages.

You notice a different photograph this time and can see how your memory has contrived to combine two images into one: it is an image of your father on his feet, holding you in his left arm, wearing a white shirt with a black tie knotted loosely around his throat, just like your grandmother who is sitting with you in her arms while you are yawning with boredom in the photograph beside it he is preoccupied with your face (which is looking up at him raptly, utterly present), he is seen in profile therefore, but instead of holding a glass and toasting the portrait of Hitler as you have thought all these years, his large palm is open around the left side of your body, as if he wanted to protect you from falling out of the crook of his arm where you are lying or to form a shield with his cupped hand over your heart. The explanation for the confusion lies in the photograph above, the one in which your father, in his dress uniform, is toasting the portrait of Hitler, the two figures have simply been blurred together and you, wedged into your father's side, along with them. And the consequence of placing that photograph at the centre of the pictures of your christening day, you are thinking, is that you, a baby whose admission to the Christian community was being celebrated, are being symbolically presented to Adolf Hitler, symbolically admitted to the Fascist community of which Adolf Hitler is the overlord, as though Adolf Hitler had become your godfather.

You go back to the corresponding image on the first page, the group picture in which you have been transposed to the right edge of the image and are therefore almost directly beneath the Nazi dagger your grandfather brought home from the Russian front, by Lake Ilmen, near Novgorod, the dagger is mounted horizontally above the crown of your head and looks as if it is related to it (a dark round point) and to your body (swathed in the flowing christening robe your body makes you think of a long white line), together dagger and baby appear to form an ideogram, the dagger which is suspended by two straps looks as though it belongs with your head and body in the same way that the tilde over the Spanish letter "ñ" belongs with the "n". The white christening robe is long like a comma, white like a blank line.

She must have realised it would be impossible to go on breathing if she did it she did it anyway her child the same age as you in your christening robe she must have felt it would be impossible to breathe she left it in the middle of the pavement anyway she must have felt as if there were an iron weight on top of her stomach her lungs must have felt like stone she kept going anyway she stopped for a second during the march (the Jews from Węgrów were marched on foot to Treblinka, the extermination camp was that close) she stopped for a second during the march and crouched carefully down she must have felt it was hard to breathe but she bent down and let go she must have felt the iron weight shift upwards and crush her lung only with crushed lungs is it possible to abandon your child on a pavement and continue walking only by tearing away the part of herself she must have felt it would be impossible to breathe without though it was also the other way around: she was quite blue around the lips even at the beginning of the march with the child in her arms her lungs close to exploding and she stopped and bent down to take in air at last that part of herself that lay in swaddling clothes the only part that counted the only part that even had lungs and a beating heart she bent down and gently released the child gently so infinitely gently and carefully that it would not hit its head and when it was done she got back to her feet and screamed mute torrents of sounds that bled she screamed and screamed without making a sound the whole way to the platform in Treblinka where time was going to stop in any case and then she opened her eyes wide and looked at the child with the stillness of a camera lens and thought that if I photograph my child with my eyes she will stick to my retina and if her eyes (the child was a girl, that much is known, the story came to light at the Marriott Hotel in New York in the course of the second International Conference of Hidden Children during the Second World War) stick to my retina my eyes and my face will have stuck in her eyes her baby eyes that are still blue green anything no matter what as long as she goes on breathing after me day in and day out and she can hear the child crying all the way along the streets of Wegrów and all the while she is marching out of the town she marches for sixteen kilometres and can hear the child though not her own heart her own heart has stopped long before she gets to the station in Sokołów where the goods wagon is waiting she must have felt it would be impossible to breathe she crouches down anyway and leaves the girl on the pavement holding her carefully round her head so it does not hit the stone and she does not close her eyes even though her lips are blue from feeling she is choking the child does not cry the child sleeps in her mother's arms the child closes her eyes but not the mother the mother opens her eyes wide and stops breathing so the girl will be able to sleep in peace and not be aware of what is happening (what is happening is that her mother has to leave her for ever) she opens her eyes wide and looks up at the front of the house above but can find no faces just curtains moving hands that let go and when she looks down at the pavement she cannot see the child because one of the women nearest her has pulled her up and is shoving her onward move keep moving so they won't notice you've left the kid the woman hisses and pushes her forward and she turns her head and can see a divide opening along the road where feet are making way for her child and the woman pulling at her keeps repeating look ahead look ahead so they won't notice the kid lying there and she looks ahead and then she can see dogs approaching her daughter nosing at her nappy the first dog has a go at the stomach and digs at her rear the second dog tears off half the ribcage eating its way from there up to the throat and the head and when she stumbles and is falling flat on her face the woman grabs hold of her at the very last minute and whispers don't faint don't faint keep going if you want her to live you keep going and when the mother hears that she stops thinking about the dogs and does not faint she thinks about the hand that was moving the curtain when she looked up and she sees the woman come down and pick up her child and pour milk from a little glass bottle into a saucepan and the child smiles at the Polish woman because her child is bright and has understood that she has to live for her mother's sake otherwise her mother will not be able to breathe and she has to be able to breathe in order to find the strength to get all the way to the station in Sokołów and she has to have the strength to get all the way to Sokołów because if she does her child will survive she knows that it is something God has promised her or that she has promised God and the woman whose hand she saw comes down and picks up the girl and wraps her in a long robe and christens her and gives her a Polish name and she can hear the names whirling up like dust in the sunlight in the church she has never seen and she can hear the Polish woman saying Krystyna or Maria or Elżbieta and then she is rocking her child and whispering Maryśka or Elka or Elunia or Ewa or Joasia or Aśka or Anna or Anula or Anka or Agnieszka or Aga or Agatka as she bathes her in a white enamel basin she is rocking her and singing her name Dorotka or Danka or Danuta or Danusa and she puts the feeding bottle between her child's lips because the Polish woman's breasts are small and dry and do not ache like hers and the Polish woman with no milk in her breasts says shush Małgorzata or Małgosia or Gosia or Gośka Gośka or why not Izabela known as Iza or Izka or Izunia because her girl will be so beautiful with thick long eyelashes or maybe Elżbieta again or Agnieszka which sounds like a whisper passing her lips that she is feeling an irresistible need to clamp together to shut in her own cries of no though Krystyna will be safest in any case Krystyna Krystyna Krystyna Krystyna Krystyna Krystyna . . . for sixteen kilometres she repeats the Polish name she has finally chosen until she is close to losing her mind and her blouse is soaking wet around her left nipple the one she would have suckled at next because she was given the right breast the last time she fed at the right breast last the last time she gave her the breast and that thought makes her want to stop breathing again stop walking stay here stay stay disappear then somehow she pulls herself together and keeps mumbling Krystyna over and over again until she can see the woman in the window and she keeps repeating the Christian name until it is lying on top of the Jewish one like cotton wool like a soft clean eiderdown lying over her living child . . .

The German nation was a body, it was sick and had to be cured, it was vital to cut away the festering sore of Jewish Bolshevism. The eight thousand Jews who lived in the town of Wegrów had been exterminated but the little girl on the pavement was like a cancer cell that had got loose and was bent on surviving by spreading along the blood vessels and lymph glands. That was the kind of thing that hung on the walls at home when you were born (between the lines, behind the pictures), it was hovering above your open fontanelle: that a newborn child was a malignant tumour in the social body that had to be gassed or shot or buried in a mass grave in the forest.

A child just like you.

A child like your child.

Everything has been tainted.

… the dance called memory
Anne Carson

On Board the *Ciudad de Cádiz*,
by Sea from Barcelona to Santa Cruz de Tenerife,
January 24–9, 1959

The First Evening (January 24, 1959)

The cries of the gulls in the port of Barcelona eventually died away, her fellow passenger lying on the other bunk is wearing only her corset, panting. There was a storm in the English Channel the last time Gertrud Söderbaum crossed the open sea, on the night of the accident. She pulls out her suitcase from under the bunk and opens it, she takes out a dress with a flared skirt in rough, moss-green taffeta and a pair of beige pumps. She tightens the narrow belt and inserts her bad leg into the wobbly shoe, the large toe is turned in and pressed against the other toes by the triangular point, the swelling around her ankle has gone down, she takes a few steps around the cabin.

In front of the mirror above the sink she runs her fingers through her hair, she is nineteen and life is still refusing to show her its face, all she can see is the mouth, her mouth and a pair of blue-green eyes in which a gold-coloured glint of suspicion can now and then be seen. She keeps adjusting her fringe, drawing out and separating the strands into tips, her hair is her weak point, thin and straight and mousey, that is how they would describe it to you (or he would with her consent) many years later when they told you what they were like when they met: *color de rata*, he said, and you thought he thought your mother's hair was nasty.

She shoves lipstick, cigarettes and her purse into the little pouch-pockets gathered up and sewn on top of the ample fabric of the skirt; she lingers over the word purse as long as over its contents, *portmonnä*, the Swedish word must surely have been borrowed from the French? They were supposed to have celebrated New Year in Paris, the pain is immediate and burns, dripped from the steam of a hot spring. Outside the cabin, while she is locking the door, she is hit by a smell of paint that pinches at her nostrils, the white iron walls have just been painted. Upstairs in the lobby a broad and open staircase with a turned balustrade of dark wood leads to the saloon and the restaurant, she walks up the staircase as though she were a princess travelling incognito, a princess on her way to an exotic island close to the coast of Africa (where her white-haired mother was bound to have been made queen), and after that she is going to be an *au pair* with the family of a Swedish diplomat in Casablanca. Gertrud Söderbaum is travelling on her own, solitariness comes naturally to her, like an instinct.

The dance floor of the *Ciudad de Cádiz* is almost empty, a couple of waiters in short jackets are lined up behind the bar, a dance band is getting ready, tuning their instruments around the white circle projected by a floodlight, a woman in a black evening dress is talking intimately with the bartender, the *artiste*, she is making expansive, deliberate gestures with a cigarette between her fingers, the fringed side panels of her straight dress tinkle with every movement, they sparkle with a glassy sheen that makes Gertrud think of a forest of conifers in the rain at night. When the waiter approaches holding his zinc tray she orders a Coca-Cola. On the other side of the panoramic windows the sun is about to set, she remembers their discussion of the term in German: *Sonnenuntergang*, the downfall of the sun (for someone intending to be a doctor he was unusually interested in linguistic matters), the dark mass of the sea appears to extend towards an abyss it keeps propelling towards infinity but which continues to remain where it is, beyond the visible horizon, the pink glow beneath is like a scream, like an echo of the cry of that enormous celestial body when it fell, and she takes pity on it against her better judgment, feeling ever so slightly sorry for the sun. She can still see the plunging globe of fire as she gets the cigarette packet out of her pocket, the bottomless abyss the whole ship seems to be travelling towards, and she is thinking that her cabin is much too far below the deck were anything to happen. The singer in her tinkling dress of nocturnal pine needles enters the circle of light while the musicians are playing the first chords, Gertrud lights a cigarette and leans back, placing the damaged leg across the healthy one, her flared green skirt is spreading over the chair like a plant, like the glossy leaves of a water lily, and she tries to listen to the song, although both the words and the rhythm are quite foreign to her; a ghost rhythm from the jazz clubs in Hastings where they used to dance together begins to steal across her sore foot, he was the only person not drinking beer, the petticoats were a white glow below the spinning skirts, she remembers, the ghost rhythm turns into a conflicting one, a counterpoint to the foreign voice, and she thinks about her friends in Uppsala, suddenly missing the record with Harry Belafonte on ("Day-o, Day-o, Daylight come and me wan' go home . . ."), though her record collection is the only thing she does miss, the shiny sleeve with its picture of the black singer against the brown cover on her bed, calypso, Jamaica, the double L.P. of Ella Fitzgerald's Cole Porter songs, a tame exoticism, far away and safe at the same time.

A soldier comes in through the glass doors, he is tall and strikingly well built and the uniform jacket with its shiny black leather belt accentuates his figure, she recognises him, it is *the interpreter*, he is wearing the same black riding boots and light-grey uniform jacket he had on at the shipping office in the port in Barcelona, she cannot see the stars on his epaulets, she is sitting too far away, although the sense of authority he exudes in those knee-high boots of his tells her he can only be an officer. Then she sees the boy who was waving off the handsome officer at the dockside, he cannot have been more than nine or ten and was accompanied by another young soldier. The singer comes to the end of her song and looks back at the pianist with a nod, Gertrud shakes out a fresh cigarette while some of the dancing couples return to their seats, the handsome officer is standing at the bar with his elbow on the counter, she recalls a round pin with a bronze camel attached to the lapel, when he helped her to order the ticket it was never made clear they would be travelling on the same day, but then there he was all of a sudden at the railing a few metres away and waving goodbye to that boy, without noticing her. She lights her cigarette, the flame makes her flush with embarrassment, as if she had deliberately given away her position, the band starts up again, playing the first chords of a familiar tune by Nat King Cole that the *artiste* is singing in Spanish, Gertrud lets go of the lighter's wheel before the entire paper cylinder is set alight and sits there in imaginary safety, her half-consumed cigarette giving off smoke under the table. But he has already turned around and is looking her way, with the beginnings of a smile at the corners of his mouth. Before long she can see the riding boots making their way towards her, the long thighs inside the grey breeches, though she is not actually seeing them, she is sensing them, because she has turned towards the stage and is staring at the pine needles glistening with rain on the singer's dress. But the same huge sky they said goodbye under in Barcelona is now arched across the distance between her and the man she knows is coming over to her, that is the light she sees him again in, is seeing him still, was he seeing her under that same sky, were they still being bathed in the noonday light of a January day in Barcelona on the dance floor of the liner? The air is so clear, like a thinly spun veil above them. She is anticipating the look in his eyes that she remembers as almost transparent blue in colour, as if he were made of water under the skin and his eyes were a gap, a crack opening onto the sea beneath them. She drops her eyes to put out the cigarette which she does with repeated taps against the ashtray, a kind of bulge suddenly forms on her lips like when she was pouting in front of the mirror earlier. The boots stop in front of her table. Nothing is smouldering any longer. Outside the shipping company offices she had screwed up her eyes at a January sun she had never seen the like of anywhere else, seconds passed then, seconds pass now. He may have forgotten, she may be alone under the high, blue, actinic light of the harbour. "Êtes-vous française?" he had asked. She looks up. Then her father's black Ford rolls to a stop between the officer and her, Tess' curl-fringed russet eyes are fluttering inside, the way they did when he ran up the beach at the summer cottage in Piteå and shook off the water from his coat, she and the cocker spaniel used to accompany the district medical officer on his hospital tours, they would sit close together, her arm around his neck, they could be waiting in the car for hours for the doctor to return, with a bag of apples in her lap and the book about the Bullerbloms she had been given by *your cousins in Skutskär, Christmas 1949*, the last Christmas but one the doctor was still alive, the clammy smell of Tess' chronic ear infection used to smother the scent of apples and make her nostrils numb. The seconds are not passing any longer, the Ford vanishes. The soldier has dark wavy hair and his eyes are all for her._

He had been surprised that she was Swedish the first time he met her, so short and with light-brown hair, not blonde, her eyes lovely but greyish green and not blue. There were some young foreigners smoking outside the offices of La Trasmediterránea, they turned round when the two of them came out and he realised they were her companions. For a second or two, however, he and the young Swedish woman had lingered there on their own, halfway between the entrance and the small group of her friends, fumbling at the silence that had immediately started spinning thin threads through the air. And now here she is again, he hesitates, allowing some of the phrases of the yearning melody being sung in that dark voice (... *aquellos ojos verdes, serenos como un lago* ...) to roll along and the girl to wait on the other side of the lengthening silence, by the shore of the lake the song refers to, because he remembers the girl's eyes as being green like a lake and as calm as well (. . . *en cuyas quietas aguas un día me miré* . . .),[20] the sun has not completely set and he sees a flash of the setting sun in the desert he is headed towards. Before long he decides that the song is the right one and that he has to arrive before it ends. He makes it, he reaches her table (. . . *aquellos ojos verdes serenos como un lago* . . .). She looks up, the shiny threads are still in place, vibrating with recognition and she says yes, she'd like to dance and she gets up and he extends his arm and offers his hand and leads her onto the dance floor (. . . *aquellos ojos verdes no saben la tristeza* . . .), he spreads the fingers of his right hand around the girl's waist (. . . *que en mi alma han dejado* . . .),[21] and holds out his left arm like a branch with his palm turned upwards (. . . *aquellos ojos verdes* . . .) and his index finger extended, so that the furrow between the thumb and the index finger (. . . *que nunca nunca* . . .) forms a cradle into which her hand, so small and white (. . . *besaré* . . .),[22] can slide.

The light from the port stays with them, a slice of bright-blue sky hovering above his black hair as they glide around. She remembers the outline of a palm tree above the handsome soldier's head in the port, and the palm that grew up to the glass ceiling of the tropical diseases ward where she was confined in the late autumn seems like an omen now. He dances well, the movements they make fit together in a natural way even though everything feels unfamiliar and new. Her not understanding the words of the song, the fact that she is on the way to *Ma's island*, that there is something odd about his long nose – it is crooked. And that he, the other one (the medical student from Heidelberg), is dead. Only the figure of her mother feels

20 "Those green eyes I remember, calm as a lake, in whose smooth waters I saw myself reflected one day."
21 "Those green eyes do not know the sadness they have left behind in my soul."
22 "Those green eyes I will never, ever kiss."

known, familiar, she is waiting at the end of the voyage surrounded by the brightly coloured plants she is forever photographing. Ma Rosa's letters arrived at the hospital regularly, once a week. The car crash happened only a few weeks after she and Felix (she thinks of his name less and less often, it means "happy") parted in England, she got letters from his parents as well, one contained a black-bordered sheet of paper with the news that their beloved son had died, the paper was thick and watermarked and she held it up to the light as if expecting to see a different set of words emerge beneath the slanting handwriting of his grieving father but the only thing to appear were the bright lines of the watermark pattern. She views her own accident as an extension of the accident that killed him. One night, not far from the station in Hamburg, she had been knocked down by a van as well, she was supposed to change trains and had gone to an all-night *Imbiss* to get food for the journey, the van failed to stop, it hit her and vanished down the alley as if it had emerged out of a wrinkle in time, Felix' death reached out to touch her like the drumbeat of a secret music and that is the music she is dancing to now, on her bad leg, with a man in uniform who knows nothing about her: that she took the postcard from Heidelberg off the wall and slipped it between the pages of her passport, that she tends to run her fingers around the hole the drawing pin left in the card, in the centre of the narrow strip of sky covering the green hills above the city's famous ruined castle and its ancient centre, Felix *the happy*, Felix *the dead*.

His eyes lap up the downy skin on the girl's cheek, even whiter under the red filter of the lamps, he is at least fifteen years older and the difference makes him suddenly heavy-footed, he feels embarrassed by his own imagined stink of camel hair, rifle grease and the barracks that is settling in a layer over that more subterranean smell of chicken soup, chlorine and pee-soaked nappies. And turpentine as well. But she says yes to a second dance, the space between their ribcages narrows and widens in time to the music, they get knocked into at one point and the sharp edge of the bronze stars that protrude from his breast pocket grazes her cheekbone leaving a tiny red spot and that redness makes lieutenant Salvador Pascual Pascó, a foreign legionnaire stationed at El Aaiún, in the Spanish Sahara, see glimpses of the last two weeks he has been on leave in his home town of Barcelona, at dawn the first lorries started unloading at the covered market on the other side of the street, from the bed where he had spent most of the nights he could watch the leaves of the plane trees quiver in the breeze, though that was in summer, during a different leave when the dawn was not damp and raw the way it had been this last time with steam floating out of the mouths of the market women, *¡Buenos días mi teniente!*,[23] the burning taste of the coffee laced with brandy he drank at one of the stalls before he took the tram home to the upper part of the city, fat Manoli and her insinuating glances, her lipstick was red above the double chin and that huge bust. Some mornings, after he had slowly turned the key in the lock, his mother would be waiting among the shadows in the darkened hall, her silhouette outlined against the whiteness of the bevelled glass panes that let in a grey gleam from the lightwell, the figure of his mother the same height as the porcelain vase on a pedestal in the right-hand corner of the hall from which peacock feathers stick out in all directions and whose ocular pattern reproduces his mother's gaze like an echo, with a sheen of the same old voluptuousness that gleams in her eyes as she interrogates the staff in the kitchen in Spanish spoken with a rough Catalan accent: (*¿Y qué hiciste con tu novio ayer? ¿Fuisteis al cine?*),[24] Remedios, her hands immersed in the washing-up bowl (*¿Te metió mano? Di, ¿dónde te la metió, arriba o abajo?*),[25] rigid and mute with mortification (*¿Y con Salvador también lo haces? Si me cuentas lo que hacéis dejaré que te quedes. Pero*

23 "Good morning, lieutenant."
24 "So what did you do with your boyfriend last night, did you go to the cinema?"
25 "Did he touch you? Tell me where he touched you, up top or down there?"

con pelos y señales ¿eh?).[26] His mother's voice drawling in the semi-darkness (*Ja has estat amb dones tota la nit, oi? Oi? Que no en tens prou amb els quatre fills que li vas fer a la Teresa? Ets un home casat, és amb la teva dona que has de jeure a les nits, allò que tens li has de ficar a ella entre les cames i no a totes aquestes pelandusques amb qui vas!*)[27]

He wants to ask what the young woman is called, to say *What's your name?* But the rhythm of the music is working against that, the beat is too fast, the singer too loud at this point and there is something cool and detached in the girl's face that refuses to accept words thrown out in haste, besides, he does not want to interrupt the dance, the contact with her waist and hand, the question will have to wait and meanwhile he is thinking that Stockholm (*Estocolmo*) is on the same latitude as Leningrad (*Leningrado*, the city his father insisted on calling *San Petersburgo*) and he thinks of Estocolmo as if it were the girl's name, a snow-covered name lying cold and white before him. When the song ends they jointly decide they do not want to dance anymore and he goes with her to the sofa she was sitting on when he offered her his arm and asks if he can join her and when she says yes to that too he sits beside her, though not too close. He asks if he can buy her a cocktail, lace her Coca-Cola with rum? She nods and he snaps his fingers to get the waiter's attention: *Dos cubalibres, por favor.*

They danced in silence, now they are readying themselves for the words that have to be said. The first words are shrouded in the slowly drifting smoke that shoots out of their mouths every now and then, like a kind of antiphon, in the interval between their breaths an olfactory zone is blended (the rough acrid odour of his untipped

26 "Are you doing it with Salvador as well? If you tell me what you get up to, I'll let you stay. I want to hear all the details."

27 "So you've been out on the town all night with your sluts again, have you? What about the four kids you made with Teresa, aren't they enough for you? And you a married man, you should be spending your nights with your wife, she's the one should be receiving that thing you've got between your legs and not all those whores you go around with!"

cigarettes (*tabaco negro*) and the sweetish smell of the long American cigarettes (*tabaco rubio*) that she smokes), and it is there, in the charged passage of air that contracts and expands between them with every drag, that they utter their names, that he asks her to show herself in the full light of her name. *Gertrud*. He asks her to repeat it, the word is a tangle of sounds he finds it impossible to unravel. *Yaretroot*. The name slithers along his tongue like a lame animal inside his mouth. *Yare-troot*. Like an exhalation, a whisper that has to escape if those soft, floundering sounds are not to be crushed against his teeth. The waiter arrives with their order, he says the drinks are called *cubalibre*, can she say that?

She has to go to battle for her name, as usual, in order to preserve the correctness of its sounds and to defend its borders, she feels like an extremely small country trampled on by larger and more powerful languages that feel entitled to distort those sounds that are like little crystals, the shards of a mirror she has learnt to see her reflection in, he, Felix, whose postcard of his hometown with the cherry trees blossoming in the foreground is still pinned up on a soft wall inside her, tried to Germanicise it, *Gertrud*, to fill it with guttural and grating sounds, he converted the soft semi-vowel (y) into an explosion (g) like two soldiers on watch closing their vocal chords with a plosive both at the beginning (g) and at the end (d), her name turned into a restricted area, an enclosure. And now she has to hear this Spaniard with his broken English and a major world language of his own about to step inside her mirror-name like a bull in a china shop and she is wondering what will become of her fragile, open-ended name. Names are after all intimate and vulnerable things, as she has been forced to learn. Ma Rosa has told her about the holiday trip she and her father took around Europe in the summer of 1935 and that her keen photographer of a father recorded with his camera, the first pictures in the holiday album of that year are views of Berlin, an open tour bus (Thien's Berolina Rundfahrten), a Luther monument, a picture of the Brandenburger

Tor without a caption, then a landscape portrait from the train, *Views from the D-Zug Berlin–München at top speed* her father had written in white crayon on the grey card of the album, the images on the page shift after that to monumental views of Munich and idyllic images of medieval Nuremberg, the interior of *the St Sebaldius Church* and a smiling Rosa *On the Castle Balcony* with a mist-shrouded Nuremberg and a black spire in the background, Bierkellers (*N.B. Crucifix and I.N.R.I. in the Bierkeller!*) and a *Monument to the 1400 Fallen from M.* with a picture of the closely engraved names in Gothic script (*OBERMEIER Josef 5.9, OBERMÜLLER Max* illegible date . . .) and then the photo of an *S.S. wedding in Nuremberg*; the couple have just left the church and are about to pass beneath an arch of arms raised in the Hitler salute, people are thronging in front of the camera, a woman, evidently elated by the scene, is caught in the moment, she is turning towards a point to the left of the photographer and shouting something at someone, lips pushed out, caught for ever in the utterance of a word the picture is unable to capture. At one of the hotels they stayed in during their trip to Germany two gentlemen in suits asked to see their passports, her father was invited to answer a few questions while her mother was to wait upstairs in their room, when her father eventually came back up he told her that they had kept his passport and they were not to leave the hotel for the time being, that they had asked him what religion he was, that they had not believed him when he denied being a Jew, or when he tried to tell them the anecdote about his surname, that the –baum ending in Söderbaum was not German but the result of one of his nineteenth-century ancestors Frenchifying the original Söderbom, o is spelt au in French, you see, he lived at a Walloon ironworks in central Sweden (he's got no idea what the word for ironworks is in German), just a snob really. *Snobbismus!* (the gentlemen had no sense of humour) Wallonia? Belgium? *Nur ein snobbistischer Vorvater, kein Jude.* The trip continued from *Munich–Venice–Munich via Lake Garda–Venice–the Dolomites.* Pictures of mountains in Merano, Bolzano, Innsbruck, *San Vigilio at*

La Garda, two *Choirboys in Venice, Padua; exchange of stamps between P.H. and the monk Pater Prius*, a picture of her father at the Lido, *Swimming in the Adriatic, 2 p.m. on St Mark's Square* and the image is full of shadows rising from the ground, black pigeons with out-stretched wings, so many and flying so close together they obscured St Mark's Basilica in the background; a gang of street children by the *Canal Grande*, Rosa in a white hat on *the Bridge of Sighs*. The final page before they leave on the plane from Berlin shows mountain views of the Dolomites, *Vipiteno, Cortina, Rosengarten. End of our 1935 holiday. Souvenir of Flight Berlin–Malmö 13/8 1935* which is a postcard of a little plane with the legend D-ANEN painted in large letters on the wings and body of the plane, the plane is flying above white cumulus clouds and seen against the ragged silhouette of some dark mountains in the background. The following holidays were spent in the Nordic countries. Under the heading *Holiday 1936* are photographs of rein-deer, waterfalls, a picnic in front of a Lapp tent *Turku, Nantali, Helsinki Finland, Suomenlinna, Abisko Station*. During *Holiday 1937* the plane would fly to Copenhagen and to the northern part of Sweden as well, there are several atmospheric pictures of Lake Hornovan presumably taken early in the morning or late in the evening in which the lake is a dazzling mirror of the sky, there is one photograph she remembers in particular: a solitary reindeer is walking along the water's edge, there is no horizon, there is just lake and the lake is a reflection of the sky: the reindeer appears to be about to step inside a dream. *Holiday 1938* was spent in Narvik and it is there that the holiday album ends. Her parents never holidayed in mainland Europe again, her father never forgave the Germans for that interrogation at the hotel, that brief but anxiety-ridden deprivation of his liberty that robbed him – a hitherto German-friendly soul, who spoke German fluently because his entire medical training had been conducted through the medium of that language (and who had been conceived during a medical congress in Vienna in the summer of 1895 besides – *my Viennese child* Grandmother Anna used to call him, *my Viennese child*) – of rather more than a few hours of his time, it was a matter of his integrity, her father had felt profoundly insulted. Then came the war and Europe turned into a battle zone, that was the same autumn she was born. The ironic aspect was that had her parents travelled around Austria or Germany in the war years the Gestapo men who had interrogated her father would probably have adopted an entirely different attitude to the name Söderbaum, because their relative Kristina Söderbaum, *die Söderbaum* as she was popularly known in Germany according to Gunnar, had by then married a film director, whatever his name was, who was Goebbel's man and made propaganda films for the Nazi regime; their relative had become a huge star – *First she slept with Goebbel's man and then she became a star!* – the films she acted in were seen by millions all over Europe although they were banned now, or at least one of them was, and even its title sounded brutal: *"Jud Süss"*, she has no idea what that film was about or what happens in it, it has never been shown in Sweden and has been banned every-where else, but Gunnar, her older brother, who feels a boundless contempt for their distant relative – an *immoral opportunist* is what he calls her – has seriously considered taking their mother's surname, Widmark, instead of their father's, because of that film – *people would leave the cinema and quite literally lynch the first Jew they encountered after that appalling film had been shown* – their name has been saddled with the U.F.A.-star's shameless collaboration (*and collaboration, both political and social, was the right word!*) with the Nazis, he said. She is proud of her surname all the same, representing as it does two generations of doctors and a lineage that stretches back to the eighteenth century, which may not be that remarkable but is more than most people can say about their surnames, and what difference does it make if one of their relatives has acquired a bad reputation? Besides, whatever Kristina Söderbaum did she managed to make a name for herself and the whole world was anti-Semitic at the time, Berlin was like Hollywood then, it was only natural she should have made her way there, and the fact that she had had a great career alone and in a foreign country was admirable in one sense, Germany was a great nation and she was ambitious and so that is where she went, besides, she feels forced to admit to herself, there's no denying that *die Söderbaum* being associated with the Nazis is a tiny bit titillating in a way, Hitler, Goebbels, "Jews", the words send delicious little shivers down her spine, no matter what they have come to mean a Söderbaum was there, on the cutting edge, hobnobbing with the great men of history, not of course that she would ever dare reveal thoughts like these to Gunnar, she's very fond of him, he's like a father to her, the father they both lost, he and she belong together, like Hansel and Gretel in the dark forest of orphanhood (though they've still got their elegant mother, that sense of having being abandoned is still present to them) and they are rather alike, not as practical and materialistic as their other two siblings, Gunnar is going to be a psychiatrist *and end up in Ulleråker* as he likes to joke, she has no intention of ending up in Ulleråker or in any other Swedish town for that matter, least of all Uppsala, she is going to have a look at the world, first the Canary Islands, then Casablanca and after that, who knows? For a while it looked as though she would end up in Heidelberg, in any case she's here now, a long way from damp woollen overcoats, galoshes and spotty young students with safe Swedish names like Göran and Hans and whatever else her admirers may have been called, here she is being courted by a Spanish officer, no youth but a man and the sea they are crossing has no borders. She says *skål!* and he replies *chin chin!* And they clink their long narrow glasses of *cubalibre* together.

Gertrud Söderbaum, she's got to be kidding! The name hits him like a thunderbolt: is she related to the German actress? To Kristina Söderbaum? The girl's face, lit from the side by a spotlight that has been switched to a bluish tone that accentuates the curve of her left cheek bone, suddenly opens up to him, as if a cloud front had been dispersed and the sun had emerged from behind it or a curtain had been drawn aside and a bright white light was shining on the cinema screen: as was true of the German film star, the broad, milk-white cheeks are a translucent sphere, an undulating terrain with the intense matt gleam of sand, as soft and porous as a sand dune, only in front of the cinema screen has he ever felt so completely absorbed: her face is like light-drenched earth that sucks you in and provides you with a frame at the same time, the way the desert does when he rides out of the fort and the sand, shimmering like old gold in the early morning, keeps extending further and further in front of him the deeper into the desert he rides; he traces the outline of the girl's face which he is looking at against the light and is at an angle towards him and can feel her face expanding all around him like an unknown and yet long-desired region, a land he has been dreaming about for ages but never visited, never surrendered to, new and at the same time as familiar as a memory; much more than the eyes, which he can also see similarities in (the outline of the eye sockets and the eyes themselves, the fleshy, slightly sagging skin over the eyelids), it is the overall shape and the white gleam of her cheeks that form the midpoint of her face, and he recalls the face of the film star under bright sunlight by the shore of a lake, wearing an azure-blue dress with a white lace collar the same shade as the glittering water in the background, the film's peculiar Agfacolor blue sky above that alien Nordic summer landscape, and he remembers that his hand had stopped wandering up Teresa's thigh in the dark of the Capitol's auditorium when he saw the actress swimming across the mirrored surface of the lake, acting sulky and scared with a natural girlishness he found astonishing, the scene felt so realistic he could see the goosebumps forming on the actress' skin under the impenetrable cover of the blue-green lake, he could feel the chilly puckered surface of her trembling flesh, he was the drifting log floating motionlessly against the light that she, Kristina, of the plump white arms, was clinging to. Only now the girl is telling him that Kristina Söderbaum isn't German but Swedish, and that all the Söderbaums are related, that the film star is some kind of cousin of hers despite the considerable difference in age, and once she has said that he can see her blush, as if she were feeling suddenly shy. In the glow of the lighter's flame he sees those green eyes shimmer and they make him think of Elias, the army doctor, as he was reading to the company from the Bible in the course of the morning's manoeuvres (for which he would later be arrested!) because all of a sudden it feels as though he understands the simile of doves bathing in milk beside a stream that they had joked about afterwards in the canteen (not that he thinks of her hair as being like a flock of goats in any way and he is no longer laughing at the smutty allusions to the regiment's goat) because her eyes are fluttering like the beat of wings and gleaming like running water at the top of that face he now perceives to be a coming home, and scenes from those old films appear to him once again: He remembers Kristina riding bareback along a beach throwing darts at a target set up at the water's edge, and he remembers how excited he was by the vision of that modern Valkyrie in a white bathing costume galloping on her white stallion alongside a stormy sea, and a somewhat unexpected association also makes him hear the sound of the ball striking the wall in *el frontón*[28] over in the Ramblas, partly because he saw so many of the films at the cinema next to the court but also because he is dressed entirely in white when he plays *pilota basca*, it would have to be that, he always strikes and receives the ball dressed in a white shirt and long white trousers as the rules dictate; it was the premiere of "*Sacrificio*" ("*Opfergang*"), he remembers now, his father had returned from Russia, white geese on the wind-lashed sea, Kristina Söderbaum is leading the white horse towards the waves, as if the waves were calling to her, as if she understood, even though she was a woman, that that is the only kind of life worth living, perilous, intoxicating, she swims out into the stormy sea until the water is almost up to her jaw bone, until someone on the shore calls

28   The game known as "pilota basca" is played on a court called a *frontón*.

to her to turn and swim back, and here this girl is – related through her name, her blood, her features to his old boyhood dream: the Valkyrie, the battle maiden.

She drops her eyes because what she has said puts her in too exposed a position, one she both aspires to and shies from, she lowers her gaze and gives a little smile instead of looking him in the eye, she rarely does that, she has lowered her gaze because the film, just like the film star who almost no-one remembers and who she has just claimed to be related to, is obscure, being a banned film about Jews, so she looks down and smiles a bit wryly as though she had mentioned the term "gas chamber", the embarrassing, the titillating, the forbidden, and she gives a little smile for him to linger over while she makes up her mind how and in what way she will continue to talk about herself, how to describe parts of her world to this com-pletely unknown person, the rooms all she is and everything she remembers are enacted in, the people who move about these rooms, who touch objects freighted with memories of a lost world, the pewter sugar bowl put out at breakfast, the round dining table made of cherry wood at which her mother attempts to maintain her former glory days as the wife of the district medical officer, her brothers and sisters around the table, Gunnar saying that the Söderbaum girl was a Nazi and he felt utterly ashamed of sharing a surname with her and he had to hear it brought up over and over again, particularly at university where more than one professor had come up to tell him, eyes glittering, about the appearance at Cinema X of Kristina Söderbaum and the German film director in the middle of the war, and she can see her mother lowering her gaze, her mother who would prefer not to discuss the subject and never boasts about anything at all, let alone a distant relative of her husband, not even to mention that the film star's father was permanent secretary of the Royal Academy of Sciences and on the Nobel Committee at the time Selma Lagerlöf was a member of the Swedish Academy, though if anything it would be that, given that a framed card signed by Selma Lagerlöf and dedicated to Grandmother Anna dating from the period when the two ladies spent time together in Falun is displayed above the elegant secretaire, and then her thoughts come to a halt at the black-painted Dala clock in the big room, whose pendulum stopped long ago. She stubs out her cigarette repeatedly in the ashtray and immediately takes out a new cigarette and brings it to her mouth, she hears the click as she opens the cap of the Zippo and the sound of the flint wheel being turned before she feels the heat of a tall flame that illuminates the area around her mouth and perhaps her eyes as she looks up and says "Thank you", she has no idea why that is what she wants, to impress him, to make him realise she is so much more than a nineteen-year-old tourist passing through and she thinks about what her friend Gunnhild would say about her turning up in Uppsala in the company of this handsome officer, how his jackboots would look at Gillet, the astonished expressions on her friends' faces, or in the overcrowded four-room apartment on Ymergatan, at the cherry-wood table, and suddenly she blushes and is grateful for the semi-darkness that helps to conceal the blush she would rather disown and has no intention of interpreting; only then the words finally come to her rescue with something she can actually allow herself to utter: *I have never seen any of her films*. But then he says he has seen all of Kristina Söderbaum's films, the first towards the end of the war, not our war but the World War, he clarifies, that would have been about 1944, he was nineteen (the same age she is now, she is thinking) the cinema was next to a court where he used to play something called *pilota basca*, she doesn't know what that is and he has to explain: you hit the ball at the front wall with your bare hand, no racket or bat, he tells her that the players usually dress all in white and she tries to imagine him dressed all in white but can only make out his sunburnt face, his nose with that remark-ably crooked bridge above the narrow moustache, and because she can see the night and in it the moon reflected outside on the ocean through the panoramic window diagonally behind him she thinks that a white shirt would make his face even darker, and the image that comes to her is of his face covered by a cloud, or by another planet, like an eclipse of the moon.

She lies in her cabin without moving that first night, her spine feels heavy and stiff as if she were pregnant already although he has only touched her hand and waist, her back heavy and aching as though an embryo were pushing against her stomach and her lungs and the base of her pelvis. She conjures up her mother, seeing the white flowers on her dress in the photograph she sent from the home for Swedish rheumatics she is currently managing on Tenerife, she imagines the island where she will be living for some time, so close to Africa but with a snow-capped mountain at its centre and black sand on its beaches. Her mother took on the position only a couple of months before she was knocked down in Hamburg. An exhilarating sense of destiny keeps her awake most of the night. At dawn the *Ciudad de Cádiz* passes the Balearic Islands.

The Second Day (January 25, 1959)

The next morning he is waiting in the dining room, breakfast is long over, but he has remained sitting amidst the sea of empty rectangular tables laid with white tablecloths, feeling like the last piece on a single-coloured chessboard. He has been waiting a long time by the time she appears, in a green outfit veined with purple, the jacket's large mother-of-pearl buttons flash with the reflections of the light that is pouring in through the panoramic window. But when she sees him she hesitates and stops a few metres inside the entrance, as though considering the possibility of sitting somewhere else, of walking towards another of all the empty tables. He rarely remembers his dreams, the hours of sleep tend to be solid gaps in his memory that he invokes by leaving a light burning while he sleeps, but a delay of some kind has just occurred and it seems to him as if the dream he should have had last night were being enacted now, as if the ocean heaving beneath them had dissolved every boundary, and time, not just this floating space, were blurring in and out of something ill-defined and ambiguous that was both inside and outside himself. And just as in the most terrifying nightmare he is having difficulty getting out those vital words that might entice her to him, all he can do is get to his feet and stand there, speechless, at attention almost. Even the waiter is rooted to the spot a little way off with a pile of plates in his hands watching the officer watching the young woman, not saying what he ought to say: that breakfast is no longer being served. She eventually comes to a decision and starts walking over to him. The waiter immediately gets on with re-laying the tables. He, on the other hand, stays where he is and waits for her to cover the nightmarish gap she has to cross, for her to get the better of the tide she is moving against, as though he were afraid that every step she took might drag her backwards, make that distance grow, so it is not until she finally reaches the edge of the table that he moves to meet her, level with the chair, and then the words finally arrive, abruptly and without forethought: "*¿Has dormido bien?*" Did you sleep well? In Spanish, and those words continue to reverberate inside him for a while because Spanish is more deeply rooted inside him than the English they were using yesterday and because that is the very thing he wants to know, the very thing he has been wondering about ever since he opened his eyes in his cabin below: whether their dance has been branded on her retina too, his face on hers like hers on his, and while their sound is still dying away he can hear for himself a note of unbridled eagerness and anxiety because, as he now realises, he is afraid of the answer. And when he gets the answer, in movements of her eyes and tosses of her head that are far from unambiguous, her very evasiveness seems to him to be the closest thing to an admission he could ever imagine, so he snaps two fingers and calls the waiter over with a hint of jubilation in his voice: "*¡Un desayuno continental* *para la señorita!*" Silence falls after that, a silence full of wordless gestures. He takes an unopened packet of Lucky Strikes from his breast pocket and tears off the metallic silver paper that seals the top and then taps the packet against the table to draw out the cigarettes that are wedged tightly together inside. Two or three of them are pushed out by the taps, arranged in various lengths, like the pipes of an organ, he offers the packet to her and she pulls out one and unexpectedly says "*pitillo*", it is one of the words he taught her yesterday when they went up on deck and lit cigarettes in the blustery wind with their hands cupped around the lighter flame, his hands on top of her small ones. Then they say nothing more, as if they were just listening to the clatter the waiter is making behind the counter, as though something, the future? he wonders, had all of a sudden been served on the table before them, amidst the ash and the crumbs he left earlier, and both of them were feeling embarrassed at already considering a future together. And once again it seems to him as though the dream he should have had during the hours of the night were being enacted now, he is watching a large space swaying up and down, populated by two mute figures of whom he is one, he is still astonished and exhilarated and feeling that he has been struck dumb, as it were, by her name, and seen in the daylight, with a flood of light coming off the sea and glancing off the white tablecloths to bring out the contours of her face – the broad, milk-white teeth, floating too, dissolving in the sheen that is diffusing a kind of landscape around itself – the similarities with the face of his youthful idol seem even more striking, and he recalls yet again the scene by the lake when the Forties film star is peering at the sun, and to offset the dizziness he feels he focuses his eyes on the short fingers on which the almost transparent skin sits a little loosely, that improbably white skin does not seem like her own but a second one, a glove made of the silken hide of an unborn calf, and the dial of her narrow watch that has twisted round her wrist to press on her artery is set against that intoxicating surface like a button. He lights the cigarette that sticks out from between two of her fingers and then follows her hand as it moves towards her mouth, and there, in the space defined by her lips, something happens to that landscape that has already unfolded inside him wider and further than he can see, its transparent gleam becomes a rounded softness and a saltiness, the consistency of the meat in a white glam, and with both his eyes and his mouth, with every drag he takes, he is absorbing that luscious swelling sculpted out of the light around her mouth and whose colour, like the cream-coloured shell of a white clam, has revealed the colour of her nipples to him with a blistering and implacable certainty.

Somewhere inside she had been hoping he would not still be sitting there the way he is, alone in the large dining room, his whole body turned towards the door and row upon row of white tables on either side of him, as though he were sitting beside a wall and he were the only way through to what lay beyond it, the waiter is also looking expectantly at her and she feels she has no alternative, she has to confront him and that space he is guarding, she does not have to enter it though, going over to join him does not have to mean anything, not really, behind him there is just a glittering strip of sea after all, a much kinder sea than the one she crossed on her way from England, for that matter; so she decides to go and sit with him even though she is not entirely sure how binding the dances and the windy strolls on deck beneath the cold January moon are or what they mean. She begins to move. Out of the corner of her eye she sees her father's car slowly roll forward alongside her.

"*Pitillo*," he repeats after her, his voice sounds different in Spanish, darker, steadier, as if he were speaking from a larger room, an entire system of rooms, a huge house filled with nooks and crannies and long corridors inhabited by people whose faces she cannot see, and what he wants as he lights her cigarette is for her to enter that unknown house as well and say what it is called in Spanish, *pitil-yo* and her way of pronouncing it makes him smile. Then she chews, swallows and smokes in turns, concentrating on the sequence of movements required to execute those actions as if she were not saying anything because she was too busy and simply did not have the time. Now and then she looks around the empty dining room as if that too were a task she has to perform, she watches the waiter disappearing into the pantry from time to time, her father's black Ford has disappeared too, and it occurs to her that they are very much alone, she is alone with the officer, really alone, and she is surprised to discover an obvious though profound pleasure in that. At the same time the word "officer" makes her think of her mother, the word insists on making a place for itself as it were at the round dining table the doctor's wife loves to lay formally for a celebratory meal, it takes a seat beside the word "hostess" – she is always the hostess, it is emblazoned across her head in the spirals of white hair that curl tightly at the back of her neck and around her forehead – and the fact that the term "officer" encounters so little resistance or, rather, the reverse, it immediately feels at home in her mother's presence, allows her to catch up with the sequence of movements that have led her to the table, as if she were only now confirming the choice her body had made when she returned to him after the night's inter- ruption, as though she knew now she wanted to stay.

That evening they choose a table close to the dance floor, taking deep drags in silence almost, they dance and smoke for most of the following night as well. The songs are in Spanish, she recognises some of them from the previous evening, the singer, however, is wearing a silver-coloured dress this time. Every movement they make serves to confirm to the future the myth of how they met, it will drag her back every time she tries to leave him: the coincidences, the names, winding a steel cable around her waist and the area around her heart. At midnight the singer steps out of the circle of light and the bartender puts on a Nat King Cole record, she has learned the words: *Aquellos ojos verdes, serenos como un lago . . .*

Her sleep is troubled, the woman she is sharing a cabin with is seasick. In the straits of Gibraltar the *Ciudad de Cádiz* is tossed by ferocious winds that reach speeds of up to fifty knots.

The Third Day (January 26, 1959)

When she arrives at the dining room the next morning he is waiting at the same table with breakfast already ordered: an electroplated coffee pot, two cups, bread, jam. Since breakfast the day before they have taken all their meals together, they have already become accustomed to eating together. He asks if he can show her around when they get to Cádiz, "*La tacita de plata*," he says and picks up the coffee cup and points to the silver pot, "that is what Cádiz is called: *tacita de plata*, the little silver cup," though he cannot explain why, because the city was once an island and is connected to the mainland by a sandbank, from a distance it seems to glisten silvery white across the bay like a silver cup, maybe? Then they remind themselves that the vessel they are sailing in is actually called the *Ciudad de Cádiz* and he says: "*Nuestro barquito de plata*, our own little silver ship." In fact the ship is new and modern, built of steel in 1950, although there is another ship that covers the Barcelona–Cádiz run, he tells her as someone who does the journey often, the *Ciudad de la Palma*, it was built in 1930 and used as a prison by the Reds in Barcelona, the prison ships were anchored in the harbour. When war broke out on July 18, 1936, the *Ciudad de la Palma* transported troops on the rebel side between the Balearics, she used to sail at night, with her hull painted black. In 1938 she was converted to a military hospital. During the battle at the river Ebro she took on board huge numbers of wounded and sick. Something somewhere has made him remember his father, maybe the receipt that is lying on the table with the date on it: January 26, it would have been his birthday were he still alive. That is why he is talking about the war.

*

They disembark at Cádiz in blazing sunshine, people turn as they walk arm in arm along the pavement, in a little square-shaped marketplace that faces south are some orange trees and she thinks about the letters from her mother and her photographs of fuchsia-coloured and purple bougainvillea and her description of some delicate, yellow ball-shaped flowers called "mimosa", they are supposed to smell just like a baby's skin, her mother writes. Though that means nothing to her. She thinks about the late doctor's orchids and amaryllis bulbs during the move from Norrland, they filled all of his old official car, the back seat as well as the space between the seats. In what kind of world can flowers outlast a person? On a narrow street with whitewashed houses Gertrud and Salvador drink *vino de Jerez* tapped straight from huge barrels, the yellow stream flows into small glasses, the taverns are smoky and smell dirty and there are no other women in them besides her. At the cathedral he flags down a carriage drawn by a white horse and cries out *¡Al castillo de Santa Catalina!* And the white horse conveys them to a promenade along the beach from where they can see a broad old fortress with a flattened top, the walls of the star-shaped castle meet at five points and it rises halfway out of the sea like a starfish the waves have washed onto the beach. On the back seat of the coach with the Atlantic wind stirring her hair, Gertrud thinks that the wind is pulling so hard at her hair it is making it long, as if a veil were growing out of the crown of her head and she feels like a bride.

It was not melodramas he preferred when he used to go as a lad to see Kristina Söderbaum's films, but war films. His leave over, his father had already returned to the front in Leningrad when he saw "*El gran rey*" ("*Der grosse König*") for the first time and he knew that the opening scene, when the mills are bombed and on fire and Kristina Söderbaum and her family are trying to escape the cannon-balls and the flames in a cart, was rooted in the personal experience of the actors and the thousands of extras who were enacting the scenes and battles of a two-hundred-year-old war, that the cloud of bursting shells and explosive charges he was watching on the screen were inspired by, though not the same as, though not contemporaneous with, the exploding bombs and artillery fire the soldiers of the Wehrmacht, and his father's battalion of Spanish volunteers along with them, had been subjected to by the Red Army, as he could see for himself in the No-Do newsreels[29] (the film clips from the various fronts of the war were the real reason he went to the cinema), just as that the actor who played Frederick the Great of Prussia had quite obviously been imitating Hitler's manner, facial expressions and gestures in his interpretation of the role. As he is sitting in the carriage with Gertrud he remembers the scene after the film star has got married to the sergeant and is slipping her arms into her new bridegroom's uniform jacket, only to have the title of "Frau Sergeant" bestowed on her as a token of respect by her bridegroom's men, and he remembers the way the newly married couple perform a frenzied whirling dance surrounded by clapping soldiers from Frederick the Great's army, because they are both drunk, not so much from the sherry they have consumed but at having met one another, and the ride through a city that used to be an island and is built on sand and the whole of the sea crossing that brought them here seem to him like the honeymoon he never took with his lawfully wedded wife.

Back on the ship they get changed, ready to dance their way through a third night. Upstairs on the dance floor he orders a bottle of champagne and they drink a toast to the memory of his father. "¡Por Salvador Pascual Juliá!" he says, "¡Presente!" After that he tries to teach her the phrase *luna de miel*.[30] Through the panoramic window they can see the sea glittering black like a mirror and they take the bottle with them out on deck. She has a mink stole over her

29   El No-Do: *Noticiarios y Documentales Cinematográficos* were newsreels that were obligatory viewing at cinemas in Spain and its protectorates and colonies before the showing of every feature film between January 1943 and 1975.
30   Honeymoon.

shoulders, it is not at all cold for January and dead calm to port. They sit under the false moonlight of a lantern, her legs crossed and in black pumps that emphasise the beautifully curved line of the upper part of her foot, and this may be the moment it happens: he asks if he can remove one of her shoes, he holds the heel as if it were the base of a crystal glass, pours champagne into the shoe, lifts it to his mouth and drinks.

The Fourth Day (January 27, 1959)

They are out on the Atlantic Ocean, the morning is calm and the sea is barely moving beyond the wake of the ship, the vessel is enveloped in the slow breathing of someone asleep. They manage to find some unoccupied deckchairs on the starboard side and sit there with their backs to the iron railing and their faces to the sun, she gets out one of those little modern cameras and asks him to take a picture of her, she is wearing a moss-green jumper over a dress with a pointed collar folded down, her shapely legs are crossed and palely naked in the sunshine, the line from her ankle to the edge where the low front end of the pumps barely covers the gaps between her toes arouses an explosive desire that pounds against his temples and in his crotch and he raises his right leg to place his booted ankle across his left knee. She must have asked one of their fellow passengers at that point to take a picture of the two of them together. Their heads are turned towards each other, their backs to the sea glinting through the railing, his right boot across his left thigh pointing towards her crossed legs, she is angling her legs to one side as if to crawl in under the protection of the boot, her right arm around his left, their joined arms firmly supported by the arm rest, they are looking into one another's eyes and laughing at each other, not at the camera. When she disembarked at the island some time later she was quick to buy a pretty photo album taller than it was wide with a crocodile-skin pattern on the outside and gold marbling on the inside of the covers that she filled with the photographs of their first year together. On the first page, beside the words *Ciudad de Cádiz, January 24–9, 1959*, a large photograph of Sal is displayed with his arms crossed and leaning against the deck railing, two smaller photographs – the size of negatives – show her leaning against the same railing, with her mink stole around her shoulders, sunglasses and a handbag hanging from her bent arm, another shows the two of them standing close together. The second large photograph on the first page shows the two of them at a round table, he has his arm around her back, and below, in her narrow slanting handwriting, are the words: *Bella Napoli 29/1*. They must have disembarked at Tenerife on January 29 as a couple, and continued dancing their very first night on the island, at a dance hall they would later return to: another photograph some way inside the album shows them locked in a close embrace on the dance floor, her arm around his neck, he is in civvies and she is wearing a striped dress, below the photograph are the words *Bella Napoli*. On the last page are some new pictures of them on the deck of another ship: the *Ciudad de la Palma, November 1959*. The album thus completes a circle, it begins and ends with a cruise to and from the island of Tenerife. In between are pictures of the foreign legionnaire in various locations, with her and Ma Rosa while he was on leave on Tenerife and Gran Canaria, in Seville and Madrid, though there are pictures too that he must have sent her of his life in the desert: on manoeuvres, hunting scenes, military drills, him drinking from a cup surrounded by his men, marches and parades. An aerial photograph of the fort (*Hagunia*). *Bullfight on the First of May* and posters of the matador Curro Girón who killed six bulls in Santa Cruz on that day. The two of them together on a beach with huge white stones, him in the water, below some black rocks. Him with two Dama gazelles that had been shot in front of the El Aaiún fort, a dead gazelle in each hand.

*

In the deckchairs the conversation switches to language lessons, it amuses him that her Spanish is so literary (*¡Hablas como Cervantes!*), she had read selected passages from *Don Quijote* in the tropical diseases ward of the hospital, with a thick square dictionary wedged alongside her on the narrow bed, in preparation for the trip to see her mother on the island with the black sand beaches, and now he is teaching her the correct pronunciation of the Spanish consonants, like the lisping sounds in *Ciudad de Cádiz* or the "j" in *ojo, ojos verdes* (green eyes, like yours) and listen to that "r". Rrrr, it is rolled. But getting the "r" to roll is difficult, the alien sound rasps against her uvular though it fails to roll at all and the guttural sound between the "o"s in *ojos* makes so much saliva form around the root of her tongue she feels as if she has to spit. He laughs at all of this. She laughs too. They communicate in borrowed languages, their thoughts tottering along as though on crutches, but so long as they can laugh together the illusion can be sustained that they understand one another deep down inside, below the surface in the realm of the unspoken, the unspoken can easily be confused with the truth.

She wants to know more about his life in the Sahara desert and he tells her about the fort, the drills in the yard, his men singing the Legionnaires' hymn as they return home at dusk (*... soy un novio de la muerte que va a unirse en brazo fuerte con tal leal compañeraaa ...*).[31] Although what he can see almost immediately are the leaves of the plane tree quivering and rustling outside a narrow balcony on a square in the Ramblas where he had slept every night of that week, the room smells of turpentine and cigarette smoke and sometimes the woman he sleeps with there while on leave wants her room-mate to join in, *maintenant avec elle, je veux le voir*,[32] (you know that the woman your father used to see on leave in Barcelona before he met

31 "I am Death's bridegroom who will be united in a lasting embrace with this the most faithful of companions ..."
32 "With her now, I want to watch."

your mother was French although she has never had a name). Wafts of chicken soup and the camphor in the wardrobes in the large flat in the upper part of the city where his mother lives drift through his head as well, and the cries of children and the sound of their little feet slapping the stone floor in the corridor at night. Though it is all flickering through his head like scenes from a film, one he does not know. Gertrud's face, that is where he is now, the woman he calls Gitt, that is all there is. He tells her that all the great soldiers have been moulded in the desert, Franco especially, the War of Liberation (*Guerra de Liberación*, can she say that?) began in Morocco, he says he was hoping for a war when he applied to serve in the Spanish Sahara, that war is the proper situation for a military man, *la guerra* (can she say that?) has been his vocation for as long as he can remember.

¡Viva la muerte! Long live Death! That cry in the desert both frightens and appeals to her, as if that frenzy for death were capable of giving him the upper hand, of subjugating it, of bending it to his will. She says that she was born one month after the beginning of the Second World War, to her war means her mother in the uniform of the women's voluntary defence service and a huge pile of children's shoes being collected for donation to the children of war-torn Finland. She wonders how the boy he waved to on the dockside fits into the picture but dares not ask. He keeps talking about the war. Finland was on the side of the Germans, he says, like Spain, side by side against the Communists. A couple of photographs show them leaning against the railing on a lower deck, he is in uniform and she is wrapped in the mink stole, everything apart from the wooden rail is painted white, even the round loudspeaker that sticks out in the background. They stand at the railing for a while staring down at the ship's wake, the strip of foam latches on to a tender place in her belly, if she were to let go she would be pulled along with it, that stretch of water would lead her to a gate by the gently flowing Neckar where two German parents are grieving for their young son. She

could see the straight path running from the gate to the main entrance, the bronze knocker with a lion's head on the white door she never got to touch, minute after minute she found herself standing at one end of the moon's watery reflection across sharp white gravel, his parents had written to her informing her of his death, it might have done them good to have met their son's last (and maybe first) love, to see their grief reflected in her eyes and in them a reflection perhaps of their son's face, she would have entered the house she has never been inside and where he had grown up, walked on thick carpets that would have meant she had to take off her shoes to display her injured leg, prove to them that she had been touched by the same fate that took their son from them. But for every minute that passed it became harder and harder to step into a garden filled with light reflected off water: so eerily still, no butterflies or bees to be seen, no trace of birds or birdsong in the air, as if there were no air at all, the air was only on her side of the gate, a little pocket of air she was inhaling in short, shallow breaths. The wind picks up, her hair is being tugged this way and that, she wants to go to the cabin below to fetch a scarf.

They eat lunch, then they sit on the port side facing the invisible African coast, the long nights and the pitch of the ship make her feel drowsy, she leans her head back from time to time and then closes her eyes so that her face is bathed in all this strangeness that is not solely the product of light as it approaches the equator, what sailors call "the Line", in the orange-tinted darkness behind her eyelids she can sense something shifting in time and space as if her conscious mind were trying to encompass every place and every generation, the attraction she feels for the soldier sitting beside her seems to be expanding all the possible connections, like a force that is making her want to catch up with those fifteen years that separate them and emerge from a shell that has been feeling more confining with every port they have left behind, his uniform alone appears to outweigh the petit-bourgeois life her mother had been busy managing at home (and had now abandoned on board a banana boat running between the Canary Islands and Copenhagen) and all its comfortably controlled prosperity an enforced tone of frugality notwithstanding (the doctor's wife's bridge evenings were only a distant echo of the grand three-course dinners with a written menu and assigned seating her mother would give as the partner of the district medical officer during her childhood); although as she remembers when a gust of wind brings with it a waft of seaweed and salt and the ship's propellor is shredding a wave with wanton violence, her maternal great-grandfather was a captain based in the port city of Sundsvall and the dark uniform of a naval officer she has seen in photographs forms a kind of opposite pole to the black-belted grey coat of the handsome legionnaire; a corridor is opening in the space between these two figures that leads straight out onto the sundrenched surface of a stretch of water that streets and houses are slowly sliding towards: the apartment and the entire building on Ymergatan that her newly widowed mother moved into with her siblings and her, the apartment that is empty now because her mother has left it for a whitewashed villa situated high up in the city of Santa Cruz, its garden coloured by incomprehensible foreign words for scents (bougainvillea, mimosa), her mother writes that there is a flame burning at night above the terrace from the chimney of a nearby oil refinery, does the smoke clash with the unimaginable scent of mimosa? Her mother writes long letters that she used to read and fall asleep over in the hospital and afterwards at home in Uppsala, in the dark-red wing-backed chair by the open fire, she writes about flowers and three-thousand-year-old trees and about the teeming rain that washes the dirt from the steep streets and carries it down to the harbour, one photograph was taken in colour, her mother's skin glistens golden-brown the way it did during the summers in Piteå when they used to play Cowboys and Indians and build little cabins under the pine trees, then she sees the half-submerged black Ford filled with rippling orchids floating behind the raised windows beside the back seat, the seas merge, her thoughts lack a shore, there is only water, water as far as the eye can see, she screws up her eyes and with a great deal of effort manages to force the water to recede, although what is behind her eyelids is not the gravel in the courtyard and the row of windows with their edged curtains – one, two, three all the way to the other side of the house – nor the ramp to the basement that served as the entrance to the bomb shelter for the entire neighbourhood and that had submarine-like doors made of iron painted grey, but endless expanses of water alternating with sand, a desert landscape with a fort outlined against the horizon that horses and camels have passed by, leaving tracks that are like the letters of the alphabet, her mother is sitting wearing a blue dress on one of the camels, the island the rocking boat is approaching has a snow-clad mountain at its centre and because she cannot understand how that can be, the snow turns into a white growth covering the top of the mountain, the brittle dropped strands of an old woman's hair, the white snow a secret phrase in the other's eyes, which is why the words he used yesterday return to her like a cold kiss: he is a legionnaire, a "Bridegroom of Death", he said, "*un novio de la muerte*", and she opens her eyes at the very moment the crest of a powerful wave makes the vessel rear and sink with a splash of steel, she shuts her eyes again immediately, there is no shoreline or horizon in her mind, against the transparent sky the black gleam of weapons, the ship's hull is crashing against a kind of rippling callosity over and over again and the shocks shift her attention to her stomach where a pit is whirling in concentric rings, she throws her head back and closes her eyes against the increasing roll of the ship, her tongue pressed up against her palate as though she had trapped something there, the vessel subjected to the same centrifugal force that is eddying in her stomach, as though the vessel, and she along with it, had been exposed to a magnetic field. The invisible African coast appears abruptly in her mind's eye, edged in crimson along with the mystery of her mother's cousin who enlisted in the British army and disappeared without trace in South Africa during the First World War, a titillating conundrum that would be brought up during the clatter of china cups around the coffee table in the little drawing room when the old ladies came to visit; she closes her eyes so tightly that her eyelids cut into her skin in an attempt to get rid of both the whirling motion in her stomach and the tossing of the ship that appear to be part of the same irresistible process, she shuts her eyes so tightly that her eyelashes are turned inwards towards the thin skin beneath her eyes, as doggedly as if she were resolved to halt the ship's headlong plunge towards that old, dark disappearance.

The periods of silence afforded by her silent sunbathing provide him with a watering hole, where he can rest the grinding, cleansing excitement the girl's proximity evokes, he runs his fingers over it, turning and twisting it this way and that until he can feel the damp-sodden cross-draught in the long corridor that is the distinguishing feature of his parental home, as though he would soon no longer need to return to his mother's home on Calle Balmes once he has spent the night with a woman other than the one he is married to. He can see the pointed tip of the girl's shoe, it has ended up at an angle to the left of his field of vision, as well as the upper part of her foot and the ankle, the nylon stocking shimmering in the sunlight on her crossed legs, and he is struck once again by the thought that Leningrad lies on roughly the same latitude as Stockholm, as though this girl, so fragile beneath that unpigmented skin, were a vessel for something much larger than herself; and he is thinking about his father and his agonising death three years earlier at the military hospital in Barcelona, what he would have thought of her, would she have reminded him of the Russian peasant girls on the Volkhov front, of the girl in the *izba* (the cottage) where he was quartered his first winter, of the peasant family who gave him the little icon, if only he had lived another three years, if only cancer had not stolen his life in that humiliating hospital bed, surrounded by the rustling of the nuns' starched aprons; and he can see a road of loose logs running through a birch forest in Novgorod, corduroy roads across the swampy ground south of Lake Ilmen, *Knüppeldämme* as the Germans called them, his father's eyes as he described the *rasputitsa* (the mud) the summer he came home on leave (the summer of 1942).

That evening she looks for him at the bar where the dance band is setting up, he is sitting in the same spot they were in yesterday. The fact that it is the last evening is preoccupying him more than the fact that she has spent a large part of the afternoon in her cabin slowly tossing some of their hours overboard from her bed. She is wearing the same green taffeta dress as she did on the first evening and he views that as a bad omen because he does not like closed circles, anything and everything that comes to an end. How is she feeling? And like the first evening she orders a Coca-Cola, without rum (not a *cubalibre*), and this new signal makes his pulse beat faster. It has been announced that the singer is unwell and so it is the pianist who is singing "*Aquellos ojos verdes*", imitating Nat King Cole's American accent. He looks at the clock, how many hours have they got left? The hours she has spent on her own seem to have locked her inside herself, her arms are crossed as she sits looking over the dance floor, disinclined to communicate with him, turned inwards and listless as though she did not want or did not have the energy to stay with him, as though she had discovered something among her things in her cabin below and changed her mind, or as though she had not only been vomiting the food and the drinks they had consumed into the sink but their time together as well, the time of long looks and shivers and the palms of their hands burning against one another as he held her close and almost grazed her lips with his mouth. He can see her now at her mother's house in Santa Cruz, smiling on the terrace like a good little girl (she has shown him a photograph of the elegant woman with snow-white hair and a matching blue silk dress with a pattern of white flowers standing amidst the hanging branches of bougainvillea), and the sight leaves him cold because he is not there, she will already have forgotten him when she is standing on that terrace, what has been might never have happened, and a peculiar effect of this prospective invisibility, his approaching non-existence in her life, is to erase the days that have passed as well, erasing his entire person, as though not just their meeting but he too had never existed, or worse, much, much worse, had been forgotten, because there is a certain compensation in memory and loss, a sweetness that is well suited to military manoeuvres and alcohol, but being erased, forgotten . . . He looks at her, sitting there with her arms crossed, gulping down one *pitillo* after another without any moderation at all, and what he had found appealing to this point, a desire comparable to his, now evokes a certain distaste (like the terrible hunger of the war, that Russian word *golod*). He is overcome with a sudden rage, the path the stifled cry would take from his lungs to his throat makes him hear the way his father kept wheezing in the hospital, his sunken ribcage would only rise at long, protracted intervals, the sounds of choking that used to erupt in that room, as if he had been underwater for a long time and had managed to get to the surface, managed for another few seconds to expel the water of that Russian lake that had trickled into his lungs at the end, the lake around which he had seen his comrades fall, men wheezing in the snow in Krasny Bor, the worst thing was to go on living, eating, sleeping and to have to come home as though nothing had happened while they remained under a wooden cross in a little dump called Mestelevo or some such name. He thinks of the crowds waiting for the arrival of the *Semiramis* at the dockside in Barcelona, the same quay from which she and he embarked four days ago, the ship was transporting a little more than three hundred members of the Division who had spent ten years in Stalin's gulags, some of the passengers had been children evacuated during the war and allowed to return by Franco, most had been soldiers who fought alongside Hitler. He decides to break the silence with that story, because it is the last night and everything already seems lost, so he tests the name *Hitler* out on her, he studies her face and sees her lips just become lax and still, her eyes have become still as well, the soldiers who were shipped home on the *Semiramis* fought with Hitler against Communism, he stresses, and tells her that the *Semiramis* had docked with the last of the "expeditionaries" at the port in Barcelona just five years ago, in April 1954, an excited crowd of people were jostling on the quay and he was among them, his own father had been one of the volunteers, but he had survived unharmed for a whole year and had been repatriated in March 1943, six months before the entire division, *la División Azul* in Spanish, was recalled, his father had been an officer in the service corps, he led convoys of ammunition and essential supplies along the Volkhov front and later along the front outside Leningrad, he also became the officer who paid out the wages. Though he did not die there, he assures her, but in Barcelona three years ago, of cancer of the mediastinum, and as he confronts her with an unfamiliar term she fails to understand, he points with his palm open to a point between his lungs, the mediastinum is the area between the lungs, he says, it includes the heart and the oesophagus and the windpipe. Her right arm suddenly drops into her lap, it had been lying across her ribcage until now as a support for the other, vertical forearm that is holding a cigarette, her hand sinks down to lie open, turned upwards, the left hand still a smoking mast with a glowing cigarette at the top. "My father died of a heart attack," she says, and that sentence unleashes a burst of energy that makes her torso twist around and the horizontal arm rise and land a little further up to the left but on top of his hand. the site of their father's deaths turns out to be the same, the hollow space inside their ribcages where the pumping susurration of the blood rises and falls towards the walls of the intestines, and the indifference she had been feeling – what was the cause of it though? – is replaced with reverence, everything falls silent around them, as though they had together entered the space inside a church.

Regiones Devastadas,[33] C/ Balmes 297, Barcelona,
Spain,
Monday, January 26, 1942

"God is on our side, never forget that," (*Dios está de nuestra parte*) says the former engineer and entrepreneur Salvador Pascual Juliá, "and He is this time as well," he emphasises; the entrepreneur, who retrained to serve as the soldier he currently is and whose war record has seen him promoted to lieutenant, has just asked his son José María, who is sitting closest to the radio set, to turn it off, as the maid Pilar is putting the soup bowls on the table (the soup she had to reheat twice because the grand military parade went on longer than expected, the trams were packed and the family got home late), and it is time to say grace. General Franco is on a state visit to Barcelona and Radio Nacional has just broadcast an extract from Mayor Mateus' speech of welcome that the family have already listened to live and in its entirety, standing among the crowd fifty or so metres from the podium on Paseo de Gracia from where *El Caudillo* reviewed the troops of war veterans filing past him on parade; the fact that General Franco is making an official visit on the third anniversary of the liberation of Barcelona, which is today, is considered a good omen by the head of the family, because this very day the passport is being despatched he will need to travel to Irún at the French border early tomorrow morning, and then on to Hendaye, the departure point for the expedition with the *División Española de Voluntarios*, also known as the *División Azul*,[34] to the Eastern front; and today is also his birthday, which the family are planning to celebrate as well.

33 Devastated Regions.
34 Spanish Volunteer Division, the unit was also called the Blue Division.

"Señor, bendice estos alimentos."[35]

Tula, his mother-in-law, who had to stay at home because of her gout, wants to hear more about the parade and asks if a Mass was held as it was in 1939 and, if so, where the altar and the huge cross were placed. There was no celebration of the Mass this time, it turns out, and the boys take over the conversation and begin to list the regiments and artillery pieces for their *abuela*. Pilar, a young girl from Zaragoza, fairly new in service and as a result perhaps a bit flushed around the cheeks, nervous about the important task of preparing this banquet (she fed the capon that had been tied up for a whole week in a wooden crate in the kitchen and has butchered and gutted the confused and depressed bird, following her mistress' recipe and her instructions to the letter, as well as having to improvise in the end because the family were so late), takes out the empty soup plates and comes back in again almost immediately with the capon the young maid had the foresight to remove from the oven half way through cooking and put back in again when the family eventually came home, golden brown and shiny with fat it has been placed beside the carving knife in front of the head of the household and is now encircled by the reflections of the sunlight playing off the crystal glasses standing on the figured damask tablecloth Señora Dolores keeps at the very back of the linen cupboard. Then Lieutenant Salvador Pascual Juliá gets to his feet and begins to twist the wire on the champagne bottle, the expensive wine a gift from his wife's relatives in Falset, in the wine-growing area of Priorat, Tarragona, which arrived together with the capon that had been alive until yesterday. Later he will remember the afternoon sun falling on the table on this last day before his departure for a training camp in Germany, during his first early spring at the Volkhov front when *the sun is cold and colourless behind a greyish sky and hangs low over our heads like a dirty cloth and that only for a short period in the middle*

35   "Lord, bless this food."

of the day, he will write in his letters, *evening comes early, as if God has suddenly grown tired of seeing our misery and is turning that dirty cloth the other way round, the back is even filthier, dingy instead of the velvet black our night skies usually are, and without a single star, for even the light of the stars is denied us*; the oblique rays of the sun that are immersing the dining room in an anachronistic midsummer light, like that of ripe wheat fields before dusk, the extraordinary flood of gold bathing the room will accompany him, together with the prismatic facets of the crystal glasses that are scattering the same light over the gleaming tablecloth, in some way he knows that already, even while he is being feted by his wife, his mother-in-law and his children. His eldest son, Salvador, known as Sal, is still feeling exhilarated by the military parade and by seeing Franco, he has already applied to the Air Force Academy and both envy and pride at his father's mission to Russia (*¡Rusia es culpable!*)[36] are reflected in the steel sheen of his blue eyes, but the seventeen-year-old is a bit too restless and daring, bordering on rash at times, too handsome for his own good besides, despite that crooked broken nose of his, the lieutenant is concerned about him; in the velvet brown eyes of José María, his younger son, who is just as excited about the great events in the city, he can detect caution, however, a suppressed anxiety, he is the more sensible of the two, more like himself, both physically and mentally, unlike the older son who he fears has too many traits in common with his own father . . . Fortunately the brothers are very close, the year they spent living together in Galicia has left its mark in many ways, deepened a brotherhood that is spiritual as well, Sal would cross fire and flood for his brother, of that he is certain, and José María will stand by him, will be his dazzling big brother's more sensible conscience, they will soon be men, the two of them,

36   "Russia is to blame!" A notorious declaration by Spanish Foreign Minister Ramón Serrano Suñer on receiving the news of Germany's attack on the Soviet Union, June 22, 1941. His phrase would become the motto of the men of the Blue Division.

he pours the sparkling wine into their glasses, and even the much younger María Rosa gets given a drop or two in the end. Then he picks up the knife and starts carving through the crispy skin of the roasted bird, beneath it the pale flesh is juicy and tender, well done the new girl Pilar, such a competent lass behind those usually lowered fair eyelashes of hers. Mother-in-law Tula is offered the first thigh but cries "*No! No vull cuixa!*" in Catalan, and as though that was the funniest thing in the world bursts into a roar of laughter that makes her large body shake in the chair, *No thigh for me, thanks.* She prefers the breast, she assures him, using the Spanish word *pechuga* instead, give the thighs to the children, she says, still in gales of laughter, and then she wants to hear more about the parade. He finds himself thinking about his mother-in-law, the mother-in-law who took in his wife and daughter when war broke out, and about the family's eventual reunion just over a year later, he is thinking about the two years his sons and Dolores and six-year-old María Rosa had to traipse along the front in Madrid in order to be close to him, an area that is now under the jurisdiction of the General Direction of Devastated Regions (*Dirección General de Regiones Devastadas*), he is remembering the houses they moved into, the rooms with the furniture and clothes of strangers in them, in the apartment in Valdemoro the table had even been laid for a party, as now, with food left over and a rock-hard crust of bread the boys used for a ball game in the corridor afterwards, he remembers the colour photo-graphs, *cromos*, that were left behind and that the boys found in the bedroom they took over, a picture of a "rat", a Russian I-16, and one of a foreign female journalist killed in Brunete, he remembers the woman's short haircut, the hand camera that almost completely covered her face like a mask, and then he remembers the hill outside the town they went on outings to in the afternoons and from where you could see the front and the fighter planes engaging in combat, José María has no desire to be a pilot, as Sal does, which makes him glad. Dolores, sitting to his left, also wants *pechuga*, he carves off the best piece and tries to catch her eye as he places it on her plate but she is still sulking: *"Tu ja has lluitat tres anys contra els rojos! Que hi vagin altres ara!"*[37] she had howled at him when his call-up papers arrived two days ago, *"Que hem de fer? Deixar que regnin obrers i porteres com fan ara a Rússia?"*[38] was his reply. She refuses to look in his direction, he can see her in semi-profile, the bright sheen of her skin beneath the plucked eyebrows shaped in an arch above her eyes, velvet brown like José María's, he looks at the long line of her nose that Sal has inherited and the narrow, heavily made-up lips that no longer laugh as readily as they used to, no longer hum songs, she wanted to be a singer and was in the papers as a teenager. Dolores feels she has had to go through so much already, too much: the terror she experienced that first year of the war when she was alone in Barcelona with their little daughter while the boys and he ended up on the side of the rebels, that awful day when she was forced to abandon the villa on Plaça Bonanova in haste when the neighbourhood church on the other side of the street, whose side elevation was visible from every window in the villa, started to burn. The La Salle brothers in the school further up the street had been the first to be visited by a patrol from the Partido Obrero de Unificación Marxista the day after the rebellion, July 19, and the headmaster was taken to the interrogation centre (the *cheka*) at the Hotel Colón, while the grocer on Bonanova Square, "major capitalist" that he was, would be confined in the *cheka* on Carrer Ganduxer, never to be seen again. His wife and daughter fled here after that, to his parents-in-law's apartment, and it was here that they suffered the greatest betrayal. Not even María Rosa, thirteen years old now, has forgotten the former caretaker and her daughter Carmen, the person who denounced Dolores' brothers, Artemio and Bienvenido, to a Red

37 "You've already spent three years fighting the Reds, let other people take them on this time."
38 "What are we to do? Are we to be ruled by labourers and women caretakers the way they are in Russia?"

patrol which led to them ending up in the *cheka* on Carrer Vallmajor, along with the neighbour on the floor above, who was taken away "for a walk" (*paseo*), executed by gunmen (*pistoleros*) and dumped on some wasteland. The same María Rosa, his daughter who is sitting on his right, is the only person whose face he cannot see, her head is bowed over her plate and her hands are resting loosely on the edge of the table, her fair hair covers her cheek with the soft sheen of billowing fields of wheat in June – June, when he will not be here – and she has barely touched her food. And because he cannot get her to look him in the eye, what sticks to his mind instead is the piece of skin that has been placed at the edge of her plate, that is what he will remember, a memory to suck on later in the trenches the Germans had dug between several residential areas in the suburbs south of Leningrad (the rough piece of skin wedged deeply into his gum, so slippery and tough he can trace every ridge on its surface with his tongue while the artillery of the besieged is firing at the residential suburb and the word *golod*, hunger, clicks against the front of his alveolar ridge with a snap of his tongue every time a sniper shoots from the besieged city). But on this his birthday, January 26, 1942, when he is still in his home town of Barcelona and has not yet got on the train to Hendaye or sworn fealty to Hitler in the German city of Hof, or arrived on the line of the Volkhov front where he will drive convoys in minus 30 degrees, his thoughts flick back to the war he has already lived and known, to the hills clad in holm oaks around Boadilla del Monte where he was transferred from the front at Casa del Campo in Madrid at the beginning of April 1937, what would become known as the battle of Brunete began for his part when he was put in charge of six members of the Guardia Civil and six Falangists and ordered to defend the front line at Boadilla del Monte while under ferocious attack from enemy planes and a protracted artillery bombardment (Núñez the Falangist who crawled under a bush to find the arm that had been blown off and bled to death under a pine tree with his upside-down arm resting on the centre of his chest as if it were a crucifix, the sphere on the dial of his watch where Christ's face should have shone), until the infantry could relieve them three days later; the rest of that July he ran supply convoys over the dusty mountain roads edged by holm oaks where the trucks would get stuck in the beds of dried-up streams, Boadilla del Monte, Romanillos, Villafranca del Castillo, back and forth over the hills and the shot-up villages under a sun that shone dully as if covered by a weeping scab, the waxy haze across the sky, the air filled to bursting with the growling of motor engines and the enemy's artillery and on the other side of the haze the stumpy Russian "rats" and their orange wingtips, light and swift as vermin "the rats" would attack their planes from below, aiming at their bellies, exactly the way rats do; heat and dust, uphill and down dale, in the dusk, to the clamour of the crickets, the heavily bullet-damaged tower of Villafranca's castle serving as a landmark in the moonlight; one convoy after the other in the scorching heat, 38 degrees in the shade, and under heavy fire (in the bakery he was ordered to set up in Villafranca del Castillo the flour would seep out of the burst sacks, hundreds of freshly baked loaves on the floor and the air filled with a fog of wasted flour), until the Germans arrived to rescue them in the middle of the month and the sky was filled with new noises, with the rattling din of Messerschmitt Bf 109s. He is remembering the cheers of the soldiers in the canteen as he swirls the contents of his glass, rolling the liquid round and round so the carbon dioxide is dissolved. By the time darkness fell on July 25 the cemetery in Brunete had ended up on their side once and for all, he remembers that night at the forefront of the battle as being filled with appalling sounds, the enemy lines so close you could hear the voices of the soldiers, the enemy's slogans, the Reds would try to convert them, to get them to come over, the pay was higher, the food better, they threw cigarettes, droned on about the class struggle, every now and then someone would burst out laughing or into song, someone would be weeping, though not the Moroccans in the Ifni Sahara company

228

who sang wailing dirges that got on his nerves, the infernal din, the infernal heat, the Brunete sector had been bombed to bits, seventeen thousand lost on their side alone during the month-long battle. But the Red Hydra was demanding still more. His call-up papers arrived two days ago, January 24, today he will be forty-six years old. Everything has been arranged, it is all settled, every month his wife Dolores will receive a salary that matches that of the Spanish Foreign Legion (the best paid company in the country) while he is in Russia and another from the German Wehrmacht, he will have to get by on his campaign pay (*Wehrsold*), the extra payment for serving at the Front (*Frontzulage*) and the clothing allowance (*Bekleidungsentschädigung*). And if God wills it he will return – back here, to this room, to its balcony and the afternoon sun, to the people sitting around the laid table, as they are now, chattering, their mouths full of food – victorious and still whole in life and limb. The cutlery clatters against the china, the little one (*la peque*) asks what's for pudding. Sunlight is streaming obliquely through the windowpanes and the last rays scatter burning gold across the lieutenant's eyes, he is restless, he is tired, he wants this protracted farewell to end so he raises his glass and proposes a toast, the words come naturally to him, unquestioned, the security he has found in the military is not so much to do with the regular wages he is paid every month as a civil servant, that is not the kind of security he values, the kind that allows him to avoid the solitary torments of the entrepreneur, it is the stability of the structure generated by concepts such as *honour*, *order*, *God* that allows him to feel calm, free, which is why he looks around at his family and exclaims in the very same phrases he has uttered in Spanish every morning at the flagpole in the barracks for the last six years: "*¡Por Dios y por la Patria!*" and "*¡Viva Cristo Rey!*"[39]

*

39 "For God and Fatherland. Long Live Christ the King!"

A few hours later and the whole family are about to attend evening Mass at their old neighbourhood church Santa Maria de la Bonanova, which is opposite the three-storey detached house they lived in before the civil war. It is evening and because street lighting is restricted to the bare minimum – the supply of gas and electricity has been drastically reduced and is subject to repeated stoppages – the boys will be walking ahead of them in charge of the carbide lamp, they have tossed for it and it is Sal's turn to carry the lamp on the way there, so he opens the valve that regulates the flow of water while the rest of the family wait inside the relative warmth of the entrance lobby, once the gas has had time to form, Sal lights the wick and a powerful white flame illuminates the concave silvery reflector. *"¡Ya podéis salir!"*[40] he shouts to the others who come out of the iron front door one by one looking dazzled and screwing up their eyes, and he adds, while his mother screens her eyes with her right hand: *"¡Perros catalanes!"*[41] That just slips out of him unbidden only once it has been said he smiles that crooked smile of his beneath the broken nose that seems more crooked than usual in the light of the acetylene gas. Though his father heard the bass voice his son put on to imitate the words of a frequently quoted priest, that does not stop him from stepping straight up to Sal, the palm of his hand open and frozen in the air, on its way to being a slap: *"¡Cuidado con las bromas que gastas!"*[42] But his wife intervenes: *"¡Deixa'l, sembla que el cop que es va fumbre a la piscina l'ha deixat una mica sonat!"*[43] Then the boy's younger sister María Rosa giggles and his hand drops until it is level with the handle of the carbide lamp which it wrenches from Sal's grasp. The carbide lamp gets passed to José María, who accepts it reluctantly and gravely. The entire family remains standing there for a while on the dimly lit pavement, alone for the whole of the long

40 "You can come out now."
41 "Catalan curs!"
42 "Be careful of making jokes like that."
43 "Just ignore him, it looks like the knock he got at the pool has made him crazy."

sloping street, alone in the entire city or so it would seem. They turn to the left in silence and start walking up Calle Balmes, José María at the front with the carbide lamp in one hand and an unlit wax candle in the other, followed by Sal and María Rosa who are also holding a wax candle each to light in church, the married couple walk arm in arm at the rear; like a sign of things to come a thick layer of frost is sparkling festively in the flickering acetylene light and in the glow of the few lit streetlamps they pass on the lengthy uphill path, the nocturnal procession reminds them all of their walk to Midnight Mass almost exactly a month ago and the recollection of Christmas raises the girl's spirits, she asks her brother to aim the lamp at the ground and says it looks like the Holy Virgin has scattered diamonds along their path. "*¿La Vírgen? ¡Pero qué cursi eres, niña!*",[44] Sal says with a snort to his younger sister in Spanish. "*¡Salvador! ¡No seas bruto, hombre!*"[45] his mother scolds, in Spanish as well. His father decides to ignore his bad behaviour this time, he has been thinking about him, his first-born son, the one who was given his name, how wild he is and unmanageable, he is remembering the boy standing on the platform last summer after he had just been put off the train transporting the first contingent of volunteers to Russia, his then sixteen-year-old son stood there straight-backed and smiling as though he did not feel an ounce of shame, he returned his deliberately severe gaze without blinking and the boy's eyes were pure and steady, unafraid, *noble*. They'll lick him into shape at the Air Force Academy in any case. The lieutenant sighs, recalling his own raised hand of a moment ago, he has only ever slapped the boys on one occasion, and that was a long while back, the reason he is going is mainly for their sake, he is grateful that Providence has so arranged it that he can fight this new war in their stead. An icy gust of wind hits them head on and makes them all hunch over as they turn in to Bonanova Avenue, Dolores winds María Rosa's scarf, which had

44   "The Holy Virgin? What a ninny you are."
45   "Salvador! Don't be so rude."

been hanging loosely around the collar of her coat, so it covers the whole of her throat and neck up to her mouth, then she pulls tight around her own head the thin lace shawl that she is wearing to go to church in a rather vain attempt to protect herself from the cold nipping at her ears, she is holding her husband's arm and walking close beside him at the same steady pace, she notices her husband looking ahead, attentive to every word and gesture of his sons and daughter, and assumes that is his way of saying goodbye, against the light of the carbide lamp they look like silhouettes in a shadow play, she thinks, as they walk in front of them, the girl far too young to become fatherless, the cold wind feels as though it were making her worries greater, lending them a greater resonance. Thank God it's not far now. When they reach Plaça Bonanova they are all breathless from the cold and their efforts and the scarf around María Rosa's mouth is wet with condensation. Before they enter the church, which is in the process of being given a completely new facade as part of the still ongoing restoration work, both the adults glance furtively at the old whitewashed and undamaged villa that beckons from one corner of the square, Sal and José María ask if they can go over and look at their former home but it is almost eight o'clock and the service is about to begin. Complete silence reigns inside though the church is only half full, the verger is lighting the lamp above the side chapel dedicated to *la Mare de Déu dels Afortunats*, the Madonna of Good Fortune, *la Vírgen de los Afortunados*, as they are supposed to say now, in Spanish, so no other priest can accuse them of being curs, it is there they will place their candles once the new parish priest (the old one, the venerable Father Lluis, was appointed to the prelacy by the Pope at the beginning of 1936 and died a martyr's death during the arson attack that almost completely destroyed the church) has blessed them. They take their seats close to the chapel and try to warm their feet by making various soundless movements and without stamping them on the floor. Then the new priest finally comes out of the sacristy, followed by a choirboy holding a smoking thurible. The lieutenant is pleased to be able to take the sacrament one last time together with his wife and children, he usually does so alone every morning, and it was alone that he took this decision. He did not sign up for the volunteer battalion until it was clear that the German attack on the Soviet Union had come to a grinding halt at Leningrad and Moscow and that the United States had been drawn into the war, and until the immediate enthusiasm that had characterised the first contingent of volunteers in Spain and that had filled the stations across the country with people cheering and saluting in July, including his own son, had waned once some of first expeditionaries returned home with limbs amputated because of the cold and, in the light of what they had to say about conditions in Russia, the number of men signing up was now far lower. The choir boy is standing below the altar, swinging the thurible back and forth, and the pendulum movement has a hypnotic quality. The gravity of the moment and the fact that General Franco has given his blessing as it were to his decision by visiting the city on this particular day, the date on which their troops liberated Barcelona, which is also his birthday, and Dolores' presence on her knees beside him, her head bowed beneath the black veil and her clasped hands resting on the prayer stool, the taste of the Communion wafer in his mouth, the memory of the births of their three children, the acrid smoke from the incense filling his lungs, the vision of the Holy Virgin in the damaged and soot-stained reredos that had been saved, allow him to conceive of this Mass as a second wedding, a secret and more holy marriage.

Then the night had passed and he took the train to Irún.

Accompanied by their three children, Dolores had brought with her the black lace shawl she wore to Mass when she waved him off at the station from the platform the next day; just before he took his seat in the compartment already filled with other war veterans who were introducing themselves and telling each other which regiments they had served in and which sections of the front they had defended during their wars, she had pressed the veil into his hand and he had accepted it with a slightly embarrassed gesture and shoved it quickly into the inside breast pocket of his coat. He has not felt bold enough until now to pull out the fragrant veil more than once, and it was not until his travelling companions had fallen asleep that he undid the top buttons of his jacket and cautiously brought it out; the shawl writhed out of his breast pocket like a tame snake until it lay across his chest, in the dim unlit compartment, illuminated solely by the sparkling stars of the frosty night and the bluish-white sliver of a waning moon, he imagined for a moment that his wife's veil was spread across his chest like blood-slicked vomit and then he quickly crumpled it and raised the lace veil to his nose, eagerly breathing in the smell with his open mouth, both because the vision frightened him and because the smell seems to satisfy a kind of thirst. He absorbs it greedily through his nostrils, the scent naturally given off by Dolores' glands is a divine blend of musk and vanilla, one he can usually detect on the sheets that have been warmed by their bodies and in her clothes – in all of them, from her coats to her nightdresses – and along the hairline at the back of her neck and the long curve that runs from her shoulder to her wrist; this lovely smell is a gift only Sal has inherited, it was there under the hair on his scalp when he would sometimes crawl into bed with them as a little boy haunted by a nightmare, it clung to his large curls and ringlets, as large and as black as a girl's, in the darkness of the bedroom; with Dolores breathing quietly on the other side of the sleeping boy he used to bury his nose in the curls and press the child's warm body to his chest. Now, in the chilly compartment whose air has been spoiled by bad breath and with loud snores erupting at regular intervals, he inhales deeply through the shawl until he begins to feel sleepy, he welcomes this sleep as both a blessing and as a guarantee of protection, because besides the notes of vanilla and musk in his wife's hair inside one of the folds of lace is the comforting scent of holy incense that must have been absorbed in the cloth from the thurible the choirboy was swinging in the church last night.

With the fragrant lace shawl crumpled up in his breast pocket (the folds have settled in concentric rings, like a black rose) Lieutenant Salvador Pascual Juliá arrives, after two weeks' training in Bavaria, on February 12 at the section of the front the Wehrmacht's 250th division of Spanish volunteers is currently defending and reports to headquarters in Grigorovo, housed in a dacha from the time of the Tsars a few kilometres north-west of Novgorod. The letters from Russia that arrive at Calle Balmes 297 in Barcelona have no despatch address because they are considered to contain military secrets and must therefore be censored, so the first thing to be censored is the name and place of residence of the letter-writer, although the envelopes do bear spectacular stamps that evoke the admiration of the caretaker (by now the caretakers are all regime-friendly *"afectos al régimen"*): *Feldpost* is written at the top of the envelope and below it a round stamp with the Nazi eagle can be made out, this has sometimes been stamped in red ink and sometimes in black, and on the left of the envelope is a large red stamp with the initials S.P. Lieutenant Salvador Pascual Juliá is fascinated by the extraordinary cold (his service record states that he arrived on the Volkhov front on February 12, 1942, the month the blockade of Leningrad claimed the largest number of victims, approximately 100,000 Leningraders died of starvation, starvation-related diseases or froze to death in those four weeks), and at finding himself in a landscape that appears to have a will of its own, the will to subdue everything living beneath snow and ice, *the cold is so severe,* he writes, *you are afraid to breathe, as though every breath could lead to pneumonia or make your heart stop,* the members of the Spanish division have little more than hay and newspapers to set against that kind of cold (down to minus fifty degrees), nor are things any better for the Germans, who provide the equipment for the Spaniards; *you make a hole in a pile of newspapers and pull it down over your head so it covers your back and chest,* he writes, *you get another pile of newspapers and insert it between your trousers and your underpants, you wrap your feet in several layers of newspaper and stuff your boots with hay, the problem is that in order to do that your boots need to be a couple of sizes bigger;* incidentally those who can – there is not enough cloth for everyone – camouflage their helmets and uniforms with bits of white sheet, the result being at best the chance to have a good laugh at one another because in combat the soldiers look as though they are walking around in night-caps. The letters always contain instructional elements, aimed mainly at his sons, and are strewn with German and Russian words and terms, mostly Russian because they can be more easily pronounced in Spanish (*Feldgrau, valenki, kolkhoz, muzhik, dacha, izba, troika, akja*). The letters are read aloud in the evenings when the family are gathered around the radio set, it is Sal who most often reads the letters to them, the German and Russian words in his father's letter are underlined and look like black secretions oozing across the sentences and spreading an alien presence through the room, almost as though a smell were seeping from the ornate handwriting of the person who is absent. Their father writes in one of the letters that he was driving some equipment past a wooden church that had an icon painted on the *outside*, which he felt was quite remarkable, it took up the entire front wall of the building, *the painted face of Christ was glowing bluish-black beneath the saddle-back roof, enthroned above the snow-covered landscape,* but the faces of the starving Russian soldiers were also a kind of black and *the inside of the uniform was black with lice,* he writes, on occasion he has seen them rush out into no-man's-land as though they wanted to be shot. The Russian prisoners and deserters who do the work for his company are, in contrast, *well fed and contented,* particularly the deserters, *los pasados,* and so are the Russian peasants who hire out their horse-drawn sleighs (*troikas*) to the Germans for 3.50 Reichsmark a day, sleighs (*trineos* in Spanish) are the best way to travel in winter when the cold freezes the oil in motor vehicles. It takes several hours to get an engine that has been turned off overnight to start again and allowing it to idle would take too much petrol. There are various kinds of sleigh, they are mainly divided into the Russian or the Finnish kind, known as *volokusha*, which are pulled by two soldiers on skis. If the snow cover is very deep and the load a smaller one, *Akjas* hauled by people are the most flexible solution and the oddest, because their shape is reminiscent of a flat-bottomed boat. The bread, however, is transported on large horse-drawn sleighs that can carry up to 300 kilos, they are made by the Germans and known as HSIs.

One morning at the end of April, as Dolores is returning home after trying on an outfit at her old seamstress' on Carrer Ganduxer, close to the villa they lived in before on Plaça Bonanova, Engracia, the caretaker, a childless widow of fifty, comes rushing out of her cubby-hole to meet her by the lifts, she is permanently in mourning for a corporal who fell at Belchite and is dressed all in black from her worn slippers to the grey-flecked top of her head she keeps covered under a kerchief, she has already called the lift for her and the rumble and creak of the machinery is echoing in the lift shaft. Confronted with the sight of the dismally thin and black-clad woman in the yellow light from the bare bulb in the cubby-hole whose smile is marred by tooth decay, Dolores is reminded of her sons saying the new caretaker is "as ugly as sin" (*La nueva portera es más fea que Picio*).

"*Buenos días, señora Pascual, mire lo que ha traído el cartero,*"[46] and the widow with the bad teeth extends a white envelope to her very gingerly, her hands cupped and held high at her ribcage, one gnarled hand above the other, as though the white envelope might fall and hurt itself or fly away like a dove from her rheumatically misshapen fists unless she is careful. Between the caretaker's swollen finger joints Dolores can see the German eagle that signals letters from Russia, the red ink gleaming between the nodules on her fingers, it

46 "Good morning, Señora Pascual, just look what the postman delivered."

is the second time today she has been struck by that ominous colour: the seamstress pricked her index finger with a pin while basting the pleats of her new spring outfit, which needed taking in at several points, and, perched on the fitting stool, she went weak at the knees with fear right then, that may also have been because she always feels alarmed by the street the seamstress lives on as she has to walk past the former location of one of those torture and interrogation centres, one of those Russian inventions that the whole of the Sarrià-Sant Gervasi district was so full of for a while and everything she had heard about the *cheka* where her brothers were imprisoned came back to her: the sloping bunks it was impossible to lie down on, the awful clashing colours on the walls and ceiling, lemon-yellow orange-red traffic-signal-green, daubed with geometric figures and lit by spotlights that were never turned off and cubes, cylinders and spirals that burrowed inside the prisoners' minds and drove them insane. Which is why the unsightly widow fails to receive the smile or the thanks she is expecting, Dolores grabs the letter instead and steps into the larger of the two cabins (beneath the bronze sign INQUILINOS, residents) the caretaker is holding open for her and shuts both glass doors behind her with a click and presses the Bakelite button for the second floor as deeply as she can. She tells Pilar who opens the door with all the signs of having run to it (out of breath, flushed, arms bare in her summer uniform, her honey-coloured eyes wide with astonishment at the repeated pressing of the bell) to heat the water, and on the double, inside her bedroom Dolores' hands are shaking so badly she has trouble getting the hook out of the eye on her skirt, it is slightly bent and tends to get stuck as you try to undo it. Things always have to play up just when that's the very last thing you need. After she has changed into her indoor clothes, a brown woollen dress the seamstress sewed for her the last autumn before the war, she heads for the kitchen with the letter in her pocket, once by the stove where the water is boiling away in an aluminium saucepan Dolores gets it out and holds the back of the envelope flat above the saucepan and then makes horizontal figures of eight in the air above the steam until the flap begins to unseal. The two previous letters her husband sent were not addressed to her but to the entire family; the first was written from the training camp in Germany, he told them about all the changes of trains and what it felt like to put on the Germans' uniform and swear allegiance to a foreign flag; the second letter was a postcard from Berlin where he had spent the night, the city was *monumental*, he wrote, children and young people were actually skating in the centre of the city! He had bought her something in a grand fashion store called Hertie. Even though this letter does not have her name on the front either, she feels in her bones that she has to break her promise to her sons and open the letter in advance and on her own, instead of waiting for the evening, today that is what she has to do, today something dreadful has occurred and her sense of foreboding is linked in some vague way both to the dangers of the freezing cold and to the brothels the Germans have set up for their soldiers, the seamstress showed her the entry made on his way home in the service record she found among the papers of her son: *Wehrmachtsbordell, Parkstrasse 4, Riga,* with the son's name and rank recorded, the signature of a doctor (*Unterschrift, Dienstgrad des Sanierenden*) and lastly a woman's name (*Der umseitig Bennante hat besucht: Maria*). Pilar is hanging clothes on the veranda outside, on the south side, at the furthest end of the long dark corridor from the kitchen where Dolores is reading the letter standing up, she can hear her singing a folk song that is all the rage, *Él vino en un barco de nombre extranjero lo encontré en el puertooo un atardeceeer . . . ,*[47] so when the doorbell rings it is Señora Dolores who goes to open it. It is Engracia once again, looking even more dreary in the light from the milky groundglass windows on the landing, and Dolores recalls for a moment the

47   "He arrived on a ship with a foreign name, we met in the harbour as the sun was setting." *Tatuaje* (The Tattooing) was a *copla* or Andalusian folk song popularised by the ballad singer Concha Piquer in 1941.

former caretaker and her daughter Carmen, who had a job at a clothing factory but helped her mother in the evenings by taking out the rubbish and so on, the girl had a boyfriend in the Confederación Nacional del Trabajo and became an anarchist herself afterwards, both mother and daughter were cheerful and had large busts, they both had large olive-green eyes with yellow-and-black veins that looked like shiny snakeskin, and real snakes were what they turned out to be, and then she recalls that phrase again, that Engracia is *as ugly as sin*, while Rosario and Carmen in their colourful dresses were saucy and charming and had something bubbly about them whenever they said hello from their cubby-hole or rang the doorbell; though she can also remember the night Carmen turned up with an inspection squad from the *cheka* on Calle Vallmajor and took away her brothers and Don Ramón on the third floor, as well as Carmen standing there yelling in the middle of the night so loudly it echoed round the whole staircase that there would be no more groping, no more filthy language (*Se acabó el 'ven aquí, guapa, tetona, que te toque el coñito*)[48] and it looked as though it was to her brother Artemio those dreadful words were directed, now he was going to have pay for the day he tried to lay an underage girl inside the caretaker's cubby-hole while her mother was away. Engracia is not smiling this time and simply says with a wounded expression that the Señora was in such a hurry she didn't have time to give her the other letter and hands her an envelope. Dolores accepts an official letter with the name of the despatcher clearly printed that turns out to be from the Air Force (*Ejército del Aire*) and thanks her more deliberately: *¡No hacía falta que se molestara, mujer!*[49] because she has read the letter from her husband and the pressure on her chest has lifted, he has not been captured, he is not wounded, he is not writing from a hospital, nor from a Russian prisoner-of-war camp, neither his feet, nor his

48 "There'll be no more of that 'bring those big titties over here so I can feel your little pussy.'"
49 "She [Engracia] shouldn't have bothered to bring the letter up."

nose . . . nor that . . . have frozen off. He writes about the snow and a frozen lake and that the peasant family in the dacha he has been quartered in have an icon on the wall they light candles to and they get the candles from him, that the stove in the *izba* raises the temperature to 30 degrees. *The peasants are happy the Germans have reopened the churches for them and want the Germans to win the war so they won't ever be forced to join the* kolkhoz, *but they also want the Germans to be more like us who treat them like ordinary people rather than animals.* There is a girl who is the same age as María Rosa, he writes, she is blonde as well, of course, all the women there are blonde, she thinks, with golden eyelashes, like Pilar, and feels a sudden pang somewhere inside.

There is a row after supper that evening as they are about to read the letter from Russia, Sal has had his application to the Air Force turned down and is in a dreadful mood and it would be that evening José María decides to challenge his brother's entitlement always to be the one to read their father's letters aloud. María Rosa suggests they solve the conflict by playing rock-paper-scissors. The first two rounds are draws, but on the third José María puts out a flat hand while Sal produces a clenched fist, so it is the younger brother who gets to read the most memorable letter of the whole correspondence, the one in which their father tells them about his mission of March 2, 1942, when he led a convoy through a snowstorm and managed to locate the 250th Reserve Battalion, known as *La Bernarda*, after driving for six hours through a landscape in which the road was constantly disappearing from view.

Extract from the Service Record of Salvador Pascual Juliá for the Year 1942

On February 7 he swears allegiance to the flag of the Third Reich at the training camp in Hof [Germany] and then leaves immediately for the Eastern Front and more specifically for

Grigorovo (Russia) arriving on February 16, there he reports to the general of the division and is posted the same day as convoy officer in the food supplies section of the commissariat. As of this date he leads convoys on both the front and rear lines. Special mention should be made of his mission on March 2 when he served under extremely challenging circumstances north of Ruitof [sic] where the Reserve Battalion of the 250th was operating without its exact location being known, although the road was impassable owing to snow and heavy winds, his orders from the commanding general were to reach the unit at any cost and then inform headquarters as to their location. After exceptional efforts to overcome all these difficulties and obstructions the Convoy Officer concerned, together with the forces under his command, succeeded in carrying out the orders referred to at 02.30 on March 3, having spent six hours traversing the first five kilometres in order to reach the battalion, and was commended by his commanding officers and the commanding officers on the staff of the 4th Section.

Spring comes to Novgorod, and the thaw that has such a devastating effect on the soil frees Lake Ilmen from its prison of ice, *la* rasputitsa *es lo peor, peor que la nieve,*[50] it is called *rasputitsa*, the thaw that turns the whole of Russia into an impassable sea of mud, motorised vehicles have to be abandoned and sleighs are used instead. The cranes return, one day he sees them flying in V-formation above mirror-surfaced pools, like flying crucifixes he writes in a letter (*parecían crucifijos volantes desde el suelo*), he thinks they are the same cranes he saw one spring above the flat landscape around Madrid, they formed the V-shape, then as now. The bright nights of summer are coming and the waterlogged landscape seems to him to be filled

50   "The *rasputitsa* is the worst of all, worse than the snow."

with staring eyes that can never close (*lagos y charcas reflejan la luz del cielo como ojos despiertos que nunca duermen*). He will be granted leave when the nights begin to get dark and the stars return. The following typed testimonial is presented in a separate document:

División Española de Voluntarios 250
Representación Estafeta 39.502

R.nr.304
R.L. Consecuente a sus respetables escritos nros.615 y 616 de fecha 17 del actual, tengo el honor de participar a V.S. que los equipos de los fallecidos sargentos de esta División DON CIPRIANO TARTILAN y DON FRANCISCO CARRERA CAÑETE, han sido recogidos por esta Representación y serán enviados a la misma de esta División en Madrid conforme ordenaba en su superior escrito habiéndose hecho cargo de los mismos el Teniente Jefe de una expedición con permiso, DON SALVADOR PASCUAL JULIÁ, para que haga entrega de los mismos y ser recibidos por sus familiares.

Lo que comunico a V.S. para su superior conocimiento.
Dios salve a España y guarde a V.S. muchos años.
Estafeta 39.502 a 24 de Agosto de 1942.
EL COMANDANTE JEFE
(*signature*)
Sr. Coronel de Estado Mayor Jefe de los Servicios de Retaguardia en
BERLIN [51]

51   Office of the 250th Reserve Battalion of the Spanish Volunteer Corps.
     Despatch 39.502
     R.no.304
     In relation to Your esteemed letters nos 615 and 616 of the 17th inst. I have the
     honour to inform Your Excellency that the items of equipment belonging to
     the fallen Sergeants of the Division DON CIPRIANO TARTILAN and DON

"*En toda Rusia no hay carreteras, los alemanes construyen carreteras de madera con troncos de abedul*", there are almost no asphalted roads in Russia, the Germans have to build roads out of birch logs, they call them *Knüppeldämme*, your back and kidneys take a heavy pounding travelling on those rolling log roads, you get blinding headaches, even the horses are affected. In winter the German engineers flush the deep snow with water to form a firm foundation, but there are still no roads, you can have no idea how awful it was the night I was supposed to locate the Reserve Battalion. It is August 27, 1942, he was met with rain when he got off the train four hours ago, the late summer showers of Barcelona falling in torrents from Tibidabo down the steep streets in Vallcarac and Sarriá-San Gervasio and washing the city clean. It has taken six days to travel through Europe from the Volkhov front, four days alone from Novgorod to Berlin. He has just been telling them about Berlin, the sketch map he was given at the registration office at the Alexander barracks is on the table, he has pointed out the overnight accommodation the Wehrmacht makes available at the various train stations (he spent the first night at Bahnhof Friedrichstrasse and the second two at Potsdamer Bahnhof, Leipziger Strasse, where he bought the presents for Dolores and María Rosa, starts at Potsdamer Platz), on the table there is a programme as well from *Grosskabaret Berolina*, a club located high above Alexanderplatz, where you can get dinner for under one Reichsmark, listen to Erich Krumm's orchestra and enjoy marvellous views over

---

FRANCISCO CARRERA CAÑETE have been collected by this office and will be despatched to the Office of the Division in Madrid, as ordered in Your letter, under the supervision of Lieutenant Colonel DON SALVADOR PASCUAL JULIÁ who has been charged with delivering these effects to the families of the fallen.
This I now make known to Your Excellency.
May God preserve Spain and protect Your Excellency for many years to come.
Despatch 39.502 24th August 1942
The OFFICER IN COMMAND
(signature)
Chief of Staff of the Rearguard Troops Stationed in BERLIN.

Berlin but where *you are not allowed to dance,* he stressed, because that is felt to be lacking in respect for the soldiers on the front. Sal asked if he had walked along Unter den Linden. Then he had to run his index finger across the map again, he did that on the very first night, he had spent the first night at Friedrichstrasse after all, *there.* The Germans have regulations about everything: Did you know you are not allowed to smoke on Unter den Linden? The effects of the two fallen sergeants sit on the desk in his study, he has had a long bath in the large, blue-tiled bathroom, tomorrow he will return the dead men's possessions to their next of kin. Behind the white curtains in the dining room, inky-grey thunder clouds are massing, a fly can sense the storm coming and is buzzing impatiently above the fruit bowl, the blue-black skin of the figs is glowing in the flat light coming in through the balcony. The people of Leningrad are not giving in to starvation, that surprises the Germans, who get their information from spies, defectors and prisoners of war, their unrelenting block-ade has not yet led to a revolt among the inhabitants of Leningrad, there is talk instead of mass deaths among the millions of people in the city, the spies the Germans send in say the corpses are piled in the streets, that it is only the extreme cold that is stopping the spread of an epidemic; he gets his information from the Germans at the central supply depot, he tells the family, despite feeling so tired after the meal and wanting to bring the conversation to an end, he drives to the central depot every other day to fetch the food supplies, Russian prisoners of war unload them once he has driven the food to their positions and the prisoners make no secret of the fact that the soldiers of the Red Army are starving as well. One of the flies lands on a fig, the sheen of the blue-black outer layer appears dulled by the storm looming behind the tulle curtains, María Rosa's hand enters his field of vision as it whisks away another fly. The captured Russian nurses who work in the Germans' military hospitals talk as well, but that is not something he can go into. He feels bloated, the blue-black figs fill him with revulsion, he has been travelling for six days, hauling the dead men's possessions between various trucks and military trains, over rolling birch-log roads and dusty railway tracks, breathing and swallowing dust for hours in stale stinking heat, dehydrated, his throat so on fire from thirst that even the sight of water brought coolness with it (all those rivers he has seen and crossed: Volkhov, Ishora, Niemen, Wisła, Oder, Rhine, Meurthe, the Meurthe beside his favourite station: Lunéville, *Villa de la luna*, Moontown, after Strasbourg and just before Nancy, already in France, that is, halfway home, many thousands of kilometres from the wooden houses in Russia, Lithuania and on the Polish steppes), the train stopped in Grodno, on the platform, surrounded by laughing German policemen in uniform, he drank foaming cold beer, it was that bitter taste that slaked his infernal thirst, he gulped down the beer while a railwayman struck the train wheels with a metal bar – clang clang clang – and the clanging was superimposed over the cries of some civilians hammering their fists on the windows of a train under guard standing beneath the blazing midday sun on a nearby siding; he wants to be lying at full length in the cool dark, his thoughts flit to the bedroom, he visualises the white sheets stretched out in the semi-darkness of the room like drifting ice-floes, sees himself dropping his neck onto the cold pillow, the whole bed sinking into a silence in which only his heart is beating, his pulse like great wings beating towards the stormy sky, wings as large as sails shearing the sky and drowning out all the din . . . Consuelo, the new maid, a spindly girl with frizzy hair, brings in the coffee cups which rattle against the side plates on a large oval tray. "So what happened to Pilar?" the lieutenant asks when the girl has gone back to the kitchen.

"*¡Pregúntaselo a ese!*"[52] his daughter shouts in reply, her arm reaching across the table to point at her eldest brother.

"*¡María Rosa!*"

52 "Why don't you ask him!"

"¡Yo no he dicho nada! ¡Además, la guerra es un aburrimiento!"[53]

The war is boring, she says. The lieutenant thinks he can still hear the clatter of the coffee cups along the corridor that begins at the door on his right and turns at an obtuse angle towards the interior of the flat like an intestine, the way he hears the clatter it sounds as if the maid had taken the empty coffee cups away again or not yet come in with them but was still on her way to the dining room, the coffee cups are there, however, on the table waiting to be filled with the piping hot coffee substitute, he can hear them clinking in the corridor all the same and in that corridor the paintings are rattling on the walls, the walls are shaking in a cloud of dust and plaster, and all of a sudden the bedroom at the other end of the long tunnel is no longer as enticing, and neither is the slinky skin-coloured nightdress he bought in Berlin . . . a whistling sound is beginning to howl from the end of the corridor as if it were being made by organ pipes in hell, combined with the drawn-out roar of his own rage, he would like to shred the air with his screams, yell it all out, yell out that the Russian doctors and their staff are eating amputated body parts, that he is returning from a war in which the enemy is being forced to eat itself, and what have they been doing *here* in the meantime, sitting round this bloody dining table? He raises his clenched fist towards his mouth and sucks on the knuckle, Tula, his mother-in-law, asks Sal to fetch the tablet box she has left in her room, Sal gets to his feet and looks his father in the eye, under the table the lieutenant moves his other hand towards his groin where he can now feel a dull pain, he asks for some water, Dolores gets up and pours water into his glass, she asks if everything is alright, but it is as if all he can hear is the pounding of his blood in his ears, a flapping of swan wings flying low over the broken crust of ice on the lake, the light over Ilmen then was greyish blue the way it is here, a low storm sky that exuded a dense, heavy silence, he could have shot the low-flying

53   "I didn't say anything. Besides, the war is boring."

swan whose wings were pounding far out over the surface of the water, as though it were the regularly pulsating pain of the sky he was hearing, and it feels as if the swan were flying somewhere in here, at the far end of the corridor that is his head, the dark winding passage, evil-smelling like the lining of an intestine. Sal comes back and walks all the way round the table to his grandmother with the little silver box he places beside her glass on the table, then he walks the whole way back to his father's chair and hands him a book.

"*¡Mire qué estoy leyendo, padre!*"[54]

The lieutenant asks to have his glass refilled and downs it in one go before looking at the book his son has put in front of him. It is Hitler's *Mi lucha*, "My Struggle", with a familiar picture of the Führer on the cover. Still with his knuckle in his mouth he looks up at his son who is looking at him proudly and expectantly. Then he drops his hand and uses it to turn the pages of the book, he can see that Sal has underlined and marked with brackets lines and entire paragraphs in the first two chapters.

La doctrina judía del marxismo rechaza el principio aristocrático de la Naturaleza y . . . Niega así en el hombre el mérito individual e impugna la importancia del nacionalismo y de la raza abrogándole con esto a la humanidad la base de su existencia y de su cultura. [. . .]
POR ESO CREO AHORA QUE AL DEFENDERME DEL JUDIO LUCHO POR LA OBRA DEL SUPREMO CREADOR.[55]

---

54   "Look what I am reading, Father."
55   The Jewish doctrine of Marxism rejects the aristocratic principle in nature. [. . .] Thus it denies the value of the individual in man, disputes the meaning of nationality and race, depriving mankind of the assumption for its existence and culture. THEREFORE, I BELIEVE TODAY THAT I AM ACTING IN THE SENSE OF THE ALMIGHTY CREATOR: BY WARDING OFF THE JEWS I AM FIGHTING FOR THE LORD'S WORK.

His son has also scribbled on the pages, and not just in the margins, but in between the blank lines: *No caridad – Justicia Social*, is his summary of Hitler's assertions on page 38, where *social justice* is doubly underlined. And not in pencil, but in ink, of course. The young whippersnapper has written his comments in indelible ink, engaging with the author, one of the greatest leaders of all time, as an equal. But the pain in his side is getting worse and the lieutenant has to get up, he smiles at his son, before plunging out into the long dark corridor feeling he is going to vomit at any moment.

The family spend two weeks in September at the health resort in Sant Hilari Sacalm, Girona, just as his wife's family have done every summer year after year, and after drinking the spa water and taking long strolls in the hills the lieutenant's kidney problems appear to ease. He begins yet another five-thousand-kilometre train journey on October 3, 1942: from Barcelona to Logroño in the north from where the expedition is due to depart, and from there to Irún/Hendaye where he is welcomed once again by the nurses of the German Red Cross, examined by doctors, offered coffee and handed eighty French francs for expenses during the journey. Then he gets on the through train to Berlin and off at the camp in Hof, where he arrives on October 5. He suffers an attack of kidney stones on October 6 and is hospitalised at the Spanish military hospital in the same city, where he remains for five days. According to his service record he is discharged on October 10 at his own request. One of the nurses of the Sanidad Militars, a Catalan woman of his own age who, like him, served at Brunete, recommends he drink as much beer as he can get hold of, beer is a diuretic, the best way of protecting oneself against another attack is to try to pee the stone out. But the lieutenant loathes beer, he drinks no alcohol at all apart from champagne on certain ceremonial occasions. Shaken by his stay in hospital and the high doses of morphine he was given he arrives on October 15 at the new headquarters of the Blue Division in Pokrovskaya, a town thirty kilometres south of Leningrad, where he reports for duty and is posted as payments officer. During his leave the section of the front the Blue Division is defending has been moved from Novgorod and the Volkhov river (a forty-kilometre-long front line) to a smaller segment (twenty-nine kilometres) divided into four sectors (from east to west: Krasny Bor, Federovskoye, Pavlovsk and Pushkin) and fortified with a complex system of trenches, the defensive line assigned to the Spaniards crosses the main road to Leningrad, the Red Army are on the other side of the Ishora river (a tributary of the Neva) in the industrial suburb of Kolpino, which contains a vital tank factory. The headquarters in Pokrovskaya, three kilometres south-east of Pushkin, is housed in a neo-classical villa with Doric pillars at the entrance that the members of the Division call *el palacete*, the little palace. But the enemy's snipers and artillery fire (*Stalin's pipe organs*, he writes) are causing heavy losses among the besiegers and creating craters as big as bullfighting arenas. From the outset the only part of the town the forces he belongs to were shooting at and bombing every evening (the bombing raids began on the dot of eight p.m.) that the Spanish war veteran could picture in his mind was the abandoned Smolny cathedral that the Communists had shut. These were the same Heinkel HE111s that laid waste to the Brunete sector in 1937, but now that the German bombers were dropping their payloads over St Petersburg the former engineer was praying that the architect Rastrelli's blue-painted masterpiece would be spared. He had even been to see another of Rastrelli's creations, the Catherine Palace, currently used by the Germans as a military hospital, one afternoon when he was visiting some wounded compatriots at the military hospital in Mestelevo, his driver, a corporal from Valladolid, offered to drive the long way round via Pushkin so he could have a look at the magnificent Rococo palace before being taken back to headquarters in Pokrovskaya. Battles had been waged in this area the first summer following the German attack on the Soviet Union and the building had been damaged in several places, the vast esplanade undermined by grenade bursts, many of the golden cupids and figures on the facade he had so often studied in a hand-coloured book in the library of his guardian, Father Aurelianos, in Sarriá were covered in grime and partly blown away, nor was there much left of the lovely blue colour Rastrelli had chosen to paint this building in, large patches had flaked away and it looked as if the whole of the colossal palace were suffering from a kind of leprosy. Inside the immense residence he could sense the wing beat of history, it was here the Romanovs were captured during the Red revolution that was the source of all the evil that was occurring now, but the former splendour in which the Tsar's family had lived had been ruined, disfigured, it was devastation that was celebrating triumph after triumph in this place, and the smoky drawing-room mirrors that were left in some of the magnificent rooms could only reveal ghostly images: white beds repeating themselves *ad aeternam* and vanishing into the depths of long, metallically gleaming tunnels. He did not get to see the famous Amber Room, however, the amber mosaics that had covered the walls and ceiling and all the other decorations in one of the rooms had been dismantled in September 1941 and carried off to Germany, so he was told by a German officer who offered to show him round. On the way back to headquarters, before they got into the car, the lieutenant got out a pack of cigarettes, the exit from the military hospital gave onto a broad, open veranda composed of black-and-white marble tiles where he stood for a while having a smoke with his driver and the officer from the division of the German Ordnungspolizei whose beat covered a neighbouring section of the front, the German, who was from Hamburg and had travelled around Spain before the war and visited the abbey at Montserrat, the extraordinary rock formations and the boys' choir (*la escolanía*) were among the many things that had profoundly inspired him, as he told him in the same excellent Spanish he had used as his guide inside the palace. The ancient Baroque gardens that surrounded it had been destroyed and were now closed off with barbed wire, while the lieutenant was attempting to restore the gardens in his imagination to their original design he was told about the four thousand fixed loudspeakers that had been installed on the streets and squares of St Petersburg since the 1920s, an urban feature that did not exist anywhere else in the world and that Hitler was intent on copying, when the wind lay in the right direction music from the thousands of loudspeakers could be heard as well as the clanking of the trams, the officer said. All of it a trick, however, according to the German, *the tram sounds were pre-recorded to make us believe that the city is unaffected by the siege, ha!* The German's company also enjoyed the dubious pleasure of frying meat at strategic points close to the battle lines although only when the wind was blowing *in the right direction,* towards the starving Bolsheviks, that was. *The Communists have come up with a nicer-sounding word for starvation as well, they call it: "dystrophy", ha ha!* The man in the green uniform was something of a ventriloquist, his laugh reverberated inwards without any trace of it on his face. Lieutenant Salvador Pascual Juliá lit another cigarette. That very day a suitably southern wind was blowing that could carry the smell of frying to the positions of the besieged and make their mouths water and their stomachs writhe with cramps, not just the rumbling stomachs of the soldiers, but also those of little children, the stomachs of boys and girls, of toothless old people, mothers' stomachs, women with mouths contorted by despair, it is as though he has not understood that before, not until this moment when he is chatting with one of the green-uniformed police officers he has seen harassing those wretched Jews on stations and streets wherever he goes. Lieutenant Salvador Pascual Juliá clicks his tongue to get rid of the harsh taste of his Philip Morris, the tobacco takes on a bitter edge when exposed to contact with air that is so cold even though it comes from more southerly latitudes, there has actually been snow in the air for the last few days, this sudden change of direction is just a temporary application of the brakes, a last road-block against winter, that much he has understood about this climate that feels so alien to him. He takes a deep drag, it will have to be the last one before he chucks the stub and starts walking to the car, the late autumn light is falling obliquely across the chess-patterned floor of the veranda and reminds him of the flooring in the lobby of the apartment building in Barcelona between the front door and the black-painted cast-iron gate to the lift although the surface area would be at least a hundred times greater here, the distance to his home suddenly feels infinitely long and utterly unmanageable, like a pressure beneath his breastbone; and it is then, while he is still reeling from that pitiless sensation, that the German officer, a broad-shouldered figure whose moss-green uniform casts a green shadow over the long row of black-and-white squares, comes out with the most appalling thing the lieutenant has heard to this point: that the starvation inside the city is so great that gangs of criminals go around hunting and killing people to sell their flesh, he had heard that from a reliable source and as a policeman, he is in a position to know, and then that stiff inward laughter was echoing again, as if it were coming from the bottom of a tin can.

Christmas and New Year and all of January come and go. Sal is now enrolled at the officer training school in Zaragoza whose entrance exam he passed with flying colours in October. At 22.25 on February 13, 1943, José María tunes the radio to 42.13 metres, the B.B.C.'s wavelength for their evening broadcast to Spain, he has a list in his hands of the various wavelengths and times, he wants to be a military man too but not a pilot or an infantryman like his brother, the front line is not what appeals to him, what he dreams of is the vital office work the war requires at the rear, which is why he is usually to be found by the radio set like any other radio ham, tuning in to different stations, indulged by his mother because he is able to find programmes that are of interest to her, such as "*La mujer en la Guerra*" ("Women at War"), a programme in Spanish broadcast by the B.B.C. several days a week after the 13.45 news bulletin. The hour is now approaching

22.30. Dolores is already seated in the armchair closest to the standard lamp with her knitting, María Rosa and Granny Tula have gone to bed. It is always a Spanish colonel who reads the war bulletin from London, as is the case this evening, although this evening the voice that takes over after the signature tune has a flat and solemn tone that instinctively makes mother and son prick up their ears: the bulletin concerns events on the Eastern front. The Blue Division is reported to have been annihilated following a massive Soviet attack three days ago, on February 10, at Krasny Bor, one of the four sectors covered by the Spanish division south of Leningrad. Dolores has literally no idea what to do, what she is supposed to do with her hands and the rest of her body, she knows even less about how to go on breathing, she has probably been screaming, but she is barely aware of that, her entire mental focus is taken up with the effort to follow what the voice that goes on talking is saying, as though hanging on every word that voice utters were the only way not to let go and fall into a huge black hole. To José María, on the other hand, it is as though the colonel had snapped his fingers and woken him from a dream: he feels wide awake, as though the world had fallen silent and only his brain were operating, in the ensuing silence he registers everything from the crackle of the broadcast to the information the voice is delivering, including its intonation, as well as the angles made by the knitting needles that have slid down beside his mother as though they were sticking out of her ribs, he also notes the colour of her face which has turned a repellent dull grey, in the midst of this strange silence, which is actually occurring outside his head, he realises that it is now up to him, in some strange way his father's life and his mother's depend on him, on what he can come up with to say. The voice drones on meanwhile, with a poorly concealed undertone of satisfaction that does not escape him: announcing that the Soviet's preparatory fire started at seven o'clock in the morning on February 10 and lasted for three hours, and that it was the Soviet *Katyushas* that caused the lion's share of the losses to that point, that this was then followed by a four-hour-long battle during which the remainder of the Division was said to have been slaughtered. Then the news bulletin is over.

"Papá está en intendencia, a las siete de la mañana nunca estaría en primera línea. Además ese coronel es republicano, dice lo que quieren los rusos."[56]

Of course! Dolores looks at her son with a gratitude that will be transformed over the years into lifelong respect, she decides she is going to listen to him instead, to her clever son who goes on to argue that the Spanish colonel is a Republican in exile and that the very fact he used the word *Katyusha* was proof positive that the news could not be trusted.

It is not until February 27 that Radio Berlin contradicts the news of the annihilation of the division of Spanish volunteers and dismisses it as Soviet propaganda. The losses among the Spanish volunteers amount to more than four thousand dead, the bulletin admits, although the emphasis is on the heroic conduct of the Spaniards and the even greater losses suffered by the Russians. In between, the family receives contradictory bits of information from Radio Nacional, reassuring reports from the military base in Barcelona where José María is sent the next morning, and a call from Sal who has spoken to the general at the military academy in Zaragoza. Eventually a letter arrives from the lieutenant dated three days after the battle at Krasny Bor. A certified copy is enclosed of a letter of commendation to be added to the lieutenant's list of distinctions which already includes the Eastern Front Medal (with the inscription "Winterschlacht im Osten 1941/42") that was pinned to his jacket when he came back on leave in August. The letter anticipates the lieutenant's return by just over a week. According to his service record he is repatriated on March 6 and crosses the border

56 "Father is in the service corps, he would never be on the front line at seven in the morning. And besides, that colonel is a Republican (in exile), he's just saying what the Russians want him to say."

between France and Spain six days later on March 12. He would have arrived home at Calle Balmes 297 at some time on March 12 or 13. Among the papers in his breast pocket is the original of the letter of commendation, the German eagle beside the signature has been stamped in mauve ink that has a lovely sheen when he puts it on the table.

Im Namen des Führers und Obersten Befehlshabers der Wehrmacht verleihe ich dem Oberleutnant Don Salvador Pascual Juliá.-Stb 250.- Span.-Freiw.-Div.- -Das Kriegsverdienstkreuz.-2 Klasse.- Mit Schwertern.- Im Felde den 1.12.1942.- der Kommandierende General.- Hansen.-General der Kavallerie.

The Visit, Ymergatan 7, Uppsala, August 2006

On March 13, 1943, as your grandfather was returning to Barcelona after serving with Hitler's army for twelve months, the Germans put up signs around the Belorussian border city of Grodno declaring that the town was free of Jews (*Judenrein*). This meant that the Jews who had been confined within the city's two ghettos since November 1, 1941 (Ghetto A inside the old town centre for skilled workers and Ghetto B in the suburb of Slobodka for non-productive Jews) had been deported. In January 1943 five transports left Grodno for Auschwitz, in February two transports departed for Treblinka (4,400 individuals). Between February 9 and 14, 1943, several so-called *P.J.-Züge* (the German abbreviation for trains of *Polnische Juden*) from Białystok and Grodno arrived at the railway junction Małkinia, south of Białystok, their destination was the extermination camp at Treblinka. On February 14 the P.J.-train with inhabitants from the Grodno ghetto left Małkinia at 11.23, it was a short journey, the train had already reached its last stop at Treblinka by 12.52. Given that your grandfather left the suburbs of Leningrad on March 6 he would have passed Grodno at some point between March 7 and 10. He could just as well have passed Grodno on February 14 and seen the train containing deported Jews waiting on a siding to make way for the military train he was travelling in, or as early as the end of January when most of the emptying of Ghetto B took place, but it is as if a great hand had put him on those military trains either before or after the P.J.-trains passed through, or could it be that the P.J.-transports were planned for the particular days when no troop transports occurred? The same could be said of Vilnius which he passed on his way to and from the front and where there were also two ghettos, and of a holiday resort outside Vilnius, in Paneriai, by a lake surrounded by pine forests and in those woods a 1.5 metre deep pit in which the inhabitants of the ghetto would be systematically shot with the onset of Operation Barbarossa, only later to be shoved onto trains instead. And at all the other stations he passed through or stopped at or changed trains in (before Vilnius there was Vitebsk and after Vilnius and Grodno came Suwałki, Treuburg (Olecko in Polish), Allenstein (Olsztyn), Dirschau (Tczew), Küstrin (Kostrzyn) on the border, there were two alternative routes at this point depending on the current state of the rail traffic: either via Berlin and Leipzig, or via Cottbus and Chemnitz, to Hof and on to Bayreuth, Nuremberg, Karlsruhe at the next national frontier, after that through occupied France where the trains with Spanish volunteers on board were greeted with clenched fists, verbal abuse and stones: Lunéville, Nancy, Troyes, Orléans, Poitiers, Tours, Bordeaux, Hendaye, Irún) there were railway junctions that led to or were close to a concentration camp or a ghetto, such as the stations in Bayreuth, Hof and Leipzig from where one could travel to Weimar's Hauptbahnhof, the railway station closest to K.L. Buchenwald (in the spring of 1943 the prisoners in the camp were forced to extend the line so that the track from Weimar led all the way to the camp). Although the transportation of forcibly deported people is going on or has gone on or will be going on throughout Europe, it is as though your grandfather, equipped with his Spanish passport and his travel permits, were able to travel along special corridors in time.

Then you become aware of the sounds from the kitchen, the large heavy wooden drawer in the cupboard that rattles the cutlery when drawn out and almost immediately afterwards the bottle of wine being uncorked, your mother comes into the living room holding the bottle and goes over to the glass cabinet where she gets out a crystal glass she pours red wine into for you. The roll of the ship, the sparkling wine they drank in the dance hall on the *Ciudad de Cádiz* and on deck, outside in the sun. She would learn to say *los rojos*, as a language exercise to begin with perhaps, then she switched to thinking *los rojos*, as time passed she would have no objection to him putting up Hitler's portrait in their home, as time passed – that is where time would take her, to a damp apartment with mottled-green tiled floors in a town, Lérida, that could barely be found on a map – she would be sitting in a white nightdress on the edge of the bed with a puppy in her arms, in the background the Hitler portrait that would later float above your open fontanelle, you are not born yet, perhaps you are already a button in her womb in this photograph: eyes drowsy with sleep, the air in the black–and–white photograph gone stale overnight, the puppy may have woken them wanting milk, the puppy's nose is pressed against her collarbone, her hair is longer, darker because she dyed it black, she is wearing a broad white head-band as she cuddles the puppy on the edge of the bed. But for the moment they are still there on the *Ciudad de Cádiz,* travelling on a silver ship, *nuestro barquito de plata.*

"*¡Mozo!*"[57] Sal – it is the fourth or fifth day of their boat trip and she is calling him Sal now – snaps his fingers and orders *champán*, it is acid and sweet at the same time, bursting with carbon dioxide. The roll of the ship, the wind, the wine that claws at their throats. For the moment they are still sitting there on deck. The waiter in a white, waist-length jacket comes over with a tray, on it a green bottle of Codorniu with a gold label that they drink in the sunshine.

"*Yo estaba en el bando nacional cuando estalló la guerra, mi padre nos llevó a Galicia (–Galicia?), Galicia, encima de Portugal*"[58] (he cups his right hand over his left as though one was the province of Galicia and the other Portugal, oblong and boxed in between Spain and the ocean, and she notices the dexterity of his beautifully bony fingers

57 "Waiter!"
58 "I ended up on the rebels' side when the [civil] war broke out; my father took us to Galicia (Galicia?), yes, Galicia, on top of Portugal."

with their square-shaped nails) *"el primer verano de guerra, mi hermano y yo jugábamos en la ría de Pontevedra y veíamos los fusilamientos, las ambulancias iban cargadas de muertos."*[59]

It is odd to think she was not even born when he watched the firing squads from his hiding place, in Galicia, she was too young and without a history, as fluid as the liquid she may have allowed to linger on her palate before letting it run down her throat, the Spanish foreign legionnaire, this *novio de la Muerte*, appeared so weighty in contrast, so filled with purpose, all she had been to that point was the future and the future suddenly felt like a cloud of gas bubbles, empty air. The man who would become your father spent part of his childhood in small towns behind the front in the region around Madrid, the towns that ended up on the battle lines were annihilated and had to be rebuilt, Franco created a ministry to that end: *Dirección Nacional de Regiones Devastadas*, the General Direction of Devastated Regions. There are devastated regions inside people as well, you think of her ribcage and the pain that would make it go stiff and spread out to devastate her childhood when her father died, her girlish chest a devastated area as well, an entire landscape just came to an end but would remain in there: the visits to the sick in the black Ford, the summers beside the sea in Piteå, the patients who stopped climbing the steps to Father's surgery, it all went up in smoke, like the fire in the Lundbergs' shoe shop she watched from the windows of the living room, she says almost all she can remember is the fire in the shoe shop and her father's funeral procession. He died of a heart attack in spring, in April, just after his birthday, the black Bakelite sign (*District Medical Officer Dr P. H. Söderbaum, entrance round the corner*) was taken down and shoved in the boot at the last minute when they moved from Piteå, Tess was sitting in her lap and still smelled of pus. Though the ship she found herself on with the

59   "The first summer during the war my brother and I used to play at the mouth of the river in Pontevedra and we watched the executions, the ambulances were filled with dead people."

foreign legionnaire many years later smelled of its recent coat of paint, through the paint-spattered iron rods in the railings she could observe the surface of the sea and that ability it has to be shattered by the breakers of storm and wind and then, with a light touch, as light as the touch of the last light of evening, to repair itself, to become blank and smooth for skies and cities to mirror themselves in.

En España las flores son para los muertos. Enseñaremos a nuestros hijos a gritar ¡Arriba España! cuando vean la bandera.[60] Everything was flowing, becoming part of an ever larger chain of events, and this weighty man, he was a man, not a youth like the others she had fallen in love with, rode across the desert, he shot gazelles. The *Ciudad de Cádiz,* their little silver ship, is sailing between two of the Canary Islands, there are not many hours left until they dock in Santa Cruz. Is this when he drinks *champán* out of her shoe? He took off the shoe that was pinching her injured foot and poured into it the local variety of sparkling wine, drank out of it, transforming the pump into a ritual cup, a vessel. You were revolted by that story when, not yet fifteen, you heard it told one Sunday around the dining table, you were living on Menorca then, a strong northerly wind was blowing beyond the balcony, maybe it was the wind that made him think of their voyage on the *Ciudad de Cádiz* in January 1959, you were sitting at the round mahogany table eating chicken roasted according to a recipe your paternal grandmother had given your mother during her only visit to the island, it was a Sunday, this was also the day you were told that you had four half-brothers and sisters. The boy your mother saw on the dockside is called Salvador, like his father and his father before him. You have never met him or any of his siblings.

"Dinner is ready," your mother says, it is hard to imagine her as the same woman in the photographs, though you still remember them together, the spirit of the *Ciudad de Cádiz* still hovered around your home on certain nights, in the best room with the records piled

60 "In Spain flowers are for the dead. We will teach our children to cry *¡Arriba España!* at the sight of the flag."

on the floor beside the ivory-white gramophone they danced like they once did in Santa Cruz, Seville or Madrid, at places that were called Bella Napoli or El Guajiro. Then she started drinking on her own and he began to hit her, even in front of you, you thought there was a link, a causal relationship that justified the punishment: that he hit her because she sometimes forgot to fetch you from school when it was dark and forgot to make food for the two of you. What made her stay with him? Was it love? What is love? You still cannot understand why he had to have Hitler's portrait in your home. Or how she could have wanted it there or have allowed it in the first place. What kept Stangl's wife, the wife of the officer in charge of Treblinka, by his side once she understood what his work involved? Was it love? What *is* love? What kept Kristina Söderbaum in Germany? Was it love? Or was it ambition? Why did your mother travel to Munich to visit the elderly film star in 1989? Was it nostalgia? Or vanity? The age-old vanity of the ambitious Söderbaum family that impelled the swift rise of a miller's son at the De Geer ironworks in Lövsta in Uppland to become an accountant, succeeded by priests and doctors and then a permanent secretary of the Royal Swedish Academy of Sciences. She was bound to have told Kristina how much your father admired her. My husband saw all your films, she would have said. Kristina Söderbaum, "the Watery Corpse of the Third Reich", had published her memoir, *Nichts bleibt immer so*, a few years before, and while they were having coffee in the living room of the two-bedroom flat the elderly film star lived in behind the Frauen-kirche, in a centrally located block of sheltered housing, your mother was given a leaflet about the launch in one of Munich's bookshops, but not a signed copy of the book because the first edition had been sold out long before. Your mother knocked on the door of Goebbels' old film star and was invited in because of her surname: Söderbaum. What makes you stay? Is it love? What *is* love? You keep chewing, she has a way of slightly raising her upper lip when she drinks, as if she did not want to get it wet or touch the wine, but the food is delicious, you are thinking about the Russian word *golod*, hunger, and about the same word in Spanish, *hambre*, you are thinking about the fact that the people in Leningrad ate their shoes, the glue on the wallpaper and then the wallpaper before they began to eat their own dead. You are thinking that it was your grandfather on the other side of the front line who fetched the food supplies for the division from the Germans' central depot and that he used to drive the essentials to the embattled battalions that first winter along the Volkhov front, the second winter he handed out the wages to the men holding the line at Leningrad so the soldiers could buy cigarettes and smoke them in the trenches while the civilians on the other side of the battle line died of starvation, pure and simple, in their hundreds of thousands. You are thinking about a passage in a book by Ingeborg Bachmann: *I'll let you in on a terrible secret: language is punishment. All things must pass inside it and there must pass away, according to their guilt and the degree of their guilt.*

Part Two

The Descendants

Làttimi. Hotel Arlechino, Piazzale Roma,
Venice, Italy,
June 2006

The different levels and steeply sloping roof of the narrow L-shaped attic room, wallpapered throughout in satins and silk brocades in various shades of pink, delighted your little girl, the hotel room was so difficult to get hold of after you were stranded at the airport in Treviso – for a while, finding anything available in the whole of Venice seemed to be impossible – that when you were finally surrounded by that rose-coloured light you felt exhilarated at first, then exhausted, at least you and he did, your husband, who immediately lay down on the double bed with backache after the long drive from Salzburg while your daughter ran up the few steps that separated the room into two skewed halves and claimed the bed niche by the window from where she could look down at the narrow canal that laps below the hotel. You could tell she was excited, she seemed to understand that she was on the periphery of a very unusual city, the strangest in Europe, a city built on water, a city that was currently sinking and being thrust towards the bottom of the lagoon, a fact, when you thought about it, that seemed strangely in keeping with the road trip across the Dolomites, Monti Pallidi, the pale mountains, a region that formed the bottom of a sea some 250 million years ago, the Tethys sea, when *the mass extinction of the living species of the earth had already occurred and no birds crossed the skies, only winged reptiles*, at least that was what it said in the travel guide you had in the bag still hanging from your right shoulder. There was a little writing desk opposite the double bed and you went over to put the handbag with the cameras and your notebook on it, you

267

swung your arm to massage the shoulder joint but did not sit on the brocade-clad baroque copy of a chair by the desk, you were too restless, still part of the forward motion that had carried you along foreign motorways, your mind's eye lingering on the asphalt ribbon between pale and peculiar limestone formations. You had left the E55 at Tolmezzo about four hours ago, you got out of the car knowing you were standing on the floor of a primeval sea and the bright light – a silvery irritation on your cornea as of fish scales glittering off a smooth expanse of water – appeared to confirm that in some uncanny way: a shimmer like a ghost of water, like the memory of the extinct Tethys sea, and the silvery particles of that memory were vibrating restlessly and anxiously in the air, as if being driven by an inner transformation: what was air might be about to become water once more. Afterwards, inside the lopsided hotel room, not even the salmon-coloured reflections off the satin drapery could extinguish the memory of that light. Your daughter had got the crayons out of her little backpack and was sitting on her bed drawing a princess outdoors, in a meadow, she was drawing the grass as you sat down beside her. The princess was happy, the line that was supposed to represent her mouth was large and upturned, her hair – drawn in pencil – was long and voluminous, more like a garland made of charcoal. The princess was wearing a long dress drawn in blue crayon, two humps stuck out of her hips that had been filled in with bright red wax crayon, the baroque cut made you think of the little princess in Veláquez' "Las Meninas". To the left of the princess your daughter had drawn two flowers, one with a blue bud (a little blue spiral) and next to it a somewhat smaller one with a red bud (a solid circle), and, to your astonishment and delight, these flowers had red roots that were growing beneath the patch of grass the princess, the flowers and the tree were standing on. The tree was on the right of the princess and its trunk, unlike the coarse brown colour you used to draw as a child, was a narrow straight pencil line that connected seven of the red roots with a green crown whose shape was reminiscent of a cloud, a cloud that was resting askew on top of the line.

"Look how lovely this is," you said to your husband, he was still resting on the bed. You sat on its edge and ran the index finger of your uninjured hand over the red roots of the flowers and the tree. He looked you in the eye, little sparks of something there, you both smiled.

Outside the afternoon was still sunny and cloudless. You crossed the square that marked the boundary beyond which all motor vehicles were forbidden and walked over a newly constructed bridge to the vaporetto stop and got on a No. 2 to St Mark's Square, the boat puttered past churches and palaces with ornate columns and domes that stood out against a velvety blue sky, and you rubbed the tops of your fingers against each other as if to feel the downy texture of that sky, the silver shade of the Tethys sea growing fainter and fainter the further down the Grand Canal you went: Ca d'Oro, Rialto, Palazzo Grassi, Accademia. Once again, as in the car, you were being propelled by a force beyond yourselves, and you let yourself be rocked by the rhythm the halts produced at every stop, when the power of the engines altered as they idled and while the propellers were carving large whirlpools in the field-green water. At Accademia a lot of passengers get on and the rear deck becomes packed. The vaporetto heads for the middle of the canal, to the right almost immediately is the outline of Santa Maria della Salute's enormous dome and the mouth of the canal that opens out like a funnel towards the lagoon and the islands. It is then you see them, suddenly and with no warning at all, hovering closely together above the breast-shaped cupola of La Salute: birds with sabre-like beaks and sharply pointed leather wings, not birds at all but reptiles. You can hear the deafening flapping of sheets or sails in a strong wind and you stick your head out over the railing. The boat is crossing back over the canal towards the stops at San Marco, the pterodactyls are gliding over the white dome of La Salute and the contour of the rooftops in La Giudecca, abruptly they change course towards the boat, the first to arrive has a round red comb on top of its head, then come the others, you can see their silhouettes from below: the stick-thin legs and the pointed beak, the oblong abdomen, the leather wings. The vaporetto is approaching the quay, the engines switch to idle, the water bubbles up in large eddies below the hull. You watch the monsters plane across the Palazzo Ducale, heading for the Lido, they are flying in formation, red swastikas painted under the wings, and in the porthole on the first plane you can see the blonde head of the German film star, she is waving at the crowds holding flowers and the clustered banners spread across the broad white steps of the picture palace. *Als wir in Venedig landeten, schien die Septembersonne, als hätte sie sich schon ein bisschen vom Frühling geliehen. Der Pilot zog eine Schleife über der Stadt. Markusplatz und Dom, Brücken, Inseln, Paläste wirkten wie vergoldet. Das Seltsamste war das Wasser, das nicht sauber war, wie ich wusste, aber dennoch glitzerte.*[61]

Whenever a Jew has had sexual intercourse with a Christian, he shall be condemned to death by hanging. You stay in your seats on the boat which gets under way again towards San Marco Giardinette, though you do not get off there either. Kristina Söderbaum and the director Veit Harlan attended the film festival in Venice in September 1940 because "*Jud Süss*" had been nominated for best film that year. In the final scene Süss the Jew has his hands tied behind his back and is shoved inside a cage with a noose around his neck, it is snowing, Süss, arrogant and autocratic until now, turns out to be a coward, terrified at the prospect of dying, his voice fractures in panic: *Take all my*

61 "When we landed in Venice, the September sun was shining as though it had borrowed a little of the spring. The pilot flew in a loop around the city. St Mark's Square and the cathedral, the bridges, islands and palaces appeared to have been gilded. The strangest thing was the water, which I knew was not clean but it glittered all the same." (Kristina Söderbaum, *Nichts bleibt immer so*)

houses, my money, but let me live. The cage is raised high above the backdrop of a town square crammed with extras dressed in seventeenth-century costume while snowflakes from a dry-ice cannon whirl in front of the camera lens and the air is completely filled with tiny whirling dots. *Ich bin unschuldig! Ich bin ein armer Jude! Lass mich leben! Lass mich leben . . . !* The base of the cage opens in the middle of the word *leben* and the dead Süss, or rather his dangling lifeless feet, fills the entire screen. An official voice finally announces: *Let this punishment be an example . . . All Jews must leave Württemberg within three days . . . may our descendants uphold this law for ever and thus keep pure the blood of their children and their children's children.* Black screen. ENDE. The engines in the vaporetto are rumbling again while idling at San Zaccaria and this time you stand up and get off, your little girl in front of you holding her father's hand, the water so high it skims the gangway. The quay looks newly washed, shiny as if it has been raining although the sky is perfectly clear, you follow the flow of people moving to the left, *Riva degli Schiavoni* you read on a sign. In 1942 *die Söderbaum* was invited back to the film festival in Venice, this time to receive the Volpi Cup for her leading role in "*Die goldene Stadt*", the golden city is Prague whose limestone buildings are said to gleam gold in the sunset. Suddenly a siren howls and the people on the quay turn around, many of the tourists stop dead, as you do, the drawn-out wail appears to be leaking from an invisible joint behind the untrustworthy blue sky, the velvet looks to you now like fragile porcelain that could be covered in cracks at any moment. The din makes your daughter's body go rigid, her father has to take her in his arms while the three of you follow the stream that continues up the stairs to a high white bridge rising from the centre of the quay. From an ornate white balustrade you look out across the lagoon with the Lido and La Giudecca in the background, but you can see nothing to explain the siren. You move over to the parapet that faces the inner city, the water in the narrow canal is greener than out in the lagoon, its course runs below and between the buildings towards the labyrinthine centre of the city, if you stretched your hand towards the red facade on your right your fingers would graze the plaster. When the siren falls silent the scarlet colour of the building expands across the silence the din has left behind and clamours for your attention, you look up at the building, it is a palace with rows of windows that are curved in an Oriental style and decorated with white pillars. Your daughter frees herself from her father's arms and comes over to you, she wants you to tell her if a princess is living behind those windows. You have no difficulty imagining a noble-woman standing there, her hair in braids and a string of pearls across her forehead, she would be holding an ermine in her arms or perhaps a squirrel monkey in a little red velvet jacket.

"There might have been a princess in there once, only now it's a hotel, do you see?" And you lean down so your head is at the same height as hers, your eyes barely above the parapet, you pass one hand, the bad one, lightly around her back, you point with the other at some capital letters in gold that you ask her to read aloud.

"DA-NIE-LI," she spells it out. The hotel's name is Danieli. *Mutter, ich höre dich, ich komme!* It was *die Söderbaum* who would be standing there in that luxury suite, looking at the lagoon with the Volpi Cup in her arms, no doubt casting her mind back over her film career, all those innocent girls led to their downfall that she had portrayed, *Mutter, ich komme sofort!* she cries as Anna, the farmer's daughter, her eyes rolling above the bog she is about to step into, *Mutter!* And she strokes her mother's gravestone with her hand, the mother whose body floated up at the same spot where the daughter is now; perhaps Kristina was recalling what she had thought about while they filmed the last scene of *"Die goldene Stadt"*, the way it felt to stroke a gravestone made of papier mâché; perhaps she was reproaching her husband, the film's director, for allowing the camera to dwell far too long on her large, unrefined hand and its thick swollen fingers, because the moonbeams a spotlight produced had lingered on her restless hand, awkwardly trying to scrape despair out of the rounded arch of the fake gravestone and made the ugliness of her hand and the emptiness of the gesture all too apparent; or was she remembering, as she stood there in the window of the hotel with the Volpi Cup in her arms, what she had been forced to think about in order to create the lump in her throat as well as that despair, which did not come at all easily and which she had to employ every means at her disposal to evoke, using memories and her voice and the silly convulsive movements of her hand, just to make the whole thing feel more or less convincing. Having to act despair when there was so much genuine despair in cinemas and everywhere else in Europe ... She may have been thinking about that while holding the trophy for best actress somewhere in that luxury suite, that her counterfeit despair had, bizarrely, gone down well; or she may have been standing there with Veit Harlan, who was embracing her from behind and enjoying the moment with her, his arms around her waist and his chin supported on her shoulder, the two of them watching dusk fall across the lagoon from the same spot at the window, they would of course have been feeling successful and happy as they stood there and she may well have asked for something at that point: that the next death by drowning could take place here in the eternal city, although sooner or later her embarrassment at the nickname the German people had given her would have made itself felt as well (*Jude! Jude!* her enraged fiancé yells accusingly below the windows of Süss' house, holding the raped and drowned body of Kristina's character in his arms): *Die Reichswasserleiche,* "the Watery Corpse of the Third Reich" (*Jude! Jude!* his eyes blazing with an authentic Nazi hatred that shines through the seventeenth-century costume), and Veit Harlan tightens his arms around the waist of his third wife in the luxury suite of the Hotel Danieli and smiles in contentment, she can feel the muscles in his face stretching, his chin becoming heavier on her right shoulder, though she does not find the nickname the least bit funny and turns around and wrinkles her forehead like a child, pouting and looking furtively up at her husband the way she does in most of her films when she wants to appear indignant. The main entrance to the Hotel Danieli is reached by water, by boat, Kristina Söderbaum wrote in her memoirs that she arrived at the Hotel Danieli on the vaporetto, she would of course have arrived by launch or in a gondola at the film festival site on the Lido.

Your family has already started walking down the steps and you follow them, the quay is at a lower level and the water of the lagoon is lapping in protracted, even pulses over the stone paving. You follow father and daughter at a distance, the child is jumping with both feet together in the puddle, making splash after splash, they walk hand in hand, she so little, he so tall. A passing American tourist says something about *acqua alta*, and it is then you understand, the tide is rising, *acqua alta*, that explains the siren. You want to catch up with them and tell them that the water is rising, but you stay back, you watch them walking ahead, hand in hand, their arms like two branches of the same trunk, your gaze in the cleft they form. It is as if you do not want to infect them, you wish you could keep the same distance from them for ever, cut them free of you, you wish that she, your little girl, were a branch on a different tree (*Baum*) than yours: *You shall not bow down to them or worship them; for I, the* LORD *your God, am a jealous God, punishing the children for the sin of the parents to the third and fourth generation of those who hate me . . .* It torments you that that little girl who is your child is of the fourth generation, the fourth and not the fifth or sixth, she is the fourth, and the pain that thought causes you sometimes leaves you paralysed, you may be able to inhibit your reflex to breathe, from a desire to step outside your own respiration as if it were somewhere you could just walk away from, but you are confined to the place that is you. Hatred, the hiss of the German *Hass*. Though who ever hated that jealous God? Not your paternal grandfather, he served the Nazis in order to serve the same jealous God and, by all accounts, with the same zeal. Did your father hate God? If he hated anything it was the priesthood, but not God, who he probably did not believe in, though he must have believed in Hitler, *the idol*, the graven image in the hall, your father believed in perverse idols, your grandfather served them, your mother consented to having representations of them in her home. All of a sudden they have disappeared, you are level with St Mark's Square and following the stream of pedestrians turning to the right, which is where you finally catch sight of them; they are both wading through what appears to be a large pool of water that has formed over the part of the square that is closest to the main entrance to the church of San Marco, half the square is flooded, just half, as though the great piazza were lurching tail-heavy towards the basilica. A great many other tourists are also splashing in the pool that has formed, sandals in their hands, all of them barefoot, exhilarated, some of them walking around aimlessly kicking the water with a dreamy expression on their faces, one or two have their heads tipped back, searching the sky, the light fades just inside the greyish-white arcades of the square, and the barefoot people are wandering around in the water like patients at an antiquated mental hospital. You do not want to take your shoes off so you step onto the walkway that runs across the short end of the piazza and move along it until you reach the centre of the pool where your child is jumping and splashing together with other children. You should be laughing, but all you care about is getting her out of the water, the pigeons at the edge of the flooded area, towards the middle of the square, fill you with revulsion, you do not want your child swimming in the same water the pigeons gargle and in which they clean their feathers and spill their droppings, the pigeons that might draw down the great birds that are still there somewhere at the back of your mind. Your husband is laughing too, when she jumps off the walkway he catches the child in both arms, he catches her little hands in the air with those lovely hands of his, it has been a long time since you came as close to him as the child is now, you have lost the desire to do so, his skin is now just the memory of a scent, your lips can only bear the child's skin. For nine months your body got used to having the rhythmic beating of two hearts inside it, she was pulled out of your womb by force but the empty place inside you is still there, unhealed. You remember the way he used to put his ear to the second heartbeat every morning and evening, the reddish-brown wooden funnel you were lent pressed against the stretched skin across your belly. Kristina Söderbaum also gave birth to her first son by Caesarean section, she stayed in bed for almost the entire pregnancy on the upper floor of a newly built villa in Bavaria, from the bed she could look out across the tall conifers in the garden through a panoramic window that was eight metres across, the pine forest was part of the room. She travelled to the glittering city on the water from that forest and was welcomed at the airport by Italian cadets dressed all in white and by women and children who threw flowers and wanted to touch her dress. *Bella Kristina!* they shouted. The son was called Kristian, it was Veit Harlan's decision, in honour of his wife, the same way your father decided you would be called Cristina, also in honour of Kristina Söderbaum.

Làttimi, you remember hours later in the narrow hotel bed that is bathed in moonlight, you are lying in the foetal position beside your daughter, the shorter strands of the hair on the crown of her head tickle your nose, the vanilla-like scent of her scalp gathers at the top of your palate and your tongue pushes against the sweetness of the smell and sucks at it, your mouth extracts nourishment from the scent, as though you were a baby at the breast. *Làttimi*, opaline, soft, semi-transparent glass, also known as *bone glass* if bone ash was used to cloud the glass, sometimes as *milk glass* if the colour is white, milk glass is a modern term but *làttimi* have been produced in Venice since the fifteenth century. In the satin-clad alcove where you lie close together the moonbeams glisten as if water were flowing across the wall. *Lacrime*, tears. They are asleep, you lie awake, your tears are flowing beyond your face, across the glossy wallpaper, in the canal below that laps against the buildings, all the way across Dorsoduro and the Canal Grande to San Samuele and Campo Santo Stefano in the neighbourhood of San Marco or in Cannareggio as well, on the other side of the train station, in the neighbourhoods around San Geremia in the former ghetto where Micòl Finzi-Contini went looking for *làttimi* to add to her collection. It has all felt so bewilderingly like happiness. The taste of the fresh fish and the white wine outdoors on the quay at Fondamenta della Misericordia (as if Mercy were a place you could dock at), your chairs just a few centimetres from the edge. The glass shop and its ornamental objects – roses, animals, glass beads. The child so happy when you stepped into the hired gondola in the middle of the night, floating as if in a dream, all three of you lit by a lantern dangling from the prow, the necklace of blue glass beads around her neck. Rio dell'Albero, rio de la Vesta, rio dei Barcaroli, rio San Moisè. The rattle of china and taps running could be heard through the open windows that gave onto the canals, tinny Italian voices from television sets. And the moon: it emerged above the ridged roofs all of a sudden as if it were looking for you, trying to tell you something or to show you, it was large and almost full and dropped shiny streets of steel onto the black water. Your husband put his arm around the child's shoulders and pressed her tightly to him.

Làttimi, *what are they? Something to eat? They're things made with milky glass. Normal glasses, champagne glasses, ampoules, dainty vases, little boxes, stuff you might find among the junk in antique dealers' shops. In Venice they call them* làttimi, *and elsewhere* opalines *or even* flûtes.

It was in September 1942 that Kristina Söderbaum flew over Venice on her way to receive the Volpi Cup. Micòl Finzi-Contini is here then too, she is a character in a novel but just as real to you as the Nazi film star Kristina Söderbaum. You can see Micòl standing in

277

the middle of the Campo Sant'Angelo as the planes emblazoned with swastikas pass overhead, she is in Venice, in the treeless water city of Venice, because her beloved brother Alberto died earlier in the spring of a malignant lymphogranuloma and the huge estate in Ferrara sometimes feels utterly unendurable without him. Whether she is inside the house or outside in the garden, she cannot get enough air, just like Alberto when he was bedridden and tethered to an oxygen bottle, the vast sky they looked at through the windows, all that oxygen above the twelve hectares of garden in Ferrara, must have felt like a particularly cruel taunt. So she has moved to the apartment of her bachelor uncles in Venice, reoccupied what used to be her study when she was writing her dissertation on Emily Dickinson at Ca' Foscari university, on the other side of the Accademia bridge. She has just left her uncles' gloomy flat on Calle di Christo when the first whine rakes across the blue-shaded haze of the sky, the alley she has come out of is as narrow as a crevasse between the brick facades, but now she is in sunshine at least, so she halts at the edge of the square to enjoy the warmth of the rays, she has time to close her eyes for a moment and recall the sun on her skin on the tennis court at home and feel the heat rising through her feet and up her legs from the solid ground, feel the steadiness seep up through her sandals from the white paving stones, a sense of stability that, unlike the green canal water that runs beneath her uncles' windows and somehow manages to dissolve every line and contour, calms the fluttering she feels inside her chest a lot of the time. The sudden longing she had felt a little while ago for the garden – a residue of the care she has taken all her life of her grandmother's *Washingtonia filifera* that had to be wrapped in hay every winter – made her go out onto her uncles' balcony and water the neglected wisteria that was growing in a large broken clay pot as well as some smaller pots containing dried-out bright-red pelargoniums, watering can in hand she stood there and kept pouring until the dry loose earth in the pots could not absorb any more, the overflow dripped into the still stream of the Rio della Verona, her eyes followed the course of the drops down towards the cloudy green water and something made her breathing tight and wheezy like poor Alberto's at the end, when not even the oxygen bottles they brought home at ever greater expense from ever more disparate and distant cities – she went to Ravenna and Bologna several times and her father was constantly sending people far and wide, both to Piacenza and to Parma, the oxygen more expensive and harder to get hold of every time – were enough to help him breathe. Her own breathing on the balcony, a form of weeping that appeared to live a subterranean life of its own in her chest, as though the vertigo felt by the drops falling towards the stream that would dissolve them had infected her: vertigo at the long lonely fall. Cancer puts out shoots and spreads through the body until the disease surges in the blood like a tide and overwhelms the entire organism. She had stood there on the balcony and watched the journey made by the overflowing drops down to the watercourse and realised that the cloudy stream slowly flowing towards the lagoon was not outside her, that that water was her interior, an interior confined in a closed system. She had come to see that both inside and outside formed a circle, the way the domestic Racial Laws and the Germans' war formed a system of intercommunicating vessels, channels that merged as they headed towards a shared goal: extermination, Jewishness a lethal cancer in her blood and the blood of her family, impossible to escape from. Anxiety has just made her flee the place that is a refuge of a kind and run out on her own from the huge gloomy flat and its elderly uncles who the Racial Laws have made idle and anxious and its old Signorina Blumenfeld who can no longer be bothered to go out with her as a chaperone, and she had run down the stairs and out onto Campo Sant'Angelo with some leftover part of that energy she used to possess when, at home in Ferrara, she would run down to the garden and the tennis court with Alberto and the large clumsy dog Jor at her heels, and in that sequence of forward movements, in the muscular exertion itself, she had found a kind of power, sufficient, now that she is standing at the edge of Campo Sant' Angelo hearing the distant whine of the plane engines shredding the sky, to summon up a form of resistance. The aircraft *die Söderbaum* is travelling in flies low along the Canal Grande, so low that the arms raised at an angle in the ancient Roman salute from the covered steps on the Rialto bridge look as though they could reach the plane's underbelly. The shadow of the swastika-emblazoned steel wings creates patches that move along the buildings and across the water that Micòl is too far away to see but she can hear the hacking of the engines that is reverberating all the more strongly now along the broad canal, and she tracks the flying artefact with her eyes, even taking a few steps towards the centre of Campo Sant' Angelo the better to watch the alarming creature, until she sees it make a graceful left turn above Palazzo Grassi and then head straight for the bell tower in San Stefano and on towards the square on which she is standing as if nailed to the paving stones, completely exposed to the plane passing above her with a deafening roar while Micòl tips her head back to catch sight perhaps of a head as blonde as her own in one of the round windows in the body of the plane. Not that that would have occurred to her, she has other things on her mind, such as a kind of premonition brought on by seeing the superiority of the German flying machine up in the sky, such as a line of Emily Dickinson's that comes back to her after all these years: *The most triumphant Bird I ever knew or met . . .* The rattling drone of the plane intensifies across the square as it performs a right turn over Sant' Angelo in order to head towards La Fenice and San Marco. *The most triumphant Bird . . .* and with that phrase the memory comes back of her disputation in the spring of 1939, when the Racial Laws that would change her life were only a year old and stopped her being awarded the *cum laude* her work had actually merited, the effect of the Racial Laws spread slowly across Italy, they were still spreading, by degrees, like a kind of *acqua alta*. She is remembering that long tail-end of winter when she took her English exam, she remembers the thick, white February fog that hovered over everything and made the Accademia bridge float like a cloud in the mist when she crossed it on her way to the library in Ca' Foscari and the little streets where she would go looking for a new opaline for her collection appear to be spaces in a dream in which you wander blindly; and she is remembering the expressions on the faces of the panel in the university hall where for a whole hour she defended "Dickinson's Use of Capitilization" and her thesis that future editions of Dickinson would reinstate the dash and the upper-case letters that had been systematically removed in all the editions of her work to this time (*As the distinguished gentlemen can see for themselves in this recently published facsimile edition, in which Martha Dickinson Bianchi, the poet's niece, had some of the original texts reproduced, such as the lines from* "Two Lengths has every Day" *that the poet wrote on the flap of an envelope and in which her unconventional use of capital letters is clearly demonstrated*). And it is as if the sound of the engine of the German plane that has wandered off course to this square and its prominent Nazi passenger she had caught a glimpse of were embodying that force which was intent on ironing out and altering Dickinson's identity, her uniqueness, a force which was trying to *Aryanise* her, and then, quite literally out of the blue, poem 43 from the 1896 edition comes to her, with the same liberating sense of illumination as when she came out of the narrow darkness of Calle di Christo a while ago and the sky cracked above her at an obtuse angle across Sant' Angelo square: *The Brain – is wider than the Sky –* the lines of the poem and all their disputed upper-case letters and those degenerate, *entartete*, dashes come in to land one by one:

The Brain – is wider than the Sky –
For – put them side by side –
The one the other will contain
With ease – and You – beside –

So Micòl remains stubbornly standing in the centre of Campo Sant'Angelo, as though she were unconcerned at being seen by beings who meant her harm, as though she were above every form of insult and threat. She watches the flying machine and its blood-red swastika until it becomes a dash and then a black dot in a text that has not yet been completed. Then she starts walking towards Campo S. Stefano via Calle dei Frati and turns left into Calle del Pestrin and from there into the little triangular Campo dei Morti where one of the antique shops she favours is located.

Giorgio Bassani's character Micòl and her entire family would be arrested exactly one year later, at the end of September 1943, during the first month of the newly inaugurated Socialist Republic, after the Germans had freed the deposed Mussolini and set up a puppet regime whose power was centred on the little town of Salò on Lake Garda. In the epilogue to *Il giardino dei Finzi-Contini* Giorgio Bassani tells us that in November the family was deported to a concentration camp in Fossoli before being sent on to Germany. You have read that the place in Germany that Jews from Ferrara were taken to is called Buchenwald. And you know that by then S.S.-Unterscharführer Kurt Seidel had been transferred to the prison and transfer point of San Sabba in Trieste because the extermination camp in Treblinka was closed down in March 1943. There, in Trieste, the trail of Kurt Seidel, the man who chose to consider himself an engineer and had Treblinka's most prominent street named after him, comes to an end, the trail peters out in a town less than two hours by car from Venice. You also know that one year after Kurt Seidel arrived, in March 1944, Erwin Hermann Lambert was called in to the former rice factory at San Sabba on the outskirts of Trieste to design, construct and install a crematorium oven like all the others he had previously designed and constructed, including the ones at Schloss Hartheim and Treblinka, the crematorium at San Sabba began operating on April 4, 1944, the same year Lambert got married to

Maria Brandstetter. The wedding may already have taken place in Linz and she accompanied her husband to Trieste and spent several weeks with him on the sixth floor of the former rice factory where the S.S. staff had their living quarters. In San Sabba they would probably have met old friends such as Christian Wirth, Franz Stangl and Kurt Seidel. Perhaps the couple went to Venice on leave and celebrated their honeymoon in the city of canals. It is quite conceivable that Kurt Seidel would have taken the opportunity on one or several of his leaves to travel around Northern Italy, including to Venice. Sometimes you imagine that he was transferred to Salò, that his innate elegance and refinement served to qualify him to be the driver of one of the officers of the S.S. troop that guarded Mussolini in the red brick villa where, surrounded by barbed wire, Il Duce lived with his faithful Clara Petacci, who, when faced with the firing squad the following year, would throw herself in front of her lover to protect him and so be struck by the first bullet. You can see Kurt Seidel driving a black Mercedes along the narrow roads around Lake Garda while the officer in the back seat plays record after record on the gramophone in his lap: Anton Bruckner's Fourth Symphony, in a Telefunken recording of June 22–24, 1939, from Hamburg with Eugen Jochum conducting; Bruckner's Fifth Symphony in a recording from 1938 with the same conductor and for the same record company, the Third Act of "Parsifal" in a recording made by the Berlin Radio Orchestra on March 31, 1942, conducted by Hans Knappertsbusch and with the soprano Elsa Larcén as Kundry and the tenor Karl Hartmann as Parsifal, and a *cracking little curiosity* the officer found in the villa he had commandeered as living quarters and that now forms part of his collection, though just for fun: a recording from the Metropolitan Opera of November 1, 1936 with the Jew Artur Bodanzky conducting and Lauritz Melchior as Siegfried and Marjorie Lawrence as Brünnhilde, *Mein Gott!* And when the high-ranking S.S. officer tires of his records he asks Kurt Seidel to turn on the radio where what gets played more often than not is in any case Bruckner and Wagner, and perhaps one of the recordings of *"Die Meistersinger von Nürnberg"* makes him think of Walther beside the Attersee, playing the prelude on his instrument down by the jetty, and that resounding version of Wagner on the accordion – nautical and tipsy as it is, the rolling pitch written into the notes almost – merges with the winding road as it comes out of small villages below sloping lemon orchards, past little harbours with white sailing boats where the inhabitants are unloading fish, the light coming and going, in and out of the tunnels excavated from the limestone, all of it must make him feel at home by the waters of this new lake which is the same turquoise colour. And you are thinking about the other women. Helene Hintersteiner left the murder castle at Hartheim for a while and gave birth to a child in Linz, a child the identity of whose father remains unknown. At Elne, in the Pyrenees, Elisabeth Eidenbenz continued to run the maternity hospital until 1944, by then it was caring primarily for Jewish women from the transfer camp in Rivesaltes. You keep thinking until your thoughts begin to spin. Last night, above the gondola, the moon had been playing with you. Now cold silvery water is flowing down the silk wallpaper in the alcove. You feel grateful nonetheless for the moon-light and the draught fanning you through the open window because the delivery room in which you gave birth to your child and to where you are returning in memory was like a crate, a cardboard box with-out a lid, the child's head was turned at the wrong angle and refusing to descend towards the birth canal although her heart rate was falling towards zero, she would never pass through the canal alive, she was imprisoned in your womb like a cat in a sack thrown into the nearest body of water, if you had lived in another age and in another place than that county hospital in southern Europe in 2001, at least one of you would have died, probably both. You can sense the blunt instruments, the forceps or that blunt hook, then the sharp ones, the pointed hook whose inner bevel has been polished to a sharp edge as well as a scissor-shaped drill with which they would have perforated

284

the cranium. At the hospital on the Catalonian coast, the same hospital where they would later sew up your torn fingertip, they performed a straightforward section of your abdomen that freed her head in a second or two – as if the same hand that had thrown the kittens into the water had changed its mind and untied the knot on the bag and let one of the cats live, just one, just her, not *the others, all the others* – so your womb remained heavy even when your healthy child was lying at your breast, and your mind was sore, as if the placenta had not been removed, as if your belly were swelling because a death were taking place within it and hands were digging into your insides with that razor-edged hook, with the saw that tore your pubic bone and ripped at your ear canals with a hateful, urgent sound. For a while during the gondola trip you felt that the dark waters of the canal led nowhere. Though the gondolier finally rowed you back to the open lagoon and left you at the same landing stage where you embarked. That quay ought also to be called *Misericordia*, mercy. Nineteen forty-two, the year of so many of the mass killings, when so many of the mass murders of the Nazis began, the number of the year is floating across all these waters like a reflection, as if you had held it up on the port side of the gondola and it were being reflected in the water, and it had been inverted the way reflections are, 1942 1492, because it was from a Spanish port that Micòl's family on her mother's side, the Herreras, were expelled, arriving in Ferrara and Venice via Rome in 1492. You are thinking about Micòl's uncles on Calle di Cristo where Micòl spent several years off and on writing her dissertation on Emily Dickinson, you are thinking about her collection of *làttimi* that was arranged in one of the windows that gave onto the Verona canal while waiting to be displayed on the mahogany shelves of her room in Ferrara, whose view over the garden and the roofs and castle of the town was like that from a transatlantic liner, according to Bassani, the opalescent glass that reminded her of the Venice mists would end up in a cupboard of its own next to the bookshelves, their books arranged according to language, English and French on the wall between the two windows from which she could see her grandmother's fibrous *Washingtonia filifera*, and a *fifth bookshelf, this one for Italian literature, classic and modern and for translations: mainly from Russian: – Pushkin, Gogol, Tolstoy, Dostoevsky, Chekhov.* And now you are remembering your own bookshelves on Marielundsgatan in Uppsala, the books lined up in the deep window recesses, the corkboard on the wall next to the white bookcase with your "butterflies": pieces of paper written on in your own hand and cuttings you pinned to the corkboard with the names of authors, book titles, relevant historical dates, arranged so as to give you a kind of overview, a synchronicity you were unable to identify in the linear order of the books. The white notes with their drawing pins in the middle fluttered in the draught from the windows during spring and summer, or every time you opened one of the two windows to let out both of your now long-dead cats. Your daughter is wedged against your ribcage in the confined space that reminds you of a ship's cabin, the walls seem to be yawing in the moonlight, the alcove is swimming in cold silvery water, you have a hollow feeling in your stomach, as if you were being dragged down by a powerful force and everything were about to sink, and you press the child close against you and bury your face in her neck, and somewhere you can hear the roar of the Tethys sea and you see a great wave washing over Micòl's books and her collection of *làttimi* topples to the floor to float around, and your butterfly collection comes loose from its silvery pins to be washed away as well, vanishing in the currents of the vast primeval sea that is returning.

The Internment Camp at Rivesaltes,
Pyrénées-Orientales, France, the Free Zone
From Friedel Bohny-Reiter's Journal

July 16, 1942

The gold of the sunset is spread out where the hills disappear into the azure. The rays are still colouring the camp and make everything seem a bit more cheerful. The little garden in front of the barrack has just been watered. The green beans are growing straight as a die. I have my dogs beside me: Cispa is observing the evening with a philosopher's gaze, and little Viana is playing in the sand. It all makes for a peaceful scene that softens the harsh impressions of the day.

Today black cars arrived at the camp – the German Commission. The people who were deported or fled from Germany are being allowed to return – their faith or National Socialism. There are not many signing up but the temptation to return to an ordered life must be great.

We are as happy as larks. Tomorrow we are having a gypsy party.

July 19, 1942, Sunday

A thousand Gypsies arrived last night. What is going to happen to them?

Gypsies are a strange people [. . .] The children have lovely, fine-featured faces, the women are stately and proud. A race of beggars, but free and proud for all that, rebels who are outcasts wherever they go.

The party was delightful. First they were given shoes, then we all went out to the large field. We sat on the ground, that lovely bare soil they are so attached to. We sang. It wasn't very tuneful, but their dark eyes shone with happiness, for once someone was looking after them and them alone.

Sunday. It is silent and empty in the K12-block. I have never felt so glad about silence before. I am almost holding my breath as I sit here so as to enjoy this wonderful silence. No-one can pursue me, I can just be myself, I am not irritating anyone, no-one has to thank me, no-one is jealous of me or admiring me. Here is where I find the grey walls that have become as dear as friends, protecting me from the gossip of the world outside and that are – silent.

July 23, 1942

Today is a grey day. The crowding, the destitution, all the people who are steadily deteriorating. They make me feel this profound sense of discouragement. What are we achieving by giving them a plate of pureed peas? Elsi telephoned me, she will not be coming for a long while – that is hard.

It is clearing up a bit, thank heavens. All this greyness, all this heaviness – I didn't think I would be able to overcome it yet again. The misery appears to be getting even worse. Though perhaps that is not the case? Every morning when I see the long, long queues of people fighting and insulting one another without any sign of fellow feeling, of caring about anyone else, I feel afraid [. . .]

And yesterday I got it thrown in my face: "Your wretched soup should have been the end of us long ago." I was overwhelmed with bitterness, a feeling I have had to endure for a very long time. Then the Spaniards walked past, they shook my hand in gratitude, they are the ones we can help.

We are lying in front of the barrack. The moon is illuminating the camp with its radiance. The stars are so tiny and so far away. I understand so well now the little girl in the fairytale who looked at the stars and cried in despair: "Stars, oh stars, are you no longer there?" [...]

July 28, 1942

We are sitting in our little office making music. It is strange how that is able to restore some of the sense of calm we are losing here. There are rumours going around besides: about the immediate future, about something unknown and secret.

New Jewish refugees – women and children – are arriving from the Occupied Zone. They were sent to the camp at Rivesaltes where their papers and food coupons were taken from them, "and here they are". The poor unfortunates have not yet realised they are in a concentration camp and they are totally confused.

Everyone comes to me. "Sister, what do you think is going to happen?" What can I reply? These poor persecuted creatures. I am not the one who decides their fate. I try to remain calm and to pass that on to them. I am deeply affected by their distress, by the misfortune that afflicts this people.

I find it very difficult working with my German colleagues. Their faces are haggard as well.

The worst thing is that the rabbis left the camp today in great haste. Can one of them really once have said, "I want to teach my co-religionists that there is wisdom to be gained in suffering"?

Rabbi Bloch fled today. It was announced that the special forces would be arriving tomorrow. The Jews have to be evacuated to another block at 5 a.m.

We are waiting impatiently for Elsi while preparing for the first of August – that is going to be a real party. A telegram arrived on the thirtieth, an hour later Elsi turned up at the camp to say goodbye for good. That shook me to the core, and left me deeply sad. But then the children appeared, as happy as ever. I don't want there to be a funereal mood. I tell them that Elsi is going away for good. One of the girls starts singing: *"España, patria mía"*. Our children from the homes arrive for tea. They sing with such enthusiasm it almost brings the barrack down around our ears. One song after another. The whole barrack is rejoicing. Overwhelmed, I looked at the little brown, occasionally round, faces – we have managed to keep them healthy to some extent, tried to make them happy with little parties so that that priceless joy the children possess should not be buried in the greyness of the camp. I will never forget the barrack filled with singing children. [...]

August 3, 1942

It is half past three in the morning. I am sitting behind a mountain of bills and books and doing one sum after the other.

All the day's events continue to play out in my head. Dark rumours were already going around the camp the previous evening. The special forces arrived. I hurried over to J-block in the morning. Everyone was lined up in front of the barrack, their faces haggard. They were all under guard. Monsieur Littaz did the roll call. Wherever I go I see worried faces. "Sister, where are they going to send us?" The nightmare is to end up in Poland. What can I say? What do I know about it? I try to console them. "Have courage, it can't get worse." I am suddenly stricken with amazement. There they all are waiting, looking anxious, but no-one is rebelling. I almost feel like screaming: "Do you think we're no better than animals ? I am not leaving, I am not leaving!" No-one moves. Have you all become so passive you are simply resigned to accept your fate as outcasts?

I go back to our barrack. My assistant fails to appear, she escaped last night with her husband. They left all their belongings behind. Madame Schwann tells me: "At 2 a.m. they rapped on our window. I watched them go for a long time, two silhouettes running away across the fields. The rain was pouring down. Now and then the plain was illuminated by flashes of lightning, I could see them clearly then, and I shivered for them."

"Your papers, if you please." Three guards are at the door to our barrack. Madame Schwann turned pale. "So it is our turn now, Sister." The guards quickly rounded up my Germans. I have to use all my strength just to remain on my feet. My arms hang uselessly at my side. I force myself to keep my eyes fixed on them. They come out of the barracks accompanied by the guards.

I simply cannot sit still. I cycle over to their barracks. When I get there they are frantically gathering together their things. The roll call is taking place in half an hour. Then I watch them walk over to F-block, hauling their belongings – there are six hundred of them. We hurry to provide each of them with something to eat. The head of the camp says that everyone will remain in F-block for the moment. No-one knows what is going to happen. We take our soup over to them, at 7 p.m. They wolf it down, more famished than ever, and start fighting over the empty pot. I feel riven with disgust. Madame Schwann, who is watching the scene, says: "In a few weeks we who have been spoiled by Swiss aid will be just like them, starving. It is appalling. What have we done to deserve this?"

I walk among the barracks. Someone yells, "Long Live Switzerland" when he sees me coming with the soup. Getting something to eat is the most important thing for many of them. Worry never stops anyone eating.

The old women from the barracks for the convalescent are lying on their straw mattresses. In the midst of this appalling shambles the faces you see everywhere are apathetic, despairing, terrified.

I sit down for a bit with our colleagues. Bertel, the poor thing, cannot stop crying. I went to speak with the head of the camp – maybe I could keep one of them.

What will the new day bring? Who will be able to sleep tonight?

It is almost 5 a.m. I am cold. A storm is raging over the barracks. The heat has disappeared. I feel drained, defenceless, now that I can do nothing to help people anymore. Why is no-one else doing anything? [...]

August 6, 1942

We went over to F-block very early. We were afraid they would be evacuating people at dawn. When we got there everyone was in a wretched state. Some had broken down, others were tormented by the waiting. Attempted suicides. People swallowed whatever they could get hold of. Entire bottles of sleeping tablets.

I got to A-block. New arrivals, from Paris and Lyon. Women weeping in despair on the trucks.

September 2, 1942

Could there be anything sadder than to see these children and know you can do nothing for them? They have to leave, they have to be handed over.

A telegram arrived from Toulouse today. Our children and our "staff" have been freed. I hurry over to the prefecture. They promise I will get a reply tomorrow. So yet one more night.

In the camp a beaming Madame Schwartzschild comes over to me. I managed to get her and her child freed. She has already been moved to J-block. But her husband has to go. By chance I hear that the convoy will be setting off early tomorrow morning. And what are we going to do about the ones with no papers? I understand enough about the way things work here to know you cannot get anywhere without tangible evidence.

I stop the commanding officer. "No, no, they have to go." I explain – there is nothing to be done. "Get me a signed paper from the prefecture." Something suddenly occurs to him and he goes to the telephone. I can hear him asking to speak to the prefecture. I am on tenterhooks. At last. Our people, our children can stay. I feel like throwing my arms around his neck. But I made do with offering him a cigarette.

The joy among our people is indescribable.

Two children from our home at Pringy come over to me. I can do nothing for them, having to watch their reaction is dreadful. Do they really have to go? I ring Toulouse. There is no-one willing to accept the call. Though they do so in the end. I hope to receive a positive response from Vichy tomorrow.

2 o'clock in the morning

A convoy of twenty children has just arrived. It was unbearable having to watch the mothers trying to find their children. Two children whose parents could not be found are sleeping with Marianne. They are all such lovely children, I dread to think what will happen to them.

6 o'clock in the morning

Twelve hundred people turn up to the roll call with their luggage. I find five children from our homes among them. I spend four hours on the telephone until I hear Maurice's voice. He promises to do all he can in Vichy. It will be difficult to arrange for me to keep the children without papers or certificates. I see them at the roll call, pale and terrified. We have to get them released. The Kommandant's car has arrived. I tackle him once again. "Well then," he says, "try and keep them in your barrack until these papers of yours arrive."

The departure is planned for 12 noon. The buses fill up. The procession seems endless, eight hundred people – seventy children.

Fortunately for us we have to keep running round. With tea, milk for the children, fruit, cheese. Everyone has something to give to the ones who are remaining. We are roasting in the sun. New trucks keep coming. They get filled one after the other. Now that everyone knows they have to go most of them are calm and keeping themselves in check. Here come our young people from the barrack for the extremely malnourished. How hard we fought for them last winter. We saved them from dying of starvation. We watched them put on weight, start planning for the future. They used to come and say goodbye to us when they left the camp to work somewhere else – beaming and full of hope, and now? I can see them sitting on the straw in the trucks, eyes empty, despairing.

12.30 p.m.

K-block is full of life. All of our children from B-block who went with Elsbeth and me on Sundays to sing to the people in the infirmary are here. I can still see them at their tables having their breakfast before leaving the children's home. They were beaming. And now? Best not to think, just work – keep running. "Who would like more tea?" "Here are your magazines," and so on. The sun is setting. The last rays are lighting up their despairing, grieving faces. They will all soon be leaving this place. Only one dark-skinned boy will remain, alone on the plain.

When I walk past the spot the next day the hard, trampled soil reminds me of the sorrowful events of the day before.

Two trucks left the camp today with some of the fortunate ones who have been "freed".

It has been possible to get twenty-five children from the *Œuvre de secours aux enfants* released. Our ones have returned to J-block. At last. For good.

This has been a hard day to bear. I am not really sure why. I still have one bright spot left and what a radiant one it is – Gusti.

September 13, 1942

It is half past midnight. We have only just got back from the station. We had been waiting there since 3 p.m. Things were dreadful today. Even in the block. Scenes, people fainting.

From 7 to 11 in the morning everyone was on their feet waiting for the roll call, under a scorching sun. Then those who were to stay were separated from those who were being sent on the convoy. I can still hear the screams of the women.

I managed to get the children of one of the mothers freed. As I tried to get them to go with me, the mother wrenched them towards her. I took them out of her arms and over to our barrack. When the mother refused to climb onto the truck the guards lifted her into it.

Then I left the block. Marianne waited for the roll call to check that none of the children we had managed to get released were taken away.

I returned to the barrack to prepare tea, soup and supplies for the journey. At 3 p.m. everything was taken on a truck to the railway station.

The first vehicle arrived, filled with people who were being forced to leave. One carriage after another was filled. Two remained empty. We waited and kept waiting. Eight, nine, ten hours passed. A rumour went around that twenty people had escaped and there were fifty missing from the list because of a miscalculation.

I returned to K-block. In the dark I could make out the group of those who were not due to leave. A search was being carried out among them for the people who had escaped, and in the empty barracks as well. Some of them were found. The others were replaced indiscriminately. I can still see the guards dragging people who were struggling frantically away to the trucks.

A Protestant woman from Belgium had arrived here with her two children to look for her husband. She was seized and had to replace the last missing person. Her screaming during the night was awful. Before they reached the railway carriage she was desperately clinging to the guards. To no avail. The iron door was shut behind her and through the bars her weeping could be heard as she blamed the whole human race. I am often afflicted with a terrible kind of fear – that those of us here have become accomplices almost in what is in truth a form of slave-trading.

On my return I came across a half-blind old woman. She must have got out of her bed to attend the roll call and couldn't find the way back to her barrack in the dark.

The next morning everything was the way it was before, apart from the weight of bitterness inside us.

Villa Saint-Jean, Banyuls-sur-Mer, France,
the Free Zone,
September 10, 1942

The train has stopped and Carmen Pedrón does not have to get up
or even lean forward to see the sign she has been waiting for since
early that morning when Nurse Friedel put her on the train, alone,
with two sick infants in a large basket, her own seven-month-old
baby in her arms and a mute three-year-old on the seat beside her; the
sun had cast long narrow shadows across the platform at Rivesaltes,
now the clock face mounted on the station building next to the sign
that says BANYULS-SUR-MER is telling her it is ten past four; after all
the stops and delays they have finally arrived, but she remains in her
sweat-drenched seat that sticks to the underside of her thigh, the joy
she has been expecting to bubble up inside her ever since they got
in the truck that drove them out of the camp has not yet made itself
felt, not during all the hours of the journey, she stays where she is
in the nauseating heat of the train compartment, a taut veil of sweat
over her face, tight as a stocking, and if she is thinking about anything
it is the milk Nurse Friedel sent with her for the boys, it turned
sour several hours ago and they may get diarrhoea now, weak as they
already are and covered in horrible eczema and scabs, she felt she
had to put the bottles in their mouths even though she could clearly
see that the consistency of the milk had begun to change and was
curdling into large, yellow lumps, which is why she is also thinking
about her fear, and that she has not been free of it, not for one single
day in the last three years, most recently her fear that the children's
cries would annoy the conductor who went off with their papers and
has still not handed them back, she is waiting for the go-ahead from

him and also for some help, perhaps, with carrying the children, she never lets go of her own girl, Jeanne, Juanita as she calls her in her heart of hearts, she is lying in the crook of her arm, the hair on the back of her neck damp from the persistent film of sweat that clings so tightly to Carmen's skin even there, Juanita is sleeping against her sweaty arm, apparently calm even though she is not being given the breast, and the girl sitting motionless and mute beside her is also calm but calm in a consuming way, there is a glacial quality to her stillness even in the pitiless heat, she is sitting there as straight as if her spine were an inflexible little stick, during the entire journey the girl has not moved a millimetre from the position Nurse Friedel put her in, she has not leant against Carmen to seek protection or consolation and she has refused anything to eat or drink, the child has been sitting there for hour after hour as if all that her grief-stricken person amounted to was a dirty blue dress she had long since abandoned. A cold draught begins to wind through the system of tunnels and shafts Carmen imagines forms the interior of her body and face, her *insides*: she does not want to think about the girl, she deliberately steers her thoughts out into the light instead, to the travel permits and identity papers that Nurse Friedel showed the conductor, he grabbed them as if his arm were an extension of the camp, a self-appointed prison guard, his face rigid with an authority that has been applied rather loosely around the edges, like a mask he has to fit over his ears with a pair of rubber bands every morning after he has shaved and polished that fascist moustache, exactly like Franco's, from out of the two narrow holes in the mask he looked through the papers in detail, he even inspected the signs the children had hanging around their necks (Angel Baquero, né mars 8 1942, Martin Dubois né juin 15 1942, Jeanne Fayos Pedrón née février 25 1942, Hannelore Kahn, née mars 20 1939); in anticipation of his return, the memory of the navy colour of the conductor's uniform prompts a sudden and irresistible longing for a sky with the same bluish-black sheen she would be able to find coolness beneath, and almost immediately it is as if everything really does go black. But then a nasty smell sets a stray spark to her awareness (Juana?) and she follows the pungent odour moving like an ice-cold breath through the dark passages she is running down on stiff, aching limbs that seem not to want to obey her, that feel swollen and mired in darkness like steaming tar around her feet, but she keeps running, running until her feet, if only with the utmost effort, come free of the sticky darkness and the stench can finally lead her out into the light again: Thank God, Juanita is still against her chest, illuminated by the light that is stabbing into Carmen's eyes, her little fist clenched around a button on her dress.

"*Madame! Reveillez-vous! Mais Madame . . . C'est incroyable, ça!*" The conductor is waving their papers over her face, the word *madame* distorting his mouth as if he were chewing on something rotten, that is where the putrid smell is coming from, the stench washes over her with every word the man utters – *Madame!* If this war and this awful life ever come to an end she never wants to be called *madame* again, the unending humiliation she has been subjected to since she fled across the border with Juan assails her with renewed and concentrated vigour, each humiliation distinct though piled one on top of the other, the way wave piled on top of wave on the filthy sand of the beach camp at Argelès, the squelching rhythm of humiliation that refuses to stop pounding inside her, its combined weight is pressing against her eyelids and the upper part of her chest and threatening to overwhelm her but then, without further ado, the uniformed man lifts the basket with both infants and sets off along the corridor, their documents fanned out in his free hand, and Carmen Pedrón gets up as quickly as she can, the burn on the underside of her thigh as the stuck skin is ripped free helps to sober her. Vacant and immobile, the grief-stricken girl remains in her seat. Carmen puts one arm round her back and lifts her gently to her feet in the empty compartment, her toes look lost in the too-big sandals that were handed out to the children in the Swiss barracks just a week ago, carefully, very carefully, as if she were guiding a sleepwalker, she takes the slack little hand, it makes her think for an instant of the quails' eggs her brother Miguel used to hunt for in the fields when they were little and lived in a tiny village in Aragon; then they slowly start moving towards the exit, step by step they stumble along the corridor, Carmen imagines the distance to be an oblong piece of material, the muffled sound of their steps the cut that is slowly unstitching it.

In the middle of the platform the conductor is tapping their papers against his hand with an I-told-you-so expression on the loose-fitting mask, as though he were not the least bit surprised that *no-one* is there to meet them and it were perfectly obvious that they will have to go back the same way they came, and they should never have been released from the fenced-off barracks they were consigned to in the first place. She has to get Hannelore down herself; for some reason it is only now as she lifts the girl and puts her own swollen feet on the train's iron steps with a child in each arm that she says the girl's name to herself, she has not dared to think of that name throughout the entire journey, as though it might make the aware-ness of everything the girl has just been through more difficult to bear. Then they are outside on the baking platform, a platform in a small town, she can already see a whitewashed church tower sticking up above a warehouse building on a siding, though that joy she had been hoping for has yet to arrive, it is still hard to breathe. The stationmaster is standing beside the conductor now and the two men are involved in an animated exchange in which they seem intent on confirming what the other thinks, she hears the word *espagnol* repeated, the boys are whimpering at the scorching heat beneath their toes although it is the little group she makes up with Jeanne and the motherless girl below the train they keep looking askance at, both uniformed men appear to be about to come to a decision, Carmen

Pedrón can see it in their gestures and their posture, in the scornful looks those indignant faces are sending her way, and that is when something snaps, those awful screams come rushing back at her from the place in which she has been trying to keep them confined all day, once again she can hear the high-pitched denials Hannelore's mother kept gasping while Nurse Friedel prised her hands from around her child – no no no – and then the long drawn-out howl that followed – noooo – as the child was wrenched away from her mother's side, from the spot between her hip and armpit where Hannelore was wedged, whimpering, then the gurgling notes at the end of the scream as the gendarmes heaved the mother up onto the bed of the truck, as though the pain were a liquid that had filled her to the brim and then flowed out of her down to the last drop. Carmen Pedrón is trembling all over at the memory of what she witnessed at the marshalling point, the darkness of the men's uniforms is beginning to stain the whole platform, their silhouettes flowing between the cracks in the paving like a kind of viscous fluid, as though the sun had suddenly set at a very oblique angle and were throwing long, narrow shadows once again across the ground, she is about to fall to her knees and say that she cannot for the life of her go back to the camp, that they might just as well shoot her and her child right here even though she knows somewhere inside her that they are not guards or soldiers, just railway staff and therefore unarmed, with no attributes of power other than their musty uniforms, only they are going to have to shoot her nonetheless, kill her with something, with their bare hands, because she cannot take any more, she is about to yell all of that in a language both men obviously despise, that word *espagnol* she saw them spit out with an incomprehensible hatred in their eyes, when, just before the drop begins, as she is tipping her head towards the sky in preparation for moving backwards, she sees a couple of figures in the distance, at the end of the platform, they are bright, in dazzling white aprons, the broad-hipped one whose fair hair is tied back and gleaming yellow in the sunshine is striding ahead, like a swan with a crown, Carmen thinks, entranced and distracted in equal measure, behind her a shorter dark-haired figure beneath a starched bonnet is pulling a kind of cart, both women are walking along the platform without haste but with an authority that could stop the sun in its course, which is what it does as well, the dark silhouettes that were soiling the ground with their malice a moment ago are congealing and shrinking back into the sombre uniforms they came from; beside the white swan who has now come alongside them the men seem both shorter and in every conceivable way weaker than the majestic figure addressing them in French, Carmen understands exactly what words the beautiful swan is uttering, but it is as if all she wants to listen to is the sound of her voice, to its deep resonant song. *Madeleine Durand.* After a while that Carmen experiences as timeless, in which time has been temporarily abolished, she remembers the piece of paper she has in her pocket with that name written on: it is what the matron of the home for little children who is to take care of them is called, Carmen had been picturing a short nervous figure like señorita Elisabeth at the maternity hospital in Elne, instead of this striking woman with a white tie below a rounded collar whose gaze seems to come from afar while harbouring a veiled understanding of everything, an all-knowing and expectant look that is rocking under the merciless sun like a wide and benevolent body of water. Madeleine Durand extends a hand towards the papers the conductor has been keeping to himself until this moment and they are passed to her with something not unlike a bow, then she moves towards Carmen Pedrón and the children close beside her while the other nurse loads the cart with the infants in their basket and unfurls a large black umbrella that had been lying at the bottom of the cart to protect them from the sun. Madeleine Durand meanwhile has bent down in front of Hannelore whose eyes remain out of reach. Durand's large log-like legs disappear beneath the white apron and the skirt that forms a broad bell around her, for several long minutes Madeleine Durand says nothing, she is just there, her entire attention focused on the introverted child, the way the glistening sea rests beside the land, waiting; something in that sea now succeeds in rekindling the light in Hannelore's eyes, could it be the whiteness in the figure of the Swan? Carmen wonders, that means that when the Swan folds her wings around the child's ribcage and lifts her into her arms the eyes of the woman and the child swim inside each other? Then the party marches off the platform, they walk towards the town down a long hill from whose brow a narrow strip of sea can be seen, carrying her child Carmen Pedrón walks behind the nurse with tears in her eyes and a name on her mind she has avoided thinking about for months, Juan, Juan Fayos, Juanita's father, Juana, Juanita who she registered as Jeanne in order to make a new beginning in this country that does not want them, Juan who was recruited to a labour group and from whom she has had no news ever since, who she knows nothing about, whether he is dead or has left her, whether he went to Mexico or is in some German prison camp, but now that name is being cried loud enough to echo inside her, Juan! For the first time in ages she would like to tell him something, about this miraculous thing that has happened to them, that they are walking freely down a street, with ordinary people around them, that the street is turning and opening out towards the sea, that there are terraced houses and a villa here and there and a beach without barbed wire or filth along the water's edge, just seaweed and fishing boats and nets drying in the sun and tall plane trees in front of the houses like in Barcelona, she has forgotten that trees exist, there is not a single tree in Rivesaltes, not one place to sit in the shade apart from the damp, stinking, vermin-filled barracks, she would like to ask him: Do you remember our street? The water trickling from the balconies after the potted plants had been watered, those drops that made the humid air a little cooler on summer evenings? And our Sunday trips to Barceloneta, remember them? But no-one is there to remember them with, hardly surprising then that she should follow the pattern of her own thoughts and begin to recall the women from the Federación Anarquista Ibérica doing shooting practice on the beach one Sunday afternoon when Juan and she turned up, she in her new red cotton dress, slightly flared at the bottom and with puffed sleeves, which took two entire Sundays to sew; that was the summer of the revolution, towards the end of August, the female militias would all be going to reinforce the Durruti column and liberate Zaragoza, the members of the unit came from all over, most of them Catalans, the rest immigrants like herself from other regions, as well as foreigners like the woman who appeared to be their instructor, Meri Ló she was called, she wore no make-up and was a little masculine, you could see she liked to wear trousers, they all did, the photographer was a woman too, a close-cropped foreigner with fair hair and a big smile who said the pictures would be published in Paris, she was taking photographs of the militias while they were shooting or pretending to shoot at some undefined target out to sea, "it's bound to be full of Fascists camouflaged as fish," Juan joked, though she remembers his laughter with a kind of fright, because it is so long since she heard it and because whenever she heard that laughter she always used to laugh herself and she can recall the sensation of laughter only vaguely now, like an intense irritation around her stomach, as impossible to control by will as the tickling in her genitals when they swelled and grew wet to receive him, it is not only his and her former lives that have vanished without trace but parts of her body as well, the capacities of her body, although at this point the memories begin to become troublesome, painful and a little embarrassing, so she backs up to the point where Meri Ló was sitting by the fire reading poems aloud with her Cuban husband, they both read the poems in a form of Spanish that sounded like Andalusian. Meri Ló sounded even stranger because she had to be American or from Australia, that was the kind of thing that made them feel they were part of something greater, something unique: people were coming from all over the world to fight alongside them! No wonder then they immediately felt as if they were drunk, on something other than wine though that was drunk too, after the training session the militia women lit a fire and laid out bread and sardines, cleaning the fish was done in a flash, several of the militia women got out pocket knives to split open the slippery silver bellies, afterwards they folded their knives and shoved them back into various pockets in their trousers, like real men, but with a look of contentment in their eyes that came from the simplicity of the gesture, the immense freedom that lay behind it; with shrill screams the gulls fought over the innards that were thrown onto the sand a few metres away and suddenly a woman called Amparo from Mataró, who she would later come across in Argelès after the retreat, wanted to practise sharpshooting at the birds, the poor woman had bad teeth, decay had hollowed out her front ones leaving little white strips of enamel that meant her bite looked like a dog's, with sparse narrow fangs, fortunately the Australian woman stopped the massacre before it could begin, What a terrible waste that would be, comrade! We need to save our bullets for the Fascists! They always called each other *comrade*, saying *comrade* raised their spirits, as though the revolution would stand or fall by the saying of the word and the old order return if ever they stopped saying it; the smoke from the bonfire blew into their faces and their eyes depending on the direction of the wind, it got into your clothes and hair, she remembers that even though the smell itself has become an abstraction, a vague something without any connection to her sense of smell, she is remembering too the slices of bread they held against the embers, the slices turned black at the edges so they had to scrape off the burnt bits, she rubbed a clove of garlic into the hard toasted bread and the taste of garlic burned and stung her tongue. They spent the entire evening with the anarchists, the sand became damper the later it got so the back of their thighs felt cold, the other women were not bothered in their blue workmen's overalls, sitting cross-legged, the way Indians sit, while she, who was wearing her new dress, had to sit at an angle with her legs held tightly together supporting herself on one of her arms that went numb from time to time or on Juan who kept slipping his arm round her waist; night arrived with stars and a full moon, they drank wine from a *bota* handed around from one person to the next, she refrained, worried about getting a stain on her dress, but Juan poured long arching streams of red wine down his throat and whispered in her ear that that was exactly what her breasts felt like when he squeezed them, like the soft wine sack of tanned hide you held high above your mouth while squeezing out the wine, he got more and more drunk as the evening progressed, exhilarated by the whole experience, the songs alone were enough to do that, they sang "*A las barricadas*" until the words rasped across their throats, and the cartridge cases were glittering in the light of the flames so they looked like jewels and some of the militia women had earrings that also sparkled like the cartridge cases they wore across their chests and everyone was laughing around that fire, everyone apart from the young Polishwoman (Putch, Putz?) who began to weep inconsolably, she had lost someone at the front in Caspe and for a while wept with such despair it felt as though the party would have to be brought to an end, she was the youngest of them all, just nineteen, the misfortune she had suffered ought to have sounded an alarm, but for some reason they went on singing and howling like mad dogs at the full moon and the reflection of the moon on the water made them think that the war was as broad and easy to walk across as that deceptive mirage that stretched out flat and without a single ripple towards the horizon, how little they knew about the war then, how little they knew about anything then. "Do you remember that night sometimes, Juan, wherever you are?" What she would really like to remember is the taste of the grilled sardines, just that, but it escapes her, it taunts her, as if she were trying to capture a sunbeam on the tip of her tongue and it just kept bouncing off now this way now that, she hasn't eaten fish in, Good Lord, what must it be, three years now? Since the innkeeper who ran a wine bar on a narrow backstreet in Portbou gave them a couple of sardine tins and a loaf of bread as food for the journey, "*¡Ahí tenéis, tortolitos, comed sardinas mientras podáis que pronto solo habrá cebolla!*"[62] She cannot recall the taste of the tinned sardines either, just the force of the wind that blew at an angle from the other side of the border while they crept along the slippery mountain trail, the wind that seemed to be trying to hurl them to their deaths, fling them into the sea foaming and hissing below them, the rocks projecting out of the water like black fangs, the entire coastline a frothing jaw ready to devour them; later on, the tins would make her feel guilty, that was when she kept them from the other refugees in the camp, hidden in her bra, from women who had nothing to feed their hungry children on, both tins ended up in her possession after the women and children were separated from the men, she kept hold of the sardine tins throughout the first few weeks in the internment camp on the beach without opening them, she wanted to save them to share with Juan even though she had no idea how or when she would see him again; she used the first tin to bribe one of the guards to take a message into the men's camp, and when they were at last able to meet each on their own side of the fence three weeks later and open the other tin and eat the contents she got diarrhoea and spent the whole night vomiting. Even though Carmen thinks about food all the time, remembered tastes simply refuse to come back to her, not even to stick to her palate for a fraction of a second, she can remember the rice casserole her sister-in-law would make for the major holidays, she used to help chop the almonds, the parsley and the garlic for *la picada* in the big stone mortar, but she can only *see* the ingredients, the tastes have vanished, she presses her tongue against her palate, but all there ever is there is the same, stale, rotting taste of her own bad breath. She is so very tired, the women in front of her may be angels, but they are still

62   "Here you are, my lovebirds, eat sardines while you can, onions is all there'll be soon enough." The phrase alludes to the saying *Contigo pan y cebolla*: "With you I can live on just bread and onions."

strangers, as strange as angels, she is tired of the strange, of being a stranger herself, she is homesick, she feels more homesick now she is walking through this little town than she ever has before, more now than that first winter when they were shoved like animals onto a beach without food and water, more now than during the few months last spring when she and Juan were released from the camp and allowed to live freely together in Toulouse, more now than in that rocky desert in Rivesaltes. Madeleine Durand turns around, still with that look that appears to see what no-one else is able to, though almost immediately she aims it in the same direction her arm is pointing: at a large villa built close to the beach about a hundred metres or so away, in the bend where the bay curves, it has two square towers and an enclosed garden with cactus plants in the front and it makes her think of the posh *torres* in Sant Gervasi where she was in service before she got a job at the shirt factory down on Vía Layetana. "*La Villa Saint-Jean!*" Madeleine Durand cries, "*notre pouponnière!*" and though Carmen smiles it is a sceptical smile she returns, just the corners of her mouth separating and stretching to the sides, the motion is almost painful, that might be from lack of practice, because what has she had to smile about or at whom, more than every now and then, more than on the rare occasion, at her poor child? She has to think back to the maternity hospital in Elne to remember herself smiling, to be able to feel that the smile came from within and had a link to that system of airways and tunnels that make up her insides; she used to smile in the breastfeeding room, they all smiled even though all of them came from the camps, they smiled when they sewed together or when they were sitting round the long table and feeding their babies while listening to the record that señorita Isabel put on every morning, always the same piece of music, always at the same time, she, Carmen would sit there with her newborn baby at one of her breasts while other women were seated on either side of her with their newborns, Paquita, María Garcia, Concha, the foreigners you could really only smile at, not talk to, they sat there while the babies sucked and pulled at their breasts, several women on the same bench, their legs thrust under a long table as if they were all lying under the same eiderdown, the winter sun poured in through the great arched windows, the rays used to caress your back and the face of the woman opposite at the same time, and it was as if all their bodies were somehow flowing into each other inside the light that hovered between them across the table, melting together in those separate beams of sunlight, as broad and long as veils pulled taut, and that delightful sensation on your skin just seemed to dissolve any differences, every boundary. She had stood in the queue at the Swiss milk hut with Hannelore's mother every morning since she arrived at Rivesaltes, and yet an abyss would divide them at the end, some undetectable difference would separate them and – snip-snap – their fates would be severed, like two pieces of meat butchered from the same part of the body, and here she was, in this place, while the other woman was sitting on the bed of a truck and heading away, away from her child. It was incomprehensible. Her dried-out lips begin to occupy a great deal of Carmen's face, dangling like lifeless scraps of meat from her mouth, they feel like a revolting appendage growing larger and larger with every step she takes, she starts to open her mouth wide, but no words or screams emerge, because what can she say? Is she supposed to cry out that her mouth is rotting or should she just scream out loud? And could those white figures up ahead understand any of it? The Swan has already passed the fence, the shorter nurse turns towards her and smiles, there no longer seems to be a need to hurry and the nurse is waiting for her, smiling beneath her white bonnet; once Carmen has caught up she escorts her along the gravel path past huge iron pots of aloe plants extending pale thorny arms, the large entrance and windows at the front of the villa appear to have been built for giants, against them Madeleine Durand's figure appears as small as a whitewashed sparrow. It is blessedly cool inside, the Swan is already making her way up the broad staircase, at the foot of the stairs is an earthenware carboy the other nurse points at: *"Toma un poco de agua, te sentará bien"*,[63] she says in a sing-song Castilian that sounds familiar to Carmen and then she holds out her arms so she can take Juanita.

María Almendro turns out to come from Bujaraloz, in the middle of the Los Monegros plain, not far from the village Juan Fayo's family is from, she has thick black frizzy hair she slicks down so it forms smooth billowing waves and has been at the children's home and lived free long enough to start to pluck her eyebrows in an even, narrow bow the way Carmen used to, before; while María is steering her swiftly through an immense though simply furnished dining room on the lower floor she tells her that the children have finished their siestas and will soon be served a snack and then go out for a walk. They come to a cleaned and recently lime-washed kitchen with big windows and a glass door that opens onto a shimmering green space at the back, there María Almendro goes on to say that they have saved her some food, Carmen is listening but has come to a stop in front of the workbench on which two huge water melons are glistening a deep green against the whitewashed wall, beside them is a large dish of ripe and almost-ripe beef tomatoes. María Almendro watches Carmen's eyes linger on the vegetables, she has also spent several years confined in various camps and knows what Carmen is feeling, so she hands Juanita back to her mother and asks if she prefers her tomato green or ripe, Carmen replies that she would like a ripe one and María Almendro chooses one that though ripe is still perfectly firm, slices it into boat-like sections and sprinkles onto them a generous amount of coarse salt from a container beside the iron range before putting the plate on the kitchen table. Carmen has not had a fresh vegetable to eat since the six-month interlude in Toulouse when she used to walk to the market just as the peasants were starting to put away their stalls and shop for bargains, she was

63 "Have some water, you'll feel better."

always given something for free, sometimes a head of cabbage, once half an armful of lavender that Juan hung from a hook above their bed instead of the crucifix; the salted juice of the tomato is spreading a pink mist down her gullet and brightening up the dark tunnels where hopelessness has echoed for so long, she can soon feel the corners of her mouth imitating the curved edges of the tomato slices: they are tilting upwards in an unforced smile and, immediately, as if she had come across flotsam on a beach, she wants to show it to her child, almost anxiously she turns her eager face towards the baby and beams a smile at her because she knows that the smile is feeble and cannot last long, it may be extinguished at any moment; then she dips her finger in the moist flesh of the last piece of tomato and strokes it over Juanita's lips that start to shine and quiver at the cold sour-sweet touch, which makes Carmen burst into a hoarse rumble of laughter, more like a wheeze. María Almendro, who is standing at the range stirring a large pot, says: *"Te hemos guardado un poco de cocido."*[64]

Her first meal of freedom leaves Carmen dazed and flat with a rumbling stomach and wind, used as she is to the daily ladleful of boiled rice, the sensations that came with the richness of the chickpea stew, in which she even found a large bit of sausage, were so stupefyingly complex that she is still sitting in front of the empty plate listening to the sounds from her stomach and intestines, astonished at the explosion of tastes she has just experienced, the way you can be astonished at the stillness that follows a cloudburst or a shower of hail, when all that remains of the storm is a gentle patter of raindrops. María Almendro has left them to go upstairs to wake the children and get them ready with the other staff. But Juanita is restless and whining impatiently, even though she has been suckling at the breast while Carmen was eating her fill for the first time since she gave

64 "We saved you a bit of the chickpea stew."

birth to her at the maternity hospital in Elne, it is stuffy in the kitchen and Carmen gets up and walks over to the open kitchen door from where there is a slight draught, although the air being drawn in is warm, outside it is really hot, the yard at the back consists largely of a kitchen garden, with neat rows of tomatoes and beans staked to pale reeds and other plants that stick out of the reddish-brown soil, row after row as far as the hill that rises behind the house where the remains of terraced grapevines begin: María told her that the estate had been a vineyard until recently, when the military forces who were encamped here until the Secours Suisse took over turned it into a barracks. A large storage shed at the very back with a steep saddle roof, close to the hill, throws a broad band of shadow across part of the grounds, a flower bed of withered or dead plants and some pots in which weeds are growing can be seen along the edge of the building, there are a couple of threadbare palm trees nearby as well, their broad old trunks ending in straggly heads of short new leaves that should have been growing in arching cascades and casting large circles of shade over the kitchen garden. But the most striking feature is a rose hedge covered from end to end in nappies, at least thirty linen cloths in tight rows across it, little pink roses stick out from under the white nappies and Carmen finds that funny and lovely at the same time, wondering if the scent of the roses permeates the linen and maybe has a beneficial effect on the children's red bottoms. She reaches a hand out to the nappy closest to her, tempted both to smell it, to discover traces of the rose scent she is now convinced has healing properties, and to stuff it inside her neckline because she has not changed Juanita since this morning on the train when she had to use the reserve nappy because the one she thought would be enough for the whole trip was filled with a greenish sticky paste she could not wipe off without water. Juanita is restive and whimpering and Carmen knows that the excrement has become stuck to her most tender parts where the skin is cracked and infected and the collection of several hours worth of urine has added ammonia to the already acidic crust of poo: she has to change Juanita, and find water, her roving eyes hunt for the tap from which the vegetables are watered, but then she realises there ought to be a sink somewhere here as well and so decides to focus her search on a wall at the very back of the shaded part that seems the right place for one. On her way over Carmen comes across a girl sitting on a low stone wall with a large empty washing basket beside her, she can be only seven or eight, and is playing *tabas* on her own, the girl can see Carmen out of the corner of her eye but does not stop playing her game, she keeps on throwing the knuckles into the air, alternately catching them with the palm and then the back of her hand, there are already two of them between her extended fingers, a King and a Hangman, there is a knuckle on her stone seat in the *Jete* position, the one that looks like a tooth with the dent being displayed, the girl throws the knuckles on the back of her hand once more and tries to pick up the jack on the stone, but before she has time to turn her palm up to catch it one of the bones falls to the gravel: the girl glances at Carmen, in keeping with the rules of the game she now has to hand the set to the next player and the girl, who has noticed Carmen's look of recognition, as though she could see moving pictures in her eyes of all the times Carmen has thrown the little bones into the air herself, offers her the five jacks but Carmen shakes her head and points by way of excuse to Juanita, who is lying in her arms and moaning persistently and while Carmen is shaking her head she can feel that newly rediscovered smile leaking away and an insight moving in in its place: she does not have the strength, because even if the baby were not writhing in her arms, she does not have the energy to play the game with the girl, because the game, like the laugh, requires something of a person she has as good as forgotten. *"No, guapa, quizás otro día,"*[65] she says then and walks over to the tiled wall where there is not the one sink she was expecting but two. When Juanita

65   "Not now, sweetheart. Maybe another day."

feels the cold water on her red buttocks the moans become shrieks, Carmen turns the tap until she gets a slow stream and holds her child's bottom in the flow until the green crust of dried excrement has begun to soften and loosen, she is rubbing the dirt away gently with two of her fingers when she hears, over the sound of Juanita's desperate weeping, María Almendro call from behind her: "*¡Quita, mujer, esto lo hacemos arriba, con agua templada! ¡Hay que ver! ¡Estos campos malditos vuelven a la gente salvaje!*"[66]

What ugly children, Carmen is thinking where she is sitting on the cement pier, there's something ugly about the little blonde girl with the ponytail too, even though she's so small, Carmen cannot quite pin down: they have all gone down to the beach for their regular walk and to eat their snack, the nurses towing long lines of uncommunicative, compliant children, Juanita is lying on her back in a basket beside Carmen, her bottom uncovered so the skin – turned yellow with the sulphate powder they sprinkled over it in the nursery room after a careful cleaning with lukewarm water and a creamy white soap – can get the air it needs, she is not sleeping but appears content to lie there like that looking at the mass of blue air above her that is crisscrossed now and then by screeching gulls; María Almendro is sitting on the bare sand surrounded by eight children, she has got children sitting and standing on both sides, at her feet and behind her back, they are all keeping close to some part of the nurse's body, as if they were afraid of being hurled into a bottomless pit if they let go or went too far away; five other children are in front of Madeleine Durand, who is feeding them biscuits from a bag, that group is closer to Carmen and the concrete dock where some fishing skiffs are tied up, in their clean socks and shoes the children are stepping on a soft bed of dried brown algae, with one exception: Hannelore is not on her feet but sitting by herself, her arms slack, in an empty space between

66 "There's no need for that, you know, we do that upstairs with warm water, it's just awful the way those bloody camps can turn us into primitives."

both groups of children, she is the only one not chewing on a biscuit or reaching a hand out for more, one of her legs is at a wide angle and the other is turned in towards her groin, her muscles loose, like rubber, her fallen socks are gleaming white inside the shoes her mother fetched from the Swiss hut the day before yesterday. Otherwise the children all appear well cared for, their hair combed, and with neatly tied rosettes in their hair or ponytails and wearing freshly pressed dresses or shorts with braces, but their eyes, Carmen thinks, there's something wrong about them; the children are standing bunched together and begging for food, the way they did in the camp, oblivious to everything except the bag of biscuits, not interested in the sea, the beach or one another, just two of them, a boy with short hair and a blonde girl with a precociously severe expression, both about five or six years old, appear to be engaged in digging in the little patch of sand in front of them, the rest reach out their hands to the nearest nurse as though their only purpose was to shove food into their mouths, the boy with the cropped fair hair is hunched over and poking cautiously at something he has found, but when Madeleine Durand calls his name with an encouraging smile and he looks up – "Well done, Henri, can you find a shell for me?" – his eyes turn out to be tired and almost feverish, with that look sick children get, and he has got bags under them as well, it's that old hunger that makes them ugly, Carmen thinks, and somewhere inside her that particular way of putting it rips a line of fire through her thoughts, the ones she usually keeps wrapped inside a grey immobilising haze, they're sick children, those thoughts go on to tell her, and then more boldly, it's that bloody hunger has ruined them, that fucking war, and as if it were all the fault of the sand she hacks with her heel at the stony brown surface that seems to lack a single redeeming feature, neither giving nor compliant, it simply offers a pure and compact resistance which makes Carmen hit the sand over and over again with her heel and the sole of her foot, strike over and over again at those bloody inflexible grains. Hannelore, who has failed to react to anything until now, not to the milk placed in front of her or the sweet biscuits they have tried to tempt her with, turns her head in Carmen's direction, a movement Carmen catches out of the corner of her eye; the girl is still sitting with one leg stretched out and the other tucked into her groin, her socks wrinkled inside the brown shoes with a strap across the front of her foot, Carmen can remember watching them both on their way back from the queue with beaming smiles, perhaps the mother thought the shoes were a guarantee against the deportations that had been announced, why would her child be entitled to the new shoes if they (the two of them) were going to be sent away the next day? From the corner of her eye Carmen has glimpsed not only the movement of her head but the quivering of Hannelore's mouth and now, while she is looking straight at the girl's face, studded as it is with little swellings, she can feel a quiver start on her own lips: beneath the girl's left eye the venom from an insect bite has spread to the eyelid and made it swell, her eyes look like two knife slits across the watery pale flesh though it is not blood flowing from the wounds but her gaze itself dissolving in a horror that is ongoing. Whatever is slowly beginning to make Hannelore's mouth buckle might be weeping, but that weeping would have to be located in regions so deep inside that the tears could never find their way out.

Extracts from Charles Haywood Dameron's Letter to His Parents, November 22, 1945[67]

Regensburg, Germany,
Thanksgiving Day, 1945

Dear Puff and Pop,

Puff in your last letter you said that you had no idea I could express myself so clearly and yet so briefly. I don't know whether to consider that a compliment or a suggestion that my letters are too short. I realise that in comparison to what many of the other boys are able to write my letters have been rather drab. There has been a reason for it. In war crimes work we have maintained a sort of self-imposed censorship. [. . .]

All I intend to do is to try to give you somewhat of a broad picture of my activities since arriving overseas.

I must admit when I first entered Paris I wondered whether there really had been a war fought over here. The only real indication was the fact that Paris was obviously not the Paris I had imagined. There were few stores open, practically no restaurants in operation and the people seemed very poor. I think I wrote you about the places in Paris that I visited. Frankly, I did not like Paris although I realize that I saw it at its worst. After I took off in the plane from Paris, it

67   The letter is reproduced in *Dameron Report: Bericht des War Crimes Investigating Teams No 6824 der U.S. Army vom 17.7.1945 über die Tötungsanstalt Hartheim (Historische Texte des Lern- und Gedenkortes Schloss Hartheim)*, eds. Brigitte Kepplinger, Irene Leitner and Andrea Kammerhofe.

was not long before I began to see very real evidence of the war which had ended only a few days before. We flew over battlefields littered with every imaginable kind of debris. When I flew over Nurnburg [sic] I saw a tangible testimonial of the power of our air force. I have never seen such utter destruction before. After a short stay in Erlangen near Nurnburg I left to join my team in southern Austria. It was located right in the middle of the so-called National redoubt where much of the last ditch resistence [sic] was expected. I was placed in command of a team of 5 officers and 8 enlisted men with the mission of investigating and reporting upon war crimes against allied nationals. That appeared to be a job which was at least germane to my civilian training. I was soon to find out that there were many problems involved which I had not anticipated. When I arrived and joined my team those 13 men were the only Americans in the town. Our mission carried us into numerous little Austrian towns, most of which were located in the mountains. Obviously to do our job effectively we had to split up into small groups, each of the groups going into different towns. It was not long before we found out that if the war had ended a few days before, these mountain dwellers were not aware of it. On many occasions my driver and I were the first American soldiers to enter these villages. The look of surprise on the faces of many of the people was enough evidence that they were unaware of the fact that the war was over. The fact that I constantly kept my hand on my pistol was evidence of the fact that I realized they didn't know it was over. In some of the towns the sight of our jeep was enough to elicit a display of white flags from the windows. In others we had more uneasy moments where we encountered a sullen, obviously indecisive population. In those cases it was merely a matter of convincing them that we were merely the advance party of thousands of (non-existent) troops who would shortly follow us into town. In many cases I didn't even know where the nearest American unit was located. [...]

Now to tell you a little something about my main mission. Of course, as you can well imagine, it consists mainly of interviewing and obtaining statements from German witnesses. Strangely enough in most of the cases I have handled there were not enough survivors of the atrocities to furnish an accurate story and we had to depend upon German witnesses. I have found that the Germans are reluctant, of course, to give information which would implicate their fellow countrymen but I have also found that they will seldom lie if asked a specific and direct question. You can well see what an opportunity this presents for us to use our imaginative powers during interrogations. [. . .]

You realize, of course, that it would be impossible for me (without writing a book) to describe to you all the cases I have covered. I will just pick out one to give you an example. Keep in mind that many people estimate that more civilians were murdered in concentration camps, etc. than there were soldiers killed in the war. It seems incredible but I am inclined to believe it. I have seen evidence of the atrocities at Dachau, Buchenwald, Mauthausen, etc. and I can tell you that the things you read in the papers about them are not exaggerated.

Do you still have the picture of the castle which I sent you back in July? Take it out and look at it again. It just looks like a rather old castle that might have belonged to royalty, doesn't it? Well, it is. But that is not all of the story. I entered that building under these circumstances. We had a tip from the U.S. Army intelligence service that some rather strange things had occurred in the building and entered it. As I entered through the main entrance there were two plaques on the wall. I had an interpreter to translate from German and this is what we read: On the first plaque was the inscription "He who is sick in body or mind should not be permitted to transmit his illness to his children." On the other we read: "Respect for great men must be impregnated upon the minds of German youth." With that as an introduction we went inside the building. I expected to find some sort of weird haunted castle like the kind one sees in the movies. But I didn't. I found the last thing that I would have expected to find. The building was being used as an orphanage and was being operated by about 20 Catholic Nuns [sic]. There were almost a hundred little orphan children in the building. It had been so used for the previous six months. I began at that moment to wonder if Army Intelligence had not made a slip. Well, I will have to make a very long story short. I can't tell you exactly how we did it but this is what we found out:

The building did formerly belong to royalty but was taken over by the German Government and operated as an insane asylum for a time. Then later a gas chamber and crematorium were installed and all incurable insane persons from the surrounding area were brought there, gassed to death, and their bodies cremated. False death certificates were made out and the victims were recited to have died a natural death. The brains were dissected and sent to Vienna. We found records to prove that over a period of less than two years more than 18,000 persons were disposed of in this manner. At first the ashes were sent to the relatives but this was later stopped because they were not too particular about whose ashes were placed in the urns, and sometimes the relatives would receive, as a result of a mistake, two urns of ashes on widely separated dates purporting to be the ashes of one dead relative. This caused an embarrassing [sic] situation and so it was stopped. They were thereafter merely cremated without the formality of sending the ashes home. As horrible as this was to my mind we were not interested in this phase of their activities because the victims were all German nationals and hence no war crime was involved. Of course there have been books written on this subject both pro & con. Many eminent doctors (European) advocate the disposition of incurable insanes. My answer to them is simple: Who is to say that an individual is incurably insane? Who knows but that that [sic] tomorrow or next week someone will not find a cure for cancer? Who knows but what tomorrow someone will discover a complete cure for "incurable" insanity? And, above all, suppose that the mother or father or sister or brother of the executioner were declared incurably insane could he then turn on the gas in the gas chamber?

But I am getting off the subject. Of course. It was too much to expect that this installation could be overlooked by Hitler's boys. There were great possibilities. And so, beginning in about 1941 many prisoners from Mauthausen and other concentration camps were brought here and executed in the same manner as the insane persons. These people were not insane. They were, for the most part, accused of no crime except that of disagreeing with Hitler and the Nazi Party. Some were executed because they were too weak to work for the German Reich any longer. Well to make a long story even shorter the only thing we couldn't prove was how many of these prisoners were executed. We proved that there were about 20,000 and my guess is that there were more than 60,000. Six months before we arrived the S.S. had completely renovated the building, including removal of the gas chamber and the crematory. The nuns and orphans were installed as a screen. But they made one mistake as most murderers do and as a result we were able to obtain the names and addresses of over 100 people who were former employees of the establishment. There is very much more to that one single case but it would take me all day to write about it. I think that I have given you enough to give you some idea about my job. [. . .]

To sum it all up I can only say that I am thankful this Thanksgiving day that I am serving in Regensburg, Germany instead of having the S.S. patrol the streets of Port Allen. Please send this letter on to Mary and request its return. I have never written her any of the details of my work either.

Love to you all

Hay

Helene Hintersteiner's Second Witness Statement Schloss Hartheim, July 6, 1945[68]

Helene Hintersteiner, after having previously made and subscribed an affidavit in this investigation on June 29, 1945, was called as a witness at Schloss Hartheim on July 6, 1945, and, after being duly sworn, testified as follows:

Q. What is your name?
A. Helene Hintersteiner.

Q. Have you made a previous statement in this investigation?
A. Yes, a long one.

Q. I now show you an object, which has previously been identified as having been found in the office of the manager of the Orphanage in Schloss Hartheim, and ask if you can identify what it is?
A. This is the plan of Schloss Hartheim, ground floor.

Q. Were you familiar with the arrangement of the ground floor of Schloss Hartheim at the time you had previously testified it was used as a crematory?
A. Yes.

---

68   Dameron Report, N.A.R.A., Record Group 549: Records of the Headquarters, U.S. Army Europe [U.S.A.EUR], War Crimes Branch, War Crimes Case Files ("Cases not tried"), 1944–1948, Box 490, Case 000-12-463 Hartheim.

Q. I now ask you to place on the document, which you have identified, any marks by which you may be able to identify it at a later date.

A. (Witness then in her own handwriting placed on the document her identifying marks).

Q. I now ask you to state what identifying marks you have placed on this document?

A. I wrote my name and the present date on this plan at the top and the bottom.

Q. I now ask you to again outline briefly in order, the various parts of the building into which the victims were taken in the process of extermination.

A. The auto drove up to the door here, which was covered by a wooden enclosure. The people got out and came through this hall and were undressed or sometimes received in this room. Then they were taken into the other room and undressed and examined, and then taken to another part of the same room to be photographed. From the room where they were photographed they were taken through the door into the next room which was the gas chamber. After they were gassed, they were taken into the two adjoining rooms, which were used as a morgue. Then the bodies to be burned were taken into the adjoining room, which contained the oven. I think, but I am not sure, that the ashes were placed right in the urns in the crematory.

Q. I refer you again to the plan you have previously identified and ask you to mark with your own hand by the letter "A", the point at which the victims entered.

A. (Witness, then with her own hand, placed on the plan the letter "A").

Q. You have mentioned previously the fact that a wooden wall was built at the entrance that you have marked with the letter "A", and I now ask you to draw in your own hand a representation of that wall.

A. (Witness, then in her own handwriting, drew a representation of this wall on the plan).

Q. I now ask you to mark this wall, which you have just drawn, with the letter "B".

A. (Witness, then in her own handwriting, placed on the plan the letter "B").

Q. What do the dotted lines which you have drawn in connection with this wall represent?

A. These designate on both ends, the doors which opened from the middle.

Q. Approximately what size was the enclosure you show surrounded by the wooden wall?

A. It was a little bit longer than the bus and also it was a little wider and higher than the bus.

Q. Was the wall which you have marked with the letter "B" constructed after you arrived here in 1940?

A. It was built right after I first started here. I saw the construction myself, it was very primitive.

Q. Do you know what the purpose of constructing this wall was?

A. They built that because at first when they brought these people in the main entrance through the courtyard, the employees were very curious, and because they wanted to keep this a secret, and so no-one could see them get out of the bus and enter the building.

Q. After the victims were brought in the door which you have marked with the letter "A" will you state where they were taken?

A. Yes, they were taken through the corridor.

Q. Will you indicate by a direction arrow and the letter "C" the corridor which you have referred to?

A. (Witness, in her own hand, placed the direction arrow and the letter "C" on the plan).

Q. Where were the victims taken then?

A. Into the room which was sometimes used as a reception room and sometimes as an undressing room.

Q. I now ask you to mark the room to which you have just referred by writing on the plan the letter "D".

A. (Witness, in her own hand, placed on the plan the letter "D").

Q. What was done in the room which you indicated by the letter "D"?

A. They were received here and the case histories of the patients were reviewed. They were also sometimes undressed here and sometimes undressed in the following room.

Q. After this process was completed, can you state where the victims were then taken?

A. They were then taken out through the same door, along the corridor to the next room.

Q. Will you indicate by marking on the plan the letter "E" what you mean when you refer to the "next" room?

A. (Witness, in her own hand, placed on the plan the letter "E").

Q. What was the purpose of bringing them into the room which you have designated as room "E"?

A. Sometimes they were brought into this room to be undressed and also to be re-examined.

Q. Do you know who did the actual undressing of the victims?
A. Yes, the male and female nurses.

Q. Were all the male and female nurses that worked here at one time or another concerned with undressing the victims?
A. The ones who were employed at the undressing were detailed to this job by Hauptmann Wirth and it is possible that different ones would be detailed to this job on different days as he ordered.

Q. Can you give the names of the nurses that you remember having served on this detail?
A. Herman Michel
   Bruno Kochan
   Anton Schrottmair [Schrottmayr]
   Gertrude Blanka [Blanke]
   Gertrude Klaehn [Klahn]
   Mitzi Whittman [Wittmann]
   Marie Raab
   Maria Hammelsboeck[Hammelsbock]
   Gretta Heider [Margarethe Haider]

   I must state at this time that people from the bureau were asked to help in the undressing of the victims. I had to help myself. This was compulsory. If I happened to say bureau by accident, I mean office.

Q. Will you indicate by another direction arrow and the letter "F" the route taken by the victims from room "D" to room "E"?
A. (Witness, then in her own hand, placed on the plan the direction arrow and the letter "F").

Q. After the undressing process was completed in room "E", will you indicate by a direction arrow and the letter "G" where the victims were next taken?

A. (Witness, then in her own hand, placed on the plan the direction arrow and the letter "G").

Q. You have just indicated that the victims were then taken to another room, will you indicate this room by the letter "H"?

A. (Witness, then in her own hand, placed on the plan the letter "H").

Q. The plan shows no door between the room "E" and the room "H", do you know whether or not there was a door between these two rooms?

A. Yes, there is still a door there, one as an entrance and one as an exit.

Q. What, if anything, was done in the room which you have indicated by the letter "H"?

A. The people were photographed in the room marked with the letter "H". The photographs were then mounted on paper. The views of the head were mounted at the top of the paper and the full length pictures of the people were mounted at the bottom of the same page.

Q. Will you now indicate by a direction arrow identified by the letter "I" the next point to which the victims were taken?

A. (Witness, then in her own hand, placed on the plan a direction arrow and the letter "I").

Q. You have just indicated that the victims were taken through a door into another room, will you indicate this room by a letter "J"?

A. (Witness, then in her own hand, placed on the plan the letter "J").

Q. What, if anything was done in the room which you have indicated by the letter "J"?
A. In this room the patients were gassed.

Q. How many people were gassed at one time?
A. Approximately 60.

Q. On an average how many times per day were people gassed?
A. Once to twice a day. That varied, sometimes there would be none gassed for a day and then the next day there would be two or three times.

Q. Was there a door in the gas room which opened into the courtyard?
A. Yes.

Q. Will you indicate that door by placing on the plan the letter "K"?
A. (Witness, then in her own hand, placed on the plan the letter "K") This door was firmly bolted shut and there was a peephole in this door.

Q. Was the general public allowed to look through this peephole?
A. It was forbidden for any of us to look through this hole, but those employed there could look into the gas chamber.

Q. Do you know what kind of gas was used in the gas room which you have indicated?
A. No, I do not know.

Q. Do you know where the gas was obtained from?
A. I do not know where they got the gas, but I have heard that a Doctor Becker from Berlin, who was a chemist, procured the gas for this place.

Q. Do you know the full name of Dr Becker?

A. I do not know, I have not seen him for years.

Q. Do you know from what office he came in Berlin?

A. From the office on Tiergartenstrasse.

Q. Were the victims killed in the gas room?

A. Yes they were destroyed in that room.

Q. Were the bodies removed from the gas room to any other point?

A. Yes.

Q. Will you indicate by a direction arrow identified by the letter "L" the route which the bodies were then taken?

A. (Witness, in her own hand, placed on the plan a direction arrow and the letter "L").

Q. The direction arrow which you have just placed on the plan proceeds through what is apparently a wall on the plan. Can you explain this?

A. At that time, there was a door there and the bodies were taken through this door into the two adjoining rooms.

Q. Will you mark by the letters "M" and "N" the rooms which you have just indicated?

A. (Witness, in her own hand, placed on the plan the letters "M" and "N").

Q. For what purpose were the rooms marked "M" and "N" used?

A. As a morgue.

Q. Do you know how long the bodies ordinarily remained in the morgue?

A. Immediately after gassing the cremating would begin. The bodies were brought from the gas chamber immediately to the morgue. For instance if they had six bodies I do not know how long it would take to cremate them, but I believe it took from one day to the other.

Q. Will you indicate by a direction arrow identified by the letter "O" the direction the bodies were then taken after they were removed from the morgue?

A. (Witness, in her own hand, placed on the plan the letter "O").

Q. You have indicated by a direction arrow that the bodies were taken to an adjoining room. I now ask you to mark that room with the letter "P".

A. (Witness, in her own hand, placed on the plan the letter "P").

Q. Will you state for what purpose the room "P" was used?

A. This room was the crematory. In this room was the oven.

Q. Do you know how many ovens there were in the crematory?

A. To my knowledge there was one oven.

Q. Do you know at what point in this room the oven was located?

A. Yes.

Q. Will you indicate as best you can remember the location of the oven by drawing a rough sketch of same, and indicating it with the letter "Q"?

A. (Witness, then in her own hand, made a rough sketch and identified same with letter "Q").

Q. Where was the chimney for the oven?

A. Out in the courtyard.

Q. Will you indicate on the plan by the letter "R" the location of the chimney to which you have just referred?

A. (Witness, in her own hand, placed on the plan the letter "R").

Q. The plan shows a set of stairs together with an opening to the outside from the room "N" and I now ask whether or not that opening was there at the time you were employed here?

A. No, they were not.

Q. You have stated in your previous testimony that a portion of the corridor around the courtyard was enclosed with a wooden partition. I now ask you to indicate this by using the numerals 1, 2 and 3.

A. (Witness, then in her own hand, placed on the plan the numerals 1, 2 and 3).

Q. Did the wooden panel run approximately from point marked 1, thence to point marked 2, and thence to point marked 3?

A. Yes. From point marked 1 across the corridor to the building there was a door. From point marked 3 to the edge of the building it was completely closed across the corridor.

Q. What was done with the ashes after the victims were cremated in room "P"?

A. Some of the ashes were placed in urns, other parts of it were taken to the attic and also some of it was hauled away.

Q. Do you know when the ashes that were taken to the attic were removed?

A. That which remained in the attic was then removed by the people from the concentration camp at the time everything was taken away from the building.

Q. When you state in the beginning of your testimony that the plan which you have identified correctly represents the plan of the ground floor of Schloss Hartheim, did you mean that it was a correct representation with the exception of the minor changes which you have noted in your testimony?

A. Yes.

I, Russel D. Legacy T/Sgt, 16152328, being first duly sworn, state that I acted as reporter in this matter and that the foregoing is a true and correct record of questions propounded to and answers given by the witness and through the interpreter, made to the best of my ability.

[Signature of Legacy]

Subscribed and sworn to before me at Alkoven, bei Linz, Austria this 17th day of July 1945.

[Facsimile stamp and signature of Dameron]

Cristal City. C/Balmes, Barcelona, Spain, May 1969

Your aunt Ana María is seeing you out, her face wedged slantwise between the dark-brown door and its frame, her tied-back hair lit up from behind by the lamp in the hall and the low rays of the morning sun from the right side of the corridor, the one that faces south; the door closes with a distinct ringing sound that seems conceited all by itself, the light is much clearer although gentle between the pale-yellow walls of the staircase where it pours in through double windows with panes of ground glass (not harsh like the light reflected off the smooth chalk-white plaster on your staircase in Lérida) and reminds you of the cream-coloured velvet hairbands some of the girls at school wear. You know that your mother has been waiting for this moment all morning, you know that she loathes the smell of stock that spreads from the kitchen through your grandmother's flat at this time of day, a revolting smell that sits like a lump in your throat and is always finding new ways to scare you, as well as the pungent odour of mothballs in the bedroom behind the curtained glass door at the end of the corridor on the shady side, you know that she loathes that long corridor, as long as an entire block, so long that you are sometimes allowed to borrow your cousins' roller skates and skate from the sunny end that begins at the balcony overlooking the inner court-yard to the shaded part where your grandparents' bedroom used to be that is always dark and looks onto the main road, once during one of the endless mornings when your older cousins were in school you even borrowed your cousin Reyes' scooter, the corridor is fairly narrow and picking up speed was difficult, and you were slightly dazzled in any case as you wobbled along from the sunny side, which meant you almost crashed into the glass door with its floral curtain that cordons off the darkened part of the passage and where no-one was supposed to be during the daytime; that was when you saw the unknown boy coming out of your grandmother's blue-painted bedroom, like a shadow that had torn itself free from the row of her statues of saints, you were able to see the boy through the semi-transparent flower-patterned cloth, because the corridor broods between patches of sunlight like a forest whose every copse and clearing belong to a different fairy tale. Even though you know you will not be taking the lovely old lift with its twin compartment, your mother has stopped in the passage between the window and the lift doors, since the accident last spring when her arm was almost cut off at the elbow as a result of a lift operator's inattention your mother refuses to enter any kind of lift at all; you know that she is looking for a cigarette in her open handbag, that that is why she is rummaging in her bag in the relative brightness provided by the high window that gives onto one of the building's lightwells – the same lightwell that supplies the kitchen, the pantry, the laundry where half-drowned clothes are permanently soaking, the cramped, unused study whose tall shelves are filled with files and the gloomy playroom on the left side of the corridor with an unchanging grey illumination. You have to wait, your gaze lingers among the tufts in her hair, you know how she teases them with a little steel comb to fluff them up across the crown of her head: you know how she draws the strands straight up and then pulls them back and down with the comb to make thick rolls of hair against her scalp, those rolls are shot through at this moment with the light from the frosted glass, revealing little nooks and crannies a tiny rat could crawl inside. Women like your grandmother and your aunt do not smoke and do not like other women smoking, you know that as you are standing there, and they would disapprove even more of the caretaker or any of the neighbours seeing a female member of the family doing so, you know that she has been told by your father not to smoke on the staircase because the caretaker is malicious and embittered the way all caretakers are, though not as envious and spiteful as the one who denounced your grandmother's brothers so they ended up in prison during the war and almost got executed by firing squad, your mother is rooting around for her cigarettes nonetheless, you watch her teetering on her spiked heels while trying to balance the open handbag on her thigh. The peephole behind you has a sliding shutter a pair of gleaming rat eyes can peer through, there is a peephole in the door opposite as well, though it is not cigarettes your mother retrieves from her bag but the tin of sugar lumps, she opens it and gives you the first cube, keeping one for herself that she rolls into the middle of her palm which is bound to be sweaty, her hand will feel sticky afterwards, you know that, you make a mental note of which hand it is, the left one, not that this is necessary, you know she does everything with her left hand, even writing. It is time for the transparent little flask with the blue label to make an appearance, she pours a few drops from it onto her piece of sugar, the way she usually does when she is really nervous and starting to breathe oddly, your sugar lump is wedged between your front teeth and beginning to melt around the edges, you take it out with two cautious fingers and ask to have a drop of the spirits that will burn your palate on your half-melted cube, although she does not always agree to this you are given a drop or two as well, you know that the liquid will hasten the dissolving of the sugar and you push the lump towards your front teeth and suck on it as if it were a slice of lemon, tiny grains flow into the gaps between your teeth where they get stuck; when she shoves the bottle back into her bag your lump has melted and formed a thick pool at the centre of your numbed tongue. No neighbours have opened their doors or called the lift as yet, a radio is on and the pipes are being flushed, the still silence that exists beneath these superficial sounds continues to hover around you until she sighs and wafts of alcohol and lemon balm alter the nature of the air on the landing and turn it chilly against your skin like the vapour that rises from the sea at your father's aunt Julia's house in the summer or the mist that accompanies you on your way to school in the mornings. The time has come to start the descent to the ground floor and the exit which is three flights down, past the caretaker's cubby-hole situated to the left of the lift. You go on ahead and plunge down the worn marble steps two at a time, just before the landing that turns at a right angle at the corner of the lift shaft you leap over four steps and the force of the jump you have to make means you collide with the wall when you land, you parry the bumps with extended arms and open palms, every jump is making your palms hotter. Behind you comes the clip-clop of your mother's iron-shod heels, you know she is running away from the smell of mothballs and stock and your grandmother's voice as she was mentioning the boy (. . . *el niño*) in the doorway halfway into her room when she thought no-one else could hear, you run down the stairs that have a dip in the middle you try to land in with your feet while the echo of your mother's heels is tumbling down the various floors, she is invisible somewhere behind the grill of the lift shaft that exposes the cables and both compartments to your eyes, and you launch yourself once again as though you were going to leap across an abyss because the staircase is so spacious and the bronze grill of the lift shaft glistens like gold in the light from the milky-white glass of the high windows and the stairs have that deep depression in the middle from everyone who has run down them and jumped on them before you and all of this combined: the sugar lump, the lift and the stairs and your grandmother's huge apartment, with its rows of closed doors and shut-in statues of saints and its large, blue-tiled bathroom with the black border at the top that makes the room look like a swimming pool with water halfway up to the ceiling and through whose window someone had climbed down the drainpipe during the war, affect you in some way that is greater than you can grasp, something you cannot control. When you reach the entrance lobby and its black-and-white marble floor-tiles, your palms are burning from all the bumps with the walls, you play hopscotch all the way over to the marble bench by the large iron and glass door where you sit and wait for the heels to catch you up, your hands tucked under your buttocks to cool the palms against the stone. On the other side of the large glass door the traffic is rushing by, you have time to count three taxis, in Barcelona all the taxis are black and yellow, the artificial leather on the seats sticks to you and is impregnated with cigarette smoke and the smell of the same aftershave, which is a smell of winter. Your mother has reached the ground floor, you watch her walk past the lifts and their shiny engraved signs (INQUILINOS[69] – the more refined lift compartment with a mirror and black Bakelite buttons in which you rise on a foldaway seat while studying your reflection, and SERVICIO[70] – a cramped little cabin in which you have stand up the whole way and can see only the bars of the lift passing floor after floor, although you are allowed to take it on your own while your father keeps tapping on the dividing wall), in the mirrors that cover the walls in the lobby you can see her face both from the front and in profile while she is walking towards you as if down a long tunnel though the caretaker does not bother to come out of her cubby-hole to say hello because it is immediately apparent that your mother is a different sort of woman to those who reside in the building, it is obvious from miles away that she is not from here, and that is not because of those tufts in her hair. Before you go through the glass door she retrieves her sunglasses from her bag and puts them on, then she closes the clasp of the handbag with a snap that bounces off the mirrors and the marble and the plaster in the curved ceiling and makes the space sound like a chapel. Then the noise of the traffic comes flooding in through the open door and drowns out all the other sounds.

Cristal City was the name of a bar, situated opposite your grandmother's residence at C/Balmes 297 (where your uncle and his family

69   Residents.
70   Staff.

– a wife and three children – lived as well), on the other side of the broad avenue down which traffic rushed towards the lower part of town, you were standing at the red light on the right-hand side with your mother, she was waiting impatiently with one hand on your shoulder because you refused to hold hers, her head and its teased hairstyle turned in the direction the cars were coming from, from *the direction of the war*, you were thinking, because your father had told you that Franco and his African soldiers had marched that way into Barcelona when they won the war, down from Tibidabo, past the villa where your father used to live and that the family were forced to leave when war broke out, as though Franco had decided to start putting things to rights in the very part of the city your father felt was home; which is why it was as if you were expecting, every time you stood at that red light, to see *El Caudillo* appear on his horse from round the bend where Balmes turned left, followed close behind by the legionnaires and the snow-white goat that was their mascot, as though it were actually the entry of the soldiers into the city that was making the traffic move faster down the sloping street and the nervous drivers so afraid they were forced to speed right before your eyes, like desperate men. You rarely turned that way, however, when you visited your grandmother Dolores in Barcelona, most often it was in the opposite direction, to the right, as seen from the entrance to *abuelita* Dolores' building, towards the square and the café-bar where you could eat *churros* dipped in warm, viscous chocolate, and the delicatessen where your mother bought tins of Russian *chatka*, a tough white crabmeat that tasted sweet, as well as the entrance to the metro, because Barcelona was not only ten times larger than your home town in surface area, it was so large that there existed a whole system of tunnels in parallel to the world to be found up above, which allowed people to move around like ants below ground on trains and where it was always night time and when you sat on one of those night trains and as you looked through the windows what you could see besides your face, hollow-eyed and grave as if you were ill or were going to be sad for the rest of your life, was a rough wall covered in the tracks left behind by water and every so often brightly lit, white-tiled platforms like huge bathing pools people came to swim in and you used to think that some of the tunnels lit by dim light bulbs might be reflecting their yellowish glow over rivers of shining black water and when you walked along the pavements above ground you used to think about those nocturnal rivers flowing beneath your feet and about everything that might be floating in that shiny black water and you used to think that there might be people swimming along down there, maybe the children your cousins told you about, and you could see their heads in the light as they swam in the water-filled tunnels as well as the much smaller heads of rats sticking out of the water and swimming in the wash made by the children or padding along the subterranean walls and ceilings away from the brightly lit trains that rumbled along the surrounding tunnels, and the people in the water kept swimming along the tunnels without getting anywhere and they had been in the water so long their lips were blue and the skin on their fingertips was all wrinkled the way many old people's skins were. Only now you were not going that way either but straight across the street, to Cristal City, to wait for your father. Your mother always prefers to sit at the counter, you climb up onto the round spinning barstool and ask to have a Coca-Cola, with ice and a slice of lemon, you begin to work up speed by launching yourself at the counter and rotating halfway round the bar, in semi-circles that spin you to and from the counter, back and forth; the walls are covered in wooden panels and there are books on shelves here and there, your mother says some of them are in English, most in Spanish, there are even books in Catalan, and she says it as though there were something very special about the fact, then her voice changes as she says in Swedish – her pitch alters when she speaks Swedish – so no-one in the bar will understand, that there is a secret room she and your father have been inside that is filled with forbidden books the bartender has to keep hidden from the police; Barcelona is not like Lérida, everything is different here, she adds, though you know that already, you never see *the boy*, for instance, in Lérida, which you ought to after all if the boy your grandmother was talking about was your brother, the one your mother told you about, who never got born and died in her belly after you were born, though the boy who came out of your grandmother's bedroom was not small, he was a couple of years older than you, and occasionally you have seen another boy who was smaller than you, maybe five years old, he disappeared into the palatial bedroom where you and your cousins sometimes play. You keep spinning in semicircles that regularly come to an abrupt halt and make your pigtail hit your back every time you come to a stop, you are wondering which boy your grandmother meant and why she was so upset when she was talking to your mother and why your father leaves you there with her whenever he goes to meet his friends at the barracks if your grandmother does not like you. The waiter is pouring Coca-Cola into a tall narrow glass and as it falls a thick layer of bubbling light-brown foam is formed, you start to sip straight-away, the gas given off by the foam tickles your upper lip before you swallow it, a spongy bubble of foam expands inside your mouth and pushes lightly against your palate, it feels like swallowing sweet air; you lick off the distinct edge of sweetness that remains on your lip and swing back round to the street, through the bar's large windows you can see the facade of the building in which your grandmother lives, the white stone balustrade of the balconies that are never used, your cousins Reyes and Elena will be coming back from school at any moment for lunch, you should be in school too, though you often stay away, not just when you are away from home like now, that familiar knot is tying itself round your stomach again when you think of your empty chair in the classroom and what Sister María Jesús is going to say about it, you spin away from the faces in the window and back to the counter with its mixed row of bottles and books, there are silver-coloured bottles with *P-o-n-c-h-e C-a-b-a-l-l-e-r-o* on, and long-necked, wide-bottomed brown bottles that say *C-a-l-i-s-a-y* and a yellow bottle with a big number encircled: *Licor 43*, next to it is a book with a photograph of a bar on the cover, the entrance could be that of any bar, like the one on your square in Lérida, beside the bar's entrance are enormous Coca-Cola caps that have been stuck on the wall, the book is called *La plaça del Diamant*, "Diamond Square", you wonder if it is a square where someone lost a diamond, you never lose things, unless it is deliberate, like when you drop them in the pond to lure the carp over. You sigh, your mother is smoking with her elbow leaning against the counter. Your cousins will have come back from school and are having to eat the horrible noodle soup you are forced to eat because of the war, you hope you will be staying on here to eat steak and chips and to be given another Coca-Cola when your father turns up, you do not know if he will arrive in uniform, sometimes he wears his uniform even when you are on holiday, the uniforms always smell of the barracks, even the dress uniform with gold buttons he had on this morning, often when you hug him something hard gets pressed against your cheek or even your eye: a button or the clasp of his belt, today he was wearing the lovely purple sash across his chest, the fringe tickles when you brush your palm along it. Having to wait is boring. María Reyes and Elena have a room filled with old toys, some are from long ago, dolls that look like dead children without any clothes on, the lips on those dolls are parted and reveal tiny square teeth, little mouse teeth, you do not like to play with dolls that look like babies, you prefer dolls that look like adults and wear ball gowns and wedding dresses, you are missing your own dolls and your dog as well, he is supposed to be staying with a farmer in the countryside while you are away, you wonder what he is doing there, whether he is barking all the time because he misses you, you are missing him, the smell of bread on his fur, he smells of rusks and biscuits, and it tickles when he licks your cheek as you hug him, you are feeling a faint regret that you did not stay with your grandmother after all so you could play with Reyes after lunch, you are almost the same age, her birthday falls on Epiphany and yours is when summer

comes to an end, though mostly you just talk because you find it hard
to come up with games that involve her dolls, she has seen the boy as
well, but only at night, she says he cries sometimes, but when you told
your father that he said she meant her little brother Nacho, though
you know she was talking about the other children, the ones who
lived there before, because the boys you have seen smell strange and
they wear old-fashioned clothes like in the films, Reyes says they are
the children from the war, the ones who went off in big black cars
in the middle of the night or hid in the metro and never came back,
though some did, like both your fathers, they spent an entire week in
a truck and were off school for a whole year, you spin back to the
view of the front of your grandmother's building and it is as though
the balustrades had become transparent and you could look inside
the rooms, as into a doll's house, everyone is inside eating their soup
without hearing the explosions, they pay them no attention, because
they are so tired of rushing down into the metro to hide whenever the
planes come, and the children do not understand what war is, just that
you have to wait all the time and be careful and eat that soup no-one
likes, the neighbours in the apartment above your grandmother's are
getting up from the table, they are hauling suitcases along the long
corridor that is so dark the figures moving along it seem to be lit
from within, a man is climbing out through the bathroom window,
on the veranda that faces the rear courtyard you can see a dog being
sick and falling flat on his face as if he were in a very bad way, the
family gave him poison before they left him behind, the soup is still
in the bowl on the table in the sunlit dining room, it is cold and the
fat has congealed, huge green blowflies are moving across it, the dog
has died and his eyes are covered with the same green flies, when the
maid mops the floor in the bedrooms at the front the water is grey,
as if ashes had been wiped up, your aunt Ana María was showing it
to your mother today: "Do you see that? It's the exhaust fumes, living
in this place is really impossible," and when you enter your grandparents' former bedroom which was the bedroom of your grandmother's

parents before that, at the time your father was living in a villa higher up and the whole of the upper part of Calle Balmes all the way to Tibidabo was made up of villas and houses with gardens, you can feel it too, that it is impossible to live here because the air never moves even though the cars drive so fast down on the street, everyone speaks quietly and walks slowly when they go inside, they stand perfectly still and just wait, and sometimes you see the shadowy boy with the curly black hair out of the corner of your eye, but only if you are standing absolutely still, and you have seen a blonde girl too now and then, she was sitting on the floor, her legs pointing in different directions, as if she were broken.

"¿Dónde lleva este camino?"
"A la gloria."[71]

The Barracks in Girona, IVth Military Region, Spain, February 1981, Evening

For a moment the gleaming espresso machine on the other side of the bar catches his eye as if that repellent metallic sheen were connected in some way with the words that have suddenly come to him about the glory the soldier trudging through the Russian snow outside Novgorod saw as the reward for his heroism: "Where does this road lead?" "To honour." Extending two fingers between which a newly lit *Ducados* is burning, Lt Col Salvador Pascual Pascó beckons to the corporal in the white waiter's jacket wiping glasses behind the bar, and the corporal who is serving on his own in the officers' mess this evening turns towards the mirror-backed drinks shelf to get down the bottle of Bacardi and fills the Lt Col's glass with no more than a thimbleful of rum, *un dedal sólo*, Coca-Cola, ice and two fresh slices of lemon. All that can be heard from the large room next door is music and the voices of the officers and the other ranks who have been gathering at the barracks ever since the coup began. T.V.E. stopped broadcasting half an hour or so ago, military marches are all that is being transmitted on Radio Nacional. He puts his cigarette down to get the watch out of his left breast pocket, he can make out the hands with some effort, half past eight, the advance party or whatever you are supposed to call the small force that seized the parliament buildings has been in there for more than two hours now, that is more than "the moment" (*un momento*) the officer in charge, a lieutenant colonel like himself, with the drawn pistol, had

71 "Where does this road lead?" "To honour." (From Enrique Errando Vilar's memoir, *Campaña de invierno. División Azul.*)

promised, the radio reporter who had been broadcasting live on the vote in congress when the members of the Civil Guard stormed the hall had time to notice the two eight-pointed stars on the lower part of the sleeve of the man acting as leader, the one who yelled "On the ground!" (*¡Al suelo!*) before firing a couple of shots in the air. No-one seems to be in any doubt that the officer in question is Antonio Tejero, the chief conspirator in the so-called *Operación Galaxia*, who has already been imprisoned for one failed coup, the radio reporter thought he recognised him – by his moustache ... Lt Col Pascual Pascó would give anything to see the expressions on the deputies' faces at this moment: Suárez and that white-collar Communist Carrillo and the rest of the rabble. He takes a deep drag that jolts his lungs though all he gets is the harsh taste of burnt grass, he had chemotherapy yesterday and his palate has been deadened to more or less everything except sweet and sour tastes, not that that is going to make him smoke any less, he tried to stop drinking and smoking for a bit as if the cancer were not enough of a pain, where does this road lead? To hell with it! He chuckles silently and takes another deep drag, he can hear the murmuring of the officers he left in the television room, they are still speculating as they wait in front of the dead screen. He tries to find his way back to last night's dream, an odd dream in which everything was glittering, it occurs to him that he should have had a sense it would be a remarkable day as early as this morning, when his service pistol thudded to the floor and jerked him violently from his sleep, there and then he should have understood that his dream foreshadowed something exceptional, a historic day, a day when the course of history would be changed. The gun had slipped out from under the pillow where it was held in place by his neck, he must have done a lot of twisting and turning to make the thing slide away like that, maybe he had come in his sleep? Ground himself against the mattress? Against Gitt's bum? She always sleeps on her side, or remains unconscious, stuffed to the gills to be more precise with red wine and valium the

345

way she is every night, of course she wouldn't have heard the thud. The sun had not yet risen when his service pistol fell off the bed, combined with the yellow glow of the nightlight, a wishy-washy twilight was making little spots of brightness on her patterned blouse as she lay there fully dressed, her head loose and tipped back and her mouth gaping as if he had gone ahead with it, carried out the threat he would hiss in her ear every so often with the muzzle of the pistol pressed to her throat: (*"¡Tú vienes conmigo! ¡Y las pequeñas! ¡Yo me muero pero vosotras venís conmigo!*),[72] he feels totally empty after he has uttered those words, as if he had spewed up the rage that lay behind them, as though it were the words themselves, or just the idea, that were driving him crazy and as long as he could get them out, everything felt less desperate and agonising. He can sleep afterwards as well, just for a bit, last night he woke up without the taste of iron in his mouth, his waking occurred like a sort of shock, although the shock was caused not by the metallic thud of the weapon against the tiled·floor, nor by the notion that the unsecured weapon could have gone off by accident, no, it was at having to leave that other place he had woken from: the dream was so tactile, so filled with the sensations of former summers that waking up was pure torture. He had also had a massive erection that made his groin ache while his throat felt wet and sticky with tears. The strangest thing was the feeling in his chest, instead of that rat bite underneath his pectoral something soft he only remembers the word for, "joy", "happiness": the joy at seeing the face of his dead cousin again, Catalina . . . the joy of, well, still having his whole life in front of him. Even now, right now, that ridiculous joy is still quivering, all expectant and naive, like a little brown sparrow in the seconds before it is pulped beneath a wheel . . . It must be decades since he so much as dreamed about her, in any case he cannot remember ever doing so before, in the dream her face radiated this light, as if the beam

72 "You're coming with me! And the girls! I may be dying, but you're all coming with me!"

346

from an arc lamp were cutting through the darkness and drawing a white circle of protection around him, that feeling has set its stamp on this entire day, an ordinary February day to begin with, cold and still misty as he drove the younger girls to school (their fair hair so dull and porous in the mist as he limped across the playground with them in tow) but lit up by the season in the dream, so that his feet felt as light as if he were wearing sandals when he arrived at the barracks and got out of the car, even his left foot felt pliant and easy at the end of the dead leg because the dream had opened the gate to the estate at La Montoliva once again and inside he could be the strapping teenager he once was, before, at some point, if it really was true that you could make an equals sign between the young man the photographs and the peculiarly wayward nature of his memories told him he had been and the person he was now. In his mind's eye an image of himself appears from the summer of 1942, the last time he saw his cousin, he is emerging from the sea in a black swimming costume, he has not yet plunged towards the bottom of the Olympic pool, his nose still looks perfectly straight, it carves a perpendicular line against the horizontal sea; he is smiling as he walks towards the camera and the proportions of his limbs, the sky, the beach and the glittering water seem to be in perfect balance, he is smiling at the point where all those lines meet, under a high sun, at the centre of everything, life stretched out before him and not yet used up. He takes a long swig of watery *cubalibre* and when his head returns to an upright position he can see himself at the window of the boys' room in Valdemoro keeping a look out for the German Stukas on their way to the front (the light filtering through the plane trees on the square outside so confusingly like the yellowish-green rays that poured into the bedroom that used to be his as a boy in Barcelona). If life really were a thread (in which case it was already resting on the very edge of the scissor-blades of the goddesses of Fate) the thread of his life had become tangled up even then, doubt had grazed him in that flat behind the rear lines the family had taken over, like a stab of pain, and made his existence uncertain (as if not only the boy in whose room he was living had left behind his books, his stamp collection and his clothes in all haste but the entire room were askew and tilting towards an invisible parallel world): the person who was seeing all this, his heart fluttering like a bird's wing, could that be really *him*?

There is a slight delay before the smell of rubber, heated dust and lubricant arrives from the shed where the bicycles were propped against the wall, she was sitting in front of him on the handlebars of the large black man's cycle they used to get out of the tool shed, he can see the whitewashed house and the tall date palm that could be made out from as far away as the main road grabbing at the sky like an open hand and the orchard of long rows of hazels and peach trees they used to seek shelter and shade beneath, in that life he could stretch his arms to the sky, swim powerful strokes, grab everything he wanted, a girl's waist, a ball, in that life neither of his arms dangled uselessly at his side because of anything as tawdry as a stroke. That summer is beyond the reach of everything his life has now become, but he would like to hold on to the place that has temporarily brightened up the darkness all the same, a darkness he carries around like a sense of heaviness in his body, as if he were a female animal teeming with young. He can remember the angle of Catalina's arm as she lay on her stomach under the hazel tree, sunspots on her forearms, the thin yellow-gold strands of her hair rose halfway up when he ran his fingers along her spine and she shivered all over, it looked like a field of wheat in miniature, the wheat fields around La Montoliva, the wheat fields around the log cabin, the *izba* his father used to write about in his letters from the Eastern Front. "Where does this road lead?" "To Russia!" "*¡Rusia es culpable!*" Serrano Suñer had yelled to the crowds gathered in Madrid in July 1941, who remembers that now the Communists have been made a legal party whose members are in the Congress of Deputies at this very moment – and, presumably, shitting their pants? He lights another cigarette from the embers of the old one and the process makes him think of his tongue entering his cousin's mouth, as if he held a glowing ember in his own, his tongue watery and burning with desire; what was completely idiotic was that he didn't appreciate the whole thing then, when he was sixteen, he wanted to be a hero at the time and go off to Russia with all the thousands of other men who were shown in the No-Do newsreels, the crowd literally flooded the Atocha station in Madrid, there were even people on the roofs of the trains, banners were hung in front of the train windows in celebration, slogans were being yelled in a frenzy. "Where does this road lead?" "To the great ideals, *Comradeship, Honour, Heroism.*" And to the big phrases: *The Crusade against Jew-Bolshevism.* He had tried to go with them, what else? He was tall and well built, he tried to fool people about his age. He takes a long swig of his drink with a weary smile no-one can see, not even the corporal in the white jacket who is rattling the bottles and the crates at the other end. He moves his good hand, the right one, to his chest, *the hollow muscle is beating* under the uniform jacket, it was the doctor at the fort in El Aaiún he borrowed that phrase from, *el corazón, Salvador, no es más que un músculo hueco.*[73] He got caught just before the train started to chug out of the station, somehow his father had managed to find him, *¡Hijo, tú no tienes edad para ser un héroe!*[74] It was his father who made the journey a few months later instead, in the depths of a freezing winter and too old, just after his forty-sixth birthday, just nine years younger than he is now, the entire family went with him to the station, he can remember his mother's chestnut-brown eyes below those ferociously plucked brows, wide and sculpted in a semi-circle like Romanesque arches, her gaze as dark as a tunnel, and like the shrill whistle of a train from the depths of that tunnel he can hear the strains of a march he would have liked to have been singing with the other volunteers as they walked through Belorussia and Estonia and Russia itself all the way to Novgorod but which he only

73   "All the heart is, Salvador, is just a hollow muscle."
74   "My boy, you're not old enough to be a hero."

got to sing many years later in Africa with the Foreign Legion. *Soy un voluntario alegre de la División Azul | que recorrí toda Europa | como si fuera un baúl.*[75] Lord, the tiredness that comes over him all of a sudden, that tiredness is the worst of it, not like the tiredness during manoeuvres or the forced marches (*Voluntario alegre que a Rusia te vas | con rancho de hierro para caminar*),[76] not a tiredness of the muscles, not even of the hollow muscle that is threatening to explode between his ribs like a bomb manufactured by E.T.A., against that kind of tiredness brass bands and marching songs and alcohol had proved pretty useful. And against the fear. *Honour Fatherland the Flag.* The big words helped. *Voluntario alegre que a Rusia te vas | contigo un gran ideal.*[77] This new tiredness comes from inside, from the nucleus of the cells, hundreds of thousands of microscopic mouths sucking all the energy out of him, lively tunes aren't much use against them.

"*¡Cabo! ¡Cambia a la cadena S.E.R.! ¡Estoy hasta los huevos de marchas!*"[78] The corporal turns immediately to the mirrored backdrop and the shelf where the transistor radio is wedged between the bottles of spirits. *You are listening to S.E.R., still reporting live.* The voice summarises the sequence of events, as it has been at regular intervals throughout the evening: at 18.22 the Chamber of Congress was stormed by a troop of Civil Guardists with a lieutenant colonel at their head, the government and the entire Chamber of Deputies were voting on whether to appoint Leopoldo Calvo Sotelo as the new prime minister (Salvador can hear a kind of rain at this point, the name entering his awareness like twinned drops, a gulf of silence in the interval between this name and that of the other Calvo Sotelo,

75 "I am a happy volunteer in our Blue Division / travelling across all of Europe / like a trunk."
76 "You happy volunteer marching towards Russia / cutting steel your only food for the journey."
77 "You happy volunteer marching towards Russia / carry with you your noble ideals."
78 "Corporal! Switch over to the S.E.R., I've had it up to here with marches."

José, who the Reds murdered in 1936 and he is thinking that perhaps it is true after all that history repeats itself, that this contemporary Calvo Sotelo will be the starting shot for a new civil war just as his namesake was in 1936.) The parliamentarians have been taken hostage along with the Cabinet in the expectation that the "competent authority, a military one, of course," (*la autoridad competente, militar, por supuesto*) "will arrive to take command". And then once again, from the transistor radio squeezed between a silver-coloured bottle of arrack and one containing anise that has a shaggy ape with a human face on the label, the recording of the shots being fired, first the three rifle shots and the shout *On the ground!* followed by several machine-gun salvos, finally the reassuring speech to the hostages in a new warmer and rounder voice: *Buenas tardes, no va a ocurrir nada pero vamos a esperar un momento a que venga la autoridad militar competente para disponer lo que tenga que ser y lo que él mismo diga a todos nosotros, o sea estense tranquilos, no sé si esto será cuestión de un cuarto de hora, veinte minutos o media hora, me imagino que no más tiempo . . . y la autoridad que hay competente, militar, por supuesto, será la que determine qué es lo que va a ocurrir, por supuesto que no pasará nada, ustedes todos tranquilos.*[79] Salvador gets out his watch again, an hour and a half has passed and that *military authority* has not turned up, only Milans del Bosch, head of the IIIrd military region, has given his backing to the leaders of the coup thus far, his tanks have occupied the streets of Valencia where a state of emergency has been declared, his eleven-point communiqué has been read out on Radio Nacional in the Valencia area every half hour since 19.00, Milans del Bosch has revoked all civil rights – such as the right to strike – he has abolished all political parties – the Communists

79 "Good evening, you are in no danger, but you will have to wait for a while until the competent military authority decides what is to be done and communicates that to us all, so keep calm. I do not know if there will be a delay of fifteen, twenty or thirty minutes, but not likely more than that . . . and the competent authority, a military one, of course – will decide what happens after that although of course you are in no danger and you can all remain calm."

will be driven underground again – the general in Barcelona on the other hand had said *we're going to wait and see* when he rang him, the telephone has been silent as the grave ever since, *we're going to wait and see*, the three-star general is going to wait and see what course the other three-star generals intend to follow as though the Fatherland were a bloody school playground, of eleven lieutenant generals only one has shown his hand. And what is the king up to? What's he waiting for? How's it all going to turn out? Salvador peers at the watch face again as if he were consulting an oyster with oracular gifts, two hours and twenty-five minutes since he got the order from Barcelona to confine everyone to barracks, nearly two hours since Milans del Bosch declared a state of emergency in Valencia. Something's wrong, why has no-one taken over from that Tejero by now, it's about bloody time. He is picturing to himself the glint of the black lacquer on the tricorne, he has no confidence in the Guardia Civil, no respect either, he knows about all the fiddles involved when it comes to smuggling goods across the country's borders. And why is the king hesitating? He's never had any confidence in him either, even when he was still a prince and visited the military academy for N.C.O.s in Talarn six years ago you could see it in him, despite the comradely attitude he adopted towards the men in the officers' mess, that he wouldn't keep his word, or uphold the oath he had sworn. And besides, it was after that visit he'd had his stroke. *Todo está atado y bien atado,*[80] Franco had said. The fuck it was, less than five years later and they've introduced a multi-party system and even the Communist party has been legalised, and what thanks do we get? The politicians are playing right into the hands of the E.T.A., 430 terror attacks last year alone, 130 dead, most of them military . . . Chaos and bloodshed every day, just like in 1936. He is imagining the expression on Prime Minister Suárez' face, that fox, while the machine guns were singing

80 "It's all done and dusted." The celebrated words Franco is supposed to have uttered on having secured the survival and continuation of his regime after his death.

in the semi-circular hall, his pointed nose as white as a lake at minus fifty degrees and his lackey Señor Gutiérrez, who cancelled the parade to commemorate the victory of *los nacionales* in 1939 and has never fought a battle in his entire life, of course agreed to abolish it once Franco was dead, what can you expect of a man who was a fifth-columnist in Madrid during the war, from fifth-columnist to a bloody turncoat isn't much of a step. Then he thinks about Carrillo living safe and secure in Moscow while his Red rabble were fighting with the partisans in France or with the Red Army in the Soviet Union. *Krasni Armi. Si las palabras sonoras, los conceptos bellos, les llevaron a la muerte o la mutilación, hay que seguir otorgando valor a esas palabras, porque si no todo sería una mierda*,[81] as his friend Tomás Salvador wrote, friend may be the term he uses but he is actually the man who sells books and papers at the newspaper stand on Plaça Catalunya, his own books as it turned out, masses of them, in different genres, thrillers, children's books, essays, *Si quiere se lo firmo, mi comandante*,[82] he told him when they met at the news-stand for the first time, he saw him looking through a book called *Camaradas 74*, he had spent two whole years with the Blue Division in Russia, it emerged, and had written two books about it: he was holding one of them in his hands, he was the one who took him to Víctor's *bodega* on Passeig de la Bonanova for the first time, a cramped little hole with a section fitted out as a bunker where the veterans would have a glass or two together from time to time, and then it turned out that the landlord *Víctor* had been considered too young to serve at the time, like himself, and had to stay at home. The stitches in his throat pull every time he leans his head back to swallow, there is barely room inside the tall narrow glass for the long nose he inherited from his mother and he has to bend the back of his neck so his forehead is

81 "Even if the sonorous words, the beautiful concepts, led them to their deaths or crippled them, we have to continue to give those words meaning, otherwise it's all just shit."
82 "I could sign it for you, if you like, my Captain."

parallel to the arched ceiling. Suddenly he feels dizzy and the room starts spinning around him and he has to pull his shoulders in, hunch his back and screw up his eyes to make it stop. When it passes it strikes him that history really is repeating itself: he was too young in 1936 and he was too young for the Blue Division a few years later, now he is too ill, the Fatherland is calling him once again, only the cancer has got there first, he has a war of his own to fight. Where does this road lead? To hell!

"*¡Cabo, ponme un cubalibre, sin ron, que estoy de servicio!*"[83] He chuckles hoarsely as if the joking has consoled him, made him feel less alone. The corporal puts a clean tumbler in front of him, no rum this time, just lemon and Coca-Cola. Salvador recalls "the Bunker" in Barcelona and wonders what's happening there right now, maybe Víctor has pulled down the blinds and is sitting inside the smoky dive with Jorge and Tomás and the other former Falangists and veterans. *Ahora que Franco ha ganado la guerra | Ahora que Franco ha ganado la guerra| Volveremos a empezar| tomaremos Gibraltar | Tómala sí un día, tómala sí un dos . . .*[84] They're probably drinking a toast to Milans del Bosch, and the man who met him when he was an infantry captain on the Volkhov Front in 1941 will be telling them an anecdote about that time, forty years on and he is a lieutenant general and maybe the man to lead the military junta that will be set up, Milans del Bosch, is he the man everybody is waiting for? He can see the wooden walls of the Bunker hung with posters of the Blue Division, photographs of soldiers on skis or sitting in a sleigh or some young Russian women in white kerchiefs with laughing children in front of a log cabin, the young lads smiling alongside the volunteers, like the ones he found among his father's things, along with a metre-long drawing of a Leningrad suburb, skilfully executed by a Spanish artillery captain from an observation point. As well as a Russian

83　"Corporal, a *cubalibre* without rum, since I'm on duty."
84　"Now Franco's won the war | We'll start again | We'll conquer Gibraltar | It might take us one day, it might take us two . . ."

icon, a gas mask and a pair of the comical snow goggles made of perforated aluminium they used to wear, that made them look like mutant mosquitoes. He remembers them showing him all their memorabilia and someone getting out a photograph of some furniture carved with pornographic images that had been in the palace of Catherine the Great at Tsarskoye Selo and the Germans (*los doiches*) who sold them made a packet from them. His father did not have photographs like that, just the one of an *izba* and a round-faced woman with high cheekbones and very pale eyes, as pale as his own maybe, as though he had been looking over there in Russia for a mother for the child he had at home rather than a woman to keep him warm at night. He thinks about the nights on the front, he thinks about the night his father died. "*Vendrá la muerte como 'la parrala', de noche,*"[85] he said just before he slipped into a coma, he was talking about Russia to the last, about the attacks they were subjected to by one or two little Russian planes every night, and you never knew if the bomb would hit the wooden cottages they were quartered in and set them alight or not, that was why they called the Red night bombers *la parrala*: maybe, maybe not. Was he worried about the lovely Russian woman in the picture when the night bombers came? He thinks about his own end and that it will also come at night and set everything alight like those pathetic Soviet plywood planes wrapped in gauze that flew low over their positions, small, highly inflammable flying machines even women flew, one direct hit was enough to make them go up like torches low over the ground before they plunged to earth, he thinks about the radiation treatments of the last few months, about the coordinates that were read out before he was left alone, strapped beneath a rotating machine in a room like a submarine filled with noises and flashing lights. Salvador raises his voice and sings a bit louder, he lifts his drink in a toast along

85 "Death comes by night, like la parrala." Alludes to a song by "La Parrala", a legendary Flamenco singer. The refrain is: "*Que sí, que sí, que sí, que sí | que no, que no, que no, que no*" – "maybe, maybe not".

with whoever is sitting around the transistor radio in the Bunker, the same way they sat round a smoking iron stove inside an *izba* at the Volkhov Front forty years ago, he knows that sooner or later someone will burst into song, because when you have walked a thousand kilometres on foot and seen your comrades fall at Krasny Bor it is your duty never to stop singing about it: *Y si nos faltara la tierra | tomaremos Inglaterra | tómala sí un día, tómala sí un dos | sentados en una barca tomaremos Dinamarca | tómala sí un día, tómala sí un dos. | Cuando entremos en Moscú | tomaremos un vermut | Tómala sí un día, tómala sí un dos | Al entrar en Leningrado | tomaremos un helado | Tómala sí un día, tómala sí un dos...*[86]

He cannot see the white-clad waiter corporal anywhere. Nor can he hear the voices out there in the mess. The lighting seems dimmer to him, as if he had awoken from a fug. Or fallen asleep inside it. He turns around, his fellow officers are standing silently in front of the television set which is no longer broadcasting music, he gets down from the stool and walks over, from the doorway he can hear a communiqué from the ministry of the interior announcing the formation of a provisional government. It has just gone nine. A captain informs him that the unit that seized T.V.E. and R.N.E. has left both buildings and that transmissions have been resumed and that the king is expected to appear at any moment. So they're calling it off! Suddenly the second part of last night's dream comes back to him as clear as day: one of those wild September storms in Barcelona, the water gushing down from the upper parts of the city and taking everything with it, he is in water up to his knees outside the white villa on Plaça Bonanova where they lived in the years before the war, his father's two trucks are there as well, the rainwater is eddying around the

86   "If we lack territory, / we'll conquer England / it may take us a day, it may take two / if we travel in a vessel we'll also conquer Denmark / it may take us a day, it may take two. / When we conquer Moscow / we'll treat ourselves to a drink / it may take us a day, it may take two / When we capture Leningrad / we'll treat ourselves to a drink / it may take us a day, it may take two."

wheels of the brown Ford they travelled to Pontevedra in, he turns towards Sarría and the mountains and sees that the whole street is sloping much more than usual, Calle Balmes and the high-rise buildings on either side of it are gaining in height as though the whole city were about to capsize. He wades as quickly as he can in the opposite direction, but he does not have the strength to go against the current and finds himself sliding with it instead, down towards the sea, huge volumes of water are rushing from Plaça Bonanova past Plaça Molina to Plaça de la Universitat and even now he has a sense that everything is lost, that the wind has turned for good and that the people who were defeated in the war forty years ago will be the victors of this night and of the future, everything will be reversed, the narratives, the words, the songs, the forbidden songs will be the victors' songs and the old hymns will be boycotted and banned and it is as if the waters in his dream are uncovering mass grave after mass grave as they tumble down.

The bartender is standing in front of him once more, Salvador looks askance at the opening in the corporal's round white collar where his Adam's apple sticks out and asks for an espresso: "*Dime chaval, ¿tú sabes qué es la muerte?*" he asks the corporal using a quotation he remembers from his friend Tomás' book. "*Una cerveza que no vas a beber,*"[87] he answers himself and waits for the young man's laugh which comes just a moment too late, more of a faint smile, in fact. He is going to go home for a bit to reassure the wife, he has decided, the barracks can be left in charge of a major for the duration.

He starts walking towards his office to fetch his cap with the two eight-pointed stars, he did not bring anything else with him to the barracks, his service weapon is at home. The corridor is broad and the effect of the dim side-lighting is to submerge the straight passage in a crepuscular gloom, the still-standing light has been transformed into a viscous silence and it is in that silent stillness that his mother

87   "Tell me, lad, do you know what Death is? A beer that cannot be drunk."

357

appears out of nowhere: he watches her haughty walk, her Persian lamb coat, her hunched spine, her low black shoes with round metal heels that clatter together with the walking stick against the brown floor tiles in triple time, heel heel stick, heel heel stick . . . He follows several metres behind her, seeing those bowed legs sticking out beneath the black sheen of the Astrakhan coat, her silvery hair gleams through the embroidered black prayer shawl, wearing all the trappings of widowhood she seems like a widowed queen, though hunchbacked and old she is impressively majestic as she strides indomitably through life, worthy of her high-sounding name: María de los Dolores. A waft from the washroom beside the kitchen in the flat on Calle Balmes brings with it the forgotten scent of Marseille soap, someone in the long succession of maids is scrubbing sheets against the washboard . . . scents keep coming to him like that now, out of nowhere, like hallucinations . . . though his mother keeps going, without bothering to check on the oblivious maid who is singing to herself by the sink. Dolores continues down the long corridor towards the hall, she opens the front door and summons the lift with its two segregated cabins, if she gets in one, he will take the other, the servants' wooden cabin without a mirror or a seat inside, he can feel the jolt in his stomach when the lift starts, going down. His mother is alive and enjoying enviably good health at a home run by nuns in Sarría, and yet she is here now, what is she doing here, at the barracks in Girona? In the middle of this historic night? The sound of his halting gait, of the dead foot sweeping the floor beneath, is superimposed over the echoing of her heels, he keeps following the tapping of the heels and stick against the tiles, even smooth taps, until the square tiles turn to asphalt and the noise of the steps falls mute, then he stops and sees her slowly crossing the court-yard of the barracks to disappear behind the guards at the barrier.

What a desolate place, the courtyard looks as forlorn as an opera house after the curtain has fallen and everyone has left the auditorium, something has just occurred here, but all the place now contains are shadows and lamps that are about to be turned off, he can see huge candelabra being lowered from an immensely high ceiling and an invisible hand snuffing out the flames one by one. His mother has vanished without trace. And everything else along with her.

A white Seat 124 he recognises as his own drives up and stops a few metres from the red-and-white barrier. His orderly gets out of the driver's seat and holds the door open for him, but he shakes his head in refusal. Then the orderly runs around the bonnet to open the passenger door. In response to the question whether he has been following the news in the last ten minutes, his orderly informs him that the nation is still waiting for the king to appear in front of the television cameras to make an announcement. He adds that some sort of state of emergency is in operation in Madrid, the streets are deserted and the bars and restaurants have closed. That is what it feels like here too, the broad Barcelona road appears to be empty and when they cross the Devil's Bridge on their way to the Santa Eugenia neighbourhood he notices that the bar at the crossroads has lowered its blinds even though it's only . . .

"What is the time?"

It is ten past eleven. Avinguda Santa Eugenia is deserted as well, everyone is behind closed doors, sheltering in front of the television set, he can sense the acrid smell of fear, a stench like old urine in a stairwell. The perfect night for a procession! Do you hear that, Franco? You and your damned court of priests and bigots. What a waste of a brilliant soldier!

"*¡Gilipollas!*"[88] he bellows without a thought for his orderly who is driving with a tense jaw and hunched shoulders as if he were about to get a telling off he has done nothing to deserve and despite the fact that the lieutenant colonel who is paralysed down one side is popular with his subordinates. But all that finally emerges is a gurgling laugh that wheezes out of the throat of the disabled soldier

88 "What a prat!"

who has now decided to direct the troop of phantoms marching along the deserted avenue. The late winter night seems ideal for a death march, a march for and of the dead, all one hundred and thirty of them are walking along, their heads blown off by terrorists tucked inside cornet-shaped hats. And thousands of others. Those shot dead and executed are coming out of the graveyards of the civil war. Franquito[89] is among their number as well, easily recognised because he is the shortest of the lot, ha ha. The gurgle of his laughter sounds like a bathtub emptying. And the water smells bad because this is the night when the ice thaws, the night when the frozen horses of Lake Ladoga are set free. Well hello, Malaparte. So you're here tonight too, you old rogue.

"También vienen todos los que fusilaron en la ría de Pontevedra, Franquito. Mi hermano y yo espiábamos tras el muro del cementerio todas las tardes. Y los reconozco. Son mis muertos. Se pegan a mí. Yo soy de la familia."[90]

The orderly does a U-turn and pulls up outside the entrance to the lieutenant colonel's apartment building. The route to the lift is staked out in a protracted sequence of movements: car doors being opened, the left leg that has to be lifted out of the car with the right hand and the paralysed right arm whose listless pendular movement has to be contained while he gets to his feet. In its illuminated slot the lift reminds him of a coffin, his measurements are already being taken, and the little jolt after he has pressed the button for the second floor makes him belch, death is bound to come quickly and unexpectedly like a jolt. And as ridiculously. He feels hugely disappointed by Death. He who was Death's handsomest legionnaire. *El novio más guapo de la Muerte.*

89 Diminutive of Franco, little Franco. The nickname was given to the very short Francisco Franco at the beginning of his career as an officer in North Africa.
90 "The people shot by the firing squads at the bay in Pontevedra are all here too, little Franco. My brother and I spied on them every afternoon behind the churchyard wall. I recognise them, they are my dead. They cling to me. I'm like one of the family now."

Once he has reached the door he does not have the energy to fish out the keys so he orders his batman to ring the bell even though he knows that the sound of it ringing at this hour will scare the life out of Gertrud (*Hertrot*). And after a while a woman's voice can be heard, a snippy voice that simply cannot believe what her eyes have shown her through the peephole.

"*¿Quién es?*"

"*¡El negro zumbón!*"[91]

There she is, his great love, half turned away as usual, towards a tiny invisible point beyond everything else that is much more distant than it is inward. But at least she is steady on her feet, lit by the chink of light from the door and watchful, as if she were waiting for an explanation as to why he has turned up with the orderly, why so late. There is no telephone in their home. Not since all the turmoil of the freezing winter of 1969, so raw and damp that pools of condensation formed beneath the beds, pools that made her weep hard, dry tears that could only be dissolved in alcohol. The endless telephone calls to Sweden pushed their finances over the brink. Just as though she had made paper boats out of the thousand-peseta notes he brought home and flushed them down the toilet.

"*¡Basta de llamadas! ¡Se acabó el teléfono!*"[92]

He has sent the orderly off to the barracks, he is to be picked up the moment anything changes.

"*Las pequenias duermen,*" Gertrud says. The little girls are asleep, beneath the long crooked nose his lips widen in a flicker of a smile. Twenty years in Spain and there are still islands of foreignness in her speech. She cannot manage the Spanish "ñ"-sound. Or the Spanish "z" for that matter. Or the raw Spanish cold. Nor the fact that they cannot afford to live in flats with central heating. She is like an entire

91 "Who is it?" "The joking negro!" This refers to a mambo in the 1951 film *Anna* starring Silvana Mangano.
92 "No more calls. The telephone is being cut off."

archipelago of foreignness, *Hertrot*. He cannot manage her Swedish name – Gertrud.

"*¿Qué pasa, es un golpe? ¿Qué va a pasar? ¡Dime!*"[93]

And what is going to happen? It's obviously a coup, is what he thinks. But instead of answering he swivels further inside the flat with the left leg trailing behind, through the open glass door to the bare living room where no-one has hung curtains in front of the windows and the balcony even though they moved in six months ago. The large beige flowers in the patterned fabric on the armchairs appear all the more obscene, fleshy and pompous as though they were trying to make up on their own for the curtains, the pictures, the floor lamps, coffee tables, carpets, books and photographs that are not there. From the doorway Gertrud asks again what is going to happen and if she will have to go to Sweden with the girls. But he is unable to reply, he has been emptied of words the same way the bookshelves are empty without his books and it is towards those dark, empty rectangles he chooses to swivel now. As it turns out, he actually finds something restful in all this emptiness. As if the emptiness were freeing him from a burden that was too heavy to bear. Though if there is one thing he does miss it would be the books. They are stacked up in the furniture store in Barcelona collecting mould in cardboard boxes. Even the copies he had bound with his first wages as an officer, newly qualified from the military training academy in Zaragoza, the faded 1942 edition with the shiny red pasteboard covers, his own name engraved in gold on the spine, *Hitler* MI LUCHA XXXXX Pascual Pascó. All in gleaming gold, even the pattern of little crosses framing the title at the top of the spine, and both his surnames at the bottom, also in gold, as he recalls that pattern he makes an association with cross stitch or sutures, with the stitches he had following the biopsy taken from his throat. Gertrud is saying she can't cope with anything

93 "What's happening? Is it a coup? What's going to happen? Tell me."

more (*¡No puedo más!*) and abandons her post at the doorway from where a puff of air reaches him almost immediately. A moment or so later and he can hear her opening and shutting the door to the little girls' bedroom. He remains standing in front of the bookcase, remembering the books he would like to be able to see now, his entire priceless collection of *Hoja de Campaña*, the Division's monthly newsletter that was written and printed in Vilnius and sent home to Barcelona by his father with a greeting jotted at the top of the envelope every now and then, and the memoirs and all the other books with a link to Russia: *Campaña de Invierno, División Azul*, a first edition from 1943, the memoirs of General Esteban Infante and Malaparte's *Kaputt*, of course, and even Juan Ackermann's deadly boring *A las órdenes de Vuecencia*, about Ackermann's experiences as an interpreter for General Muñoz Grandes, the first leader of the Division, and the new arrival *Archipiélago Gulag* the author got the Nobel prize for, even if he was obliged to turn it down and never collected it, the poor fellow, though of course that is what Bolshevism is about: *coercion, injustice and the deprivation of liberty*, his father's generation had understood that even before 1936, that was why they went to war, for Christ's sake. Twice into the bargain! He thinks about the lakes and the birches and the midges and the mud. And about the woman in the photograph he discovered a few months after his father's death. A close-up, a portrait. As if she had been his mistress. Is the woman still alive? Does she still sometimes think about his father in her cottage? Some night when she is lying belly to belly with a Bolshevik whose mouth reeks of vodka? Does she remember then with a sense of relief that the Spanish officer she was protected by during the war was a Christian and a teetotaller. Was she the one who gave him the icon he came back with? The one hanging above the sofa, along with the pewter Wehrmacht dagger and the Dama gazelles from the Sahara desert? Did she even survive the war? The living room feels stuffy and airless, maybe because the television set is on and giving off a blue light. It is only then that he sees her, sunk into one of the armchairs, half-swallowed by the gaudy splendour of the floral fabric: the rebellious daughter, in semi-profile, one eye on the intersection of coloured lines on the television screen and the other on him, as if she were wall-eyed though she isn't, as if she were a painting by Picasso. They slide past each other that way, in full and semi-profile, offering each other only half a face, just one eye, just one part, just nothing, no words spoken, no voice. But he was the one who gave her life, he gave her her name, with all due ceremony, at a baptismal font, the water dripped on to her fontanelle and made her scream as though the blessed water had cracked her skull, she screamed so much the sunlit dome above them trembled and dust rained down against the light, like a promise of snow, like the snow that would fall that Christmas, the first one, when Gertrud hung red curtains in front of the windows and they danced through the nights, belly to belly, mouth to mouth in the cramped space between the paraffin stove and the brown rib-backed chair on which the gramophone was set, *like the prisoners the Tatars tie alive to corpses, until the dead body devours the living one*, as was stated somewhere in Malaparte, the grey gramophone with the ivory handle whose loudspeaker lid was padded with fluffy fabric that shone like gold, like the inside of a coffin; and his newborn daughter Catalina screamed, enveloped in cascades of gauze, she was supposed to be called Cristina, but then his beautiful cousin died and his newborn daughter had to take over the dead woman's name. How she howled when she got the blessed water on her head. From the depths of the folds of that white Christening robe she screamed so hard the walls of the church shook, as if the name were being etched with the diamond needle of the gramophone.

"¡*Caterineta . . . !*" That is what she is called nowadays, Caterina in Catalan, the name rattles with a rusty sound across his vocal chords, as if a cock were crowing for some kind of dawn even though it's only . . . he takes the oracular shell from his left pocket but can see nothing, what he can see is the baby that kept so close to his face, seeking his throat, that first Christmas in Lérida, trying to find the pulse in his neck, the way puppies and kittens do; but the person she is now refuses to give an inch, the new name she demands everyone call her by and which he had used to get her attention has left her unmoved, rather the reverse, his throat is still a windswept place, forlorn and singed following the radiation treatment like a burnt-down forest, just as desolate and knobbly. He sits down. He turns towards the other armchair, he and his daughter are sitting armrest to armrest like two travellers on their way somewhere. He will remember this night all his life, he thinks. But what will she remember? What? The crooked smile that keeps all of life at bay is pulling at the corners of her mouth with the same force he used to pull the tube out of his armpit yesterday, long before the bag with the bright-red cytotoxic drug was empty. And nowadays there has to be a coup for her even to come home at night. That theatre director must have been in a hurry to pack and would have sent the whole troupe home. No more Shakespeare in Catalan. Which is a pity. *Because I am a national socialist, in this country that means I'm a Catalanist.* How many times has he said that to her, the echo of his own howls is vibrating in his head. Is that what she will remember? The howling. *Because if I've told you once I've told you a thousand times that Hitler was democratically elected. Democratically. Are you listening?* The impatience that would get the better of him when she failed to understand, as if the knowledge he had acquired should have been transferred automatically when he gave life to her. *Ara l'hivern del nostre deshonor s'ha convertit en gloriós estiu amb aquest sol de York.*[94] The theatre director's red cloak that brushed the outdoor stage in front of the Romanesque church last summer when he went to see his daughter act (the daughter who keeps looking for new names), above that solitary figure the starry skies high and heavy like velvet, a sky that

94 "Now is the winter of our discontent made glorious summer by this sun of York." (William Shakespeare, *Richard III*.)

weighed more than the earth. Summer, summer night, soon there will be no more of either.

Nothing. I'll be seeing nothing soon. Not her eye in the armchair or at the dining table. In the watery darkness he thinks about the look she gave him when he was making fun of a war widow, he remembers it from in front, a hard look aimed at him with both eyes, which are green with a ring of gold in the centre. The gold ring sparkled with hatred. Though hate is white instead, white pus, it strikes him. What is that stuff that glints like gold in a person's eyes? Just pigment. Christ above, how tired he feels. He tries to gather his thoughts, when will the king make his announcement and what will happen to the girl sitting there? She will continue to receive a pension as long as she is studying at least. At the word pension that ring of hate is lit up again and shining on the pile of applications for a widow's pension that began to pour in after the new laws were passed, standing beside his desk in the Military Government (Gobierno Militar) in Barcelona was the dignified figure of the indomitable Red widow whose application for a pension he had managed to turn down time after time. The thought of that room slams into him like a defeat, it is the antithesis of everything he has ever believed in or loved, manoeuvres, the hard physical training, the horses, the looks of respect and admiration from his men, the nights under the open sky. Something groans like a wounded animal, but he has no idea where the sound is coming from.

"*Hace cuarenta años que se acabó la guerra ¿cómo puedes seguir castigando a una pobre vieja?*[95] the girl who is his daughter demanded on that occasion. Does he regret anything? The children he abandoned before she was born, does he regret leaving them? Francisco has become a drug addict, he had lost several teeth when he visited him in the hospital, he lay there toothless and so far gone he could not even come up with a word of reproach. If only he were transparent

95   "It's been forty years since the war ended, how can you go on punishing that poor old woman?"

like a book and everything had been written out, plainly visible. It is all going to disappear with him instead. (Grains of sand as sharp as glass wedged under his nails, deep lines scored in the sand, a wave washes it all away). He cannot remember what he replied that time. Though now he knows the answer, now he can say it aloud: What would be the point of winning the war if we forgot? *Defence*, that's what it is called, that is what I'm doing. Defending *the world as I knew it*.

His daughter is saying something, the one who now wants to be called Caterina, who believes she has moved away from home by changing her name (only names are not empty words, they're not a room you can just leave, names are wild and unfathomable things there is no way out of). She opens her mouth to speak beneath that long nose that is far too like his own and asks *if he knows anything*. He feels glad, almost euphoric. When did she last say anything to him at all? Does he know anything? That question is an admission on her part that he may possess information about things (about life) that could be worth something. *The world the way I see it.* The exertion that is required to stop existence from coming apart. *Todo está atado y bien atado.* You can't understand that at her age. He hadn't understood it either.

The coloured pattern of vertical and horizontal lines is still on the mute television screen, there is no flag yet to be seen fluttering in the wind with the national emblem on, they sit there expecting to see the face of the young king, to hear his monotonous voice announcing the date of a new *desfile de la Victoria*.[96] But May is in another part of the world to February, in the southern hemisphere of time, because time is round like a globe. By the time Franco marched into Madrid on May 19, 1939, the family had already moved back into a liberated Barcelona, his father still in shock at what he had lived through in Brunete, the commandeered flat in Valdemoro

96 Victory Parade.

would echo emptily once more, they left the furnishings exactly as they had found them the year before. He went into the other boy's room and opened the middle drawer of the chest, using both hands he carefully laid inside the V-necked grey jumper with a white pattern that he had folded and refolded with great pains to ensure it lay nice and flat when the drawer was opened, the V-neck symmetrically in the centre of the jumper, like two fingers making the victory sign. So he would know who had won. There were no engines droning across the sky now and the plane trees swayed silently outside the window because all the birds had been shot with catapults and eaten. It could be that the invisible boy survived. Or he might be one of those marching soundlessly down there on the avenue.

His daughter has relapsed into muteness, she is looking at the bare windows, the *tramontana* is howling through the chinks, it must be freezing outside. He is thinking about a comfortable gentleman's room that smells of cigars and where anecdotes are told after dinner, where they drink claret at the house of a diplomat in Helsinki and tell stories about the front in the Ukraine or Poland and he remembers the one about the wounded elk that had dragged itself across the Gulf of Finland to the president's home and was sent off by ambulance in the middle of the night: that bastard Malaparte could definitely write. He remembers the story about the wisteria plants on the roof of the presidential palace in Warsaw that the Nazi governor's wife had arranged to have painted over the original Italian frescoes. But table talk of that kind lacks the force to keep him there, he plunges back into the ambulance scene instead, if there is anything that scares the life out of him it is ambulances, in Pontevedra they shuttled back and forth between *la ría* and the churchyard, crammed with the bodies of the executed. Like Curzio Malaparte, he too has stories to tell. Ever since the day he read *Kaputt* that book has come to define everything the Eastern Front means to him, the letters his father had sent them from behind the lines at Novgorod notwithstanding. Lake Ilmen would become the vast Ladoga and its hundreds of frozen horses' heads. Even José María's face would be taken over by the Italian jester, the resemblance to his brother was so striking it distorted his perception of reality: the eyes were the same under those black eyebrows, the straight narrow nose was the same and so was the sneer lying in wait on those thin lips . . . as though the defector Malaparte were his closest relative, as though a twist of fate were determined to show him an image of himself through the resemblance. Because in many ways a defector is what he also was, a defector when he used to speak Catalan with his Catalan soldiers more than twenty years ago, long before it became politically correct, and when he danced *sardanes* dressed in his captain's uniform and while he was living with a woman who was not his wife, a much younger woman from a non-Catholic part of the world; he was an offence in the eyes of that court of fools and flabby armchair generals that surrounded the Leader, and he would have been one in the eyes of the Leader himself, because the general had become a dried-out old mummy (a bigot he had always been, and sexually inhibited besides), blinded by forty years of peace, and as dry grains of sand flowed down the great face of War to fly out and up like a veil around Her head, he realised that War was the great illusion that had gathered all those ideals beneath its skirts, while Peace was the woman lying beneath you when desire had run its course, a woman you believed at best you loved. Peace was always what was left the moment after, when you are abandoned to the mercy of your own tawdry dreams. Forty years of Peace had perverted and besmirched the purity of the Victory that *El Caudillo* had won for them, the mass graves and the overcrowded graveyards had led to an army of parasites and black frocks crawling over the country like a flock of crows on a newly harvested wheat field. Out of the corner of his eye he can see the priest who gave his father the last rites, he comes gliding into a room that already smells of mothballs and old furniture. He can see his father as he lay dying in the large bed with its tall headboard made of wood that was almost black, his pallid grey face and sunken cheeks and his mouth like a crater beneath the cross of ash the priest was drawing on his brow, as though he were refusing to die in the protective enclosure of his bed and had chosen instead to surrender the surface of his face to all the front lines he had experienced, from Brunete to Valdemoro and Volkhov and Leningrad, that grey skin was wide and endless like a film screen on which God, his father's God, was intent on projecting the suffering of humanity. From beyond the large balcony came the repetitive growling of the traffic along Calle Balmes, it was 1956 and the sight was hard to bear, his eyes sought out the cup-like ornaments on the ends of the headboard, his father's grandchildren would later play with the wooden cups at the head and end of the bed and set the wooden finials that looked like champagne goblets spinning, but in the spring of 1956 all the bed's component parts remained immobile, firmly glued in place, and his father would spend a long time lying in the large bedroom that looked out over the sloping street, the wide bedroom with its high ceiling like a chapel that smelled of ingrained dust the way a church does, without making a sound as he lay there dying day after day apart from the odd wheeze and groan. What he left behind were the Wehrmacht uniform and the medals and the letters from Novgorod and the ones from the hospital in Vilnius. And the photograph of an anonymous Russian woman he had found hidden in a silver cigarette case a few weeks later, his father a renegade too in a sense, who had been sent home early because of a Jewess. Throughout all the years he outlived the second expedition of the Blue Division he would assure them that the Jewess he picked up at gunpoint and took to the Spanish military hospital in Vilnius was not particularly pretty. *That is not why I did it*, he said. *Not at all.*

The Visit, Ymergatan 7, Uppsala, Sweden
August 2006, Evening

You know now that the boy your grandmother was whispering about in the doorway to her saint-cluttered bedroom was her first grandchild, the one who had been the apple of her and her husband's eyes and often used to sleep in their double bed at the beginning of the Fifties (his little feet entangled in the nightdress that got rucked up between granny's thighs), the one named Salvador, the same boy Gertrud saw from the deck of the *Ciudad de Cádiz*, waving goodbye to the handsome foreign legionnaire at the port in Barcelona. Gertrud is in the kitchen getting dessert ready, next to the silver bowl and its motley assortment of sweets the photograph album is open to the page where your father is raising a glass to the Hitler portrait on your Christening day; Gertrud does not smoke anymore, as she is doing in many of the photographs in the album or as she did when you were in Cristal City, soundlessly, with barely audible puffs and using the same hand with which she would take a swig from the glass every now and then, the white often self-consuming cylinder wedged between her index and middle fingers; that day at the Cristal City bar-cum-bookshop it was spring, winter and its paraffin stoves and mist on the windowpanes were behind you, the light of the high blue sky and the trip itself from Lérida to Barcelona, the mountain road up to Borjas Blancas, where you always stopped to buy the local speciality, a sponge cake that was as fluffy as foam and snow-white, dusted with icing sugar that stuck to the tip of your nose and sometimes to the inside of your nostrils so it was almost as if you were inhaling it, felt like a presentiment of summer, as if the snow-covered sponge were the last outpost of winter and you were heading towards the long days of open balconies when you could escape the pain of going to school and when you could spend an entire month at your father's aunt Julia's newly built two-storeyed villa on the Garraf coast; you know now that Franco's troops approached Barcelona from the west on two fronts in January 1939 from the very same Garraf coast and from Borjas Blancas, your father at the wheel of his white Seat 124, as though a large part of his life were being spent retracing the steps of the general he admired (the years in Africa, the routes of the triumphal entry). You also know now that the little blue flask containing Agua del Carmen your mother always had in her handbag was a decoction consisting of 80 per cent alcohol flavoured with lemon balm and other herbs that was popularly known as *anti-hysteric water*, advertising images of the time show smiling housewives in pastel-coloured dressing gowns and sporting broad hairbands and backcombed hair holding up the blessed little bottle; you know now that the lift accident in which she almost lost her right arm damaged the vertebrae in her neck and that your mother suffered excruciating pain for many years that no-one was able to explain, because they concentrated exclusively on the injuries to the arm and no X-ray was ever taken of her neck. One day you came home from school to find a blonde woman in the doorway with her arm in a sling, the manually operated lift at the Berlitz school your mother taught at had been started by the operator while she was still closing the doors and her right arm could not move out of the way in time, it got trapped in the gap between the cabin and the floor and it was only because the mechanism was so ancient and underpowered that the obstruction – her shoulder – was able to stop the lift without her arm being torn off; it would not be long before an itch started up beneath the rigid casing, by then the open wound was giving off a sour-sweet odour reminiscent of the stink that used to stick to Tessy's coat after he had been rolling around on top of a rotting animal cadaver. The day she opened the door with her arm in a sling she was wearing a wig, she may have gone with your father straight to the hairdresser's when they came out of the Red Cross hospital, the same hospital the gipsy woman (*la gitana*) had run into in bare feet with her dying child in her arms one morning when you were on your way to school, your father has his arm around your mother's waist and she is feeling a bit dizzy while high on morphine besides, the sling is a shiny white against the khaki of his uniform, the hairdresser helps her put on the wigs he points to, your father is smiling, the right corner of his mouth turned up and amusement in his eyes, she stands in front of the mirror and pouts to make her lovely already plump mouth even plumper; you now know that your mother had been wanting a wig for ages and that your father was trying to cheer her up on the day the inattention of the lift operator almost cost her her arm, you know now that they were able to try out the wigs at home, they were not something he could have afforded on his officer's salary at the time, it would be several more years before she would have a wig of her own, but on the day a blonde woman with her arm in a sling opened the door your first thought was that she was an emissary, a sort of contemporary angel who had alighted in your home, got the landing wrong and sprained her wing, sent to announce that your mother had been taken up to heaven. You are remembering her as well the winter it snowed in Lérida and there was ice among the oleander bushes on Plaça Ricardo Viñas, the kind you would nowadays call "wet snow" using the Swedish term *blötsnö* (then it was just snow, *nieve*), she was holding Tessy and wearing that odd zebra coat of hers that no-one else in the whole town had and none of them would ever dream of wearing, your mother wrapped in a stiff, hard zebra skin, the dog beside her in its mottled black-and-white coat, you in your navy-blue woollen uniform coat different in some essential way from them both, though she was so beautiful in any case, your mother, in that flashy coat. The river of cars on the other side of the square served as an acoustic barrier, a sea whose water had solidified and whose waves had taken on the monstrous shapes of cars and buses.

The page with the Hitler photograph is still open on the table, it is like a drain in the room, and your Christening robe is shining at the centre of the grey films of silver emulsion. You turn your eyes towards the shelves. There are still some books that belonged to your father on them and one or two more that were part of their shared library, most of them were lost in the moves, they turned mouldy and were damaged in a variety of unsuitable storage places, Malaparte's *La piel* survived the many years spent in a barn with stains and bite marks but not *Kaputt*, the rats' teeth and their urine have rendered it illegible. You know that Mercè Rodoreda's *Aloma* may have been one of the books the bartender at Cristal City kept in the secret room behind the toilets, a revised edition was published in the same year you and Gertrud were waiting for your father to come and meet you after the Victory parade, the great military parade in May, it may have been placed among the bottles, alongside *La plaça del Diamant* ("Diamond Square") and why not *Jardí vora el mar* ("Garden beside the Sea"), published in 1967, a title that would have made you long for your father's aunt Julia's summer house and its old mimosa trees beneath which you would learn to ride a bike that summer. Mercè Rodoreda might have been in Cristal City too at some point , she was allowed to join the official convoy of politicians and some thirty or so intellectuals, who had been given travel permits by the Generalitat, the Catalan government, that crossed the border at the end of January 1939, she fled in a windowless mobile library that had served at the front and was pocked with machine-gun rounds. At the time you and your parents used to visit Cristal City Rodoreda had just bought a *pied-à-terre* forty or so numbers further up, at Calle Balmes 343, she might have popped in to Cristal City now and then when she came over from Geneva to meet her publisher, the writer Joan Sales; if you had noticed her then she would probably have reminded you of your grandmother, they were both born at the beginning of the twentieth century (Rosa in 1905 and Mercè in 1908) and had the same striking white hair, although the frozen waves of Mercè Rodoreda's stiffened mane appear to have been cut short and back-combed in all the photographs whereas your grandmother's hair was as fine as silk and severely tied back in an elegant chignon. And you had silkworms then that you kept in a shoebox and fed with large heart-shaped mulberry leaves, inside the darkness of the shoebox the short, fat, waxy-yellow worms spun white cocoons that reminded you of Moumoú's hair; you used to gently brush the long fragile strands of her hair before plaiting them and then undoing the plaits only to retie them again and run through the strands with both a comb and your fingers while their tips were remembering the matte cocoons the silkworms turned into. You are thinking that the two women may have taken the same train on the section of the journey between Geneva and Barcelona, Rodoreda would have got on that train in Geneva when she travelled to Barcelona, she too lived close to the central station in a neighbourhood that, interestingly, is called St Gervais, just like the part of Barcelona she grew up in, Sant Gervasi de Cassoles, originally Sant Gervasi was a separate village, the channel of the stream that ran through the village would later become the long and sloping Calle Balmes, the same road down which the rainwater still finds its way from Tibidabo to the sea during the autumn and spring rains. You also preferred the train to the buses you would have to sit still on for two whole days, the train provided bumpy and scary crossings between the carriages and long corridors in which you could wander, looking out through the windows in various directions while the landscape outside was constantly changing. The Nordexpress arrived in Basel from Hamburg at 8 a.m., and then you and your mother would pick up the coats you had used as blankets during the night and leave the compartment to have breakfast in the dining car, most of the tables inside were window tables, the linen tablecloths were starched and the china cups had thickened, rounded rims you deliberately crashed your teeth against, beyond the large rectangular windows would be vast spaces filled with hills and mountains and houses with hipped roofs that were weighed down by snow and gardens you hardly ever saw children playing in though if you did they looked like brownies, the roads and the villages that could be seen from the train were also fantastically small, as though the real world had been turned into a miniature painting and the landscape outside were a railway model. It is January, you have spent Christmas and New Year with relatives in different parts of Sweden, and now you are slowly making your way home across Europe, in order to cross the strait to Copenhagen the whole train has to roll onto a ferry, parked cars surrounded the long line of carriages when you got off in the middle of the night, frozen stiff and dazzled by the glare of the light on the car deck you wove between the cars in zig-zags to find the sliding door behind which was a flight of iron steps that led up to the ship's cafeteria, your mother had to pull the heavy iron door to the side, in the doorway you were hit by a freezing cross-draught, the door slammed behind you and shut out the smells of exhaust fumes and machine oil, in front of you the steep steps were suspended in the air: "Remember, it's staircase F!" your mother said, "otherwise we'll never find our way back." "F F F!" you panted on your way up the iron staircase so as to memorise the way the air felt as it blew vertically down onto your lower lip from your upper teeth when you pronounced the letter F, like in *Flood, Felt, Fat*, F, like in *Flood, Felt, Fat* . . . until the steep hanging staircase came to an end and you were on an upper deck in the comfortable part of the ship where there were no draughts and where you had to queue for a sandwich made with sour black bread that had tiny naked headless shrimps on it that almost made you vomit. That all took place the first night, yesterday evening you took the night train from a large dark station in a place called Hamburg and you will continue on by train all the way from here to Barcelona. Since taking your seats in the dining car this morning the train has kept moving in and out of tunnels, you count them on your extended fingers and hold your breath every time it turns black outside the windows, because the lamps on the dark wooden panels on the walls and on the ceiling above give off a faint yellow glow that immerses the restaurant car in a muddy light that makes you think of water, light-brown stagnant water like the water in the pond the carp swim around in on the square below your home in Lérida, that is why you fill your lungs and mouth with air and hold your breath and look at the shiny windows that have suddenly turned into mirrors in which you try to make out the imaginary fishes and the drowned children you are already seeing in your mind's eye, and when the train comes out of the tunnel your puffed-out cheeks cave in and your breath goes out in an audible burst whose recoil makes you bounce against the back of the seat and the force of the movement startles your mother who is smoking in silence and she asks what you are up to; then she orders more coffee and an Orangina for you. The tunnels seem to be over now and a grey and even winter light is pouring into the carriage so you get out your sketch pad and rest your head in your hand as you start thinking about what you are going to draw. When the waiter returns with his round metallic tray the train slows and begins to brake with a long drawn-out squeal on its way into a large station. *G-e-n-è-v-e C-o-rnavin* you manage to decipher because you are good at reading; people are gathered in front of the train doors on the platform below, you can see an old woman with a light-coloured coat and wavy white hair you confuse with your grandmother at first sight even though you know that Moumoú is still in Uppsala where she waved goodbye to you. Beneath the cream-coloured coat the old lady is wearing dark trousers that leave her ankles visible and flat black shoes, the kind of shoes without heels that Moumoú would never wear, not long trousers either or white socks inside the shoes for that matter, the resemblance was deceptive and you forget her shortly afterwards. On the sketch pad a train landscape is evolving of rails and mountains and villages, and a tunnel that is a black hole in the side of the mountain and a river and a bridge for the train to cross over; you are weighing up whether to make it summer, though, because if it is winter most of it would have to stay white and then there wouldn't be much for you to colour in. You look up in search of some kind of confirmation from out there in the real world but the train is still in the station and all there is to see are the dark columns on the platform; at that very moment the same white-haired old lady you so recently caught sight of enters the dining car, she remains standing at the entrance for a little while, wearing that light-coloured coat and carrying a large brown handbag in one hand, the whole carriage smells of snow and she is the one, along with that coat of hers, that has brought in the cold sweet scent enveloping you as she sits opposite your table, on the other side of the aisle, the crisp smell is soon dispersed, however, by the fumes of burnt dust given off by the radiators combined with toasted bread and cigarette smoke. You want to have a proper look at her: it seems as though she cannot quite make up her mind, she glances around the car, her eyebrows are very close to her eyes and are just thin lines, but her face does not look old, she may not even be that old because she has only got two wrinkles, they are deep ones and carve two semi-circles around her mouth that appear to stretch the corners and make it look as though she is about to smile. The train is pulling out of the iron and glass arches of the station and it is in the bright daylight that comes flooding into the carriage that your eyes meet, you refuse to look away and the old lady smiles broadly at that, then her eyes slide across to the sketch pad you have in front of you and she nods almost imperceptibly as though she had reached some kind of understanding with you and the very next moment she leans over to the large brown bag she has placed on the floor, as she does so a large piece of silver jewellery protrudes from her neckline to hang for a few seconds in the air from a silver chain she is wearing around her neck, it looks like a fish a child might have drawn, flat and schematic; then she is upright again and placing the bag in her lap, from it she takes a pad and a fountain pen and nods at you, as if to suggest she is going to do the same thing as you; the woman performs a kind of pantomime that in combination with her ruffled white hair make you think of circuses and clowns, and clowns make you ill at ease, they are so mute and blank and attract blows and violence the way sweets attract wasps. The waiter comes and his metallic tray is in the way as he serves the white-haired woman from the same kind of silver pot your mother was given, when finally he moves out of your field of vision the white-haired lady is sipping at her cup then she moves the cup and saucer carefully aside so as not to make any mess and the next moment she unscrews the cap of the fountain pen and pulls the paper towards her, she drops her eyes to one side, and then she is looking up at you and blinking, a little bemused, as though she had been about to forget you; then she starts writing, not drawing, and, as if she had shut a door, is lost in thought, shutting you out. She is writing to Obi, of course, for a fraction of a second Mercè Rodoreda's hand hesitates about which address she should write in the top left hand corner, something she never fails to do, she usually writes *19 rue du Vidollet, Genève*, their shared official address, only now she is on a train on her way to Barcelona instead of in the little two-room flat where she lives on her own even though the apartment is registered in the name of her partner, under his real name, Joan Prat, not the one he adopted, his former *nom de plume*, Armand Obiols; nor is she seated in *la chambre de bonne* on rue du Cherche-Midi in Paris she has kept on since the war and where she and Obi meet up from time to time, no, she is *on the move*, she is travelling, hurtling across a moving landscape, and the movement is opening rooms and holes in time, making both fluid, like now as the jolting of the train takes her back to the windowless mobile library (the forward motion inside stifling semi-darkness) they escaped in to France almost thirty years ago: that's right, in two weeks time it will be exactly thirty years since Franco's troops began the advance on Barcelona and half a million people raced to get out of the country, including Obiols and her, who did not know one another then; that is what she has been thinking about all morning, that thirty years have passed and that Obi, unlike her, has not been back to Barcelona, not once since they fled across the Pyrenees at the end of January 1939; she is seeing glimpses of the days they spent at the large estate a few kilometres from the mountain pass at La Vajol, the light coloured by the mountain's dull greenery around the magnificent country house the Generalitat placed at their disposal, because they were still being treated with dignity at the beginning, at Agullana they had a real bed and a hot meal every day, and that first evening they could even sit around a fire and have discussions and live up to their official titles of "intellectuals" or *escriptors catalans*, they spent most of the day on the terrace with its view over the slopes covered in holm oaks, planning the next issue of *Revista de Catalunya*, in fairly high spirits in fact, they even squabbled good-naturedly about where it should be published: Perpignan? Toulouse? Paris? Mexico? As though the whole world lay open before them, they should have known better, the mobile library that brought them there from Barcelona had been a kind of omen after all. And still they had no idea what real hunger was, some old wine remained in the estate's cellars they could fortify themselves with and helped make that characteristic laughter ring; Obi and she had barely exchanged a word until then although she had noticed him long before the stop in a bombed-out Figueres where everything was chaos and the sense of defeat tangible and there were endless queues outside the passport office the Republican government had set up in the city, someone (it would have been Anna Murià, wouldn't it? Or was it Francesc Trabal?) introduced them while they were standing outside the bullet-scarred library van ("Armand Obiols, Mercè Rodoreda"), she can still see the word BIBLIOBUS in large white letters beside his head, high above her own as he is a head taller than her; after that she had begun to employ that loud ringing laugh of hers to attract his attention, whether it was appropriate or not, she smiles self-mockingly, regretting nothing though, because she likes to think of herself as a shrilly crowing blackcock, an androgynous blackcock, *un gallo lira*, as Spanish so prettily has it, a creature of the woods with red eyebrows and tail feathers in the shape of a lyre. On the other side of the rime-covered glass panes night had fallen and the north wind was moaning and tearing at the leaves of the holm oaks that were silvery on the underside, the estate was so isolated among those mountains it made you think of how the wolves must have howled all around it once upon a time; they were indoors on rib-backed chairs in a circle around the fireplace in the large kitchen, her sweater and her hair reeking of the choking smoke given off by the firewood, Armand was sitting with his legs crossed opposite her on the far side of the circle, closest to the woodpile by the wall, the flames were reflected in his glasses, the dark horn rims angled towards her, she was watching the movements of his lips as if in a trance, she traced the shape of his jaws and mouth, rapt at the voice that came out of it: that fire was already consuming everything inside her that could burn, even then. She picks up a sugar cube and puts it between her teeth and bites it while it is still hard so it separates into halves. On the morning of the second day one or two members of parliament appeared at the estate, including Rovira i Virgili, the writer and journalist who would publish his journal entries about the escape the following year in Buenos Aires, his group had spent the night in a ruin in a desolate area with the ominous-sounding name of Cantallops ("Wolfsong"), somewhere to the right of the road that led to Le Perthus, on the other side, that is, of the same road where they were now, he explained, and this group, including his wife and child, were on their way here: that was the beginning of the end of relative comfort, Rovira i Virgili appeared to be upset by the jokey mood that prevailed on the terrace, by the carafe of old wine that was being handed round and by the air-dried pieces of ham they were sucking on sybaritically *as if they were pralines* (as he later wrote in his memoirs) because on their farm (*in the village where the wolves were howling?* someone asked, *yes, that's right*) they had had no food at all and nowhere to sleep either, he was also envious of "the office" that had been set up in one of the rooms in the estate where a typewriter ran hot from dawn to dusk, spitting out lists of the names of people who needed passports and travel permits; shortly afterwards more parliamentarians and other unanticipated guests would arrive seeking shelter and assistance, from fifty their numbers swelled to two, three hundred in the course of a single night, people were lying on their cardboard suitcases all over the place, women, children, old people; it was, of course, true as Rovira i Virgili later wrote, she had not given up her bed to anyone and maybe none of the other intellectuals had either, that might seem selfish in retrospect, though she may have had her reasons at the time, or maybe not, just her instincts, the instinct for self-preservation was just as strong when she was young, in any case she was hungry and annoyed because there was no more food, there was just water, though it was fresh and clear as crystal (as Rovira i Virgili also wrote, and that was definitely true), at the time she would no doubt have managed to persuade herself she was relieved that her son Jordi had escaped having to go through all the things these frightened and hungry children were forced to endure, though she might have been feeling guilty at not having her child with her like many of the other women, most of whom were housewives it has to be said, while she was an independent person, a professional woman, a writer who had been awarded the prestigious Crexell prize the year before . . . She really does not regret anything, though, things were hard enough without Jordi, her currently repudiated son Jordi who she wants nothing to do with, who she does not write to or visit anymore and whose letters she refuses to read, best not think about him at the moment, she would rather think about those first days in France, before the German occupation. And there she has the beginning of her letter after all, so she writes: *Perla, estimat, te n'adones que aquest any és el trenta aniversari de la Retirada, sí, però també de Roissy? 30 anys, es diu ràpidament,*[97] thirty years, how easily those words can be written

97 "Do you remember, my darling, that it is thirty years since the Retreat, but thirty years, too, since Roissy? Thirty years, that is so easily said."

down, thirty years since the Retreat and that first period in France, at an estate in Roissy-en-Brie where they were provided with a refuge in which to live and work, and where it was all secrets and palpitations and making love in the open air, between the trees; how greedy her sensory palps had been, like little sucking cups on the inside of her fingers, and their mouths that could never get enough, and the palms of their hands hot, so hot, as though they had never moved from that kitchen in Agulla; later on, when finally they were able to share the same bed at night, they even sought each other out in sleep, like somnambulists, and made love blind, pushing into each other while still dozing as though not even sleep could separate them. She sips at her cup, the coffee has cooled and the breakfasts at Roissy come back to her, she can see their faces around the oblong table they all sat together at to begin with. She pours fresh and hotter coffee into the cup. Obiols was a married man, just as she was a married women, and they both had children they had left behind in Barcelona, his mother-in-law and his wife's brother were in the building too among the exiled writers and Trabal said he was defending his sister's honour, but really he was as jealous as a dog after their dalliance in Prague during the International Pen Club meeting the year before, so she ended up being the one, it was mainly her, to be frozen out and she can feel the shame burning even now at not being allowed to sit at the same table at mealtimes. *Mai de la vida!* Never again, as Obi has scoffed all these years, whenever a return home, even a temporary one, was mentioned, never ever, not even if Franco died would he set foot in their blinkered and narrow-minded homeland again, that would be like forgiving and forgetting it all, all the humiliations, the books that never got written most of all. She tries to find a last wave of warmth in the china she is holding in both hands while seeing in her mind's eye an image of Obi in Vienna, at the boarding house behind the Stephansdom where she sends her letters, he is lying fully clothed on the bed and reading, surrounded by bare walls that have continued to remain impersonal despite all the years he has lived in that plain hotel room, more than ten years now, it must have been in 1958 he got that first translation job there ... The endlessly provisional nature of the life they have lived; something, maybe the snow outside and all the clattering of spoons in the dining car, the metallic reflections from the electroplated coffee pot on the table, makes her remember the ringing of the bells that came pouring in through the open window one Sunday morning at the end of July, in the apartment he had rented for her first visit to Vienna that lay on a secluded street in the eighth district. The church bells began ringing long after she had awoken, a dull white light was streaming across the bed through the thin curtain when she opened her eyes and she stayed where she was, wide awake and perfectly still, turned towards his back and with her eyes fixed on the folds of the curtain in which a torpid bee had entangled itself, she remembers the way that bee captured her interest, that she tried to imagine where it had come from, whether it was from a window box on one of the balconies overlooking the rear courtyard, those central European courtyards she found so appealing, or if it had flown all the way from the wisteria around the corner ... The wisteria, oh that's right! It was on Feldgasse, that was the name of the street, Feldgasse, she can recall that so clearly, the name of the other street, the one on which the apartment was, she can no longer remember, but the building was situated at the crossing of both streets, she remembers its somewhat pompous ochre-coloured front with a small triangular gable above each window; it was really hot that summer even though July was turning into August, the windows in the neighbourhood were always open, hot and muggy the way it could never get in Geneva, though in Barcelona most definitely, the curtains used to flutter out of the buildings like streamers or sails, sometimes they were delicate pieces of gauze, sometimes shimmering golden damask cloths that flapped heavily and remained hanging outside the windowsills (like something organic and soft the building had let go of, like hair or mucus, like something cast out, like *a form of address*, she is thinking,

384

an extended *scream*); sounds too came out of the windows: from the second floor violin music could be heard every day, an exquisite short piece with two variations that someone, a young girl with long light-brown hair, it would turn out, used to practise every afternoon, she can remember wandering barefoot around the apartment while the girl was playing, how she would lean her whole body against the wall in the living room in an attempt to find coolness there and take the weight off her legs which swelled and ached with the heat while also getting closer to the sonorous violin which filled the stuffy rooms with air; *Air varié*, that is what the girl said when after a week Obi and she knocked on the door to ask the name of the piece she kept playing, *von Oskar Riedling*, she said; she spoke in German, naturally, the Austrians spoke a softer version of the language than the Germans, according to Obi, it sounded throatier but had fewer of those hissing sounds, those sibilants that had struck terror all over Europe and could still make the hair on the back of her neck stand up, could she have stayed there? Should she have done? It wasn't just the language, the impenetrable German language with its alarming combinations of sounds and aggressively open vowels, in Vienna she had missed Lake Geneva besides. She remembers how she used to lean out over that street whose name she has forgotten, her elbows on the sill beneath one of those gable-topped windows, and the feeling arrives with the abruptness and intensity of a hot flush: that was the summer the ice broke, back home in Geneva she would finally start work on a novel, the first since *Aloma*, she wrote in a frenzy, she wrote without let-up throughout all of September, then she left it alone for several years, but it was the one, the story of the gardener, that would become the opening of *Diamond Square*, written in a kind of delirium between February and September the following year, although even then in that empty, echoing apartment in Vienna, at the window where she can see herself (while also seeing Obi's naked upper body at the back of the room, propped against the pillows on the bed, his neck supported by the headboard), she could feel the words beginning to crack open, the process that presaged the years of good writing, the end of the internal paralysis (*el gran maresme*), only now she is stuck again, her novel about a family is refusing to come, and the worst of it is: she has lost interest. She sighs heavily and rests her head against her hand while her eyes sweep over the flickering landscape she is not looking at, what she is seeing is the light that made the asphalt glisten in the afternoons when the sun shone from the other end of that Vienna street, where the square with the fountain and the green benches lay, the whole district is slowly coming back to her, she can also remember the sounds and the smell of woodchips and sawdust that rose from a carpentry workshop on the ground floor, the neighbourhood was a quiet one, the red trams rattled past a couple of streets away, very few cars went by, the neighbour girl used to play, it was lovely, the music rippled through the air, music was the water of Vienna, all those open windows from which you could hear the notes of violins or pianos, though that water was too abstract, claustrophobic, there were no vast aquatic expanses with the Alps in the background, no cafés along the lakefront, no Perle du Lac where you could sit and watch the water changing after an exhausting writing session the way you could in Geneva. Then she recalls once again the buzzing of the bee in the curtain in the bedroom at the very back of the apartment that Sunday morning in 1959, the downy sheen of the insect's body as she walked to the window and shook the curtain out and watched the bee vanish upwards in spirals between the walls of the buildings around the inner courtyard, *fly to the wisteria*, she said, *fly!* The wisteria she was sending the bee to was four floors high, the massive roots had cracked the paving stones in front of the entrance to the building and with its pipe-like clusters of lilac-blue flowers it towered above the pavement like a gigantic organ in which insects and birds rustled and sang, even the crickets used to chirp in the neighbouring wall, Obi and she would always stop on the pavement in front of the building's little fenced yard when they returned from their nocturnal walks, they would stand there next to the overfilled rubbish bins and listen to the crickets' song because it brought with it a waft of the Mediterranean, the whole stretch of pavement in front of the building with the wisteria was a parenthesis full of the skies and sounds of lost summer nights, and there they even felt grateful for the humid night air that touched both their memories and their skin with sticky hands. It must have been at least fifty years old, older than their exile, she is thinking, in her grandfather's garden in Sant Gervasi the wisteria always bloomed in spring, between March and April, in all of Catalonia the wisteria blooms in the spring and not in late summer the way it did on that side street in Vienna. And all the same Faulkner writes that *there was a wistaria vine blooming for the second time that summer,* how odd, she cannot recall a single summer when the wisteria across the pergola of her childhood home had flowered, she can remember her grandfather toiling away at the bare branches in winter, during pruning season, and the way the branches would remain bare beneath the lilac-blue bunches when April arrived and they celebrated her birthday, but never that it flowered in summer. Bathed in the white light from the snow fields outside the train the coffee has grown cold, a sharp white light that takes her back once again to the bedroom in Vienna and its white cotton curtains and the downy bumble bee with the velvet body and faceted eyes. She can see herself standing by the curtain, the slip she had slept in was sticking to her back, she tore it off as she would still have been able to do ten years earlier, in Toulouse, Bordeaux or Paris, to meet him in an embrace, but that time was past, so much distance between their bodies even then, the sweat did not matter, it was not a sign of intimacy, only words built bridges between them nowadays, they usually smelled of ink and had been scratched onto a bit of paper, and even so it is the image of that morning that comes to her over and over, like a series of shots in a film, her getting back into bed, the way the soft mattress gave in the middle and made her roll into him, the way she lay there in silence, her face level with the skin over his shoulder blade, and that it was chapped and she would have liked to rub it with a cream that smelled of honey, a sour smell came off his neck instead; so sad, all of it, she is thinking about the shiny diamond pattern that had grown over their skin, a roughness that made you think of bark, time marking their hides the way it does the inside of a tree, ring upon ring, and under the skin the bodily fluids are turning sour, the currents of blood and lymph that travel blindly beneath it clouding over like stagnant water, that sour smell was like a secret clock and a path into the darkness too. *Et ecce infantia mea olim mortua est et ego vivo,*[98] she mumbles and instinctively brings her wrist to her nose to sniff though she can detect no smell, neither of old nor young skin, not even the scent of lily of the valley from the perfume (Muguette) she sprinkled on this morning before she put on her coat and ordered a taxi to the station, as though even her body only existed on paper, in what she wrote, and only there, and yet: *et ego vivo,* she feels so alive despite her sixty-one years, *et ego vivo*; in Latin the words seem to have a heightened presence, now she is thinking about it: uttered in a dead language the phrase actually becomes horrendous: *et ego vivo,* as though something incorporeal (*incorpori*), time itself, human time, the tragic time of humanity, so inferior to the soulless cyclical time of flowers and plants, were speaking, is that why she keeps dreaming about *Death in Spring*? Is she going to have to go back to that dismal, godless place again? No, she is not, she'll stick with the novel about a family, she has already written several chapters, after all, during her previous trip to Barcelona she even came across the housekeeper from her earlier version, the old woman was walking down Carrer de Santaló carrying a basket of food, who knows? Maybe she'll find a beginning for the novel this time as well, her talks with Señor Sales are always inspiring in a way, if she had a good title at least, the right title can carry the whole text, set it free even, she's going to take it up with

98   "And behold my childhood is long dead and yet I live." (Augustine)

Sales, that's the sort of thing he's good at. The girl diagonally opposite has been drawing a landscape on her pad, she can make out mountains and a black spot that has to be a tunnel and the drawing reminds her of a sketch she made and that she kept on her desk for a whole year while writing *La mort i la primavera*[99] of the *Cleft Mountain*, and the *Lord's Castle* at the top and the village with the houses that are painted pink each spring before the wisteria flowers, and she had drawn the *River* diagonally across the page from edge to edge like a pointed hook, and the *Tree Cemetery* up on the mountain slope where people were buried alive inside the trunks, and the *Horse Paddock* and the *Abattoir* down by the riverbank where the old people butcher horses every day . . . That world has never really been laid to rest in the seven years since she sent off the manuscript in the hope of winning the Sant Jordi Prize, not that she did, even though Obi really believed in it and had praised so many parts of the text, like that sentence about the bees: *És una frase de gran categoria, una de les millors que s'han escrit sobre les abelles, sense un adjectiu, neta i natural i precisa,*[100] how did it go, the sentence about bees? . . . *de les abelles que havien passejat tanta mel enlaire . . .* the bees that had filled the length and breadth of the air with honey. Though of course, it could be, as he says, that it was the jury that was incompetent and there was nothing wrong with the novel, in any case the novel still wants something from her, it wants her to go back and rummage around and add bits, to extend and expand it and let the atrocities start up again. The train passes into a tunnel and she thinks about the river that runs beneath the ground through the village in *La mort i la primavera* it is a dark story and she has to feel dark inside to be able to enter it, what does it want from her this time? *Diamond Square* is into a sixth edition, she is writing like the devil, writing and writing

99 *Death in Spring* by Mercè Rodoreda.
100 "That is a top-notch sentence, among the best ever written about bees, without a single adjective, clean, exact and natural." (Joan Prat to Mercè Rodoreda in a letter from Vienna dated February 28, 1962.)

like there is no tomorrow, life is good, she sniffs a bit at the phrase, but it is true nonetheless, she never stops writing, and she has begun to make money from her books, so: life is good. But Obiols, such a well-read and astute reader, one of their most prominent intellectuals when war broke out and through all the years of exile, a poet in his innermost being, what he cannot forgive are the books that did not get written, that he became a writer with no works to his name; she is remembering all the years she was unable to write, when she could literally not hold a pen, her arm paralysed, deformed on the inside as though she had sustained an internal war wound, and that twenty years passed between *Aloma* and *Diamond Square*, that her writer's block eased only gradually and after enormous effort, via a long and roundabout journey through painting and poems, it was only after the short stories that she could finally tackle a novel again; she remembers when Obi and she sent in poems to els Jocs Florals at the same time, and that she won three years in a row and had finished an entire collection of poetry while he kept struggling with a single unfinished poem, that was when he officially renounced his pseudonym and became Joan Prat, when he exchanged his authorial ambitions for Unesco's statutes: *Since wars begin in the minds of men, it is in the minds of men that the defences of peace must be constructed*: he took on longer and longer commissions, translating full-time, and one day he uttered the words that have continued to prey on her far more than she could ever have imagined at the time: *you keep writing*, he said, *I'll work for the two of us*. Maybe it is the light in the tunnels that make her think about that now, the claustrophobic submarine light in the drab dining car induces a feeling of suffocation as she thinks about him locked into his technical translations year in and year out, each new day another scoop of cement down his throat. Was it Obi she had in mind when she invented that awful ritual in *La mort i la primavera*? She cannot recall having thought of him at the time but that is what it feels like now, it is Obi she sees when she thinks about the scene in which the narrator's father has pink-

coloured cement shoved down his throat, *to stop his soul escaping*.
And then along come the women and sew him into the tree while
he is still alive. She looks down at her hands that have held every
kind of needle, the train has left the tunnels behind and is passing
through an open landscape, it is snowing, huge flakes floating on the
other side of the glass, like the white butterflies in the *Tree Cemetery*,
hundreds of thousands of flickering souls that can find no peace;
even after all these years it is always the war she thinks of when she
sees snow, snow is an acquaintance she made during wartime, she
is remembering the lace blouses she did as piece-work in the freezing
attic flat on the rue du Cherche-Midi while Armand was working as
an interpreter for the Germans in the Lindeman camp, and remembering the silky sable fur that is still hanging in the wardrobe on
rue du Vidollet even though she can no longer bring herself to wear
it; she was able to survive the war winters in Paris thanks to that
unknown Russian woman's fur coat, she was a Jewess, that much
she knows, and that she took her own life with Veronal. She picks
up the fountain pen, the nib poised a few centimetres above the
paper, but what does she want to write to him? What *can* she write
to him? Their letters are mostly about her manuscripts nowadays,
everything else, apart from matters to do with her health, is met
with silence, sometimes she wonders if he has someone else in
Vienna, it has been over ten years since he accepted that first commission and moved there, it might be a colleague, one of the translators,
or a young secretary, someone still capable of making him feel
desired and admired. Not that she is going to think about that now,
a dead end, as the English say, that is a path she is not going down,
sometimes she sees herself standing in an immense garden that is
a labyrinth most of whose paths she has explored and she is lost at
the centre, bogged down *en un punto muerto*, it is Spanish she thinks
of this time, at an impasse . . . The girl is about to leave, her mother
has got up from the table and the girl is gathering her things together,
now that she realises this is the last time she will see her she studies

the girl more closely, she also studies the mother: pretty, not tall, not yet thirty, how old can the girl be? She can't even be nine yet, she's got a long way left before that dreadful year when all children die, that's the way she usually puts it, that all children die when they are twelve, something happens then to make childhood end, the grace period she has allotted the girl stretches out before her mind's eye like a sunlit field though she knows that at the very edge of the horizon the fall is waiting in the form of that long black rim, a long black coffin in which her grandfather lay on the *lit de parade*, the air made unbearable by the reek of stearine candles, white lilies and lilacs . . . the spindly girl is moving down the corridor and she can see her at full length, the child turns around one last time before leaving the dining car, the whites of her eyes shimmering blue beneath the long even fringe, as though she wanted to say goodbye, it can't be that long since she learned to read and write, she is even younger than Jordi was when she said goodbye to him that misty dawn with a promise to return soon, in just a few short months, she said, at the beginning of summer, you'll see, when granny's garden is at its loveliest. And he knew better than she that it was a lie . . . *El camió va sortir de Barcelona amb nosaltres a dalt i una maleta de cartó lligada amb un cordill, i va enfilar la carretera blanca que duia a l'engany.*[101] He was ten years old that January morning and twenty when she saw him again. He has lost her once more because he is dead to her now, she has not written a letter to him for almost three years, and there will be no visits to see him with presents and treats this time either, at first, when he had the impertinence to start making difficulties about his father's money and contest the inheritance, she became ill, ill with something that must have been grief, a delayed grief, the grief she never allowed herself to feel during those first years of exile, those lost years, she remembers her ovary being

101 "The truck left Barcelona with us in the bed and a cardboard suitcase tied with string, and we drove the white coastal road straight towards that lie." (*Diamond Square*, Mercè Rodoreda.)

removed in Toulouse, maybe she was never meant to be a mother and she can never have been meant to marry her own maternal uncle, and he should never have come back from America with a small fortune; in any case it is not a matter her publisher or anyone else should get mixed up in, God have mercy on him if he tries to mediate between her and Jordi like he did last time. She is thinking about the little *pied-à-terre* on Calle Balmes where she will be staying for a couple of days, from the living-room window she can look out over the little park shaped like a stepladder that has been laid out, where her parental home once stood, she remembers a drawing she made of the front of the house and the garden when she was seven, with larger-than-life flower pots and in the foreground the pile of stones and plants and the bust of the great Jacint Verdaguer on the very top that her grandfather had built, she had drawn it all in red crayon, and above the house a mysterious balloon was flying that was either getting closer or moving away, as if even then she felt her world was too small though she knows that it wasn't at the time, her grandfather was still alive and he used to sit with her on his lap and his spectacles pushed back over his eyebrows, like a second pair of eyes, and he would hold forth about flowers or teach her the poem *Canigó* or something else, even if that particular image is not a true memory but the memory rather of a photograph she always kept with her, but she does remember the day she did the drawing: it was in winter, that must be why the garden was so bare, she was sitting in the dining-room drawing, she remembers the afternoon light from the huge window she had at her back, as well as the light from the large lamp above the dining table, the one with spirals of wrought iron and a green frill around it, that lamp was always more interesting than the food and she would often sit with her head tilted upwards dreaming about that lamp, that must have been the balloon you could set off in to all the places her grandfather told her about, to Zanzibar and its slave market, and to America, where Uncle Joan had emigrated and become rich. Oh no, so we're back to that again. If the sun is shining and there is no wind she will go and sit on a bench there tomorrow and remember the house and the garden for a while, she likes to think that the soil in their garden is the same, that it is still lying there, free, under the open sky, receiving the sunlight and the wind and the rain as it did before, and even if it has been transformed into a small ladder-shaped strip of earth wedged between two high-rise blocks the sky over the spot is the same. The waiter comes over to ask if there is anything she would like, she orders a Vichy water and lets him clear the table, her fingers have grown stiff and feel cold, she puts down the pen and massages them for a while, her temples as well, she closes her eyes and tries to focus on the letter so she can get it over with, because she has suddenly lost any desire, any inclination to write to Obi, she usually writes at this time of day, and when she doesn't she feels ill at ease, that is the worst thing about journeys, she ends up feeling cut off from her writing which feels like being outside herself, as if she had been turned inside out, like a stocking, maybe she should read instead, different texts oxygenate one another, what she writes is nourished by other works, she takes out the book from her bag and immediately feels calmer, *Absalom, Absalom!* The opening scene is quite marvellous, like a long tracking shot: the room and the two people in it are uncovered sentence by sentence, it starts with the light (a September afternoon) and the time of day, *From little after two o'clock until almost sundown,* the blinds have been drawn for forty-three years, the eye that is registering all the details makes you feel the stuffy air, the dust grating between their teeth in the gloom . . . She is reading it slowly in English, it was after the third or fourth time of reading she started paying attention to the details and looking up unfamiliar words, including the name of the climbing plant outside the window, *wistaria*: *There was a wistaria vine blooming for the second time that summer on a wooden trellis before one window,* which turned out to be the same as the plant in Vienna, *wisteria sinensis* in Latin. And she wants to tell Obi about all of it now, that she is reading yet another novel by William Faulkner, one she likes more than *Sartoris* and more than *The Sound and the Fury*, and that it is so odd to think that the book was published in 1936, *that year* of all years, so something good came of it all nonetheless. In another part of the world, it is true. And to think it is set in a civil war, one that was at least as appalling as ours. The opening scene is unique, I think I have read it ten times, and you know how slowly I read in English, after a long long presentation of the light in the room (drawn blinds, *the savage quiet September sun,* the foully sweet smell of overripe wisteria that is trickling inside) comes the description of Rosa Coldfield, a diminutive old maid dressed entirely in black, she is the one who has kept the blinds drawn in that room for forty-three years and is now sitting perched on a high chair which makes her look like a crucified child (. . . *and the rank smell of female old flesh long embattled in virginity while the wan haggard face watched him above the faint triangle of lace at wrists and throat from the too tall chair in which she resembled a crucified child.*) This is the best thing I've read in years, you realise . . .

Your grandmother's diary can also be found on the shelf where the photograph albums are lined up, the only thing she failed to destroy towards the end of her life, the padded cover in a kind of moss-green velvet is smudged by fingerprints and spots and is crammed with loose leaves that have been inserted between the pages: letters, newspaper clippings and the odd congratulatory telegram, because the telegrams actually have a folder of their own that appears to have been made of real crocodile skin and has the word TELEGRAM engraved on it in ornate gold lettering. There are some large sheets of coloured drawings starting with your maternal grandparents' marriage, June 30, 1938. The surviving diary runs from 1934 to 1946. The last pages are covered with a variety of newspaper items.

A photograph of your great-grandmother from a newspaper whose name has been cut away, a date has been inserted by hand: 1935

70th Birthday
On Sunday, June 9, Fru Addy Widmark celebrates her seventieth birthday. Fru Widmark, who is still fit and vigorous, was chairwoman of Sundsvall's Association of Conservative Women from its very beginnings until she moved from the city in 1926. Fru Widmark currently resides in Tureberg and still plays an active role in political life. She has been chairwoman and is now deputy chairwoman of Sollentuna's Conservative Women's Association [...]

Nås – 1937 (date entered by hand)
The Nås Association of Middle-Class Women arranged a substantial programme for their autumn gathering held on Tuesday evening at Hjärpholn's boarding house; the event was particularly well attended. The main speaker of the evening was Fru Elsa Nelson from Lund, who gave a highly informative speech entitled "Some Social Issues in Political Life". The speaker, who was welcomed to Nås by Fru Söderbaum, the chairwoman of the Association and wife of the medical officer, presented a report on some of the major issues that were decided at this year's parliamentary session, including such matters as the size of the population, the home loan system and the position of the Right on these matters. She went on to discuss another important social issue: the training of domestic staff. This issue would be a difficult one to resolve, according to the speaker, because domestic staff had formed a trade union under the aegis of the Social Democrats and were thus in opposition to the Conservatives. A preliminary report on the training of domestic staff had been published last year. This report met with some astonishment as it only covered the training of domestic staff in the towns and cities; indeed, it should have focused primarily on the rural areas and their circumstances. It was, however, vital that the

recommendations of the report were implemented because if domestic staff receive a good occupational training they will gain increased social standing, The speaker concluded by describing how the training of domestic staff was arranged in Germany, Denmark and Norway.

There are some photographs of your grandfather in the context of his various appointments as district medical officer and a small news item which makes it clear he was involved with the Red Cross.

On Saturday evening (12.02.1938) Nås' Red Cross Association arranged an evening's entertainment at the Ordenshus to benefit the children's home they are planning to establish. A welcome speech was made by the chairman of the Association Dr P. H. Söderbaum. This was followed by a lovely fairy play performed by schoolchildren and a solo vocal performance by Fru Anna-Greta Rooth. There was also folk dancing to fiddle music and singing by the Nås district choir. An informative film about the Red Cross was shown at the end. The performers received fervent applause from the sizeable audience.

VÄSTERDALARNA – A Farewell Party for P. H. Söderbaum, who is moving from Nås to Piteå
A farewell party for District Medical Officer P. H. Söderbaum who will be leaving Nås on April 1 to take up an appointment in Piteå was held on Sunday evening at a subscription supper at Hjärpholn's boarding house. Some seventy people attended and Dr Söderbaum was celebrated with a duet performed by Fru Anna-Greta Rooth and Fru Ingeborg Mattsson, by a solo from cantor O. Wallin and with several speeches. Speaking on behalf of the Nås' district council, master builder A. O. Andersson declared: "Great grief and dismay were felt throughout the parish when death snatched Dr Alldin so hastily away

from us and we missed him greatly. At the time people wondered whether any other doctor could ever fill Dr Alldin's shoes. Then Dr Söderbaum arrived and people decided that the new doctor would probably be very good. His friendly and accessible manner with patients helped him to gain the trust of local people and over the years that trust has only grown. Testimony to his considerable interest in local affairs is provided by the public baths whose construction was at his initiative, and as chairman of its management committee he has succeeded in making the baths financially viable and seen the baths being used much more frequently than anyone dared to hope. For your medical achievements on behalf of the local district the only recompense we could possibly offer is a heartfelt . . ." [. . .] this speech was followed by one by Lars Olsson-Gezelius, from Järna, thanking him on behalf of the management of the infirmary for all his good work and all that they had achieved together. The speaker went on to declare that it was primarily thanks to the doctor that the infirmary in Nås was considered to be one of the best in the county. Speaking on behalf of the residents of Floda [. . .]

Among other loose papers is a ballot paper for the Progressive Conservative Party from which it emerges that Dr P. H. Söderbaum stood as the candidate for Piteå in the County Council elections. That must have been after their move from Nås to Piteå in 1938.

PITEÅ-LOTTA WITH PRACTICAL SKILLS [102]
Written by hand: In Varberg 1950
During the "lotta"-training course held in Varberg, which was overwhelmingly attended by girls from Norrland, Britta Ydén fled the enemy so fast under fire that she twisted her ankle.

102 Translator's note: "lotta" is the popular Swedish term for a member of the Swedish Women's Voluntary Defence Service, a division of the Home Guard.

But fellow-"lotta" Rosa Söderbaum from Piteå was quickly on hand to help and as the wife of a doctor she soon managed to get Britta Ydén fighting fit again – or fairly fit at least. The training course, which will soon be over, has been run by chief-"lotta" Anna Strandberg from Kiruna who tells us that this summer more than two thousand "lottas" are being trained all around the country. Varberg and Gotland have proved to be the most popular course centres for the girls from Norrland.

A WARM FAREWELL WAS BID TO FRU
SÖDERBAUM BY MEMBERS OF THE WOMEN'S
VOLUNTARY DEFENCE SERVICE AND THE
HOME GUARD
The "lottas" of Piteå held a formal and especially memorable social evening in the Church Hall last Monday. The chairwoman of the association Fru Maja Wikström, the head of Luleå's air force-"lottas" Fru Aina Tornberg, the district commander of the Home Guard L. S. Fredriksson and Home Guard commander Harry Lindgren honoured the local association with their presence in order to express their gratitude and appreciation for its former and much-admired chairwoman Fru Rosa Söderbaum, who is moving down south.

You are remembering your grandmother sitting in the afternoon sun in the armchair of the living room in Lérida while crocheting granny stars for bedspreads, slippers and dolls' dresses, inside the square of sunlight streaming in from the balcony she would crochet bedspreads for all the beds in your home: the first thing she made was completely white and took a long time to complete, or several trips, she would often come to visit late in the spring and stay for months, the open-work yarn fabric would lie in heavy folds in her lap and slowly grow longer and longer, as if it were being secreted from her

399

body, until one day it hung in long sweeps on either side of her and covered her legs like a full skirt, and that lent your already striking and elegant grandmother a bride-like and majestic quality as she sat there in the armchair. You often used to watch the way she worked, following the path made by the crochet hook in and out of the loops, which she called chain stitch, there were also *slip stitches* and *double crochet* and *magic rings. We are going to start Granny's square with a magic ring:* she spun the thread twice around her left index finger to form a loop, held the hook in her right hand like a pen and then made the hook crawl in and out of the stitches in a rippling, reptilian way: *We go in and pick up the thread – pull it through the hole, go in, pull through the hole, go in – pull through, and then we've got three chain stitches, do you see?* When she had a pile of granny squares in front of her she would ask you if you wanted to *sew the stars together?* But you never wanted to, you tried to imagine instead what it would be like to sew together all the shining points in the night sky, would the stars get closer to each other like when your grandmother pulled the loop around her finger to make a magic ring? Would all the stars be drawn together and sewn into a gigantic silver ball and shine with a cold metallic light stronger than the sun? You are remembering a drawing in which you drew stars on a white sky, some clearly defined stitches at the centre of the stars from where threads hung from the celestial bodies with a darning needle swaying at one end: they were escaped stars, stars that didn't want to be sewn together or couldn't be sewn together, stars that were as afraid of being pricked with darning needles as you were of the syringe that lay in its stainless-steel dish on the topmost shelf of the bathroom cupboard. The dreaded penicillin you so loathed. Why were you always ill? As soon as autumn arrived you had to be injected. Earache and sore throats and fever. If you had to stay home from school your grandmother would be sitting there in the armchair crocheting starry squares for the white bedspread, the crotchet hook was always twining nervously between her fingertips because in order to slip the stitches through the *magic ring* your grandmother had to put on her glasses, they made her blue eyes stick out and look much bigger, and sometimes you were allowed to borrow them so you could run through the building with those thick spectacles on and then shallow oblong dips would open in the green floor and when you ran through them your whole body used to bounce just like when the car hit an air pocket which always gave you a delightfully ticklish sensation at the top of your stomach. You are also remembering her corsets, in skin-coloured nylon with stiffened glossy sections in various patterns that made her pelvis shine like a bowl, in the summer you would take your siesta together in the almost complete dark of the nursery, the darkness was meant to keep out the unbearable heat of midday, you lay beside her, naked and sweating like a human grub and right up next to the nylon corset because the coils of the mattress gave way in the middle of the bed. She was a barrier against evil, against your parents' rows and against boredom. And she called your mother Lillan,[103] which was a great mystery, because you could not conceive of your mother having a different body to the one she had as your mother, of her having been a child, what the adults said about growing up was like a magic ring: a hole from which everything started, a hole in the middle of existence, how could bodies grow and why could you never see the growing when it happened, while it was going on? Growing, the transformations of the body, could only be seen in photographs. It was a matter of trust, of having faith in the alleged continuity between the bodies outside and inside the photographs. You sometimes call your mother Lillan as well, because so many things pass across her face when you do, a flash shoots through it that is the proof of a past life, her face becomes transparent, it is like looking out of a huge window and seeing clouds driven by a strong wind, the clouds make the wind visible. Who took the picture of you and your father? The picture in which he is holding you on your Christening

103 Translator's note: very approximately "Little Lass".

day. When he is raising his glass to Adolf Hitler. Was it Gertrud or Rosa? Lillan or Moumoú? She says it would probably have been Rosa though she can't remember, the camera was hers, she always brought it with her from Sweden, it was usually her, sometimes she would take pictures with it, but that was mostly when Rosa wanted to be in the picture as well, apart from that it would mainly have been Rosa taking the pictures. Why was the photograph of Hitler hung at various sites in your home throughout the 1960s? I don't really know, it had to do with your father's history. What do you mean? With his father and Russia, you know. Your grandfather was very devout, you know, he brought back that icon with him, it was enormously important to Salvador because it symbolised the Eastern Front, your grandfather brought back that icon and a brown stone that had a figure engraved on it with outstretched arms that Salvador showed me when we first met, on the boat, it was a crudely carved figure of Christ, rather hideous really, it had horrible eyes and its mouth was a huge gaping hole, it was just a rock, but it had been polished to suggest the shape of a cross, your grandfather always had it on him during the war in Russia and afterwards at home in Spain as well, he used to hold it in his hands to calm his nerves, it had been thrown up in some explosion and your grandfather had found it, it was said to be more than a thousand years old, it had been your grandfather's lucky stone, then Salvador lost it while riding in the desert, he was very sad about that, that was towards the end of his time in the Sahara, he told me that on one of his last leaves, when he came to Tenerife to see me.

"The Florida of Europe", Empuriabrava, Girona, Spain, June 1977

"A nice *Sonnenuntergang*, isn't it?" And then a short bright laugh with an almost feminine ring. Summoning a quiet smile while raising his eyebrows a little, the man on the bench turns and twists his shoulders so he can offer his hand without having to get up, Lars Gunnar Widmark, the reverberations of the rabbit laugh visible on his broadly smiling mouth, links his hand to that of the man whose name is Kurt even though he always thinks of him as *the German engineer*, employing an almost absurdly redundant adjective as the majority of the holiday homes around the canals are owned or rented by Germans, perhaps it is just the name Kurt, when pronounced in Swedish, that Lars Gunnar Widmark finds problematic (he can't bring himself to imitate the German pronunciation with its burred "r"). In Swedish Kurt sounds perky in his ears and better suited to a clown than this imposing seventy-year-old whose long and lanky silhouette he found himself wanting to search out as soon as they had parked the car and begun unloading it just a couple of hours ago, so once all the luggage had been stowed in the apartment and Karin and the twins were getting out their toiletry bags and the bottles of nail varnish he took the chance, grabbed his binoculars and left the family with their feet propped against the low balcony wall, little white tufts of cotton wool between their toes, a bit bird-like that, he thought, as they sat there in a row with their legs bent and their up-pointing knees glistening in the sunlight, Karin in a turquoise bikini and the twins in pink: three brightly coloured canaries on the same perch. He had immediately headed for the canals along the coastline where there were fewer buildings, that was where he had first seen him, last summer, the man who would become *the German engineer* was standing on one of the undeveloped plots of land near the arms of the harbour that stuck out into the sea, Lars Gunnar Widmark was walking along the beach with the binoculars hanging around his neck and his left hand resting on them, ready to raise them to his eyes the moment he saw a pair of wings. The barely ten-year-old canal city was still being developed in an area of brackish water that was one of Europe's prime stopover sites for migrating birds on their way to Africa and back, after a long walk when all he had seen was a common black-headed gull flying towards him along the waterline he reached the boundary where the land that had been subdivided into plots gave way to marshes, bogs and the odd remaining rice paddy, and then all of a sudden there they were in front of him, a vast colony of flamingos, their legs long pink tubes glistening against the water, their wings a perfect flaming red in the sunrise, an overwhelming and intoxicating vision, like seeing a firestorm or maybe a bomb explosion (Lars Gunnar Widmark has never seen a bomb other than on the television news or in a film), which is why he could not help walking over to the older man who turned out to have been following in his footsteps at a distance, "Flamingos!" he gasped, once he had turned around and closed the distance to a point where he could be heard, at the slim white-haired man who also had a pair of binoculars around his neck, "There! You can't miss them!" They began saying hello to each other whenever they met after that morning although that had only happened a few times. Lars Gunnar Widmark had no real idea where the German's home was to be found among all the terraced houses bordering the square-shaped enclosure that consisted entirely of water ("the anti-square" as he was amused to call the rectangular *cul-de-sac* that served as a kind of turning point for the few yachts that lay moored below the houses, this anti-square gave Lars Gunnar Widmark, a psychiatrist in a university town in Central Sweden, a feeling of vertigo, the square was underpinned by nothing more than water, a mutable element in constant motion, even though the enclosed plane might have looked cosy and safe it was actually a bottomless abyss, an opening towards the irrational, a direct path to the unconscious and to the womb he had shared with a twin who had died while being born), only the colour of the paint on the shutters distinguished one house from another, but it was here that he had come across him on a couple of late afternoons, when it had begun to cool down, on a solitary bench positioned so it faced the straight-sided pond that sent shivers down Lars Gunnar Widmark's spine; he and his wife Karin were renting a bungalow on one of the main canals, the one called Port Alegre, a broad, straight stretch of water with an almost direct connection to the sea. Lars Gunnar Widmark's greeting lingers in the air, along with the echo of his rabbit laugh, to be coloured in the ensuing seconds of silence by the cherry-red shutters in one of the houses the last rays of the setting sun are clinging to, the sun really is *going under*, as that hair-raising German phrase would have it, a phrase that is diametrically opposed to the morning rites of the Navajo Indians that so inspired Jung, it is these rituals that make the sun rise, faith may be able to move mountains but language, a single word, can encompass the downfall of the entire world (hence the rabbit laugh that slipped out after the greeting). The German engineer is hesitating, he is looking at him in semi-profile, a faint gleam in his eyes that Lars Gunnar Widmark chooses to interpret as an invitation to take a seat even though he has not made the least move to shift the folded local newspaper (*Los Sitios, Gerona* Lars Gunnar Widmark is able to make out the title) lying beside him on the bench, the word *ecologistas* on the front page is one Lars Gunnar understands, below it an image of a stork with extended wings against a background he recognises as the Bay of Roses, democracy has literally just been hatched in this country but would appear to be vigorous, Karin and he had raised a glass to it on the veranda in Norby only a couple of weeks ago, toasting Spain's first democratic elections in forty-one years and the definitive departure of the old dictator, which was practically the same as toasting the bungalow they rented and that Karin had refused to rent again if the Right won or the military mounted a coup (she stuck by the ideals of her youth with the same constancy with which she applied moisturising cream to her face every morning and evening), and the same as toasting his birdwatching early in the mornings along the shore and inside the marshlands, turned towards the sloping outline of the lesser Pyrenees, the young ridged mountains on which grew pines and holm oaks, rosemary bushes and olive groves in stone-fenced terraces; all of it untenable in the long term though, once she had realised that the canal town was a German enclave Karin wanted to leave, the whole place seemed like a delusion to her, like a psychosis: an artificial town whose streets were made of water, built beside the sea but surrounded by marshy swamps and inhabited by rich Germans who looked down on the indigenous population, and to cap it all there were those strange birds, large, brightly coloured, frightening, that seemed not to belong here either but in Africa, "it's like finding myself in one of my patient's nightmares," she had said a couple of nights ago outside on the broad balcony where they remained sitting after the twins had gone to bed. "But what about these skies?" he had answered, because the stars were out and the night was moonless and suspended above them with the sheen and texture of velvet. The bright summer nights of the Nordic countries would have to be a delusion of a kind too, wouldn't they? "Being surrounded by those Germans, rubbing shoulders with them while I'm on holiday, feels like I'm going behind my patients' backs. The Florida of Europe! I was expecting to meet, if not Americans, then the English and the Dutch and the French at least, I never had any idea we'd end up in a German colony." "But we're not rubbing shoulders with any Germans," he had retorted, because from the very start he had managed to keep secret his laconic conversations with *the German engineer*, "wouldn't it be rather odd for people like us, as the professional explorers of the *individual* human psyche that *we* are, to be ruled by prejudices and generalisations about other human beings?" "*We?* Your patients are little more to you than cases to be fitted into diagnostic categories and all you do is deaden their pain with lobotomising treatments," she said then in an increasingly shrill tone, "if either of us is an explorer of the individual human psyche it would be me, *I'm* the one who listens to their stories, *I'm* the one who takes on their pain and carries it here, *here!*" (and she struck her fist hard against the broad bony valley between her breasts and, while his eyes had become fixed on the stitches and the rectangular pattern of the crocheted white tunic she was wearing, in reality a system of holes that were hooked into each other, and thus held together, by means of thin loops of yarn, he was remembering the story that had so upset her a couple of months ago, the one about the Polish-Jewish mother who used to dye her child's dark hair with hydrogen peroxide in the middle of the night). "Only you're attracted to them, aren't you, to the Germans? Just look at this wine we're drinking: *Sangre de Toro*" (at this point she had rapped the bottle with her fingertips while slurring the Spanish name that was written in gold letters above the black silhouette of a bull, and the hint of contempt he had felt left him ill at ease). "Why does it have to be called *blood*? Instead of grape juice pure and simple, extracted solely through the bloodless, peaceful, beautiful, stamping of bare feet? This perpetual Freudian attraction to barbarity, this fascination with Thanatos. We're not here for the birds, we're here for the Germans instead, aren't we? You're morbid and this whole place is morbid, it's an affront. Just look at the name of the canal we're living on: Port Alegre! Isn't that a Brazilian city? It's as if they decided to have fun drawing a map of their entire ghastly history into the bargain, highlighting all the places it was enacted and even where they went into hiding. Like that vile Stangl creature they caught a few years ago who'd been working at a car factory in São Paulo for God knows how many years. A diabolical game of hide and seek –

you're never going to get us! Ha ha!" (She had been waving both arms in the air while twisting her jaws to the left and then the right in a repellent grimace). "They might just as well call all the canals they haven't got round to building yet Treblinka, Łódź and Sobibor!" (Then she put her hand to her mouth as if she had bitten her tongue, and although those names had sounded horrendous as they were hurled out across the water he found the gesture silly and theatrical.) But the conversation had taken a new turn as an inexplicable glow could suddenly be made out beyond the stone piers that clasped the sea like pincers, at first the rapidly brightening orange light had alarmed them, but when they saw the moon emerge like a colossal salmon-coloured sphere above the water line, understanding dawned, she got to her feet and said she wanted to be naked in the light of that moon and pulled off the crocheted tunic to stand with her legs wide apart facing the heavenly body that was rising swiftly towards its zenith and getting smaller and whiter the further it rose, and he could see her back, suddenly whole without the voids and the pattern of the yarn stitches, while he was watching the reflection of the moon reach across the open sea and slowly intrude into their canal, like quicksilver trying to find its way to the point where she was standing with her back to him, her arms crossed, as if she were praying to be taken up by that light or carried off and away from their balcony and from all the evils of the world, and she tipped her head back as if she wanted to meet the night with the whole of her body and her mouth open wide and remained standing like that in the moonlight for some time (while he was thinking about the phrase *the naked ones* he had recently come across in a controversial book, that was how the commanding officer at Treblinka had referred to the victims as they queued naked along a narrow upward-sloping corridor to the gas chambers), until she clasped her arms around her body and said she was feeling cold, that she didn't want to feel cold; then he had finally promised, minutes before thrusting inside her on the bed she said was covered in sand-grains, that they would find a bungalow in Roses instead, where the French holidayed, next year, when they could afford a yacht that could take him to the marshes before sunrise even though he knew full well that the sound of the engine would cause a commotion among the birds and that any move to Roses would be impossible to combine with his birdwatching, but that disturbing discussion under the open sky (he refused to think of it as a row) or perhaps just the full-bodied barbaric wine they had been drinking deliberately and methodically since sunset, had made them both hot and soft on the inside, Karin's mucous membranes in particular felt soft between the sheets the high humidity here made damp, they enfolded him in a flowing, frictionless way that rarely occurred upstairs in their detached house in Norby where the rooms smelled of pine and everything was so grounded and safe, so dry and fixed and routine and monotonous without any swamps or canals or Spaniards waking up from a long war or guilty Germans who scared the life out of him. Kurt chose that moment to get out a long, narrow cigarette packet from his breast pocket while continuing to regard him from the side and with that glint still in his eyes that Lars Gunnar Widmark suspected might be contempt, from the packet the German extracted a long cigarrillo-like number with dark-brown paper and a gold-coloured band around the filter, then he lit it with a Zippo that gave off an immediate odour of petrol even though the cigarillo smelled sweet as though it were made from blonde tobacco rather than the aroma of cigar Lars Gunnar had been expecting, he did not smoke himself and never had and felt an instinctive resistance to sharing a bench with the man who might have given him two separate signals that he was not welcome: the newspaper was still occupying part of the spot that should have been offered to him and added to it now was this sweetish smoke the evening breeze that blew from inland was sending straight at him but Lars Gunnar Widmark had reasons of his own for sticking with the German engineer and chose to ignore the signals of rejection and remain focused on their most recent conversation of a year ago, even as he was being forced to confront this bottomless pit filled with water, because few things create bonds as powerful as sharing the memory of a place and quite by chance this particular German who he had spoken to early one morning on the beach and who shared his interest in birds was familiar with the spot where his brother Henrik had drowned seven years ago, the German engineer had actually dived down to the same limestone formation 117 metres below the surface of the water that was called the Schwarze Brücke or Schwarze Wand, a diving spot that claimed victims every year, mostly among advanced divers such as Henrik had been, and now there was this Kurt who evidently dived as well; that had emerged one morning shortly after their first conversation when he came across him wearing a diving suit, two black silhouettes that grew larger against the white sand as they crossed the long stretch of beach at a diagonal, Kurt was in the company of another man who appeared considerably younger when he got closer, he said hello without stopping; that evening Lars Gunnar Widmark had happened to find him sitting on the bench and he had gone up to him and told him almost at once that his brother had also been a diver until he drowned in an Austrian lake seven years ago. Kurt had reacted calmly with the same lack of concern as on the morning when Lars Gunnar had shouted he would see flamingos if he kept going straight on, without considering that – as Lars Gunnar Widmark would subsequently realise – the German had been living in this European Florida since the holiday complex was first built and that the sight of a flock of flamingos would hardly be a novelty to him. "I know that lake I have dived there myself, die schwarze Wand is a dangerous place," he had said in response, his gaze elsewhere, somewhere far away. Initially Lars Gunnar Widmark had felt stunned by the coincidence but gradually, while sitting on the bench beside the older man whose eyes were looking without seeing, fixed on the lightly rippling surface of the water in front of them, the shock turned into a kind of exhilaration, as though the fact that this almost complete stranger had dived in the same waters where his younger brother had lost his life made his brother less dead or the unknown man less of a stranger, a relation almost, so he asked Kurt to tell him about the mysterious allure of that place for divers, what could make people risk their lives over and over again, it would have to be dark at those kind of depths, what was there to see? Unusual fish? "No fish down there, just ice-cold water and a deep green light and your own heartbeat," was the only reply he made and his words gave Lars Gunnar Widmark the creeps. There were several crosses along the beach and one protruding from the water that had a wreath of roses on it at the little village called Weyregg, where his brother's corpse was waiting for him, the roses were made of weather-beaten plastic that had faded and lent the whole place a macabre and depressing air, while beneath the water the shoreline was covered in round, smooth stones as large as ostrich eggs and Lars Gunnar Widmark could not help finding a symbolic meaning in the resemblance: the stones were the eggs of death and it was that unquiet bluish green lake, so different from the dark waters of the lakes he was used to, that had laid them. The police constable who accompanied him to the beach from where the divers swam to the point where they could dive down to the Black Wall had informed him when they first met that a preliminary investigation had been set up because they had discovered that all the valves on Henrik's oxygen bottles had been closed and there was reason to suspect that a crime had been committed. This had upset him even more than the news of his brother's death. He checked in to a small hotel in the neighbouring village, he had no desire to stay in Weyregg itself where a plaque announced that Gustav Mahler had spent one summer as a guest. During the two days the investigation lasted he had driven around the Attersee from end to end, every so often little clusters of houses and villas would appear along the narrow winding road that followed the waterline without deviating from it, although he did not stop for the most part but kept driving from one village to the next with the car radio on and his thoughts flickering furiously around his brother's remembered image, scenes from their child-hood kept popping into his mind, minor details he thought he had forgotten, the group picture of the whole family in front of the summer cottage, all four children in swimming costumes, Henrik and he had headbands with feathers in them and wore war paint like Indians, those swimming trunks had now lost what *oskuld* they used to possess ("*oskuld*" was a word he had always disliked in Swedish, he preferred the English version: innocence), it was while he was thinking about his brother's swimming trunks that he came to see them as a precursor, a larval form of the black wetsuit, as close-fitting as a second skin, that would drag him down into the depths; and, as he lay sleepless in the hotel bed after he had rung home and said goodnight to the twins and spoken to Karin with the receiver wedged for so long between his ear and his shoulder that it left red marks, he was thinking that now he would not just have to put up with his dead twin brother who had died beside him in the womb (skin to skin, face to face, face to bum, face to spine, feet to mouth . . . was he the one, who had come out first, that pulled the umbilical cord around his twin's throat so he choked to death?), the twin brother he quite literally carried on his shoulders and who was part of his persona, inasmuch as the dead twin stood for the other half of his name, Lars, Lars was the dead one, he was Gunnar, and as a child he had often wondered how his parents had decided who would be called what and why; under the hotel duvet which smelled of chlorine he was wondering not so much who or why someone might have wanted to kill his living younger brother – the idea of his being a murder victim sounded so far fetched and absurd he refused to take it on board – as how Henrik should be borne in his memory, borne so he would be safe from that hideous and brutal death that had begun to seep like poison backwards through his life to taint all the images he could remember, as though Henrik, more than anyone else, had been marked for death from the outset. The police shut down the inquiry shortly afterwards, he got the message when he returned to the hotel on the afternoon of the second day, having driven around half the circumference of the lake while Mahler's *"Kindertotenlieder"*, which could suddenly be heard on the car radio (an eerie Jungian synchronicity), was animating the landscape he was seeing and at the same time not seeing; the investigators had worked out that Henrik must have closed the valves himself when, at a depth of sixty or seventy metres, he realised that his regulator had frozen in the icy-cold water and that he would never be able to get back up to the surface again. This information fitted in much better with the image he had of Henrik before he had been to that beach where the lake laid its eggs, Henrik was the kind of person who made decisions quickly and stuck by them, a person who knew immediately which side he was going to be on and why; unlike himself, Henrik was the one who never dithered and he had clearly not done so down there on the Black Wall and he found a measure of peace in knowing that because it helped to restore the image he had of Henrik and by extension of himself. He had to drive a few more kilometres along the now-familiar lakeside road to find roses, receptive for the first time to the overwhelming beauty of the three-peaked mountain that loomed above the left side of the road, he bought the roses in a larger village on the opposite side of the lake but did not drive back to the grisly shore where an unsuspecting Henrik had entered the water to meet his death, an impulse made him stop the car in a lay-by instead, under that imposing mountain he had driven beneath and seen in the distance, and walk out on to a jetty from where he threw the roses one by one into the water, they were all for Henrik and yet they weren't, the roses were white like the snow they had shoved inside each other's collars every winter until they were grown up and went their separate ways and like the fermented milk they had eaten for breakfast in the kitchen at home and like their shared mother's hair, the roses he threw into that crystal-clear bluish-green water were for Henrik but also for all the other *tote Kinder* who had died because of that lake, because there was no-one who did not carry their childhood self at the heart of their adult most often ruined, lost or victimised soul. "You know," Lars Gunnar Widmark said as he sat on the bench, "a couple of years ago I went to a medical congress in Vienna, I am a psychiatrist as you may remember, and of course we visited Sigmund Freud's home which has recently been converted into a museum. It was a fantastic experience to see all the objects one had seen in pictures stand there live in the room where he received his patients, wrote his books and smoked the cigars that would end up killing him" (rabbit laugh), "he developed cancer in his mouth, did you know that? Anyway, among others there were pictures of his friend and follower Princess Marie Bonaparte with that fluffy dog of hers which is often seen in pictures with Freud, it was thanks to her great fortune that Freud and his family could flee to London together with his books, sculptures and his famous couch – saved him to a dignified death in a nice big house with a garden instead of in an infamous ghetto or even worse, one of those extermination camps (*Vernichtungslager, stimmt?*) where four of his sisters, left in Vienna, ended up nevertheless, as did the sisters of another genius, Franz Kafka, which reminds me by the way of the coincidence, or let us call it an ironic sense of justice, that Freud's cabinet in Vienna was restored in its original place soon after all those trials held in Israel and in your country against Nazi criminals, I especially recall the one in Düsseldorf a few years ago against the man who ran one of those extermination camps, Treblinka, have you read about it? Well, I am sorry, I'm getting to the point, don't worry. Have you ever been to Vienna? Well, the Berggasse is a quiet and bright slopey street, me and my colleagues walked down it with a sense of worship, of course, then we went up the same stairs as Sigmund Freud himself had done for more than forty years and so many of his immortal patients and followers, I remember that at the entrance we had to press a round brass bell exactly as all his visitors might have done, it shone like a sun in the upper middle part of the dark varnished door, finally we walked into the waiting room, it was more like a bourgeois

... how do you call it, sitting room, with sculptures and works of art on the walls and a big window overlooking a backyard with a lonely tree in the middle, the same yard and the same kind of wide window, from wall to wall, that was in Freud's cabinet, situated in the next room, his desk beside it receiving all the light from the whitewashed walls of the houses that surrounded the backyard (the flat is on the first floor), and when I went in there, after recognising immediately some of the objects from the pictures I had seen since my years as a student, my eyes searched for the one and only thing that would prove to me the authenticity of the reconstruction of Freud's cabinet, if that one and only object hung where I had seen it hanging in a completely astonishing and bewildering way in so many photographs then it would mean that I could trust the rest of the things exhibited in the room where one of the brightest minds of the century, of one hundred centuries" (rabbit laugh) "had worked and developed the most revealing ideas of the human mind, and you know what? It was there, that amazing object hanging in just such an enigmatic way: what I am talking about is a small rectangular glass mirror with a modest frame that hung from one of the handles of that big bright window, do you understand what I mean? A mirror in the only place you wouldn't expect it to be because a window is something meant to let the light in and at the same time let you look out, then that small mirror, not much bigger than a human face, hanging there in the middle of the glass pane in such a way that when you stood in front of that window maybe expecting to observe the outside (the sunlight leaving traces on the whitewashed walls of the backyard, the branches of the tree, a rectangular piece of a clear blue sky) you just stood in front of your own face, and a face, as we all know, is an invitation, or perhaps a temptation, like that cobbled lakeside where you went in to dive to the Black Wall, the human face, with its eyes full of water, is the waterside from where you can look into the self, what poets call the soul, and you know what? This place where we are sitting now reminds me of that mirror hanging in the middle of the window in Freud's cabinet, it simply does." The contempt had vanished from Kurt's eyes, he was looking at him with circumspection now, a touch confused or maybe concerned, he was staring at him as if trying to gauge who he was actually dealing with, as though for the first time in the few conversations they had had he were taking him seriously, with a seriousness that was not welcome and that made him pull back those long legs, bare from the knee down beneath a pair of beige-coloured shorts, that he had stretched out in front of him, one sandal-shod foot crossed over the other, as if to observe his own sinewy well-shaped feet, unusually good-looking and well cared for in a man of his age, as if they were ageing at their own, slower pace, the nails on the toes lacking that yellowish shade of horn you find in many old people, there were no imperfections on his sunburned legs either, neither varicose veins nor scars; his feet were now under the bench which had the effect of making Kurt sit up straighter and therefore taller in relation to Lars Gunnar, the thick stubble a gleaming white across his scalp, although he made no attempt to use his position to subdue as it were his companion with an arrogant look or a devastating comment but avoided meeting his eyes instead, as if he had something else to think about, focused once more, those few moments of confusion or it may have been anxiety, over with, gone for good, and he confirmed his superiority by getting out a new cigarillo from his breast pocket, so the stink of petrol and the sweetish cigarette smell wrapped itself around them once again as if the two of them were in a glass bowl, more acrid now the wind had dropped as the sun continued to set. Both men remained sitting there side by side in silence, their eyes lost in the smooth rectangle of water that lay in front of them, framed by the white terraced houses, and all of a sudden Lars Gunnar Widmark knew that the innermost being of the old man, who he was and what he had experienced – there could be no doubt he would have gone through the war one way or another – was as inaccessible as the Black Wall at the bottom of the Attersee; and then he thought about

Henrik and that they were not really as unlike one another as he had believed. Then Kurt exhaled a cloud of smoke from that healthy mouth of his, untouched by cancer, and said: "The flamingos left, you will not see flamingos this year."

Topography

Bad Ischl, Austria
A traditional spa and holiday resort in the heart of the lake district in the Salzkammergut in Austria, where Emperor Franz Josef maintained a summer residence for sixty years. It was here too that the King-Emperor signed the declaration of war in August 1914.

Haus Schoberstein, beside the Attersee, Salzkammergut, Austria
Rest and recreation centre for the employees of Aktion T4, the secret euthanasia programme, which was run directly from the Führer's private chancellery on Berlin's Tiergarten. In addition to serving the holidaying workers of the Third Reich's forced-euthanasia clinics and extermination camps, it would also in the course of the war house the records of Hitler's chancellery.

Unterach am Attersee, Austria
Holiday resort on the opposite shore of the Attersee.

Schloss Hartheim, Austria
One of the centres in which the Nazi's euthanasia programme was put into operation.

Lambach, close to Attersee, Austria
Adolf Hitler lived here as a child.

Château Bardou, Maternity Hospital in Elne, Pyrénées-Orientales, France, The Free Zone
Maternity clinic run by *Secours Suisse aux Enfants* (a Swiss aid organisation that became part of the Red Cross in 1942) on the borderland

with Spain. The hospital took in women from the camps on the beaches such as Argelès and St Cyprien, where France interned the half million Republicans fleeing from Franco's troops in Spain.

The Internment Camp at Rivesaltes, Pyrénées-Orientales, France
Spaniards (refugees from the Spanish Civil War and subsequently from the Franco dictatorship), Roma, stateless persons and Jews from all over Europe were interned here. From 1942 onwards thousands of people were deported from the camp to Auschwitz.

Villa Saint-Jean, Banyuls-sur-Mer, France
A nursery and care centre for the most severely malnourished small children from the internment camp at Rivesaltes. The centre was run by the Swiss woman Madeleine Durand as a subdivision of the maternity hospital in Elne.

Pontevedra, Spain
Town in the province of Galicia. The province was a stronghold for Franco's troops throughout the Spanish Civil War.

Calle Balmes 33, Lérida, Spain
The narrator's childhood home.

Calle Balmes 297, Barcelona, Spain
The childhood home of the narrator's father.

Cristal City Bar, Calle Balmes 294, Barcelona, Spain
A meeting place for writers and intellectuals in Barcelona. The bar served as a bookshop and library, and made books that were banned during Franco's dictatorship clandestinely available.

On Board the Ciudad de Cádiz
A ship on the regular service between Barcelona and Santa Cruz de Tenerife.

"The Florida of Europe", Empuriabrava, Girona, Spain
A canal city created towards the end of the 1970s in a region of
brackish water that sustains a great deal of birdlife (as a stopping
point for migrating birds on their way to and from Africa). The villas
and bungalows had their own moorages and access to the sea. It soon
became the mainly German colony it has remained.

Venice, Italy
Several of the films in which Kristina Söderbaum starred won
prizes at the Venice Film Festival, including the then unknown *"Jud
Süss"*, which was premiered in September 1940 and seen by millions
of cinema-goers throughout Europe. The film is still banned in
Germany and many other countries, and its anti-Semitism was so
powerful that showings could lead, according to people such as
Imre Kertész, to pogroms breaking out, for example in Hungary. For
the 1942 film *"Die goldene Stadt"*, whose xenophobia was aimed at
the Slavic races as represented by the Czechs of Prague, Kristina
Söderbaum was awarded the Volpi Cup for the best performance by
an actress in a leading role. Venice is also the location for sections
of the 1962 novel *"Il giardino dei Finzi-Contini"* by the Italian author
Giorgio Bassani which depicts the fate of the Jewish Finzi-Contini
family from the accession of Mussolini to the deportation of the
family during the Second World War.

Ymergatan 7, Uppsala, Sweden
The home in which the narrator's mother would live after spending
twenty years abroad.

Dramatis Personae

KURT SEIDEL – employee of the euthanasia programme and stationed at the extermination camp in Treblinka; after the camp was shut down he served in Trieste, Italy – no further information about his life and death is available

HELENE HINTERSTEINER – secretary to the hospital director Dr Rudolph Lonauer and office administrator at Schloss Hartheim

BRUNO BRUCKNER – institute photographer responsible for making photographic records of the so-called patients who were exterminated at Schloss Hartheim, as well as of the studies carried out by the medical staff

MARIA RAAB – nurse

HUBERT GOMERSKI – cremator

ROSA HAAS – cleaner employed at Schloss Hartheim, which was close to where she lived.

ANNELIESE NEUBECK – typist

GERTRUD BLANKE – nurse

CHARLES HAYWOOD DAMERON – U.S. Army officer charged with investigating German war crimes during the Second World War, including those committed at Schloss Hartheim

ELISABETH EIDENBENZ – Swiss volunteer and matron of the maternity hospital at Elne

RANDI TOMMESSEN – Swiss-Norwegian nurse and volunteer at the maternity hospital

FRIEDEL BOHNY-REITER – Swiss nurse at the internment camp at Rivesaltes, near the Spanish border

MADELEINE DURAND – matron of Villa Saint-Jean, a children's home for malnourished children from the internment camp at Rivesaltes

CARMEN PEDRÓN – a Spanish refugee who arrives at the Villa Saint-Jean with her newborn child

GERTRUD SÖDERBAUM – the narrator's mother

ROSA SÖDERBAUM (MA ROSA, MOUMOÚ) – the narrator's maternal grandmother

P. H. SÖDERBAUM – the narrator's maternal grandfather

LARS GUNNAR WIDMARK – the narrator's maternal uncle

SALVADOR PASCUAL PASCÓ (SAL) – the narrator's father

SALVADOR PASCUAL JULIÁ – the narrator's paternal grandfather

MARÍA DE LOS DOLORES (DOLORES) – the narrator's paternal grandmother

JOSÉ MARÍA – the narrator's paternal uncle

MARÍA ROSA – the narrator's paternal aunt

ANA MARÍA SAMBOLA – married to the narrator's paternal uncle José María

MERCÈ RODOREDA – Catalan writer whose major literary breakthrough came with *La plaça del Diamant* – a depiction of the struggle of a working-class woman to survive during and after the Spanish civil war

KRISTINA SÖDERBAUM – Swedish actress, one of Nazi Germany's major film stars and married to Veit Harlan, Goebbels' main collaborator in the film industry; distantly related to the narrator's mother

MICÒL FINZI-CONTINI – fictional character in Giorgio Bassani's novel *Il giardino dei Finzi-Contini*, about a Jewish family in Italy

Sources

Quotations or adaptations occur in the novel from the following sources:

Augustinus, *Confessiones*, Book I

Bachmann, Ingeborg, *Malina* (translation by Frank Perry of German text available online)

Bassani, Giorgio, *The Garden of the Finzi-Continis* (translated by Jamie McKendrick, Penguin, 2007)

Bohny-Reiter, Friedel, *Journal de Rivesaltes 1941–42*, Editions Zoe, Carouge-Geneve 1993 (translation into Swedish by Anna Petronella Foultier)

Carson, Anne, *The Beauty of the Husband*

Dameron, Charles Haywood, letter to his parents, November 22, 1945, *Dameron Report: Bericht des War Crimes Investigating Teams No 6824 der U.S. Army vom 17.7.1945 über die Tötungsanstalt Hartheim (Historische Texte des Lern- und Gedenkortes Schloss Hartheim)*, eds. Brigitte Kepplinger, Irene Leitner and Andrea Kammerhofe, Studien Verlag, Innsbruck 2012

Helene Hintersteiner's Witness Statement, *Dameron Report, NARA, Record Group 549: Records of the Headquarters, U.S. Army Europe [USAEUR], War Crimes Branch, War Crimes Case Files ("Cases not tried"), 1944–48, Box 490, Case 000-12-463 Hartheim*

Dickinson, Emily, "The most triumphant bird I ever knew or met"; "The Brain"

Faulkner, William, *Absalom ! Absalom !*, Random House, New York, 1936 & Chatto & Windus, London

Higginson, Thomas Wentworth, "Emily Dickinson's Letters", *Atlantic Monthly*, October 1891

Huxley, Thomas Henry, "Agnosticism and Christianity", *Collected Essays, vol. V, Science and Christian Tradition*, Macmillan, London, 1893

Malaparte, Curzio, *Kaputt*, Casella, Naples, 1944

Prado, Fidel, "El novio de la muerte", 1921

Rodoreda, Mercè, (*La plaça del Diamant*) – *La mort i la primavera*, eds. Carme Arnau, Fundació Mercè Rodoreda, Institut d'Estudis Catalans, Barcelona, 1997

Salvador, Tomas, *Camaradas 74*, Plaza & Janes Editores, Barcelona, 1975

Shakespeare, William, *Richard III*

Söderbaum, Kristina, *Nichts bleibt immer so*, Herbig Verlag, Bayreuth, 1983

Talleyrand, Charles-Maurice, *Mémoires du prince de Talleyrand*, Calmann-Lévy, Paris, 1891

Utrera, Adolfo och Nilo Menendez, "Aquellos ojos verdes" 1929

Vilar, Enrique Errando, *Campaña de invierno*, División Azul, José Perona, Madrid, 1943

Waldrop, Rosmarie, *Curves to the Apple*, New Directions, New York, 2006

CATERINA PASCUAL SÖDERBAUM, 1962–2015, lived between Sweden and Spain and worked as a translator of Swedish literature into Spanish. Her first book, a collection of short stories entitled *Sonetten om andningen* ("The Sonnet on Breathing"), won Sweden's Catapult Prize for best first work of fiction. *The Oblique Place* was to be her last novel, and was awarded the prestigious Sveriges Radios Novel Prize posthumously, in 2017.

FRANK PERRY has translated many of Sweden's leading novelists, poets and dramatists. His work has won the Swedish Academy prize and the drama translation prize of the Writer's Guild of Sweden. His translation of Lina Wolff's *Brett Easton Ellis and the Other Dogs* was the 2017 winner of the Oxford-Weidenfeld Prize.